David Wishart studied Classics at Edinburgh University. He then taught Latin and Greek in school for four years and after this retrained as a teacher of EFL. He lived and worked abroad for eleven years, working in Kuwait, Greece and Saudi Arabia, and now lives with his family in Scotland.

Praise for David Wishart:

'As ever, Wishart takes true historical events and blends them into a concoction so pacy that you hardly notice all the interesting details of Roman life being slipped in there ... Salve! To this latest from the top toga-wearing 'tec of Roman times!' *Highland News Group*

'[I]t is evident that Wishart is a fine scholar and perfectly at home in the period.' *Sunday Times*

'Tales of treachery, betrayal and murder always make good reading, but Carnoustie author David Wishart's novels have an extra dimension – they are set in ancient Rome ... David takes real people and weaves his novels around them ... For while the dramatis personae have Roman names and live in Roman times, they speak in modern English which is both familiar and natural.' *Dundee Courier & Advertiser*

'Witty, engrossing and ribald ... it misses nothing in its evocation of a bygone time and place' *Independent on Sunday*

'Once again Wishart gives us an Ancient Rome that would have disgusted Romulus and Remus, but also one that throbs with vibrant if voracious life.' *Northern Echo*

D0544270

Old Bones

David Wishart

NEW ENGLISH LIBRARY
Hodder & Stoughton

British Library Cataloguing in Publication Data
A Catalogue record of this book is available from the British Library.

ISBN 0 340 76884 3

Typeset by Palimpsest Book Production Limited,
Polmont, Stirlingshire
Printed and bound in Great Britain by
Clays Ltd, St Ives plc.

Hodder and Stoughton
A division of Hodder Headline
338 Euston Road
London NW1 3BH

To the CALS department of the University of Dundee, not forgetting the Gorilla Upstairs; and to Kathryn and Gary Colner, with thanks for the use of their Tuscan cottage

DRAMATIS PERSONAE

CORVINUS'S HOUSEHOLD AND FAMILY

Alexis: particularly sharp slave-of-all-work
Bathyllus: the bald, hernia-suffering major-domo
Corydon: a mule
Hilarion, Publius Salvius: a Hippocratic doctor
Lysias: the family coachman
Marilla, Valeria ('the Princess'): Corvinus's and Perilla's adopted daughter
Meton: the anarchic chef
Perilla, Rufia: Corvinus's wife
Phormio: Priscus and Vipsania's avant-garde chef
Priscus, Titus Helvius: the tombs nut; Corvinus's stepfather
Vipsania: Corvinus's mother

VETULISCUM

Arruns, Larcius: Nepos's litigious neighbour
Baro: Vipena's foreman
Clusinus, Titus: Vetuliscum's most unpopular resident; Vesia's husband
Holconius, Publius: Sicinia's cousin; a wine-shipper, resident in Pompeii
Mamilius, Quintus: a nonagenarian legionary veteran. His son is Decimus
Navius, Attus: the murdered man. His father and grandfather are Gaius and Velthur Navius respectively
Nepos, Aulus Licinius: Priscus and Vipsania's host
Papatius, Larth: innkeeper and vinegrower; Thupeltha's husband

Publius: Arruns's nephew
Ramutha and Tanaquil: Vipena's unmarried sisters
Sicinia Rufina: Attus Navius's mother
Thupeltha: the owner of the wineshop; Papatius's wife
Vesia: Titus Clusinus's wife. Her children are Trebbia and Sextus
Vipena, Gnaeus: augur and vinegrower

CAERE, PYRGI AND ROME

Arria Metella: Aulus Bubo's wife
Aternius, Gaius: Caeretan lawyer; Cominius's nephew
Bubo, Aulus Herminius: a second-hand goods dealer in Caere
Bubo, Publius Herminius ('The Owl'): his brother; owner of a business in Rome
Caelius Crispus: a seedy Roman acquaintance of Corvinus's, now attached to the praetor's office in Rome
Cominius, Quintus: the Caeretan mayor ('the Cominii' refers to Cominius and his nephew Aternius)
Lippillus, Decimus Flavonius: a Watch Commander friend of Corvinus's
Perennius, Titus: a former business acquaintance of Aternius's
Pullia: Aulus Bubo's girlfriend
Tolumnius, Titus: owner of a potter's yard. His brother is Gaius, a ship's captain
Veluscius, Marcus: a former accountant

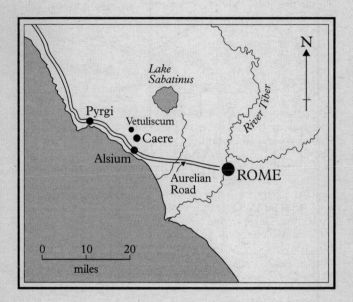

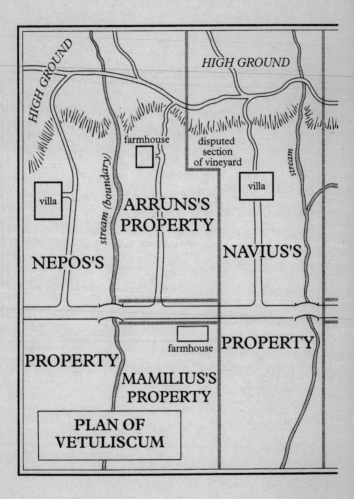

HIGH GROUND

HIGH GROUND

farmhouse

disputed
section
of vineyard

stream (boundary)

stream

villa

villa

ARRUNS'S
PROPERTY

NAVIUS'S

NEPOS'S

PROPERTY

farmhouse

PROPERTY

MAMILIUS'S
PROPERTY

PLAN OF
VETULISCUM

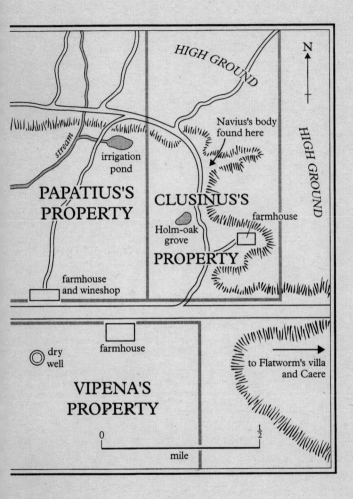

1

The big black bugger at the head of the line was smart, which was probably why he'd landed the job in the first place. He didn't give up, either, even with a breadcrumb three times his size and twice the size of the hole he was trying to put it down. As I watched he pulled it clear and chewed at it one more time. Then, lifting it off the ground, he set his back legs against a loose stone chipping, twisted his body and shoved.

The breadcrumb shot through, smooth as cream, to be grabbed by his pals down below and hustled off to wherever the hell they were stashing the stuff. You could almost hear the cheers.

I tore up a bit more of the loaf and watched the little guys behind him pounce on the falling crumbs. Scale's an amazing thing. To an ant, one lunchtime roll's as much bread as you could make from the contents of an Ostian grain barge. Squirrelled away at the rate these bastards had been going it'd last them to the Winter Festival, easy.

'Hey, Perilla,' I said.

The lady looked up from her book. The early afternoon sun, shining through a gap in the trellised vine, caught on her hair. She'd had Phryne fix it up in a simpler style than she usually wore it back home in Athens: when you're on holiday out in the sticks with no one to dress up for sartorial elegance tends to go by the board. Comatic elegance. Whatever. If you could call this a holiday. Personally I thought we'd been suckered into two months' worth of thumb-twiddling, but then that's Mother for you.

'Yes, Marcus?' Tetchy; tetchy as hell: she must've hit one of the juicy bits.

'You think ants throw parties?' I could hear her teeth grate. Well, maybe it did need a context to make it halfway sensible. 'I mean, breadcrumbs only keep underground for so long. It'd save a lot of waste, especially if the different nests worked out a rota.'

'Marcus, why don't you go out for a walk if you're bored?'

'Who said I was bored?'

'It's a logical assumption. People who live full and active lives don't spend their afternoons throwing bread to the ants.'

'Is that so, now?' I brushed a few more days' supply of formic corn dole from my tunic and reached for the wine jug.

'That is so.' She set the book down altogether. 'Nor do they spend them getting stewed on the terrace.'

Uh-oh. 'Don't knock it, lady. It has its points.' I poured. Yeah, well, the quality of the wine was one plus at least to set against Mother's dragging us all the way from Greece: Caeretan might not have the name of its big brothers to the south, but drunk on its home ground it was still pretty good stuff. 'And personally, I can think of worse things to do.'

'Indeed?' She picked up the book again and unrolled it.

I sneaked a look at the title. Scratch the juicy bits; it was Aulus Caecina's *Etruscan History*, solid stuff, and par for the course. Perilla's your original conscientious tourist: if it moves she'll read it into submission. Jupiter knew where she'd got Caecina from, mind, because Gnaeus Lentulus whose villa we were currently borrowing was no highbrow; when we'd been at school together the kids had nicknamed him Flatworm, and the name still fitted. A library the guy had – no self-respecting country villa is completely bookless – but Perilla had taken one look at it and quietly closed the cabinet. I had a glance myself, later, and I wasn't surprised: most of the books were the sort of illustrated instruction manuals that eat through their rollers and leave scorch marks on the shelves.

I took an appreciative mouthful of the wine. I hadn't been kidding: there were far worse ways to spend an afternoon when you're stuck out in the country than sitting in the shade of a trellised vine feeding the ants and making a hole in Flatworm's twenty-year-old Caeretan. I could've been out tomb-bashing with Priscus, for a start . . .

'If I'd known you'd be at a loose end this early in the holiday we could have gone into Caere with your stepfather to look at the tombs,' Perilla said. 'It's what we're here for, after all.'

I winced and set the cup down. It wouldn't do a blind bit of good, I knew, but it had to be done. For the umpteenth time. A lovely lady, Perilla, a peerless wife and clever as they come, but sometimes her grasp of the eternal verities would disgrace a clam. These born educators are all the same: they just cannot believe however often you tell them that a diet of temples, statues and the like brings normal people out in hives.

'Lady, would you watch my lips for a moment, please?'

I said. Caecina dipped; not seriously, but it'd have to do. 'Short of slugging me with a particularly hefty club and tying me behind a brace of bullocks there is absolutely no way that you are going to get me within spitting distance of any tombs. Mother may've used Priscus's annual tomb-bash as a come-on with you but she sure as hell didn't try it with me because she's a smart enough cookie to know her limitations. Now is that clear or should I draw you a picture?'

Perilla sniffed and turned back to her book. At which point the mule joined us.

He came strolling up the terrace steps like he owned the place, chewing on what looked like half the ornamental shrub that Lentulus had planted in an old wine jar by the gate. When he saw us he stopped, grinned and carefully lifted his tail . . .

'Corydon! *No!*'

I caught one glimpse of our adopted daughter Marilla's horrified face as she rounded the trellis corner, just as the bugger deposited his load on the gleaming flagstones.

'I'm sorry.' Marilla had grabbed the brute's bridle and was hanging on with all the proprietorial tenacity of the fourteen-year-old animal lover. 'He got away from me as we were coming up the drive.'

'Uh . . . yeah.' Jupiter! Our major-domo Bathyllus would have a fit! In the two days we'd been here even the sparrows had learned that crapping on the little guy's preserve was a short cut to suicide. 'Where did you pick that thing up from, Princess? If it's not a stupid question?'

'He was wandering about at the foot of our road.' Marilla was stroking the mule's nose while the brute went on grinning like a drain. Accident, nothing: from the satisfied look in the moth-eaten bastard's eye I'd bet he'd been holding himself in for days, just waiting his chance. 'I think he must've slipped his tether.'

I glanced at Perilla. The lady was stiff as hell, but the tips of her ears were pink. A good sign. Maybe the mule would live after all. Certainly having the Princess on his side didn't do any harm.

'"Corydon"?' I said.

Marilla blushed. 'Well, I had to call him something.'

'Marilla, you are *not* keeping him.' Perilla rolled Aulus Caecina up with a snap and laid him on the table beside her. 'Not even temporarily. He was probably on his way home. Take him straight to Alexis. He can find the owner for you.'

Yeah. I'd go for that. Alexis was the smartest of our skivvies, and unlike Bathyllus he didn't regard animals as some sort of divine scourge sent to mess up his nice clean universe. The Princess was right about the tether, too. Although it was the proper length the end looked ragged. Either it had slipped or – more likely – the evil bastard had pulled the knot out specially just so he could come up and shit all over our terrace.

Marilla was looking at me with those big brown eyes of hers. I sighed. Well, it had to be done. And mules, even this fugitive from a glue factory, were expensive animals.

'Perilla's right, Princess,' I said. 'Take him round to Alexis.'

'But—'

'Go ahead. And the next time you find a stray elephant drinking from the birdbath I swear I'll let you keep it.'

She turned and went moping off round the edge of the villa towards the kitchen garden where Alexis would be potting up sprouts or whatever the hell keen gardeners like him did in their spare time. The mule followed her, stopping to tear down a large chunk of trellising on the way. Probably storing up fresh ammunition.

I let her get out of earshot before I turned back to Perilla.

'Okay, lady,' I said. 'You can let your hair down now.'

Perilla smiled. 'Was it that obvious?'

'Only to me.'

'It really wasn't funny.' She glanced at the pile of dung steaming away next to the pristine whitewashed wall and started to giggle. 'Bathyllus will be furious.'

'We can tell him Mother's tame doctor recommended it as a cure for baldness.'

The giggle changed to a laugh, and I got up and kissed her; which was exactly when Bathyllus himself softshoed out looking serious as hell.

'Excuse me for interrupting, sir,' he said. Odd. He hadn't even glanced at Corydon's offering, and that was odd, too, if you like: selective astigmatism may be one of the little guy's cultivated virtues, but selectively purblind he isn't, and he'd practically stepped in the stuff. We hadn't got the disapproving stare we're usually treated to when he catches us breaching his personal code of ethics, either.

Weird. *Definitely* weird.

'Oh, hi, Bathyllus.' I straightened while Perilla adjusted her mantle and put on her stiff Roman matron pose. 'Just the man. We, ah, seem to have had a bit of an accident here.' I didn't look at Perilla, but I heard the lady grunt. 'You want to bring a brush and dustpan, maybe?'

He fizzed for a while like Bathyllus never does. 'Yes, sir,' he said. 'Certainly. In a moment.'

Still the perfect butler. Jupiter! There was something badly wrong here. I'd expected the biggest blow-out since Etna last erupted and I hadn't got even a sniff. So far as Bathyllus could ever look six yards out of the game the little guy was doing just that. I stopped grinning. Whatever this was, it was no joke.

'Hey, sunshine,' I said. 'You okay?'

'Yes, sir.' He cleared his throat. 'We've had a message from Licinius Nepos. Your stepfather has just committed a murder.'

I stared at him, my lower jaw scraping the terrace.

'He has *what*?'

'Killed someone, sir.' Bathyllus hesitated. 'One of the locals. With a knife, as I understand.'

Shit.

2

Nepos's villa wasn't far, no more than a couple of miles down the road in the opposite direction from Caere, at the end of a string of smaller properties with the collective name of Vetuliscum. Nepos was an old friend of my father's; Mother and Priscus stayed with him whenever the annual tomb-bash took them to Caere, and we'd've been doing the same if I hadn't remembered about Flatworm's place. In herself Mother's okay, just, but she had her mad chef Phormio with her, and sure as eggs are eggs we'd've been poisoned inside a week. The fact that this time she'd added a parasitic Hippocratic doctor to her entourage didn't help much, either. If Phormio hadn't got us that bastard would've for sure; mad chefs are bad enough, but Hippocratics get you both ends of the digestive process and expect you to thank them while you're throwing up and dumping down. If you can speak at all, that is.

I'd done the walk for fun the day before, but this time I was in a hurry and I took a horse. My brain was buzzing all the way. This thing didn't make sense, because Priscus wouldn't hurt a fly. Priscus *couldn't* hurt a fly: the old bugger would've taken three days to find the fly-swatter, by which time he'd've forgotten what he wanted it for and wandered off instead down one of his esoteric byways chasing rogue Oscan datives. Mother, sure; I'd've believed Mother, easy, only if she ever decided to murder someone she wouldn't get caught; but *Priscus*? No way. It had to be a mistake.

Nepos was waiting for me at the door. The old guy looked worried as hell, which was a bad sign; even from the little I'd seen of him I had a lot of time for Nepos. He was no fool, for a start. Unlike Flatworm who only used his country villa for alfresco screwing purposes and wouldn't recognise an endive outside a salad if it jumped up and bit him he was a real countryman who knew his ground and what to do with it. How to make it pay, too, and that was what counted. Ask any farmer.

'Come on up, Corvinus,' he said. 'Titus is still a bit shocked and not quite himself, I'm afraid. And of course that damned Greek fellow would choose this morning to go into Caere.'

Yeah, well; that was one good thing, anyway. A doctor might've finished the poor sap off altogether, and personally I could do without Hilarion's company. It just showed you how stupid names can be. Cheerful was something the guy most definitely wasn't.

We went upstairs: like with a lot of the big working villas the living accommodation was two floors up, where things were quieter and less messy. Priscus was lying on a couch in the main sitting-room with Mother beside him on a chair. I'd expected under the circumstances she'd be frayed at the edges, but she looked much as she always did: half her age, impeccably made up and poised as hell. If the Germans ever poured across the Rhine and fought their way looting and pillaging to Rome they'd find Mother sitting in the atrium waiting to serve them honeyed wine and upside-down cake. She'd insist the buggers wiped their boots on the mat before they came in, too.

She raised her cheek for me to kiss.

'Marcus, how lovely,' she said. 'It's good of you to come so promptly. Isn't it, Titus?'

'Mmmaaa!' Even under normal conditions Priscus was like something you'd find under the lid of a mummy case. Now the guy looked like he wouldn't even make the first five dynasties. He was wiry, mind. Whoever had put Priscus together might only have used string and glue, but all the bits were there and fully functional. Except whatever organ handles common sense, of course, but then you can't have everything. 'Hello, Marcus, my boy! Bit of a bugger, this, isn't it?'

'*Titus!*' Mother looked shocked, as well she might: personally I'd have bet a gold piece to a poke in the eye that the unworldly old prune didn't even know the word, let alone use it. *Not quite himself* was right.

I sat down on one of the other couches.

'So, Stepfather,' I said. 'Who did you kill?'

'He didn't kill anyone!' Mother snapped. 'Don't be silly!'

I sighed. 'Okay. So who *didn't* you kill?'

'A young fellow by the name of Attus Navius.' That was Nepos, and he sounded tired. 'He owns – owned – the land on either side of the Caere road two along from me, between Mamilius's place and Papatius's wineshop.'

'Uh-huh.' I knew where he was, at least with the wineshop: that I'd already found (surprise!). And Mamilius's would be the farmhouse that fronted on to the road just before the bridge that marked the edge of Nepos's property. 'That where it happened?'

'No.' Nepos had obviously decided to give me the

details himself. Very wise, with Priscus as the only other option. 'You know Clusinus's track?' I shook my head. 'You'll've passed it on your way here. The first on the right as you come into Vetuliscum.'

I remembered the track now. It branched off just past the point where the line of rough country bordering the road to the north opened out into Vetuliscum proper. 'Leads up into the hills?'

Nepos grunted. 'That's the lad. Navius was up there in a gully a few hundred yards beyond the farm proper, stabbed through the heart. Titus was caught, ah' – he cleared his throat – 'standing over him with the knife still in his hand.'

Jupiter with little bells on! I looked at Priscus in total disbelief. The guy gave an ovine bleat and tried a louche grin that didn't work.

'I'd just . . . mmmaaa! . . . found him, Marcus, you see,' he explained. 'The whole thing was an accident. The purest chance.'

'Yeah,' I said. 'That I'd sort of assumed. And the knife?'

'I pulled it out of the body.'

Oh, joy in the morning! I wasn't hearing this, surely: no one could be that stupid, not even Priscus!

'You did *what?*' I said.

'Pulled it out, Marcus. I thought perhaps . . .'

Holy gods alive! 'You stupid old bugger!'

'*Marcus!*' That was Mother.

'At which point,' Nepos went on in his toneless voice, 'Clusinus comes waltzing down the hill, jumps to the obvious conclusion and makes a citizen's arrest.' His eyes closed as if in pain. 'Finish, end of story.'

I really didn't believe this. Or – scratch that – I wouldn't't've believed it if the fall guy had been anyone else but Priscus. Even so it took a lot of swallowing.

'What the hell were you doing up there in the first place, Stepfather?' I said. 'I thought you were going tomb-bashing in Caere this morning.'

'He was.' Nepos's eyes were still closed.

'Then why . . . ?'

'Don't ask, Corvinus.' Nepos again. 'Just . . . don't . . . bloody . . . *ask*!'

Priscus had the grace to look embarrassed. 'I, ah, seem to have taken the wrong turning,' he said.

I stared at him. 'Priscus, that is a sodding cart-track, right? It leads nowhere, and it does it in totally the wrong direction. Last but not least, you must've been back and forwards to Caere by the road a hundred times. So don't tell me—'

'I was thinking,' Priscus said with great dignity, 'of other things.'

Jupiter save us! 'It's a pity you weren't thinking of other things when you pulled the fucking knife out and waved it over the fucking corpse!'

Nepos made a choking sound, and Mother gave him her best glare. Then she turned back to me.

'Marcus, dear,' she said coolly. 'I appreciate you're upset over this, as we all are, but that is no excuse for bad language. Titus is simply an unfortunate victim of circumstances.'

I sighed: that wasn't exactly the phrase I'd've used. *Complete bloody prat* came closer, but calling a spade a spade wouldn't help things any. The thing was done, and there was an end to it.

'Okay,' I said. 'So what happens now?'

Nepos had opened his eyes again; I expected he might have agreed with me on terminology, but arguing with Mother is like mud-wrestling eels. 'Titus has been released into my custody, naturally,' he said, 'but a report has gone to Quintus Cominius, the Caeretan mayor. No doubt Navius's mother Sicinia Rufina will be pressing charges shortly.'

'The guy wasn't married?'

'He was only in his early twenties. He came into the property when his father died last year.'

I sat back. Jupiter, this was a real bummer! Sure, being a Roman knight there was no way that Priscus would be hauled off to the local slammer, but even so it looked pretty bleak for the poor sap. If he were convicted – and being caught red-handed made that likely – a hefty fine was the best he could expect, with exile a fair possibility. Something had to be done, and fast.

'This Navius,' I said. 'Did he have any enemies?'

'No.' Nepos hesitated. 'None that I'm aware of.'

'What's that supposed to mean?'

'Just what it says. He was a nice enough lad, a bit of a spoiled pup the way they all are at that age. He'd a taste for wine and an eye for the girls, but there was no real harm in him.' Yeah. That sounded familiar. I was glad Perilla wasn't here to see my blushes. 'And he'd the makings of a farmer, even if he did raise a few temperatures in the neighbourhood.'

'Yeah?' I pricked up my ears. 'What kind of temperatures?'

Nepos chuckled. 'Farmers – and I'd include myself, for my sins – have pretty fixed views on things, Corvinus. We don't like them questioned, certainly not by youngsters. I'm talking farming methods, you understand. Young Attus Navius had some ideas that weren't too popular locally, and being the lad he was he didn't mind spouting them in public. Oh, he got up quite a few noses. But not far enough to get himself killed, nowhere near it.'

'Uh-huh.' Yeah, well. That sounded familiar too. Farmers

are like everyone else; they don't like smartass kids still wet behind the ears telling them where they've been going wrong for the past fifty years, and the kids – being kids – will naturally slug on regardless. Still, I shelved that little nugget for future reference. 'So how about this Clusinus?'

'Ah.' Nepos had pulled up a chair himself by now. He leaned back frowning. 'I thought you might be interested in him.'

'You bet I'm interested. The corpse was on his land and he turned up from nowhere just at the perfect time. And if Meataxe here didn't kill the guy he makes as good a starting point as any.'

'Mmmaaa!' Priscus waved a protesting claw. 'My boy, I really wish you wouldn't be so facetious.'

'I think we should let Marcus handle this, dear.' That was Mother, of course. She was looking brighter, and I had the distinct impression she was beginning to enjoy herself. 'Tiresome or not, he does know what he's doing in situations like these. It comes from having a warped brain.'

Ouch.

Nepos had steepled his fingers. He was still frowning. 'Clusinus is a bit of a queer fish,' he said. 'He's no farmer, to begin with, or not a proper one as people round here would understand the term. Oh, his land isn't all that good, of course – a lot of it's no better than broken country and scrub – but he could do a lot more with it than he does. A hell of a lot more, in fact. Which doesn't exactly endear him locally. To make matters worse he keeps goats, and you know what arable farmers and vinegrowers think of *them*.' Yeah, I did, even a city boy like me: goats'll eat anything they can get their teeth into. They're no respecters of boundary lines, either.

If Clusinus wasn't overcareful about little details like
hurdles – and I had the impression, somehow, that he
wouldn't be – then his caprine pals could make him
very unpopular indeed. 'Not to put too fine a point on
it, the fellow's a complete wastrel. He spends more time
hunting than looking after his farm. Which was what he
had been doing, in fact, when he came upon Titus and
the body.'

'Uh-huh. You happen to know if he'd caught anything?'

Nepos gave me a sharp look: like I say, the guy was no
fool. 'Now that is a thought,' he said slowly. 'No, I don't.
But he was certainly empty-handed when he brought
Titus in.'

I turned to the Mad Axeman himself. 'Priscus?'

'Mmmaaa?'

'Was Clusinus carrying anything in the way of game,
did you notice?' Not a flicker. Jupiter! The guy might be
able to tell a labial fricative from a plosive but I'd met
with smarter frying pans. I tried again. 'A hare or two,
maybe? Dragging a boar behind him with a spear in its
gullet, perhaps?'

'Come on, Titus, dear,' Mother prompted. 'You can
remember.'

Priscus's brow furrowed, then cleared. 'Mmmaaa. Yes,
Marcus, he was indeed. A brace of bustard; *tetrax*, if I
recall correctly, not the heavier *tarda* variety, although I
do believe one can find *otis tarda* occasionally in—'

'Yeah. Yeah, fine.' Bugger; there went that idea. Well,
at least he'd noticed; I wouldn't even have laid bets on the
boar. 'One more thing, Nepos. What about the murder
weapon?'

'I have it here.' Nepos got up and went over to a storage
chest in the corner of the room. He came back with a

bone-hilted knife with a blade six or seven inches long. 'Clusinus wanted to keep it, but I told the fellow I'd give it to Cominius myself.'

It wasn't anything special, the sort of thing you could pick up anywhere for a few copper coins. Nothing any self-respecting Roman knight would look at twice. I hoped Cominius would spot that, too.

'You mind if I hang on to it for a while?' I said.

'Not as long as you're careful with it.'

'Priscus?'

'Mmmaaa. Carry on, my boy.'

'Right.' I stood up and tucked it into the belt of my tunic. 'If you'll excuse me I'll go and have a look at the scene of the crime.'

'You're not eating with us, Marcus?' Mother said. 'I'm sure Nepos would send the coach for Perilla and your daughter. And Phormio's promised us some marrow-bone and emmer broth. So strengthening.'

But I was already on my way out.

3

I rode down Nepos's carriage drive and turned left on to the main drag. This time I paid more attention to the scenery, especially to the bit between Mamilius's farmhouse and the wineshop. For all Nepos had talked about Navius's fancy new ideas I couldn't see much difference between his property and the rest except that it was mostly planted out with vines. Then again, maybe I was missing something.

Papatius's wineshop looked tempting but I earmarked it for later. That was a pleasure to be savoured: I'd already checked out the wine and it was as good as Flatworm's best, easy. Mrs Papatius wasn't bad either. The lady wasn't in evidence but there was an old guy gnarled as an olive stump sitting on one of the benches under the trellis. I gave him a wave and he lifted his cup in salute. Well, at least the natives were friendly, and that was a good sign: friendly natives tend to have loose mouths. If my luck held he'd still be there when I got back.

There was one other house between Papatius's and Clusinus's farm, on the other side of the road. Its terrace had been empty when I'd passed before, but now there were a pair of middle-aged spinster types in residence.

I gave them another cheery wave and got a brace of glares in return that all but froze my balls to the saddle. Yeah, well: *some* of the natives were friendly. These two beauties looked like their faces would crack if they so much as simpered. They were wearing headscarves so I couldn't see their hair, but I wouldn't lay any bets that it wasn't the kind that had fangs and hissed.

I turned left up Clusinus's track. Looking around, I could see what Nepos had meant: the guy was no farmer, that was sure. The fields on either side were an anonymous sea of burned stubble from the wheat harvest, but there were vines on the slopes beyond to the right before the broken country began that even to my city boy's eye looked scraggy, like they'd been left to do whatever they liked. About three hundred yards up, the track split. A side branch led to what had to be the farmhouse; the other carried straight on towards the high ground to the north. I'd just turned the horse up this second branch when a girl wrapped in a cloak and carrying a basket came down the first.

We both looked round together. I had a glimpse of dark hair framing a heart-shaped face and black, anxious eyes; then she was hurrying back the way I'd come, towards the main road. I watched her go until she was out of sight. Even with the cloak wrapped round her she was a stunner.

Uh-huh. An eye for the girls, Nepos had said. Maybe I'd just seen why young Navius was so far off his own patch. I clicked my tongue and sent the horse on up the track and past a grove of holm-oaks. Where the ground started to rise there was a ragged orchard of apple and pear trees. Goats were wandering under the shade of the unpruned branches, grazing on the stubble of what had obviously been another wheat crop. The trees themselves had hurdles round them, but from the condition of the fruit Clusinus would've done better to let the evil-smelling horned bastards have their wicked way and then sold them on as kebabs.

Nepos's gully was screened by a cleft of hill-slope from the track proper which carried on up to the higher ground, and barring a few scuff marks and a spot or two of dried blood there wasn't much to see. It crossed my mind that I hadn't asked Nepos what they'd done with the body. I'd've liked to have seen it for myself – a stab through the heart's a stab through the heart, sure, but there might've been other things to notice – but presumably it'd either been taken home or directly to the undertaker's in Caere. I kicked around for a while in the hopes of picking up a clue, but the place was clean. No scraps of cloth ripped from the murderer's tunic, no mysterious messages scrawled in the dust by the dying man's finger. No nothing, in fact, which was about all I could've reasonably expected. What you saw was what you got.

Well, there wasn't any point in sticking around here, and at least I'd got the girl. If I hurried, I might pick her up again on the way back. And if not there was the wineshop.

The old man was still there. 'Old' didn't do him justice; he would've given Tithonus a run for his wrinkles, maybe even Saturn as well. The guy could shift it, too. As I tied the horse up where the bastard couldn't reach the grapes hanging from the trellis and made my way over he poured the last of his jug into his cup and swallowed it down like it was barley water.

'Hey, Grampa,' I said. 'You manage another one of those?'

I'd been kidding, or half kidding, but he grinned at me, turned round and shouted, 'Thupeltha!'

Mrs Papatius came out. So that was her name. She was certainly something, big as a man, easy, a Praxiteles Juno squared with the biceps of an Amazon. Women like that, you don't leer, you marvel.

I'd sat down next to the old bugger on the door side of the bench. Turning, and finding myself face to face, as it were, with a pair of breasts that were practically army ordnance grade, I swallowed hard.

'Uh ... you want to bring us another jug, sister?' I said.

She picked up the empty and disappeared with it inside. A minute or so later, she reappeared with a full one, planked it down on the table and went back in again. All without so much as a smile. I got the distinct impression that our Thupeltha was a lady of few words, which wasn't surprising because the way she moved more than made up for them. Who needs ordinary conversational skills when you're put together like an Archimedean City-taker?

Ah, well, fantasy over and back to the job in hand. I turned to Tithonus and poured for both of us.

'Marcus Corvinus,' I said.

'Quintus Mamilius.' The guy was still grinning. I'd expected him to be toothless but he had practically the whole set. They were in good shape, too. 'Quite a looker, Thupeltha, isn't she?'

'Yeah.' I let the first swallow of Caeretan slip past my tonsils. Beautiful! 'She makes nice wine, too.'

'That's Papatius. Best vintner in the district. With his brains and her ...' Mamilius stopped. 'Aye. Well, Corvinus, like you say it's good wine.'

'You're ex-army.' It wasn't a question: you get to spot

these guys, and Mamilius had *legion* written all over him. Not just because of the amount of booze he could shift, either, although that helped. It's a funny thing, but I've never met an army man who couldn't drink two jugs to my one.

He nodded. 'Senior centurion with the Grabbers. I fought with the emperor and his brother against the Raeti.'

I whistled, impressed. 'Is that so, now?' Jupiter, old was right! I wasn't sure of the exact date, but the Wart's campaign against the Raeti must've been a good forty-five years back. And if this guy had been a senior centurion at the time then he'd be pushing ninety. 'You farm the place up the road?'

'Aye. Have done since my discharge.'

'You, uh' – I paused. I didn't want to be personal, but hell! I was genuinely interested – 'you farm it alone?'

Mamilius shrugged and topped up the cups. I wondered if I could keep up the pace. 'I've a son and a couple of lads. They do most of the heavy work these days.'

'"Lads"?'

'Slaves. I bought them about thirty, thirty-five years back.'

'Uh-huh.' I sipped my wine. Well, it was all relative, I supposed. 'You know Attus Navius?'

Mamilius sank a straight quarter-pint before answering. It may've been my imagination, but I felt he'd taken a sort of mental step backwards.

'Aye,' he said shortly.

'You care to tell me about him, maybe?'

He reached for the wine jug and topped up both our cups again; his needed it, mine didn't. I noticed his hand was rock-steady. Built like a rock, too.

'You're the knight's stepson, right?' he said. 'Helvius Priscus's. The man Clusinus caught with the body.'

There wasn't any point in denying it. Vetuliscum was a small place, and even if we had only been here for a couple of days I'd've bet the locals knew already what we put on our porridge in the morning.

'Yeah,' I said. 'That's right.'

He grunted. 'And naturally you're out to prove he didn't do it. True?'

'You ever meet Priscus, Mamilius?'

The guy obviously hadn't expected a question. He paused with the cup halfway to his mouth. 'No. Can't say I have.'

'Take my word for it, then. The cack-handed old bugger couldn't stab anyone if he tried between now and Winter Festival.'

Mamilius's eyes opened wide. Then, slowly, he began to laugh. It was like hearing a superannuated wolf choke on a duck.

'Aye,' he said finally. 'Well, maybe that's as good a defence as any. You're right, killing a man takes practice. Even so you'll have an uphill struggle proving it.'

'You think so?'

'I know so.' He took a swallow of wine then set the cup down. 'Put it like this, Corvinus. Whoever killed Navius wasn't just passing through. Your stepfather doesn't belong here. If he did it, then fine, but if he didn't then it was one of the locals. If you'd lived here all your life which solution would you prefer? Even if it was the wrong one?'

I frowned. Shit, that was something I hadn't thought of, but the guy was right, straight down the line. Forget objectivity and the pure desire for justice; as far as the Vetuliscans were concerned if they could stick Priscus

with the rap, guilty or not, then everyone'd be happy.
Everyone but Priscus, sure, but then he didn't matter
because like Mamilius said he was an outsider, and
a Roman aristo at that. Corvinus with his questions
was going to be as popular locally as a flea in a
barbershop.

Mamilius was watching me.

'Me,' he said, 'I was born in Tusculum.'

'Is that so?' I sat back.

'That's so. Like I said, I got the farm as my discharge
settlement forty-three years back when most of these
bastards weren't even a gleam in their fathers' eyes, and
I'm still a stranger. You believe that, Corvinus?'

Yeah, I'd believe it. Farming communities're no different from the Roman aristocracy: you're either family or
you ain't, and if you ain't then all your money and all
your goodwill and community spirit won't buy you in,
ever. There was an edge of bitterness about Mamilius
that I could understand.

'So.' He topped the wine cups up again. The level in
the jug had slipped by half in ten minutes, and he'd had
most of it. Jupiter, if I could sink the stuff like that when
I hit ninety then I'd call myself a drinker. 'What do you
want to know about Navius?'

'Who killed the guy.'

He chuckled. 'Aye. No doubt. Well, that's one thing I
can't tell you. Try me with something easier.'

'Okay.' I thought of the woman with the basket. 'Clusinus.
He got a daughter, maybe?'

An expression I couldn't quite place rearranged the
wrinkles on Mamilius's face, so fast it was gone almost
before I realised it was there. 'Aye,' he said. 'He's got
two children. A girl and a boy. The girl's just turned
six.'

Uh-huh. Bright-Eyes hadn't been any six-year-old, that was for sure. 'His wife, then,' I said. 'She small, slim, dark hair, dark eyes?'

He nodded. 'That's Vesia.'

Shit; this could be tricky. 'Navius was found on Clusinus's land. I understand that he had, uh, a liking for feminine company. I wondered whether maybe you thought there might be a possibility that he might've conceivably dropped by for a visit. A social visit.'

Mamilius had picked up his cup but he wasn't drinking. He didn't say anything for a long time, just sat looking at me like I'd crawled out from under a rock, and nonagenarian or not his look had me sweating. Finally, he put the cup down.

'No, I don't,' he said. Just that, but the tone told me the subject was closed. Closed, locked and buried.

'Uh, yeah. Yeah, right.' I swallowed. Sure, the question had had to be asked, but the country isn't Rome. Cast aspersions on the local womenfolk and you're liable to lose your teeth, fast; and I reckoned I'd just come within spitting distance of losing mine. 'Fine, pal, fine. That's all I wanted to know.'

His hand bunched round the wine cup, and I had the unpleasant feeling that he'd rather it was my throat. 'Listen, Corvinus,' he said. 'Vesia's a good woman and a good wife, right? She could've left that shiftless bastard years ago for someone better but she didn't. And if she ever did take up with anyone else it wouldn't be effing Attus Navius. Besides—'

He stopped speaking. Suddenly, like his mouth had just welded up. I waited, but there was nothing else. He picked up the wine cup, emptied it at a gulp and poured us some more.

Time for a change of subject. Or at least the same

subject from a different angle. 'So what was Navius doing up Clusinus's road in the first place?' I said.

'He wasn't necessarily up Clusinus's road at all. Not as such.'

I frowned. 'You've got me there, pal.'

'When it leaves Clusinus's property the track turns left and follows the foothills. The Navius place is on the slopes to the west, and the track runs past it. Navius could just as well've been coming the other way and heading for the main road.'

Yeah. That was something I hadn't thought of, not knowing the topography, but it made sense. If the guy had been going to Caere, say, it would've been six of one and half a dozen of the other which way he went, especially if he were on foot. Shit. Maybe the fact that he'd been knifed on Clusinus's land wasn't relevant after all. Still, that was something I could check: if he had taken the main road there was a chance that he'd been seen. By one or both of the Gorgons, maybe. These two had looked the type who wouldn't miss much.

'Uh, the pair of ladies in the house along the road,' I said. 'Who would they be, now?'

'The Gruesomes?' Yeah, well, I'd been close, and Mamilius's temper seemed to have improved now we'd got off Vesia. 'Gnaeus Vipena's sisters. The elder one's Tanaquil, the younger's Ramutha.'

'Good old Etruscan names.'

'Believe it.' He chuckled like a badly greased hinge. 'Good old Etruscan family. With the accent on "old". Vipena's the local augur, and he's got a family tree that goes back to the time of the Tarquins. So he claims, anyway. They even speak Etruscan at home.'

'Yeah?' Shit, that was really weird: no one, but *no one* spoke Etruscan these days barring the Wart's nephew

Claudius, and that guy was barking crazy in any language. 'That all there is of them? Just the three?'

'Vipena's never married. And no one with any sense would want to bed either of these vinegary bitches.'

'Uh-huh.' I looked up. The sun was well over to the right-hand side of the trellis. It was getting late, and Perilla would be more than curious about what the hell was going on. 'One last thing, friend. For now, at least.' I took the knife I'd got from Nepos out of my belt. 'You recognise this at all?'

Mamilius took it from me and turned it over in his gnarled fingers. 'This what the lad was killed with?'

'Yeah.'

He shrugged and handed it back. 'Could be his own,' he said. 'Navius had one like that, sure, but so does half the district.' He reached into his own belt and pulled one out that was practically a ringer, its blade honed almost concave and sharp as a razor. 'Gaius Tullius the cutler over in Caere makes them by the dozen.'

Ah, well; another bummer. Still, I couldn't really expect that whoever had shoved his knife into the guy would've left it there to be traced back. And if the knife was Navius's own, of course, the murderer'd probably have been keen to get rid of it anyway. 'Would anyone know for sure?' I said. 'If it was his, I mean?'

Mamilius hesitated. Again I got that fleeting impression that he was going to say something and decided against it. 'Your best bet would be the lad's mother,' he said. 'But maybe under the circumstances that's not such a hot idea.'

'Yeah.' I got up and took a silver piece out of my purse to pay for the wine. 'Well, it doesn't matter. I'd best be getting back. Thanks for the information, friend.'

'You're welcome. Any time.'

*   *   *

The Gruesomes weren't in evidence when I rode past. Maybe it was just as well: I doubted if they would've taken too kindly to a strange man trespassing on their virgin modesty. This was a job for Perilla – or maybe for both of us, since I might want to follow up that one question with others. We could sort of drop by by accident tomorrow.

Meanwhile I had a lot to think about. Like for example what Mamilius had been very careful not to say about Attus Navius.

4

Perilla was still on the terrace with Aulus Caecina when I got back, but she rolled him up when she saw me and lifted her mouth for the traditional welcome-home smacker. Bathyllus was hovering with the wine tray as per standing orders. I sat down and let him pour me a belt of Flatworm's best.

'Well, Marcus?' Perilla said.

I gave her the basic run-down.

'What on earth did he think he was doing?' she said when I'd finished. 'The silly, *silly* man!'

'Yeah, that's our Priscus.' I downed a swallow of the Caeretan. 'The guy ought to wear ear plugs to stop the wind blowing through.'

'So what can we do?'

I shrugged. 'Find the real killer. Oh, sure, the chances are when the case comes to court the jury'll take one look at the poor old bugger and throw it out the window, but if they don't then Priscus could be in real trouble. On the other hand if I can give them the guy who did it neatly parcelled up with a bow round him then we're laughing.'

'Corvinus, we are on holiday! I am not going to sit

at home twiddling my thumbs while you go traipsing around digging the dirt. Let alone wash the blood off you when you get your silly head bashed in for being, to use your own expression, a smartass.'

I was shocked. You don't expect language like that from respectable Roman matrons, certainly not when they've got Perilla's wide vocabulary.

'Uh, yeah,' I said. 'Well, actually—'

'And what about Marilla? The poor girl's tucked away most of the time in the Alban Hills. When she goes on holiday she expects a bit of excitement.'

I tried not to grin. The Princess loved it up at Perilla's Aunt Marcia's with the sheep and the chickens; it was why we'd left her there instead of dragging her off to Athens after we'd adopted her, and although Marcia would've surrendered her without a murmur losing the kid would've hit the old girl hard.

'Yeah,' I said. 'All those tombs. And I hear the smart set in Rome are coming to Caere this year instead of going to boring old Baiae. In fact, they say that the Wart's travelling up specially from Capri for the annual cheese-rolling festival.'

'Corvinus, there is no such thing as an annual cheese-rolling festival!'

'There is now, lady. As of this year. That and goat-pitching. The local Caeretan Committee for the Propagation of Tourism's reviving all the traditional Etruscan sports. King Porsenna of Clusium was the Etruscan League's all-comers' goat-pitching champion five years running. Your pal Caecina didn't mention that?'

'Corvinus . . .' Perilla's lips were beginning to tremble.

'Then there's Guess How Many Hedgehogs in the Amphora, the five-a-side Pass-the-Bean, Juggling the Marrow and Sausage . . .'

'Marcus, stop it!'

'. . . the Wives of the Committee of Ten Freestyle Naked Mud-Wrestling, the launderers' guild's Spot the False Nose Competition, the . . .'

'*Marcus!*'

'. . . fluteplayers' Eat All the Doughnuts You Can Manage In One Breath, and finally the Mule and Monkey Hundred Yard Hurdles. Yeah. You're quite right, Perilla. Maybe the kid would miss out.'

'What's the Mule and Monkey Hundred Yard Hurdles, Corvinus?'

I turned round. Marilla had come out on to the terrace with Corydon in tow.

'Oh, hi, Bright-Eyes,' I said, ignoring Perilla creased up in the other chair. 'Sorry. Joke. I thought Alexis was getting rid of that moth-eaten couch cover.'

'He hasn't found the owner yet.' Marilla helped herself to a handful of early grapes from the bowl on the table and fed half of them to Corydon. 'Who did Priscus kill?'

'A guy called Attus Navius. Only he didn't.'

She looked disappointed. 'There was no murder after all?'

'No, Princess. There was a murder all right. But Priscus didn't do it.'

'Then who did?'

'I don't know. That's what I'm trying to find out.' I glanced at Perilla. She'd stopped hugging her ribs and she was a better colour. Also she wasn't grouchy any more. 'We.'

'"We"?' Perilla said.

'Uh, yeah.' I took a fortifying swig of wine. 'That's what I was going to say before you sidetracked me, lady. Hold the thumb-twiddling. I need your social skills to butter up a couple of elderly spinsters tomorrow. You think you can manage that?'

'I don't know, Corvinus. I might if I were given a good enough reason.'

Yeah, well; that was fair. I told her about the roads difficulty. 'If Ramutha and Tanaquil didn't see Navius then it doesn't prove anything, one way or the other. But if they did then it's a fair bet he was headed for Clusinus's place as such, or at least had business on the guy's property. And the combination of his reputation for a roving eye, the honey I saw with the basket and Clusinus being off hunting is too good to pass up.'

'Corvinus, you said Mamilius discounted that possibility.'

'Yeah.' I topped the cup up from the jug. 'But I wouldn't necessarily take what that old guy said as hard fact. Oh, he wasn't lying, but where this Vesia's concerned he obviously has stars in his eyes. It happens more often than you'd think with these regular army types, boiled leather slit-your-throat-if-you-cross-them one minute, soft as Suburan grandmothers the next. And he didn't like young Navius at all.'

'What makes you think that?'

'Nothing specific, exactly. He didn't actually say anything bad about the guy, but I'd bet a barrel of fish sauce to a corn plaster he was holding himself in. In fact for all the impression he gave of being ready and eager to spill the local beans, when it came to it old Mamilius was pretty tight-mouthed.' I took another swallow of wine. 'Ah, hell. Leave it for the moment. What time's dinner?'

'Early. I thought we'd have it out here. Meton's making a hare and squash casserole.'

'Great.' I looked at Marilla, who was feeding more grapes to her pal the mule. The bastard was being good as gold at present, but I didn't trust him an inch. 'Alexis struck out, you say, Bright-Eyes?'

'He's been trying all afternoon, asking round the local farms, but no one he's talked to so far knows anything about it.' She stroked Corydon's neck while he tucked into our cream-of-the-crop dessert. 'Corvinus, can't we keep him if he isn't claimed? He wouldn't be any trouble.'

Gods alive. One look at the set of the bugger's ears and the permanent sneer on his face would be enough to convince any reasonable person just how valid that prediction was. But then where animals were concerned the Princess wasn't a reasonable person. Corydon could've been guilty of the muline equivalent of first-degree sacrilege, multiple murder and five separate counts of grand larceny and in her eyes he'd still be a snow-white innocent. Sure, if he kept at it then Alexis would come up trumps eventually, but there was a big stretch of country out there, and it was filled to bursting with small farms, especially the flat land between us and the coast. If Corydon was a real stray we could be talking long term, and I had a sneaking suspicion that that would be bad news. I felt like the guy in the story that the king gave an elephant to and who couldn't get rid of it.

The Princess was still looking at me. I swallowed and put my best judgment aside. 'Yeah, well,' I said. 'Give it two days. Tomorrow and the next. If Alexis still hasn't had any luck then subject to later developments I reckon we'll've done all we could. Deal, Princess?'

'Deal.' She kissed me solemnly. 'Come on, Corydon. Let's see if we can find you a lettuce.'

They started off in the direction of the kitchen garden. That took them past Perilla, who was still sitting with Caecina in her lap. The mule's head snaked round . . .

Perilla squealed.

'*Corydon!*' The Princess was pulling at Caecina's end-roller while the mule's teeth got busy editing the text. '*Bad* boy! Drop it! *Drop!*'

There was a ripping sound, then silence except for the rhythmic chomping of jaws and a sort of muline snigger. Shit. There went a lifetime's work, three hundred years' worth of collated scholarship and the entire recorded achievements of a once-proud nation.

'Oh, Perilla, I'm sorry!' Bright-Eyes was still tugging at the bit of Caecina which projected from the mule's mouth. The mule pulled it away from her with a jerk of his head and carried on eating. 'He didn't know what it was!'

I don't think I've ever been so proud of Perilla. At this point anyone else but the Princess – including me – would've been a small glowing pile of ash on the flagstones and all the wildlife for miles would be headed at speed in the general direction of Parthia. Jupiter alone knew what would've happened to the mule. But not an eyelid did the lady bat.

'Never mind, dear,' she said. 'It can't be helped.'

Marilla led Corydon off, still busy with his textual criticism. I gave her a couple of minutes then sneaked a glance at Perilla. She was staring out over the plain towards Pyrgi and the coast in the distance.

'Corvinus, you've heard of Cilnius Maecenas, I suppose?' she said after a while.

I cleared my throat nervously. It was quiet; too quiet, like there'd just been an earthquake and the world hadn't decided yet whether it was still in one piece. 'Uh, yeah. Yeah, sure. Augustus's pal. What about him?'

'He wrote poetry in his spare time. He's also supposed to have introduced the eating of donkey flesh as a delicacy at banquets.'

Uh-huh. 'Is that right, now?'

'His poetry was considered to be trite, badly con-structed, trivial in theme and totally unoriginal.' Perilla picked up a half-eaten book-roller from the ground and set it carefully on the table beside her. 'Personally I think he's grossly underrated.'

'Yeah?'

'Yes. I thought I might just tell you that.'

'Uh, yeah.' Jupiter! 'Thanks, Perilla.'

'And no quips about that animal having excellent taste in literature, please. I'm not up to them at present.'

'It never even occurred to me, lady.'

'Good.' She brushed the papyrus fragments from her mantle and stood up. 'Now I think I'll just go upstairs for five minutes and have a quiet scream.'

She left.

Ah, well. You win some, you lose some. Grinning, I reached for the wine jug.

5

Perilla and I went to Nepos's next day via the spinsters'. We took the coach: left to myself I'd've walked, and unlike your standard Roman matron Perilla is a pretty willing and competent hoofer, but I'd bet that the Gruesomes were sticklers for the proprieties, and if we'd turned up on the doorstep sweaty and covered with dust we'd just have got another of these hundred-candelabra stares and the bum's rush. Lysias the coachman had been warned to do things right for once, with no slouching in the box scratching his armpit while the master opened his own door, and he rose to the occasion. We pulled up in front of Ramutha and Tanaquil's terrace like visiting royalty and de-carriaged in style.

The sisters were shelling beans; whatever arcane practices the augur's household indulged in they sure as hell weren't Pythagorean-based. Close up, I could see what Mamilius had meant by vinegary: personally I'd never actually come across such a thing as a life-sized pickled gherkin before, but if I ever did I reckon it would've been tough to spot the difference.

'Yes?' said the psoriatic one with the mole. Friendly as hell. You'd've thought we'd come specially to steal the spoons.

Perilla introduced us while I kept to the background and smiled. Bringing the lady with me had been a stroke of genius: you could almost hear the crackle as the ice melted.

'And so we thought, or rather Marcus thought,' she finished, 'that we would take the liberty of paying a brief visit. It's so important, don't you feel, when one is on holiday, to make the acquaintance of the right type of people.'

They blossomed like December roses. The one with the mole – that was Tanaquil, the elder; Ramutha was the eggbound hen – even patted her iron-hard bun. We were whisked inside and plied with honey wine and cinnamon cake. The cake wasn't bad, but the honey wine set my teeth on edge. Jupiter, I hate that stuff!

Perilla did most of the talking, which was fine by me. Half an hour in we'd covered, in order, what a terrible place Rome was (parties going on until all hours, ten o'clock at night, sometimes, so they'd heard, would that be right, now?), how Athens wasn't much better (Perilla's contribution, much appreciated), how things had deteriorated since they were girls forty years ago ('But you're much too young, Perilla my dear, to remember that!'), how even in a quiet, decent place like Vetuliscum people nowadays actually had the bad manners to get *murdered* . . .

'But then of course,' Tanaquil said with a sniff, 'he brought it on himself.'

'It's his mother I feel sorry for.' Ramutha was cutting another slice of cinnamon cake. 'Such a *nice* woman! *Her* side of the family always was most respectable.'

I bit down hard on my tongue. I noticed that Perilla, her job done, had her eyes lowered and was sipping her honey wine.

'*Most* respectable.' Tanaquil's thin lips were pursed above the rim of her cup. 'I really do not understand why that brazen hussy's husband doesn't take a stick to her.'

'Quite.' Ramutha nodded. 'It's just a mercy there are no children.'

I frowned; something was screwy here. The 'no children' bit didn't square for a start, and Mamilius might've gone slightly over the top but not that much. 'Uh ... I'm sorry,' I said, 'but are we talking about Vesia? Titus Clusinus's wife?'

Tanaquil sucked in her breath and shot me a look that made my scrotum crawl.

'We most certainly are not!' she snapped.

'The very idea!' Ramutha sawed viciously at the cake. 'Valerius Corvinus, you surprise me!'

Jupiter! 'Right. Right.' I was nodding so hard I thought my head might fall off. 'So ... ah ... who?'

'Why, that woman down the road, of course.' Ramutha's voice was pure undiluted venom. 'Larth Papatius's wife.'

I almost dropped my cup. 'You mean *Thupeltha*?'

'You know her?' Tanaquil was glaring at me like I'd blown my nose in my napkin.

'Ah ... yeah, well, not personally, of course, but—'

'By reputation,' Ramutha finished. She dumped the slice of cake on Perilla's plate. 'Indeed. I'm not at all surprised.'

'Hell, she's practically old enough to be the kid's mother!'

Tanaquil smiled grimly. 'You're quite right to be shocked, Valerius Corvinus,' she said. 'We all were when it started. Shocked and appalled.'

'It, uh, had been going on for a while, then?'

'A year. Perhaps longer,' Ramutha said. 'Certainly

before the boy's father passed away. I wouldn't be
surprised, myself, if the shame of it didn't hurry the
poor man into his grave before his time. Scandalous,
quite scandalous.' She leaned across the table, and her
voice dropped to barely a whisper. 'And, of course, it
wasn't the first time, either.'

'Yeah?'

'A butcher in Caere. Just after they were first married.
They say his death was an accident, but you can believe
that if you like.'

'Uh . . . the guy died?'

'Found with his neck broken at the bottom of a ravine.'
She sat back and beamed at me. 'The investigation was
most cursory.'

'A strong man, Larth Papatius.' Tanaquil chewed on a
morsel of cake. 'And not the most evenly tempered. One
must be charitable and feel some sympathy for the boy,
naturally, but a husband does have rights, and he acted
most properly.'

Perilla had raised her eyes, startled. I felt pretty knocked
back myself.

'Ah . . . hang on, there,' I said. 'You're saying *Papatius*
killed Navius?'

Tanaquil frowned. 'But of course he did. We saw him
ourselves.'

Jupiter! 'You *what*?'

'Not the actual killing, of course.' Ramutha gave an
acidulous sniff. 'We saw him as he went past.'

'He was following Navius' – Tanaquil bared her brown
teeth at me – 'who was following the woman, no doubt to
one of their assignations. Oh, she was *quite* blatant about
it, wasn't she, Ramutha?'

'*Quite* blatant,' Ramutha agreed. She lifted her cup
and sipped delicately. 'Personally, I don't blame Larth

Papatius in the slightest. All that surprises me is that he didn't kill his wife at the same time.'

Oh, gods! Oh dear, sweet gods!

Tanaquil picked up the knife and leaned forward, smiling. 'More cake?' she said.

6

Ten minutes later we were in the carriage heading for Nepos's. I was still feeling like someone had clouted me from behind with a blackjack.

'It can't be that obvious,' I said.

'Of course it can, Marcus.' Perilla was looking relaxed. 'Crimes of passion are the commonest type. Husband murders lover, lover murders husband, wife murders husband . . .'

'Since when were you an expert, lady?'

'Admit it. You feel cheated.'

'Damn right I feel cheated! And that pair of harpies are cracked as a cut-price Corinthian vase!'

'They seemed quite sensible to me. Not exactly my type, but—'

My fist hit the cushion. 'Jupiter, Perilla! Papatius couldn't have done it!'

'Why not?' Yeah. Good question. I didn't answer. 'Marcus, the thing's solved. Papatius killed the boy out of jealousy. All Priscus has to do is subpoena Tanaquil and Ramutha and have them tell their story to the judge. As far as we're concerned we can forget about it and get on with our holiday.'

'Looking round tombs?'

'Not all the time, no. Caere has some wonderful old temples.'

'Jupiter on a bloody see-saw!'

Perilla smiled. 'At least Priscus'll be pleased when you tell him. He must be very worried.'

'Priscus has probably forgotten all about it by this time. Where everyday things like murder are concerned the guy's got the attention span of a gnat.'

'Marcus, you're grousing.'

'I am not—' I stopped. 'Yeah, okay. But we don't stay to lunch, right? I've had about all I can take for one day without adding food poisoning to the list.'

She leaned over and kissed me. 'All right,' she said. 'Is that Thupeltha, by the way?'

I looked out of the carriage window. We were passing the wineshop. Mamilius was sitting on the outside bench and Thupeltha had just put a jug of wine down beside him. Over in the far corner of the terrace a big bald-headed guy was lashing a fugitive vine tendril to the trellis. He looked up momentarily, then went on with what he was doing. Obviously the landlord himself, and what Tanaquil had said about him being a powerful man was right. Even his muscles had muscles.

'Yeah,' I said. 'That's her.'

'Then I see what your spinster friends meant. Men would find her very attractive.'

'You think so?'

'Oh, Corvinus!'

I grinned. 'Uh, yeah. All right, then, she's okay. A bit obvious.'

'And you were right about something else. If Navius was only in his early twenties then she is old enough to be his mother. She must be thirty-five if she's a day. That's interesting.'

'It is?'

'How many women do you know who take lovers younger than themselves? Present company excepted, of course.'

I gave another grin: Perilla's got eighteen months on me, although it doesn't show. 'Quite a few, as a matter of fact.'

'In the long term? And much younger?'

'Sure. Only in that case there's usually some sort of quid pro quo. The woman's generally ugly and loaded and the kid's a stud on his uppers. Nothing wrong with that. Both parties get what they're looking for, they're both happy and it's no concern of anyone else's.'

'But, Marcus, in this case Thupeltha isn't ugly, she's hardly, I would imagine, loaded, Navius strikes me as rather a mother's boy despite his reputation and as the owner of quite a sizeable property in his own right he can scarcely be described as on his uppers. Besides, I would assume that Papatius would be quite concerned, for one. And lastly this is not Rome or Athens. Liaisons like that belong to a more sophisticated world. They simply don't happen out in the country.'

Jupiter! When you translated that into simple Latin it actually made sense. 'You making something out of this, lady?'

'Not really. But it's worth thinking about, isn't it?'

'Yeah.' I frowned. 'Yeah, it is.'

When we arrived at Nepos's his foreman was in the yard supervising the daubing of the empty wine jars with pitch ready for the up-and-coming grape harvest, but he took time off to show us up. Nepos himself,

Mother and Priscus were all in the atrium, as well as
Mother's doctor hanger-on, the unhilarious Hilarion. I'd
only met the guy once, but he'd given me a pain in my
back molars the minute I'd set eyes on him.

'Marcus, dear.' Mother came over and turned her
cheek for me to kiss. She was wearing a stunning yellow Coan silk mantle and she smelled of the hyacinth
perfume that goes for a gold piece the bottle in the
pricey Saeptan shops, if you can get it. 'And Perilla.
How lovely.'

'We just dropped by to see how Meataxe was doing,' I
said.

'Helvius Priscus is bearing up very well.' That was
Hilarion. The guy was stroking his beard like it was a cat
that had fastened itself to his expensive lambswool tunic.
'Although there is still a certain overpreponderance of
phlegm in the brain that I am at present combating with
hot mustard poultices.'

'Is that right, now?' I said. I turned to Priscus. He was
lying on one of the couches with a squishy bag of gunk
tied to his forehead. 'How's the boy, Priscus?'

'Mmmaaa . . .'

Hilarion coughed. 'The patient has also, temporarily,
been forbidden to speak,' he said, 'the shock of yesterday having significantly depleted the air content of the
blood vessels which, as you are no doubt aware, Valerius
Corvinus, is essential to rational thought. To that end he
has been forbidden lettuce and restricted to a diet of
boiled pulses.'

'Yeah?' Jupiter! In my strictly non-medical opinion
keeping Priscus off the salads and zipping up his mouth
weren't going to do a hell of a lot of good as far as
improving his mental thought processes was concerned.
And if air in the brain had anything to do with intelligence

then the old bugger must've been starved of it at birth. 'You sure he wouldn't be better off in Caere, bashing tombs?'

'With the wind in the south and a superfluity of cerebral phlegm?' Hilarion gave what passed with him for a wry chuckle. The first time I'd heard it I'd thought the guy was pegging out. 'Hardly, hardly. My dear sir, I have no wish to offend, but you're obviously not a doctor.'

'Don't be silly, Marcus,' Mother said. She'd been listening to the old quack with dewy eyes and hands reverently clasped, and in a woman of Mother's intelligence it was sickening to watch. 'Hilarion knows what he's talking about. He is a genius.'

'Is that so?' Yeah, sure; and I was Asclepius's grandmother. I turned to the guy and gave him my best smile. 'Let me just say one thing, pal. If we're talking about wind then the only relevant bit around here is—'

'*Marcus!*'

Fortunately for family amity Nepos put his oar in at this point.

'Corvinus, my dear fellow,' he said, 'why don't you and I go along to my study for a while, eh?'

I let myself be led off; all the more willingly because Nepos picked up a jug of Falernian and a couple of cups on the way. That medical bastard would probably claim that, me being of a choleric, that is hot and dry, disposition Falernian was the worst thing I could inflict on my system. As far as I was concerned Hilarion could take the whole Hippocratic corpus and use it as an enema.

'Well, now,' Nepos said when we were ensconced on a pair of reading couches with the Falernian between us. 'And how's the investigation going?'

I took a swig. Caeretan's fine in its way, like I said,

but its big brother from down south definitely has the edge. Nectar. 'Not bad. In fact it may be all over.' I told him what the Gruesomes had just told us about Navius, Thupeltha and Papatius. 'That make sense to you, Nepos?'

He shrugged. 'It doesn't surprise me, certainly, although I knew nothing about the affair myself. Remember, I'm no Vetuliscan, I'm not one for gossip and I don't see much of the locals. Barring that old bastard Arruns, naturally, but that's another story.'

'Arruns?'

'Larcius Arruns. My immediate neighbour. You won't have met the fellow yet, but he's quite a character.' Nepos chuckled into his wine. 'Too much of a character for my delicate taste, to be truthful.'

'Uh-huh.' My ears had pricked up. *Immediate neighbour*, right? So he'd be a neighbour, too, of Navius, on the other side from Papatius, and Nepos's tone hadn't exactly been all sweetness and light. If the Papatius angle fell through this Arruns might be interesting. 'So why doesn't the affair surprise you?'

'Oh, anyone could see it coming, my dear fellow. Thupeltha's got red blood in her veins, Navius was a good-looking lad and Papatius isn't a man I'd like to cross. There's a story about a Caeretan butcher—'

'Yeah. The girls told me that one. Is it true?'

'As far as the basic facts are concerned, yes.' Nepos frowned. 'Beyond that I don't know. Certainly the fellow was found dead of a broken neck halfway to Caere, but he'd left the wineshop drunk and it was a filthy night in the middle of winter. He could easily have strayed off the road. Whether there was ever anything between him and the woman your guess is as good as mine, and as for actual foul play . . .' He shrugged.

'Uh-huh.' I took a swallow of the Falernian. 'What sort of a guy is this Papatius? In himself, I mean. You think he's capable of murder?'

'Possibly. Under the proper circumstances.'

'You care to tell me what these are?'

'I doubt if I can. Papatius isn't an easy chap to pigeon-hole. Thirty days out of the month he's as easy-going a man as you could wish to meet. The thirty-first' – Nepos turned his cup in his hands – 'well, you know these flash rainstorms we get this time of year, Corvinus; one minute blue sky, the next all hell let loose. Papatius is a bit like that.'

'Yeah?' So. That fitted with the Gruesomes' story, anyway. And if the guy's wife was carrying on with Navius an impulse killing was a definite possibility.

'We'd an incident a year or so back, for example. I was in the wineshop myself, as it happens. Stranger up from Pyrgi took on more wine than he could handle and began to get a bit abusive. Papatius let the man rant for a while, then he gets up and without a word of warning smacks the fellow in the mouth.' He chuckled. 'Breaks his jaw for him, one punch, then sits down like nothing's happened and leaves us to pick up the pieces.'

'Uh-huh. Jealousy?'

'Oh, it had nothing to do with Thupeltha, my dear fellow! Woman wasn't even there at the time. In bed with a bad cold, had been for days.'

'They, uh, get on well together? Papatius and his wife?'

'As far as I know, publicly at least. In business terms the marriage is an ideal arrangement. Thupeltha owns the wineshop and the land, Papatius is the best damn vinegrower in the district, partly hard graft but that's never enough with vines. Whatever the fellow's got – and remember the wine business is chancy at best – it's very close to magic. Between them he and Thupeltha are coining money hand over fist.'

I sat back. Yeah. That little nugget was interesting. Also it fitted in with a couple of other things that'd been bugging me about Navius's murder. Maybe when I got Perilla alone I'd try them out on her.

'Okay,' I said. 'Tell me about this Larcius Arruns.'

Nepos chuckled. 'Now he really is a Vetuliscan. The family's been here at least since Deucalion's flood, probably a lot longer. If you're looking for someone to add to your list of suspects then I recommend Larcius Arruns to your attention. And guilty or not, speaking personally I wouldn't be sorry to lose him in the slightest.'

'Yeah? How so?'

Nepos reached for the wine jug and topped up our cups. 'Because, my dear fellow, he's a crusty, litigious old bugger. We share a perennial boundary stream, and you know how precious these things are. I've fought tooth and nail ever since I bought this place over my fair share of the irrigation rights, but the wretched man won't give an inch.'

'Uh-huh.' I could understand the exasperation in his voice: all-year-round water is as precious to a farmer as gold. 'I thought irrigation rights were written into the deeds.'

'Of course they are. But the word of the law's one thing, implementing it's another matter, especially if you want to stay on neighbourly terms. And it's not just me. He has court cases pending with half Vetuliscum for one reason or another.'

'What about Navius?'

'Oh, my dear fellow, that's a very old chestnut! Practically a family feud. There's a stretch of vineyard on the edge of Navius's property that Navius's grandfather bought from Arruns's father fifty years back. Arruns has always claimed the sale was bogus and the vineyard still belongs to him.'

'The sale's on record?'

'Certainly.'

'So?'

'Arruns claims the deed is forged, that his father never sold the land and Navius's grandfather swindled him.'

'That's no reason to murder the grandson.'

'Agreed. But then stranger things have happened.'

I grunted. Yeah, well, it was possible: these old country feuds had nothing to do with logic. Maybe Arruns had the right of it and the land was his after all. Or maybe, like Nepos said, the guy was just a litigious old bugger who got a kick out of mixing it with the neighbours. Still, it was another strand. Not that I needed one at present. I swallowed the last of my wine and put down the cup.

'Okay,' I said. 'You've done what you set out to do.'

Nepos laughed. 'And what might that be?'

'Cooled me down. I might even let that phoney bastard Hilarion live after all. Let's go and rejoin the party.'

'Fine. Oh. Before we do that I've one small bit of news myself.'

'Yeah? And what's that?'

'Quintus Cominius is sending an investigator of his own. His nephew, as a matter of fact. Chap called Gaius Aternius.'

I stared at him. Hell. Hell's bloody teeth.

7

We got back about two hours later, in time for a late
lunch. Nepos had pressed us to stay, and his side of the
table would've been safe enough, but Mother would've
found ways and means of getting me to eat the whacky
stuff, and with Phormio and Hilarion both slugging for
the home team I wasn't risking food poisoning for no
one. We had fennel omelette, rissoles and braised chickpeas. Marilla bolted hers and dashed off to do whatever
the hell fourteen-year-old kids find so fascinating, leaving
us to our wine (me) and fresh-squeezed cellar-cooled
grape juice (Perilla).

'So, Marcus,' Perilla said. 'What was Licinius Nepos
saying?'

I told her. 'I owe you an apology, lady. Papatius is the
murderer after all.'

'Unless Tanaquil and Ramutha are lying about seeing
him pass their house that morning.'

'Why should they lie? Sure, they might invent a juicy
bit of scandal just for the fun of repeating it, but they've
got no down on Papatius. Quite the reverse.'

'We've only got their word for it that Navius and

Thupeltha were lovers. Nepos didn't confirm that, did he?'

'No. But it hangs together, especially looking back to what Mamilius told me. Or didn't tell me, rather. Navius was involved with someone. If it wasn't Vesia then Thupeltha's a fair bet, especially if the lady's that way inclined.'

Perilla sighed. 'Corvinus, don't exaggerate. We know of one lover and even he is questionable. Also, don't forget what I said about older women.'

'Yeah. But the butcher still died.'

'Possibly by accident. Keep to the facts. When it comes down to it your only reasons for choosing Papatius derive from gossip passed on by two biased, spiteful and thoroughly unpleasant old women.'

I grinned. 'Hey, lady! Last I heard you were all for the case being solved. You changed your mind or something?'

'No. But I have been thinking things over and I'm simply putting them into perspective.' Perilla took a sip of her grape juice. 'Certainly Papatius is the prime suspect, and he may well be guilty, but his guilt is by no means either self-evident or proven. It involves too many assumptions based on too few facts.'

'Yeah.' I shifted on the couch. 'That's the problem I'm having. Even given that Navius and Thupeltha were an item and that Papatius had both an opportunity and a motive, two things still jar. First, why the hell Clusinus's property?'

'Pardon?'

'Come on, Perilla! If the two were screwing then why choose there to do it? Papatius's farm and Navius's share a boundary. They could've met somewhere along that stretch, or anywhere either side of it. Why go in the other direction and risk a third party muscling in?'

'Privacy? You said yourself that Clusinus's farm is quite wild. And by all reports he doesn't spend all that much time there.'

'Fine. But if they wanted privacy then all they'd have to do would be go up into the hills. You're begging the question, lady. Clusinus's was a conscious choice. I'm asking you why.'

'I don't know, Corvinus. You're the sleuth.'

'Yeah.' I frowned. 'Problem is, if Thupeltha's the girl-friend and not Vesia then I don't have an answer either.'

'What was the second thing?'

'The Gruesomes said the affair'd been going on for a year, minimum. So if they are right and Papatius topped the guy because of it then why has it taken him so long?'

'Perhaps he didn't know.'

'It's possible, sure. But in a small place like Vetuliscum? And with folk like Tanaquil and Ramutha ready to drop some pretty big hints?'

'All right. Then perhaps he was making his mind up to it.'

'Perilla, this is the guy who's already supposed to have broken a butcher's neck for him. And even if that was an accident there's the business of the loose-mouthed lout from Pyrgi. Papatius is no shrinking violet. Maiming-stroke-killing his wife's lover right off or holding back for a month or so I could understand; but brooding over it for a year? No way. Besides, there's another reason why he wouldn't've done it at any time.'

'And that is?'

'Nepos told me the land and the wineshop are in Thupeltha's name. As things are, as a team they've got a good thing going. Papatius is no sponger, he pulls more than his weight growing the vines and making the wine, but when it comes down to it his wife holds the purse strings.'

Perilla stared at me. 'You're saying Papatius *knew*?'

'About the affair? Sure. Or at least it wouldn't surprise me.'

'And he let it go on?

'Lady, this is the country, remember; land's important, priorities are different. As a couple they're doing well. If Papatius kicked up a stink or forced a break than they'd both lose out, sure, but he'd be the harder hit. He wouldn't be the first husband who's turned a blind eye for reasons of his own.'

Perilla was quiet for a long time. Then she said; 'I suppose it does make some sort of sense. But what kind of man would tolerate a situation like that?'

I shrugged. 'Like I say, it's a question of priorities. And if Thupeltha was discreet, like she seems to have been, then there's no reason why it shouldn't go on indefinitely.'

'Marcus, theory's one thing, proof's another. How do you go about proving something like that?'

'Simple.' I drained the cup and got to my feet. 'I talk to the lady.'

'Now?'

'Sure. Why not? Besides, if anyone knows what actually happened in this business it's Thupeltha. The sooner I have a word with her the better.'

This time I walked. It was a glorious day, and although the countryside isn't my bag a quiet stroll followed by a jug of good wine and a chat with a good-looking woman aren't to be sneered at. Murder investigation or not, I was looking forward to this.

If Papatius had been around I'd've put things off,

naturally, but there was no sign of him. Mamilius neither: the terrace was empty. I went inside.

Thupeltha was standing by the kitchen table, skinning a hare. She looked up at me and frowned. I caught a strong whiff of perfume, the cheap-and-cheerful stuff you can buy in any small town for a silver piece the pint that smells like dried lavender with overtones of cat.

'Wine?' she said.

Yeah, well, we were making some progress. That was the first time I'd heard the lady speak. Maybe if I stuck around we might get the length of sentences.

'Please,' I said. 'No hurry, though, sister. I can wait.'

She shrugged and turned back to the hare, working its hind legs through the belly-slit. Then she took a firm hold of the neck and tugged. The skin came off with a ripping sound that set my teeth on edge. She laid the skinned animal down and wiped her hands on a scrap of bloody cloth.

'Want to go outside while I bring it?' she said.

'Don't bother.' There were benches against the walls with folding tables beside them. I chose the one nearest the door and sat on it. 'Here'll do fine.'

'Suit yourself.' She dropped the cloth and collected a cup from the dresser, then pulled a wine jar from the rack on the wall and upended it into a jug with about as little effort as if the thing had been empty. Jupiter, the lady was strong! If Papatius was someone to be reckoned with then his wife wasn't far behind.

She set the jug and cup down beside me and went back to the table. Then she picked up a cleaver and began jointing the hare as if I'd stopped existing. Yeah, well, I'd known already she was no conversationalist. This was going to be an uphill struggle. I lifted the cup and sipped.

'Nice wine,' I said.

The cleaver came down hard, severing the hare's spine. I waited. No other answer. I tried again.

'The name's Marcus Corvinus. I'm looking into Attus Navius's murder.'

'I know.' *So what?* her tone said, and she hadn't so much as glanced in my direction. Carefully, she put the point of the cleaver against the hare's breastbone.

'I understand you were friendly with him.'

The cleaver paused. Thupeltha turned round slowly, like a trireme bringing round its ram.

'Who told you that?' she said. 'Those two old bitches down the road?'

Now it was my turn to shrug. 'Were you?'

'Tell them from me they can stuff their long noses up their own backsides.' She pushed down hard. Bone crunched. 'As for you, you can drink up and go.'

I sighed. 'Listen, lady. Under normal circumstances I couldn't care less. But my stepfather's facing a murder rap, and if he didn't do it, which he didn't, then I intend to find out who did. You were the last person to see Navius alive, which makes you a prime witness. At the very least. You understand?' Her eyes shifted, but she didn't answer. She moved over to the vegetable basket by the door and pulled out a bunch of turnips. 'You were seen following him in the direction of Clusinus's farm. Half an hour later the guy was dead.'

Thupeltha paused. 'You think I killed him?' Her face was as expressionless as her voice.

'No.' I laid the knife I'd got from Nepos on the table in front of me. 'You recognise this?'

She put down the turnips and came over. I thought she'd pick the knife up but she didn't; only looked.

'It's Attus's,' she said.

'You're sure?'

'I've never been one for lying, Corvinus, and I won't start now. That's Attus's knife. You can believe me or not.'

I put the thing back in my belt. 'Okay. You know where it was found?'

'I can guess. Between his ribs, yes?'

Well, the lady was cool enough. 'You any idea who put it there?'

'Of course.'

Jupiter! I blinked. That had come out so flat I thought I'd misheard somehow, or she'd misunderstood the question.

'Uh . . . hold on,' I said. 'Are you telling me you actually saw the murder?'

'No. I said I knew who was responsible for Attus's death. There's a difference.'

'Okay. So who?'

'Attus himself.'

I sat back. 'You're claiming it was *suicide*?'

'No.'

'Jupiter, lady! Then what . . . ?'

Her thick lips twisted in a grin. 'I'm not claiming it was suicide, Corvinus, I'm telling you it was.'

Shit. This was something I hadn't expected. 'Hang on. If you didn't see Navius die then how the hell do you know he killed himself?'

Another shrug. If I hadn't known the pair had been lovers I'd've thought she couldn't care less. She pulled the turnips towards her, picked up a small vegetable knife from the table and began to top and tail them.

'Thupeltha?' I said when it didn't look like I was going to get any more of an answer. 'What makes you so sure Navius committed suicide?'

The blade – it was paper-thin, and honed so sharp I could've shaved with it – slipped through the turnip's flesh like a sigh.

'Because when he left me he said that was what he was going to do.'

8

'You want to tell me about it from the beginning?' I said quietly.

Another shrug; I had the idea that whatever I suggested would be received with the same total lack of interest. She pulled up a stool and sat down. The stool creaked beneath her weight.

'The cats are quite right,' she said. 'The affair started eighteen months ago, at the Spring Festival.'

'Who started it?'

She smiled, suddenly and unexpectedly. Helen might've smiled like that when Paris suggested a trip to Troy. She'd've been a few stones lighter, mind, but the effect would've been the same. I felt my hair crinkle. 'He did, Corvinus,' she said. 'Let's get that clear from the start. I'm no cradle-snatcher.'

I nodded. Yeah, that made sense. It fitted in with the picture I was building up of Attus Navius, too: 'He made the running all the way, right?'

'Not all the way. He was a nice enough boy, good-looking, very polite. To me, at least. And he was good in bed, too, when we got that far. Which was about three days in.'

'Uh-huh.' I sipped my wine and tried to match her matter-of-fact tone. 'Did your husband know what was going on?'

'Naturally. I told him myself. I always do.'

Jupiter! 'And he didn't mind?'

She sighed. 'Corvinus, understand this. All Larth is interested in are his vines. Or my vines, if we want to be accurate. We don't sleep together. I won't say we never have, but it hasn't happened all that often because Larth just isn't that way inclined. Or any other way for that matter, if that's what you're thinking.'

'You have an arrangement.'

'We have an arrangement. I'm up front with him, I never take more than one lover at a time and in every other way I'm a good wife. In return he leaves me alone and spends his time making the best wine in the district from my grapes.'

'Sounds like a fair bargain to me.'

'Don't sneer, Corvinus. It suits both of us and we're happy enough. Larth's only interfered once, and he was quite right to do so.'

'The butcher from Caere?'

'Juno, you have been busy! The cats again, was it?' I didn't answer. 'That's right. The man's name was Marcus Poetelius, not that it matters. He couldn't keep his mouth shut.'

'So your husband shut it for him?'

She ignored me. 'That's my first condition, and his. The second is that there's no long-term commitment either side. Poetelius broke the rules.'

'What about gossip?'

'There's always gossip, however careful you are. I don't mind it, within reason, and nor does Larth. If it gives sad old women like the cats any fun then they're welcome. Men're a different thing. If Larth heard a man say one word against me, or even heard of it, he'd kill him. Everyone around here knows that, and the threat's enough.'

'Only with this guy Poetelius it wasn't.'

'No.' That was all, but the implication was clear. Jupiter, this was weird.

'So Navius broke the rules as well,' I said quietly.

'Attus was no braggart. Not by nature, at least.'

'The second of the conditions, then. He wanted a long-term commitment.'

She nodded. 'You're clever, Corvinus,' she said. 'Very clever. Yes. He wanted me to divorce Papatius and marry him.'

'And when you refused he threatened to kill himself.'

'He did more than threaten. I told you.'

'Yeah.' I took a sip of wine. It tasted sour. 'One question. Where did this happen?'

Her eyes shifted. 'A few hundred yards down from where he was found. There's a grove of holm-oaks just—'

'Yeah. I know where you are. You met there often?'

For the first time she looked uncomfortable. 'No.'

'So why this time?' No answer. 'Was it your choice or his?'

'It was mine.'

There was something wrong here. Thupeltha might not be lying but she wasn't telling the whole truth, either. I was being deliberately shut out of a whole chunk of the story, and whatever that was it was crucial.

A different venue, not Navius's choice, on someone else's land . . .

. . . and then I had it. Shit! I'd been a fool!

'You hadn't gone there to meet Navius at all,' I said. 'You'd gone to see Clusinus.'

There was a long silence. Finally, Thupeltha got up, walked towards the door and leaned against the jamb with her back to me.

'Clever's right,' she said.

'One lover at a time. You'd already given Navius the brush-off and Clusinus was the guy's replacement. Navius knew, and he didn't like it. He followed you and tried to persuade you to change your mind.'

She still hadn't turned. 'He'd been working in the corner of his property beside the road,' she said. Her voice was flat, expressionless. 'He saw me leave. I didn't see him until I was at the grove.'

''Was Clusinus there already?'

'No. I was early. I turned round and there he was.'

'And then you had your argument and the kid threatened to kill himself.' She nodded. 'He make any other threats?'

She went very still. 'Such as what?'

'To make a meal of the situation in public. To blow the whistle on you and Clusinus.'

She whipped round, glaring. 'Why should he do that?'

'Jealousy's a good enough reason, lady.' I held her eyes. 'And I get the impression it's the sort of thing he might do.'

'He might. Or might've done, rather. But in the event he didn't, did he?'

That came out cold as a Riphaean winter. Jupiter, the poor bastard!

'Okay,' I said. 'What happened next?'

'When he saw I wasn't going to change my mind he left me and ran off. That was the last I saw of him.'

'Uh-huh. And what—?'

She put a finger to her lips and glanced quickly over her shoulder. A man came in, pushing past her like she was just an obstacle in the way; the bald-headed guy I'd seen fixing the vine. He was carrying a truss of early grapes. He set them on the table, nodded to me but ignored Thupeltha, then fetched a cup from the dresser and poured wine into it direct from the flask. I noticed he lifted it easily with one hand.

Thupeltha had picked up her knife again and was back to slicing turnips.

'Nice day,' I said.

Papatius grunted, sat down and drank. Obviously a born communicator like his wife.

'The name's Valerius Corvinus.' I waited. Nothing. 'Helvius Priscus's stepson.'

'Is that so?' The tone showed he'd have been just about as interested if I'd said my name was Tiberius Caesar.

'I've been asking your wife some questions about Attus Navius.' Thupeltha's eyes flicked up, then down again. She went over to the unlit stove and began laying it with sticks and charcoal. 'She's been very helpful.'

'Navius is dead. There's an end of it.' Papatius drained his cup and got up to pour another. Deliberately, I leaned back so that the knife in my belt was visible. Papatius glanced at it without interest, then away. He came back to the bench and sat down.

'Yeah,' I said. 'That's the point, pal. Only there are different kinds of dead, and I'm still not sure which category he fits into, murdered or suicide.'

'You say you've asked Thupeltha. She'll've told you clear enough.' He took a swallow of wine. 'The boy killed himself.'

'Uh-huh.' I emptied my own cup and refilled it from the jug. 'Yeah, well, that's still a moot point. Sure, he might've threatened it, but no one saw him actually die. Or did they?'

He set the cup down slowly. 'What do you mean?'

'Vipena's sisters saw you follow him up the road towards Clusinus's place. I just thought maybe you might've—'

I stopped. Thupeltha's head had come up and she was staring at Papatius, her mouth open.

Shit! She hadn't known! *Thupeltha hadn't known!*

Papatius didn't move. He didn't look at Thupeltha, either; his eyes were fixed on me.

'Maybe I might've what, Corvinus?' he said. His voice was level; too level.

My brain was racing. 'Uh, seen something.'

'I was going that way, sure.' He was looking at me like he would've cheerfully hauled out my guts and strangled me with them; he could've done it, too. 'But I wasn't following Navius. I was on my way into Caere. If it's any business of yours. And I didn't see nothing.'

'Yeah. Yeah, right.' Jupiter! 'That's fine, pal. It was just an idea.'

'Then another time keep your ideas to yourself.'

'I'll do that. I most certainly will.' I finished off the cup and got to my feet; there was still a quarter of the jug left, but I'd got what I came for and I had the impression I'd outstayed my welcome. Papatius hadn't moved, but he was sending out what definitely felt like bad vibes. 'Thanks. I'll see you around.'

I'd got as far as the door when Thupeltha called out: 'Corvinus!'

I turned. 'Yeah?'

'That'll be a silver piece. For the wine.'

'Oh. Right. Sure.' I took the coin out of my purse and laid it on the table. 'Nice talking to you both.'

There was no answer from either of them. I left.

I was sorry I wasn't a fly on the wall. With me

out of the way the next ten minutes would've been interesting.

As I walked back, I thought about where all that had got me, apart from within spitting distance of a few busted ribs. Sure, Navius could've killed himself like Thupeltha had said. Suicide made a lot of sense; all there was against it as a solution was its simplicity, and I wasn't stupid enough or vain enough to take that as a valid argument. It fitted with the nature of the wound, for a start – I wouldn't care to slit my throat myself, and cutting your wrists is messy and too long-drawn-out – and also with Navius's character, as far as I'd been able to piece it out. Killing himself was just the sort of stupid thing the moonstruck young bubblehead might've done, and he'd had the knife to do it with. Last but not least, he'd told Thupeltha he was going to finish things, and whatever faults that lady had I didn't think lying was one of them. Not out of any moral compunction, mind; the bitch just couldn't be bothered to make the effort.

Okay, so if Thupeltha was telling the truth suicide was possible, maybe even likely. What about murder, which was equally likely? In that case we were back to suspects. Thupeltha herself would've been capable, sure, physically and mentally, and she'd had both the motive and the opportunity. Papatius was an even better candidate in both categories, especially now; that claim to've been going into Caere had rung as fake as a lead penny. When he turned up Clusinus's road he could've left the track and taken to the higher ground to the right where the scrub would hide him. From there he'd be able to see what was going on; hear it, too, if the argument had developed into a shouting match. As for motive, the guy had that in spades. Forget the jealousy angle; Thupeltha had said it didn't figure, and I believed her. If Papatius had killed Navius it wasn't because the kid had been screwing his wife; it was because he'd just been threatening to spread the word around. And that got rid of the problem of the year's delay, too. Lastly, the fact that Thupeltha hadn't known he was following her – and she hadn't, that I'd swear to – meant that the lady could genuinely think the kid had killed himself like he'd said he would, because she'd no reason to suspect otherwise.

It would work. Sure it would, especially since there was still the outside possibility that Thupeltha might change her mind and marry the kid after all, taking the farm with her ...

Yeah. I liked Papatius. I liked him a lot. He was definitely a possibility.

There was no sign of Perilla when I got back, but Bathyllus was waiting for me on the terrace with the wine tray.

'Hey, little guy.' I took the cup from him. 'Where's the mistress?'

'Getting changed, sir.'

He had his grave look on again. Uh-oh. This looked like trouble. I sat down on the nearest chair.

'Don't tell me, sunshine. Corydon's broken into the library and he's browsing through Flatworm's pornography collection.'

Bathyllus didn't smile. Not that I'd expected him to; the guy had all the sense of humour of a grapefruit. 'No, sir,' he said. 'It's more serious than that, I'm afraid.'

'Meton's put too much fish pickle in the sauce? You've run out of spoon polish?'

Not a flicker. Trouble was right. 'Neither, sir.' He

cleared his throat. 'We've just had a message from Licinius Nepos. There's been another death. Your mother's doctor friend.'

'*Hilarion?*' I set the cup down.

Jupiter!

9

They'd put Hilarion in a corner of the wine cellar on the north side of the villa's ground floor, where it was nice and cool.

'One of my slaves found him in the hills just north of here.' Nepos was frowning down at the body on the stretcher.

'Uh-huh.' Gently, I examined the guy's head. Whatever he'd been clouted with had been pretty effective. The back of the skull was stove in like an eggshell. 'What was he doing up there?'

'Walking. He usually takes – took – a constitutional after lunch, and he went that way more often than not.'

'It couldn't've been an accident? He couldn't have fallen or been hit by a falling rock?'

'Not a chance.' Nepos shook his head. 'He was lying on the path. There're no overhanging cliffs there. No big rocks near the body, either.'

'Uh-huh. This path you mentioned. That'd be the one that runs round the top of the farms and down by Clusinus's place, right?'

'That's it, Corvinus. I understand the fellow made the circuit and came back along the main road.'

So. He hadn't gone all that far before he was killed. And if he'd left just after lunch that put the time of death mid-afternoon at the latest. 'Would this be common knowledge?' I said.

Nepos shrugged. 'You knew him yourself. He lived by routine. And most of Vetuliscum uses that track, for one reason or another.'

I stared at the dead man. Shit, it didn't make sense. Who the hell would want to kill Hilarion? Apart from being a pompous self-opinionated bugger with all the charm of a wet poultice he was a complete nonentity. And being a stranger he had no local connections at all.

Unless he'd seen something, of course. Like Navius's murder . . .

Only that didn't make any sense either. Navius had died halfway through the morning, Hilarion took his constitutional in the afternoon and besides the guy had been in Caere all day; to my certain knowledge he hadn't got back until the early evening. Mind you, that only covered one end of it.

'Uh, what time did he leave yesterday, by the way?' I said. 'You remember?'

'*Yesterday?*' Nepos gave me a sharp look. 'Ah. I see. Quite so. Very early, just after dawn, in fact.' His lips twisted. 'Something to do with cool air and the balance of the humours.'

Well, it had been worth checking. And even if he had set out later Hilarion was no Priscus: he wouldn't've taken any wrong turnings. Still, it was a thought. And as far as I could see it was the only possible explanation.

'I don't know about relatives,' Nepos was saying. 'Nor does your mother. In any case a delay's out of the question this time of year. We'll arrange the funeral ourselves.'

'Yeah.' I sighed. I hadn't liked the guy, but I wouldn't've wished him ill, not with any seriousness. And there was something pathetic about the small figure on the stretcher. 'Okay. Let's go and join the rest.'

We went back up to the dining-room: it was practically dinner-time now, and this time Perilla and I would have to stay out of pure politeness. Ah, well; with a death in the house not even Mother would have the nerve to force any of Phormio's gunk on me.

There was a stranger on one of the couches: a big, handsome guy in his late thirties wearing a sharp mantle that must've come from one of the best shops in Rome. Wearing it well, too.

'Ah, Aternius, you've arrived,' Nepos said. 'My apologies. Your uncle did say you'd be coming today but what with poor Hilarion's death I quite forgot.' He turned to me. 'Gaius Aternius is the fellow I mentioned to you, Corvinus. The mayor's nephew. He'll be looking into our little problem. Aternius, this is Marcus Valerius Corvinus, Helvius Priscus's stepson.'

'And Vipsania's son?' Aternius looked at Mother, lying next to Priscus; death or not, she was stunning as ever. 'That I can hardly believe.'

Uh-oh. I had the feeling already that I wasn't going to like this guy one bit. He had the kind of built-in smarm that makes my skin crawl.

'Is that right, now, pal?' I said, taking my place next to Perilla. 'You like to see the birth certificate, maybe?'

'*Marcus!*' Mother snapped. Perilla was glaring at me too: female solidarity. Priscus was out of it as usual, communing with the ceiling inlay.

I held my hands up, palm out. 'Okay. Okay,' I said. 'Forget I spoke.'

Nepos had taken the host's couch. He gave a signal to

the waiting slaves and the boys went out to bring in the eats. 'You'll be staying here, Aternius, until this business is concluded, naturally,' he said.

'For tonight, certainly, if it's not inconvenient under the circumstances. I'd be delighted. Especially with such charming fellow-guests.' His teeth flashed in Mother's direction in a hundred-candelabra smile. They were pearly white and even, and I'd just bet he had all thirty-two of the little darlings. Although a reduction in the number could be arranged. 'I doubt if I need impose on you for longer.'

'You're very welcome however long you wish to stay. I'm grateful that your uncle is taking an interest in the affair.'

'Election coming up, is it?' I said. Needle, needle.

Aternius's eyes narrowed. 'As a matter of fact it is, Valerius Cercinus,' he said.

Bastard. 'That's "Corvinus", friend.'

'My apologies.' He turned to Mother. 'So. How do you like our little backwater, Vipsania?'

I'd've thought Mother would be pretty subdued with her doctor pal lying stiff and cold two floors down, but she was practically glowing. 'I think it's charming,' she said. 'So unspoiled. Of course with all this nonsense Titus and I haven't really had much chance recently to see around. No more than a tomb or two. Isn't that right, Titus?'

'Mmmaaa?' Priscus's eyes peeled themselves off the decor and blinked at her. 'Certainly, my dear. Just what I was about to say myself.'

'You haven't been up to Lake Sabatinus yet?'

'No, I don't think so.'

'Oh, but you must go there! It's absolutely beautiful, and no more than half a day's ride away. I have some friends with a villa at the lake edge. I'd be most happy to take you. And your husband, naturally. They'd be glad to put us up, I'm sure.' He gave another dazzling smile. 'We could go tomorrow, in fact.'

'I rather think we'll be burning poor Hilarion tomorrow.' Mother was dry.

'Ah. Yes, of course. The day after, perhaps?'

Jupiter, I didn't believe this! The guy had to have an ego the size of the Capitol. 'Uh, hold on, friend,' I said. 'I thought you were here on a murder investigation?'

He didn't even have the grace to look fazed. 'Oh, that?' He waved his hand dismissively. 'I doubt if that'll be much of an obstacle, Corvinus, not now in the light of the wineshop woman's evidence. Your wife told me that you'd got the full story from her this afternoon.'

'Is that so, now?' I glanced at Perilla. Her ears were pink and she wasn't looking at me. Guilty; guilty as hell. So the smarmy bugger had got round her, too. Jupiter, wait till I got that lady home! 'Yeah, well, it could've been suicide, sure. But now Hilarion's got his head beaten in I'd say the odds on murder have shortened considerably.' I saw Mother wince; well, it served her right. 'I'm sure Perilla pointed that out to you too when she gave you her bootlegged run-down.'

'Actually she—'

He was interrupted by the slaves wheeling in the starters. I kept a leery eye on the plates, but most of them seemed all right: the usual crudities, olives, hard-boiled pea-hen's eggs, chickpeas with fennel. There was only one whacky dish that I could see, a sort of terrine made up of grey mush and green veins. It had 'Phormio' written all over it.

'Uh . . . what's that stuff, Mother?' I pointed, keeping my finger well clear in case it bit.

'That?' Mother's perfect eyebrows lifted. 'Oh, that's fermented wild emmer purée in aspic with dandelion and burdock, Marcus. Do be sure to have some. It's very good for you.'

Yeah. I'd just bet. Thank the gods I'd asked.

'No, I'll pass, thanks,' I said and reached for a pea-hen's egg.

She sniffed. 'Suit yourself, dear.'

'I'll try some, if I may.' Aternius transferred a large spoonful of the glop on to his plate. 'It looks absolutely delicious.'

Mother gave him a beaming smile of approbation. Crawler!

I put the egg down. This was going to be good. I noticed that Nepos and Perilla, too, were looking on in horrified fascination. Aternius scooped up half the glop, opened his mouth, popped it in, closed his eyes and chewed. Any moment now . . .

Seconds passed. Nothing. I didn't believe this.

'Excellent.' He spooned up what was left and ladled more on to his plate. 'You must let me have the recipe.'

There was a terrible silence.

'You, ah, liked it, my dear chap?' Nepos said finally. He was looking sick. 'Genuinely?'

Aternius's spoon paused.

'Of course. Shouldn't I have?'

'Jupiter!' Nepos muttered, and reached for the chickpeas.

Well, I'd seen everything now. The guy must have a palate like a strip of wash-leather. I dipped the pea-hen's egg in fish pickle and bit into it . . .

Holy sweet immortal ever-living gods!

'Nice, aren't they, dear?' That was Mother, watching

me while I choked. 'They're Phormio's latest discovery. Eggs stuffed with pepper, anchovies, stem ginger and crushed juniper berries.'

Luckily the wine slave had been doing the rounds. I grabbed my wine cup, sank a straight quarter-pint and held it up for more. It didn't quite kill the taste, but at least it put out the fire in my throat. Some of it, anyway. I wiped my streaming eyes with my napkin. Jupiter, that had been a bad one! I wondered if whoever had brained Hilarion might be persuaded to take a free crack at Phormio. I might even add Mother to the list.

Aternius picked up one of the eggs and popped it into his mouth whole. Well, the guy had guts, I'd give him that. Or at least he had at the moment. Come four o'clock in the morning I wouldn't lay any bets.

'So, Valerius Corvinus,' he said, chewing, 'it's your view that Attus Navius was definitely murdered, yes?'

'Yeah.' I was watching him fascinated. 'I'd say that was a reasonable assumption.'

Nepos's spoon with its load of chickpeas paused halfway to his mouth. I noticed he'd been pretty careful to sample one first. Quite right. With Phormio loose in the kitchen you didn't take anything for granted. And after the pea-hen's eggs nothing was safe.

'Gentlemen,' he said, 'do we have to talk murder at the table?'

Mother selected an olive. 'Personally I find it fascinating,' she said. Holy Mars in spangles! That was news to me! Any time in the past I'd brought up anything visceral round the dinner table I'd been slapped down. But she had her eyes on Smooth-Chops Aternius, and they were looking positively melting. The way to Mother's heart is definitely through your stomach. Right through. 'You have a forensic connection yourself, Gaius Aternius?'

'I'm a practising lawyer, yes.' The bastard was chewing on his egg like it was something actually edible. 'Although mostly I deal with the property side. Conveyancing and so on. I'm only doing Uncle Quintus a favour here.'

'Good qualifications,' I said. 'Shuffling paper and an uncle who's the local mayor.'

Perilla gave me a glare. She'd been pretty quiet since I'd nailed her for blabbing, but she was obviously coming out of her shell now. 'Marcus, what is wrong with you?' she said. 'You've been terribly rude all evening.'

'Don't exaggerate, lady. The evening hasn't started yet and I'm just warming up.'

She sniffed and turned away.

'Marcus, stop it.' Mother again, and seriously peeved. She turned to Aternius. 'He's really a lot more intelligent than he sounds. Or rather, not quite so unintelligent.' Ouch. 'And he does seem to have the sort of warped mentality that makes him good at solving puzzles.'

'So I understood from your wife, Valerius Corvinus.' This time I was the one who got the teeth. A shame his uncle couldn't take that white and bottle it. He'd have every political candidate in Italy beating a path to his door with his electioneering mantle under his arm. 'In fact she tells me that you've already solved this particular one.'

'Uh, come again?' I said cautiously.

'Forgive me, Gaius Aternius.' Perilla's voice cut across his. There was a flash of movement as a spider in the corner scuttled up its web and disappeared into a crevice. 'But I said nothing of the sort.'

'Not in so many words.' Smile. 'But the conclusion was inescapable.'

I sat up. I was seriously worried now. 'Hang on there, pal! I haven't solved anything!'

'Of course you have.' Smile again. 'And in only two days. I was most impressed, as my uncle will also be. I'll be taking Larth Papatius into Caere first thing tomorrow.'

'You're arresting *Papatius*?' Jupiter! I didn't believe this!

'Of course. He murdered Navius, didn't he?'

'Uh-uh.' I shook my head. 'He *could've* murdered Navius. There's a slight but significant semantic difference there, friend. In case you didn't notice.'

Aternius sighed. 'Corvinus, you're being far too cautious.' He counted on his fingers. 'One: Papatius was seen by two reliable witnesses following the dead man. Two: his wife was having an affair with same. Three: he has a history of violence, possibly even involving murder. Four: his wife owns the property they jointly occupy. Should they divorce it will revert to her absolute control. With that amount of evidence against him any court in the empire would convict him.'

Shit, that wife of mine had been busy right enough. One application of smarm and she'd passed on the lot. We would *definitely* be having words. 'Okay. So what about Hilarion? He couldn't've known anything about the murder. He wasn't even in Vetuliscum at the time. So why did he die?'

Aternius's brows went down. 'How the hell should I know?' he said.

Well, at least the guy was human after all, or part-human: the exasperation was genuine. 'That's my point, sunshine. Before you can claim to have solved anything you've got to be able to answer all the questions. And that one's the biggie.'

'I would have thought you'd be relieved that the second murder clears your stepfather absolutely of suspicion.

And no doubt we'll find out the whys of the case when we interrogate the man.'

My blood went cold. 'Torture?'

Aternius looked pained. 'He's a citizen, Corvinus. Torturing citizens is illegal.'

'Yeah. Yeah, sure.' If you've got a stripe to your mantle, or if it's the best lambswool and freshly laundered like this guy's. Hicks from the sticks with calluses on their hands whose normal sartorial level is a sweaty tunic are something else, especially if they're murder suspects. 'Okay, I'll rephrase that. You mean after he's accidentally fallen down a few flights of stairs in the local militia building.'

'I think we can assume the relevant authorities know their own business best.' That came out stiff as hell. 'And I'm afraid I rather resent your tone.'

'Stick around, pal. It gets worse.'

'I think perhaps we should change the subject.' That was Nepos. 'These friends of yours with a villa by Lake Sabatinus, Aternius. They wouldn't be young Oppius Mucro and his wife, would they?'

Ah, hell; I was obviously outnumbered here and I might as well save my breath. I settled back on my couch and reached for the olives. Smooth-Chops here had made up his mind, and there wasn't anything I could do about it for the moment. Besides, he might be right.

Nevertheless, I'd be there the next day when he took Papatius. I owed my conscience that, at least.

10

I was down at the wineshop bright and early, although I didn't go in. Aternius turned up eventually, with two big bruisers in tow. He gave me a look that was about as far the wrong side of friendly as you can get.

'Valerius Corvinus,' he said. 'I'm surprised to see you here.'

I shrugged. 'Just dropping in for a breakfast cup of wine, pal. Don't mind me. You go ahead if you feel you have to.'

I stood aside to let him pass. He signalled to the bruisers and pushed open the door. I followed them inside.

It was too early for customers. Papatius was sitting at the table over his breakfast porridge, Thupeltha was frying a couple of eggs on the stove. She looked up, saw me and her eyes widened.

Papatius put his spoon down slowly. He didn't say anything, but then it was pretty obvious we hadn't come for social chit-chat.

'Larth Papatius,' Aternius said. 'My name is Gaius Aternius. I am taking you to Caere to answer questions concerning the deaths of Attus Navius and Publius Salvius Hilarion. You'll come with me now, please.'

Jupiter, the guy was fast! I didn't even have time to blink before he was out of his chair and halfway across the room. I'd thought he was making for the door, but his hands reached for Aternius's throat.

Aternius took a step to the side and coolly planted a smacker behind the guy's ear. Papatius went down like a poleaxed ox and the two bruisers were on him in a second. They weren't gentle, either.

I had to admit as arrests went it was pretty slick. Mind you, I might've expected that Smooth-Chops would be able to handle himself. It went with the image. Sickening.

The bruisers had lifted Papatius up and were dusting him down. If that's what you'd term covertly beating the living shit out of someone.

'Uh, you think maybe that's enough, boys?' I said mildly. 'I'd say at a guess the guy's pretty well restrained.'

They looked at me, then at Aternius. He nodded. They stepped back, although they kept a grip on Papatius's arms.

Thupeltha hadn't moved. I'd thought she might've slammed one of us with the egg pan or screamed abuse, but she didn't. She didn't say anything at all.

'This is your doing.' Papatius was glaring at me. He was crouched over – one of the big boys had kneed him in the balls – and bleeding from a split lip. 'Why don't you mind your own fucking business?'

'Detection of murder is every honest man's business,' Aternius said. 'I'm very grateful to Valerius Corvinus.'

Papatius spat out a tooth. 'I had nothing to do with it. And who's this Salvius Hilarion?'

'A doctor,' I said. 'He was killed yesterday afternoon.'

'I was picking grapes all yesterday afternoon. You saw me come in yourself.'

'I only saw the one bunch, pal. To be absolutely truthful.'

'I packed the rest in sawdust to take in to Rome today! Holy Jupiter, you can check if you like! They're in the wagon round the side!'

I looked at Aternius. He didn't bat an eyelid. 'You could've picked them at any time,' he said.

The big guy scowled. 'You don't know much about the fresh fruit business. Rome's twenty-five miles away and that's a twelve-hour drive already. You don't pick until you're ready to transport, not when you're talking prime table quality. The profit margin may be bigger when you sell at city prices but so's the competition.'

'Man's got a point,' I said. 'Me, I'd check.'

'I don't need to. I'm sure they're there right enough, although perhaps not quite as fresh as he claims.' Aternius smiled at me and turned back to Papatius. 'Also that you're sufficiently clever to have arranged an alibi in advance. And in any case, you certainly killed Navius. You were seen following him.'

'For the gods' sakes! I was on my way to Caere! I told that to your tame purple-striper monkey here!'

Ouch.

'Fine.' Aternius shrugged. 'Just give me the name of someone who can vouch for the fact of your presence there and when we've confirmed your claim you'll be released with my apologies.' He waited. Papatius said nothing. 'Precisely. Take him away.'

The big boys hustled the guy out. Aternius turned at the door.

'I'm sorry we don't see eye to eye on this, Corvinus,' he said. 'However, I do thank you most sincerely for your help. You have my admiration, and my congratulations.

We'll meet again soon, no doubt, and I hope in more congenial circumstances.'

Then he was gone. I was left facing Thupeltha across the kitchen table. She was still holding the frying pan. She put it down and without a word calmly poured two cups of wine from the jug on the dresser.

'Uh, I'm sorry about this,' I said. 'It wasn't my idea.'

She handed me one of the cups and sat down. 'He didn't do it,' she said.

'You sure of that, lady?'

No answer; Thupeltha just sipped her own wine.

'Did he go to Caere? Like he said?'

'I don't know. He might've done. It's what he told me, too, when you left yesterday.'

I took a swallow. 'Okay,' I said. 'So we start fresh. Level with me and I'll do what I can.'

'I've told you the truth, Valerius Corvinus. All the truth. I can't tell you any more.'

I wouldn't've bet on that, but I let it go. Now wasn't the time. 'Let's have it again,' I said. 'Just to check.'

She set the cup down. 'I arranged to meet Clusinus at the oak grove mid-morning. I set out from here early, like I told you.'

'Papatius was here? He knew where you were going?'

'He knew. Or he knew about Clusinus, anyway. He was in the yard round the side, boiling up pitch for the wine jars. He saw me go, but he didn't say anything.'

'Uh-huh. Then?'

'I went to the grove. I was looking round, like I told you, when Navius showed up. I hadn't known he was following me, and he took me by surprise. We had an argument. I told him my decision stood – the affair'd been over for almost a month – and he tried to make me change my mind.'

'Did he know about Clusinus too?'

'Not from me. But he'd guessed it from where we were. And Clusinus has had other girlfriends in the past.'

'How did he take it?'

Thupeltha shrugged. 'How do you think? He wasn't exactly happy. He threatened that if I didn't agree to divorce Larth and marry him he'd tell everyone we'd been screwing and I'd passed him up for Clusinus. Then when I still refused he drew his knife and told me he'd kill himself. I laughed and told him not to be a fool. He ran off. I waited around for Clusinus, and when he didn't come I went home. End of story.'

'You didn't see Papatius? At any time?'

'No. He wasn't there when I got back, either, but that wasn't unusual.'

'What about the pitch?'

She looked at me blankly. 'What?'

'You said he was boiling pitch for the wine jars. He'd just left it?'

She was frowning now. 'Yes. The fire had gone out.'

'What about the wine jars? Were they done?'

Thupeltha stood up. 'Corvinus, leave me alone, okay? I'm sick of questions and I'm sick of you. Just go away and don't come back.'

What else could I do? I left.

Perilla would be gone into Caere by now with Nepos and Priscus to act as the family rep at Hilarion's funeral, and she'd taken Marilla with her, so I had the rest of the day to myself. I'd thought carefully about what was the best way to spend it and I'd decided on a walk round Vetuliscum, calling in on the locals I hadn't met yet: Nepos's pal Arruns, for a start, the Gruesomes' brother Vipena, maybe even Navius's mother if I had the nerve. Vesia . . .

And Clusinus. There was one guy I really had to meet.

I could check out that track in the hills, too. That seemed to be figuring quite a lot, and I'd only seen the stretch at Clusinus's end.

Outside the wineshop, I turned towards Nepos's. The road up to Arruns's place would be the one on the right after Mamilius's farmhouse, before the bridge.

That little scene with Papatius, and the talk with Thupeltha, had been interesting. The guy was lying about going to Caere, that was certain: Aternius had been quite right about that, and he'd handled it well. If you're facing a murder rap and someone asks you for a name to prove you were where you said you were you don't mess around, and if Papatius wouldn't give one the obvious implication was that he couldn't. On the other hand he'd gone somewhere, in a hell of a hurry: farmers don't up sticks and leave jobs half done without good reason, especially this time of year when they're working to a tight schedule. And he hadn't told Thupeltha, either; she'd got the point about the pitch, sure she had, and it had rocked her. That's the problem with these open marriages: you get used to knowing everything, and when one partner holds out it's worse than if they've been cheating all along.

So what was Papatius doing that was so bad he wouldn't even admit it to his wife? Scratch the obvious: Thupeltha had already told me that the guy had no interest in sex, and in her position she couldn't well complain anyway. Taken with the fact that the Gruesomes had definitely seen him following Navius, plus his own Caere story, the only alternative was the one we'd started with: that Papatius had secretly gone up Clusinus's track after Navius and his wife, listened in to the argument at the grove, followed the guy and murdered him. In which case, the bastard being already in the hands of the law, finish, end of story . . .

Only why should Papatius follow his wife at all? He already knew about Clusinus and presumably he didn't care if the couple were meeting. And as for Navius, he knew the guy was a spent coin who didn't matter any more.

Unless he thought Navius meant to cause trouble, as indeed the guy did; in which case we were back to square one, with Papatius as the killer . . .

Shit. My head was going round. What I needed was wine. I should've brought a travelling flask and filled it up at Thupeltha's before she threw me out.

Someone shouted. I looked up. I was passing Mamilius's place, and the old guy was out in the yard in front pitching wine jars; it seemed that was the in job at the moment, although that was hardly surprising with the main grape harvest coming up. There was another man with him, maybe one of the 'lads' he'd mentioned buying thirty years back.

'Hey, Corvinus!' he said. 'Out for a stroll?'

'Yeah.' I went over. 'How's it going, pal?'

He put down the pitch brush and wiped the worst of the muck off his hands with a scrap of rag. 'Time for a cup of wine?'

There are gods after all, and sometimes they listen. 'Sure,' I said.

'Good. I could do with a break. This is my son Decimus. Say hello to Marcus Corvinus, Decimus. Nicely, now.'

The other guy – he was fifty, easy, but built like a barn door – raised his eyes from the jar he was working on and the hairs rose on the back of my neck.

'Urrrgguu,' he said, and held out a hand like a tile.

Shit. It took all the nerve I had to take it and give it the shake he was waiting for. 'Uh, hi, Decimus,' I said. 'Doing all right?'

No answer. I reckoned Decimus had given his all already.

'We'll go up to the terrace.' Mamilius threw down the rag. 'You manage on your own for a bit, lad?'

The guy turned back to the pitch bucket. I followed Mamilius up the terrace steps.

'Sit yourself down, Corvinus,' he said. 'I'll bring the jug.'

'Fine.' There were two rickety basketwork chairs next to a plank table. I pulled one up and sat on it.

Mamilius came back with a plate of sliced cheese, a wine jug and two cups. 'It's not Papatius's, but it's drinkable,' he said. 'The cheese is mine as well. I keep some sheep up in the hills.' He poured. 'Your health.'

'Health.' I took a swallow. He was right; Papatius's had it beat six ways from nothing, but it was a good swigging wine. And like I said it came as the answer to a prayer. The cheese was good, too.

Mamilius lowered himself into the other chair, slowly; the old bugger might be fit as a flea and tough as boiled leather, but he was still ninety or as close as dammit and I'd bet he didn't bend as well as he used to. 'So,' he said. 'How's the investigation coming?'

'They've arrested Papatius.'

He gave me a sharp look. 'They've done *what*?'

'Less than an hour ago. Nothing to do with me. A guy called Gaius Aternius.'

'The lawyer? Quintus Cominius's nephew?' Mamilius's lips twisted and he spat.

I grinned. Mamilius clearly didn't have much time for Smooth-Chops either. 'You don't think Papatius did it?'

He picked up his wine cup and put it to his lips. The Adam's apple bobbed up and down in his scrawny throat. Finally he put down the empty cup, wiped his mouth and reached for the jug. 'I know nothing about anything, Corvinus,' he said, 'but for what it's worth I don't think the killer was Larth Papatius. Especially with that doctor friend of your stepfather's dead.'

'You heard about that?'

'The whole of Vetuliscum knew an hour after the body was found. Aye, I heard about it.'

'Okay. So if not Papatius then who?'

Mamilius shrugged. 'Jupiter knows, and personally I couldn't care less. When you get to my age death isn't so important any more.'

Yeah, well, I supposed he had a point. He had to be less than a shuffle away from the urn himself, and legionary First Spears aren't exactly renowned for their sensitivity. We sat in silence drinking our wine.

Finally he nodded towards the yard.

'He's a good lad, Decimus,' he said. 'Slow, of course, but he's willing and he does what he's told. His mother died twenty-seven years back this Winter Festival. He idolised her.'

'Yeah?' I looked down at Decimus. The guy was heaving the heavy wine jars around like they weighed nothing at all, and my balls shrank. *Slow*. Not the word I'd've used, but he was the old bugger's son, after all. Insanity's the one thing I can't take. If I ever go that way myself I hope they'll have the grace to slit my wrists. 'He the only one you've got?'

Mamilius hesitated, then picked up the wine jug and refilled our wine cups. 'I had a granddaughter,' he said. 'Not Decimus's; she belonged to my other son, Sextus. He was an optio with my old legion in Germany.'

'Is that right, now?'

'He was married to a local girl. Not officially, of course, you can't do that in the Eagles, but that was what it amounted to.' He emptied his cup and poured again. I didn't say a word. 'They caught the fever, both of them, and died of it. Mamilia survived. She was eighteen months. That was sixteen years ago.' Cup, mouth, jug. He wasn't looking at me now; he could've been talking to himself. I didn't dare breathe. 'She'd nowhere else to go so she came here. Lived here with Decimus and me until just under two years back. Then she died.' He sank half the cupful of wine and topped it up again, then sat staring blankly into space. I waited. 'You asked me about Attus Navius, Corvinus. I'll tell you. I hope the bastard's frying in hell.'

11

I left Mamilius drinking his way down the jug – not
that it seemed to be having much effect on him – and
carried on up the road towards Arruns's turn-off. Shit,
this was getting complicated. For a guy only just turned
twenty Attus Navius had had a real talent for making
enemies. Mamilius hadn't said how his granddaughter
had died, but from what I knew already of the lad's
reputation I could make a good guess. I just wondered
what little goodies Larcius Arruns had in store for me.
If I was really unlucky he'd admit to harbouring deep,
implacable feelings of hatred towards the kid ever since
he'd caught him apple-scrumping.

I spotted Arruns almost straight off. He was fifty yards
over to the left of the track at the edge of a field of
cabbages, waist-deep in a ditch and hacking away with
a spade. I went on over. He glanced up, then put his head
back down and carried on with what he was doing.

'Uh, excuse me, Granddad,' I said when it was rapidly
becoming clear that a view of his bald patch was all the
guy was going to give me. 'Your name Larcius Arruns?'

The man's chin came up. He lowered the spade slowly
and stood glaring.

'Who wants to know?' he said.

I'd expected a hick accent, but there were good vowels there. I remembered what Nepos had said about the guy coming from an old family. He wasn't as ancient as Mamilius, nowhere near, but he was no chicken all the same: I'd guess sixty, sixty-five. And he'd been a strong man in his day. The muscles and sinews on his naked chest and arms stood out like cords.

'The name's Corvinus,' I said. 'Marcus Valerius Corvinus. I'm staying at Gnaeus Lentulus's place down the Caere road.'

Arruns cleared his throat and spat into the ditch. 'So,' he said. 'Another Roman. Why can't you bastards all just go to hell where you belong and leave us in peace?'

Jupiter on wheels! 'Uh, yeah.' I stepped back a pace. 'Right.' *And I love you too, sunshine*, I thought. Well, I could see already what Nepos had meant. Friendly, welcoming and accommodating were three things this bugger wasn't. 'My mother and stepfather are staying with your neighbour Licinius Nepos.'

Arruns's brows went down. 'Neighbour? He's no neighbour of mine.' He looked away and jabbed savagely with the spade at the earth in the bottom of the ditch. 'The man's a damned parvenu. He's only been here five minutes and he's telling me I can't use my own bloody water. Romans!' He straightened suddenly and pitched the shovelful of dirt over the side of the ditch. Half of it landed on my sandals; no accident, either.

This was going to be a tough one. Still, there was no point putting things off. 'Ah ... I don't suppose you'd maybe consider taking a break and talking to me for a bit, sir?' I said in my politest voice. 'About Attus Navius?'

The spade paused in mid-stroke and Arruns looked up sharply.

'Navius? What's your business with Navius?'

'My stepfather found his body. I'm, ah, investigating the death.'

'Are you, now?' He gave me a long considering look. You could've used the set of his mouth to pick locks with, but I thought I could see a faint twinkle in his eye. 'All right. Ask away. But I've got work to do. These ditches don't clear themselves and the rains're coming. There's a mattock over there; give me a hand and I'll talk all you like. Deal?'

Hell's teeth. Purple-stripers don't do manual work; it's in the Twelve Tables. Still, I was being called, and I knew it. Also that if I backed off I could kiss whatever co-operation the old bugger was willing to give me goodbye. 'Sure,' I said, going over to the mattock and picking it up. 'Deal.'

He grunted: I got the impression he hadn't expected me to take him up on the offer, or maybe with a lot more bad grace. 'Good. You break, I'll shovel.'

I jumped down into the ditch and started hacking away. The guy had a point about the rains: this time of year, late summer early autumn, the weather turned pretty unchancy, with sudden thunderstorms sweeping down from the hills and dumping their load on the lower slopes. After the long drought the earth was powder-dry and the result could be a flash-flood that swept away the topsoil and everything growing in it. If the ditches at the edges of the fields weren't cleared out good and deep a farmer could be in real trouble.

He watched me for a minute, then grunted again and bent down to clear the earth I'd dislodged.

'Navius was a smart-mouthed pup,' he said, 'but he'd the makings of a good farmer. He's done a lot for the property since he took it over. Cleared new land, dug drain-shafts above the hill terraces. Done it himself, too, with his own hands. One thing about Attus Navius: he wasn't afraid to get his hands dirty. Not like his poser of a father or your two Roman friends.'

'Uh-huh.' I shifted my grip on the mattock. Hell, this was no joke. I could feel the blisters rising already, and the tunic was sticking to my back. 'Nepos said the guy had some fancy ideas where farming was concerned.'

Arruns threw another shovelful of earth on to the field. 'He put a few noses out of joint.'

'Whose, for example?'

'The ones you'd expect. Larth Papatius's and Gnaeus Vipena's.'

'Yeah?' I was careful not to stop digging. 'Why theirs in particular?'

'They're the big commercial vinegrowers. The rest of us don't sell our wine, or not enough of it to make any odds. We grow mainly grain and pulses.'

I dislodged a stone and rolled it towards him with the blade of the mattock. 'These fancy ideas, now,' I said. 'What exactly are we talking about?'

'Vennunculans for Apians. And compluviate trussing.'

'Uh, you care to run that past me again, pal?' I leaned on the mattock and grinned at him. 'In Latin this time?'

Arruns grinned back as he hefted my stone up and over the edge: he had about a quarter of Mamilius's teeth, and they weren't in too good shape, either. 'If you want to fit in at Vetuliscum, Corvinus,' he said, 'you'll have to broaden your vocabulary. Vennunculan and Apian are vine varieties. Most of the vines you'll see here are Apians. You get Vennunculans a lot on the big estates in Campania, round about Pompeii. And compluviate trussing means the vines are grown up a four-sided frame instead of along a yoked line.'

'So?'

'It's the old argument, quality against quantity.' Arruns leaned on his spade; Jupiter, the guy wasn't even sweating! 'You can't have both. Vinegrowers around here have always gone for the first, like the big boys further south in the Falernian and Caecuban areas. Apians aren't high croppers but the grapes're top quality, and grown in a yoked line they ripen evenly and all together. Vennunculans give you twice the yield, maybe three times with compluviate trussing. With Apians and yoke-training you can press maybe twenty, twenty-five jars the acre, say a hundred and twenty gallons of prime juice. Vennunculans'll give you twice that, maybe three hundred in a good year, but the grapes're rubbish and the wine's piss. Good enough for the mass market but no more. You understand now?'

I shook my head. 'Uh-uh. Oh, sure, I can see that Navius might've been breaking with tradition in going for a wider market but that was his business. He could plant whatever vines he wanted on his own property and grow them how he liked.'

Arruns laughed. 'You're no vinegrower, Corvinus, that's certain. Vines take five years to mature. Five years from now Navius would've been selling his wine as Caeretan, and it would've been junk. Worse, he'd've had three times as much as any other vinegrower in the region. He'd've made a killing for the first four, maybe five years when he sold to the wholesalers and the jars were kept in bulk storage, but how long do you think the price of Caeretan would've held once it started to reach the customers and the market woke up? Then there's the knock-on effect. Vinegrowing's a

chancy business to start with. Who's going to take the
risk of producing a low-yield quality wine if they might
end up having to sell it at mass-market prices? So they
plant Vennunculans themselves or give up and grow
beans. The local quality wine industry'd be dead inside
ten years. And for the commercial growers like Vipena
and Papatius that's no joke.'

Shit. I saw what the guy was getting at now, and con-
sciously or not he'd opened up a completely new can of
worms. The wine business gave Papatius another reason
for killing Navius that had nothing to do with Thupeltha.
And it started up another hare: the Gruesomes' brother
Vipena. Complicated was right.

I hacked out another few feet of ditch. I was
getting blisters now for certain, but I knew better
than to complain. The old bugger was turning almost
friendly, and he was keeping up his end of the
bargain. Maybe I could risk something closer to
the bone.

'Uh, Nepos said you had a family feud going with
Navius,' I said carefully.

Uh-oh; silence. Arruns started shovelling again. The
scowl was back.

'Is that right, now?' he said finally.

I put my head down and didn't answer.

Arruns grunted. 'You're talking about the terraces on
the slopes north-east of here,' he said.

'Yeah?'

'Fifty years ago the boy's grandfather claimed he'd
bought them from my father. The bastard was lying.'

Fifty years! Shit! They certainly had long memories in
the country. I risked a glance at him.

'Your father denied the purchase?'

That got me a glare. 'My father was dead, Corvinus.

The month after he died old Velthur Navius – that was the grandfather – produced a forged bill of sale.'

'It'd have to be witnessed, surely.'

'It was witnessed.' Arruns stabbed at the pile of earth. 'The witness was lying too. My father never sold anything. That's our land still, and if you want to call wanting it back a feud then you go ahead. It's none of your business, anyway. Or that plummy bastard Nepos's.'

Ouch. I'd obviously touched a nerve and it was time to back off. 'One more question. Quintus Mamilius.'

'Yes?' Arruns straightened. 'What about him?'

'He had a granddaughter, died a while back. You know what of?'

'She died in childbirth. The baby as well.'

Yeah. That's what I thought the answer would be. Still, it was good to have it confirmed. 'Who was the father? Attus Navius?'

That got me a long look, and not a friendly one either. 'Now that really isn't your business, Roman,' Arruns said quietly.

'Uh, right.' I put down the mattock and got out of the ditch. 'Thanks for your help.'

He grunted and went back to his shovelling. As I walked away he called over: 'Corvinus!'

I turned. 'Yeah?'

'Put some oil on those blisters.'

I grinned and waved, then set off up the track towards the high ground.

12

I found the hill track easily. It ran behind Arruns's farmhouse through high, broken countryside cut by ravines screened by ilex and holm-oaks and littered with huge rocks of red tufa covered with bright yellow and orange lichen. Pretty wild stuff, and nice if you like that sort of thing. Me, I prefer concrete and paving slabs where the only wildlife around are the muggers and hookers.

I carried on back along the track towards Navius's property. I could see now, with my newly acquired farmer's eyes, what Arruns had meant: most of the ground from the hill slopes to across the Caere road was planted with vines, but they were being grown against supports more like scaffolding tunnels than the linked lines of crosses I'd seen elsewhere. In another five years there'd be a hell of a lot of grapes down there, and at triple the yield they'd make a hell of a lot of wine. Navius would've sold it, too: the wine market in Rome is growing year by year, and although a lot of cheap stuff is starting to come in from the big commercial vineyards in Spain and Gaul supply and demand have a long way to go before they balance. Also there's the question of transport. Having to hire space on cargo boats and carts can raise your operating costs sky-high, and there's always the danger you'll have nothing to show for it in the end but slops: cheap wines don't keep, they don't travel well, and even Suburan punters won't pay good money for vinegar. If Navius could've produced even a half-decent swigging wine in bulk this close to Rome he'd've been laughing.

Laughing partly at other folks' expense, and at the expense of Caeretan's reputation. That was the rub. I didn't underestimate what Arruns had told me: we were dealing with livelihoods here, not just of individuals but of families, and in the country the family's vital. The question was, had the severity of the threat been a good enough reason to kill the guy? Because if it had then things looked even blacker for Papatius.

The track branched to the right, and I could see a villa further down the slope. That would be the Navius place. Well, it had to be done sooner or later, and at least with Priscus off the hook the dead boy's mother might be more ready to talk to me. What had Mamilius said her name was? It began with an 'S': Sulpicia, Sedilia . . .

I couldn't remember. I'd just have to play it by ear.

I took the right fork and came down the hill through the vine terraces. The villa was easily as big as Nepos's and it looked prosperous, with half a dozen slaves in the yard and a busy feel to it. I went up to the nearest guy – he was plaiting a wicker grape basket – and introduced myself.

'The mistress at home?' I said.

'Yes, sir. She's in the garden. If you'd like to follow me?' The guy was pretty cool, but polite enough; maybe the news that Meataxe Priscus hadn't zeroed the young master after all had got here ahead of me. I hoped so.

There ain't nothing more embarrassing than paying a social call on the mother of someone your relative's been accused of putting underground before his time.

'Thanks, pal.' I fell in beside him. 'You mind telling me the lady's name, by the way?'

The slave gave me a funny look.

'Sicinia,' he said. 'Sicinia Rufina.'

Yeah. That had been it. Two names, too: we were dealing with quality here. I wished I had a clothes brush to brush some of Arruns's ditch off my tunic.

The basket-plaiter led me through a gate in a neatly clipped hedge and into a rose garden. Prosperous was right: it was laid out with gravel paths, and besides the roses there were fig and plum trees and beds of ornamental herbs. There was even a marble fountain decorated with passable cupids sitting on dolphins.

The lady was ensconced in a natty little gazebo overlooking the garden. I saw her stiffen when she saw me coming, but she was polite enough when I told her my name. She must've been in her late forties, but she'd been a looker once and her pure white mantle wasn't Caere make.

'Won't you sit down, Valerius Corvinus?' she said. 'Lucius. Tell Crito to bring us some wine. And grape juice for me.'

The slave left. I pulled up the gazebo's other chair.

'Well, Valerius Corvinus.' She leaned back. 'And what can I do for you?'

I cleared my throat. 'First my condolences. I'm sorry about your son.'

'Yes. Attus was a good boy.' She stared past me at the roses. 'A very good boy. I'll miss him very much. You'll no doubt be relieved, however, that your stepfather is no longer under suspicion of his murder?'

'Uh, yeah.' I felt uncomfortable. Well, at least that was out of the way. 'You know Larth Papatius has been arrested?'

'So Gaius Aternius informed me.' Her lips tightened.

'He stopped by this morning?'

'Oh, yes. His family and ours are old friends; very old friends indeed. Aternius's uncle went to school with my late husband.'

'That'd be Quintus Cominius, the Caeretan mayor?' She nodded. So. That explained the high-level proprietorial interest in the case. I was surprised, though, that Smooth-Chops hadn't mentioned it.

'I'm only sorry that something can't be done about that wife of his.' Sicinia's voice took on a distinct edge. 'That's where the real responsibility lies.'

It took me a moment to realise she was talking about Thupeltha. 'You think so?' I said cautiously.

'Corvinus, I hope I am a charitable person, but I'm afraid I can't help hating that woman. Having got her hooks into poor Attus she had him besotted with her, and then she dropped him like a used rag. If anyone is responsible for my son's death it's she. I could even, if I'm to be completely honest with you, have a small spark of sympathy for her husband.'

Uh-huh. 'You think she led your son on?'

'My son was barely twenty-one years old. She is almost twice that. He had very little experience of the world, she had a great deal. What is your opinion?'

My opinion was that the lady was suffering from a bad case of astigmatism, but I wasn't going to say so. And for all I knew she could be right. I'd only Thupeltha's word for things, after all. I moved on to more delicate ground. 'Could she have had, uh, a motive for seducing your son do you think, Sicinia Rufina? Apart from sex, that is?'

Sicinia closed her eyes briefly: I had the idea that the word 'sex' wasn't used all that much in the Navius household. 'Attus was quite a wealthy young man,' she said, 'well connected, especially on my side, and with good prospects. I hesitate to say she initiated the affair for purely mercenary reasons, especially given the outcome, but I would not discount them altogether. It certainly wouldn't be the first time that had been tried.'

The house slave appeared with the wine tray. I noticed that the jug and the cups were good quality silver, and Sicinia's grape juice came in a Syrian glass beaker. We were moving in high circles here, no provincial tat; the lady had taste, and evidently the money to indulge it. I hadn't missed that 'especially on my side', either.

The guy poured and left, and I took a swig . . .

The wine burst into song on my tongue. Jupiter! This was no home-made Caeretan. Obviously whatever Navius's opinions were on growing cheapo grapes they didn't affect what he kept in his own cellar.

Sicinia had been watching me, a slight smile on her lips.

'You like the wine?' she said.

'Yeah.' I took another mouthful. Liquid velvet! 'Falernian, right? And top-of-the-range stuff.'

'Indeed. Thirty years old, or so I'm told, although I take very little interest in wine myself, at any level. My cousin sends it.'

'Your cousin knows his wines.'

The smile broadened. 'He should. Unlike my late husband, you see, I'm not from this region: my family come from Campania, Pompeii originally, and we've been in the wine business for years, on the trading rather than the production side. My cousin is the present head of the firm. He specialises in the quality varieties, especially Falernian and Faustinian. This is one of his best.' She indicated the jug. 'Do help yourself, please.'

I didn't wait to be asked twice. 'You said it wasn't the first time a woman had got involved with your son?' I prompted gently as I topped up my cup.

'That is so.' Sicinia sipped her grape juice. 'One of our neighbours had a granddaughter.' Her voice was genteelly disapproving. 'A pleasant enough girl, but half foreign, very obviously so. You know the type, Corvinus: large, busty, blonde-haired, blue-eyed, quite impossible. He – the grandfather – was under the impression that the girl had some sort of a claim on Attus; ridiculous, of course, the boy was hardly more than a child. And there would have been almost no dowry to speak of. Gaius – my late husband, he was alive then – sent him off with a flea in his ear.'

The hairs lifted just a little on my neck.

'Uh, just a question, Sicinia Rufina,' I said, 'and forgive me for asking it: but how did your husband die?'

There was a pause. 'He was out riding,' she said finally. 'He fell from his horse, hit his head and never regained consciousness. That was almost exactly a year ago.'

The prickling grew stronger. Shit; and I'd somehow got the impression from the sisters that the guy had died of a fever or something similar. A head injury, eh? That was interesting. *Might* be interesting.

Sicinia was frowning. 'Our family has always been . . . I hesitate to say clumsy, but certainly accident-prone. On the male side, at any rate. Indeed Navius himself is' – she stopped – 'was recovering from a broken forearm occasioned when he fell down the hayloft ladder last month.'

'Yeah?' I pricked up my ears. That was interesting too. 'Were there any witnesses?'

That got me a glare; accidents, seemingly, were one thing, but any suggestion of foul play was bad form. 'I was present myself, as it happens. He simply misplaced a foot. He found the convalescence very irksome. Attus always was a very energetic boy, and he actually enjoyed physical labour. That was something I often found difficult to understand.'

Yeah; she would. 'Did your son have any other enemies? Or people who might wish him ill, rather?' I said when her mouth opened to protest: precious darlings like Attus Navius clearly couldn't have enemies from first principles.

'Of course not. Attus was very popular. There's that dreadful old man Larcius Arruns who insists that he owns two of our vineyard terraces, but he was always an embarrassment rather than a danger, and to give him his due I don't believe he would stoop to violence. Not that Attus's death would have improved his position to the slightest degree.' Sicinia frowned again. 'Valerius Corvinus, am I to understand from your question that you *don't* believe Larth Papatius killed my son?'

Uh-uh. Astigmatic or not the lady was no fool. I gave her the simple truth.

'I don't know,' I said. 'Sure, I'm nine-tenths certain he did, and the more I find out the more things point that way, but there's still that last tenth. How about you? Have you any views yourself?'

She was quiet for a long time. Finally she gave the ghost of a smile. 'No,' she said. 'To be honest, I have not. But I do know that whoever murdered Attus was quite mad. He was a lovely boy, he had everything to live for, he'd offended no one and he would have grown up a credit to our family and to Vetuliscum. His murder was completely without sense, an insult to rationality in any form. And whoever was responsible for it, catching them will not bring him back.'

Yeah; that last bit was true enough, but as far as a mad killer went I wasn't taking any bets. Whoever had put Navius away – and Hilarion – had done it for a reason.

There wasn't much else to say. I thanked her for the wine and left.

13

The morning was wearing on and I was getting peckish. I decided to give Clusinus a miss for the moment and rejoin the main road, call in at the Gruesomes' in passing in the hopes of catching Vipena, then go home for a quick bath, something to eat and a jug on the terrace while I waited for the family to come back; sleuthing was all very well, but a holiday's a holiday, and you don't want to kill yourself over it. Besides, when I finally met Vesia I wanted to look my snappy sartorial best.

The sisters were on the terrace as usual: peas this time instead of beans. They sniffed a bit when they saw my tunic, and a bit more when they caught my scent – a couple of hours' strenuous walking in the September heat overlaid by a spell of ditching is enough to put paid to the most persistent of bath oils, and I stank like a camel – but Perilla's influence still lingered and they were politeness itself.

'Gnaeus is inside, Valerius Corvinus,' Tanaquil said, 'talking to our foreman. Just go through.'

'Inside' was an exaggeration: the ground floor, at this point at least, was an unroofed work area. I walked through the small cobbled entrance court into what was

obviously the main fermenting yard. The wide necks of
half a dozen huge buried vats projected above the floor,
and a slave with a long-handled brush and a bucket of hot
water was on his knees next to one of them scrubbing at
its innards.

'The boss around, pal?' I said.

He jerked his thumb to the left. There was a big
conduit running about three feet above the floor with
an arrangement of sluices and piping at the near end
that fed directly into the vats, its other end disappearing
through a hole in the wall into the next section of the
yard. Beside the connecting door was a stack of wine
jars. I glanced at them in passing and noticed that the
potter's stamps were botched: the letters in the centre
had come out clear, but the two either side were a mess.
Vipena must've got them cheap in a job lot. Yeah, well:
soothsayers and augurs, you've got to get up early to
be ahead of those guys. Every one I've ever met with is
near enough to skin a flint.

I went through. This was where the press was, and I
could see why it was unroofed too: the press was huge,
with a wooden lever fully thirty feet long. There were
two guys there: a squat bruiser with a broken nose who
I took to be the foreman and a tall thin vinegary-looking
man who looked so like the Gruesomes that he had to
be Vipena.

'Hi,' I said to this guy. 'Sorry about the interruption,
but your sisters said just to come on in. My name's
Marcus Valerius Corvinus.'

'Ah.' The thin man put his hand out. 'Yes, they told
me that you and your wife had visited yesterday. I'm
delighted to make your acquaintance.'

'Uh, likewise.' I took the hand. It felt like wash-leather,
which was par for the guy's skin texture in general.

Vipena turned to the bruiser. 'We'll talk later, Baro,' he said. 'The gods willing.'

Jupiter! Well, he was in the business, after all.

The bruiser left. I glanced around with interest.

'So this is where it all happens, right?'

Vipena gave me a quick sideways look. 'Where what all happens?'

'Making the wine.'

'Ah, yes!' He smiled, or maybe it was dyspepsia. 'To be sure! Lord Bacchus's gift. You've never seen a winery before?'

'Uh-uh.' I shook my head. 'I tend to be more into the consuming side of things.'

'It's simple enough. The grapes are loaded into the press here and the juice extracted. It flows along the conduit into the vats next door where it is fermented. Wine ferments best in the open air, exposed to the elements, Valerius Corvinus; that is what gives it its character and its body.'

'Yeah?'

'Indeed. After pressing the portions of the pulp mat which overflow the press are cut around and pressed separately: were the juices to be mixed the resultant wine could have rather a chalybeate tang.'

'"Chalybeate"?'

'It would taste like an iron skillet. Not that I've ever tasted an iron skillet, of course.' He sniffed. 'My apologies. A small joke.'

'Uh, yeah. Yeah, right.' Jupiter! Or Bacchus, rather. Well, I'd asked for the guided tour, and if I'd got it I couldn't blame anyone but myself. It was a shame Perilla wasn't there; she loves that kind of high-tech stuff. I pointed to a series of deep cisterns ranged along the wall with spigoted lead pipes projecting from them at waist level. Underneath the cisterns there was an iron grid like you see in bakers' shops to hold the burning charcoal. 'So what're these things for?'

'Oh, we don't use these very often. They're a stage in a sub-process which it would be tedious to explain.' He took my arm. 'Shall we go out and join my sisters?'

'Uh, yeah. Yeah, okay,' I said. There was something adrift somewhere, but whatever it was I couldn't quite put my finger on it. 'If I'm not interrupting your work.'

'If you are then it was foreordained, and so not your fault.' Jupiter! A weird bugger, this guy, but then he was a soothsayer after all when he wasn't pressing skillets, and these bastards are half out of their skulls at the best of times. It comes of spending a large chunk of your life up to your wrists in sheep guts reading livers.

We went back outside. The girls were still slitting pea-pods, but they put the bowl away and brought out the honey wine and cake. The four of us settled down for what promised to be a not-so-jolly chinwag.

'So, Corvinus, you must be settling in at Vetuliscum quite nicely now.' Vipena poured me some honey wine. 'Becoming – if you'll excuse yet another joke – somewhat of an "old hand".' Another sniff, longer this time, followed by a snuffle which I decided must be his professional equivalent of a belly laugh.

Jupiter! And *joke*? Well, maybe I was missing something. 'Yeah,' I said. 'It must be all of four days. And two murders kind of let you get a feel for a place.'

'Indeed. Indeed.' Vipena sipped his wine. I didn't: reckoned I'd been poisoned enough by that stuff already these past two days. How any self-respecting winemaker can drink that bilge, let alone serve it to guests, just beats me. 'A sadly misguided young man, Attus Navius. In more ways than one.' He shook his head slowly. 'I hear they've arrested Larth Papatius.'

'Yeah. This morning.'

'The gods be good to him, then. It would have been better if he had controlled his wife instead of killing her lover, but there' – he sighed – 'we are all in the hands of fate.'

'Yeah.' I paused. 'Uh ... you said, "in more ways than one".'

The yellow poached-egg eyes came up. 'I beg your pardon?'

'You said that Navius was misguided "in more ways than one". I know the one, at least I think I do. But what was the other way?'

He stared at me for a long time. Then he blinked and turned away.

'Just a figure of speech, Corvinus,' he said finally.

Sure; and I was Porsenna's grandmother. Still, I let it pass for the moment ...

Which was lucky, because at that point Tanaquil leaned forward and said something to the guy in Etruscan: I remembered that Mamilius had said they spoke it at home. I only caught two words: *lupuce* and *tular*. The first you can't be around Priscus for long without knowing, the second Jupiter knew where I'd picked up but I knew that too.

'Uh, what's that about boundaries?' I said. 'And who's dead?'

Vipena's jaw dropped and he went pasty white.

'You speak Etruscan?'

I shook my head. 'Uh-uh. Two or three words, that's all. My stepfather's the one for dead languages. He's—'

I stopped: Vipena was holding up a hand like Jupiter himself preparing to smite the ungodly with a thunder-bolt.

'Etruscan is *not* a dead language!' he snapped. 'Not yet! But if it is moribund then it is the fault of you Romans!' Shit, that was a change-around! One minute the guy had all the drive and force of a wilted lettuce, now you could've shoved a knife between his teeth, given him a sign saying 'no prisoners' and used him as a model for Hannibal before Cannae. 'And as for your stepfather desecrating our ancestors' tombs that is sheer blasphemy!'

Uh-oh; there went the spittle and the manic gleam. We had serious problems here. Time for bridge-building. 'Hey, hold on, pal!' I said mildly. 'Priscus doesn't break in. He just borrows the keys and lurks. And he doesn't touch anything, either. The owners are welcome to frisk him when he comes out.'

I might as well've saved my breath. Vipena's eyes were blazing. It was like watching a praying mantis suddenly metamorphose into a very tetchy basilisk.

'Our history is not a sideshow! And he may not steal himself, but he encourages others to do so!'

Yeah, well, the guy had a point: the more shady antique shops in Rome were full of bits and pieces that had probably seen the inside of a tomb somewhere if you went back far enough. And a lot of the tombs Priscus visited had already been cleaned out over the past hundred years by entrepreneurs working nights and weren't worth the trouble bricking up again. The bastards may not have gone to the length of lifting the paintings off the walls, but it was only a matter of time before someone developed the technique.

Ramutha had her hand on Vipena's arm. He was literally shaking with rage. 'I think you should go, Valerius Corvinus,' she said.

That made two of us. If I stuck around any longer a

curse was the least I could expect to be hit with. I stood up. 'Uh, yeah. Right,' I said. 'Thanks for the—'

'No.' Vipena was taking deep breaths. 'No. Wait. My apologies.' Wheeze. 'I get . . . rather upset over the – ah – cavalier way your ancestors treated mine.' Wheeze. 'Of course it's not your fault, either individually or collectively.' Wheeze. 'I'm speaking cosmically, of course.'

'Cosmically.' Jupiter on wheels! Still, I sat down again. 'Is that right, now?'

The guy picked up his wine cup and took a long swig. Under it I could see his Adam's apple working as the honey wine slipped past his tonsils. I winced. Finally he set the cup down empty and wiped his lips. Foul stuff or not, it seemed to have done the trick and the manic glare was gone. Now he just looked like a mad dishcloth.

'Perhaps if I explain,' he said.

'Uh, yeah. Go ahead, pal.' Well, anything was better than being on the receiving end of another Wrath of God speech. And if it calmed him down to speak cosmically, then that was fine with me.

'The limits to the Etruscan race's existence were set long ago. We were allotted ten cycles of time. The ninth ended at the death of your Julius Caesar, and the tenth cannot have long to run; perhaps I may see it end myself. When that happens everything will be gone: not simply independence but history, language, way of life. Perhaps even the Etruscan name itself. Everything. Gone and irrecoverable. Imagine, if you can, your Rome in the same position, Corvinus. How would you feel? How would you view the culture responsible for its death, and the representatives of that culture?' I didn't say anything. Vipena sighed. 'Well, let it pass. As to your question, or questions, rather. I was concealing no

great secret. The well near the boundary I share –
shared – with Navius dried up recently. I hoped that
I could persuade him to rent me at least partial water
rights to the perennial stream that flows through his own
land some twenty yards from my own. He refused, and
I count that decision "misguided" in the sense that we
were neighbours and the advantage to me would far
outweigh the loss to him. Tanaquil was simply advising
me to tell you that.'

'Okay,' I said. 'And *lupuce* – "he's dead"?'

'Latin and Etruscan share an axiom, Corvinus: "Speak
of the dead nothing but good." It's a fine rule, and one I
try to put into practice. I was therefore reluctant to speak
ill of Navius. Tanaquil disagreed; it was her opinion that,
Navius being dead, information concerning a quarrel
which shows him up in a poor light cannot possibly
harm him.' He cleared his throat. 'And now if you'll
excuse me I really must go and talk with Baro.' He stood
up. 'I've enjoyed our meeting. You and your charming
wife will be most welcome should you choose to call at
any time.'

I said my goodbyes and left.

On the way home I thought about that last little
gem. Sure, it was plausible, if you twisted it a little,
looked at it sideways and allowed for the wind, but
that was the point; otherwise it stank. My gut feeling
was that Vipena had been lying through a hole in his
fillet. Language is one thing, tone of voice is another;
I'd got the distinct impression that whatever Tanaquil
had said she'd been warning him, not advising him.
And whatever the ins and outs of it, the admission of a
quarrel was yet another indication that everything wasn't
all sweetness and light in Vetuliscum where Navius and

his neighbours were concerned. Whatever his mother might tell me, the guy wasn't popular. And somehow, some*why*, his unpopularity had killed him.

14

Perilla had arrived back just before I did, so while she got changed out of her formal mantle and purified herself from the funeral I got Bathyllus to lay us out a cold lunch and a jug of wine on the terrace.

'Hey, little guy,' I said while he dished out the cheese and olives. 'Where's the Princess disappeared to?'

Bathyllus sniffed. 'She went straight out with the mule, sir,' he said. The tone that went into the penultimate word would've fitted a loathsome disease. Like I said, Bathyllus is no animal lover.

'She's missing a meal?' Jupiter! That would be enough to bring the end of Vipena's tenth *saeculum* on.

'No, sir. She took half a loaf and a bagful of sliced sausage with her.'

Half a loaf and a bagful of sliced sausage, eh? Yeah, that made a lot more sense. As did taking Corydon. I grinned and settled back in my chair with my feet propped against the terrace wall. Today was the day the brute's probation ran out, and subject to the original owner turning up to claim him he was officially ours, for which read Marilla's. We'd done all we could. Alexis had tramped about the countryside for three days asking at every farm, but no one had bitten. I didn't blame them; if I'd finally managed to get shot of the bugger I'd be keeping quiet too.

I was tucking into what the Princess had left of the sausage when Perilla came out, looking cool in her lightest lounging tunic. She leaned over and kissed the back of my neck.

'So, Marcus. And how was your day?' she said.

I gave her the full details while she made inroads on the cold pickled tongue with sweet-sour sauce that Meton had sent up. 'So we've got too many suspects,' I finished. 'Every time I talk to someone I find another reason why Navius should be dead and why they could've killed him.'

'What about Hilarion?'

'Shit, Perilla, I can't even begin to guess about Hilarion! His death fits in, sure, but the gods know where. Leave him out for now.'

'All right.' She reached for a stuffed olive. 'So let's go through the various motives for murdering Navius.'

Fair enough. It was about time I got them all straight in my own head anyway. I pushed away the sausage plate and filled myself a cup of proper brain food.

'Okay,' I said. 'We'll start with the biggie, Larth Papatius. Points for: all the circumstantial stuff we'd got already, plus this new angle that Arruns handed me. Papatius has two motives for murdering Navius, unconnected but reinforcing each other. One, the kid threatened to blow the whistle on Thupeltha, not just about his own affair with her but Clusinus's as well. Papatius had already killed a man for that, although after all this time we'd be hard pushed to make that stick, so a second murder's well within the grounds of possibility. Agreed?'

'Agreed.' Perilla sipped her grape juice. 'There's one

thing more, Marcus. The Clusinus affair is still going on, or I assume it is. If Navius had made it public then Papatius's everyday relations with Clusinus would be under considerable strain. To say the least. In a small community like Vetuliscum that would be an important factor.'

'Right. If nobody talked about it it didn't exist, and eventually, Thupeltha being the lady she is, it'd probably go away of its own accord. Letting Navius dig the dirt in public would open up a whole new can of worms. As motives go they don't come much bigger.' I took a swallow of wine. 'Two. Navius's plans for his property. These hit Papatius where it really hurts. The guy may not care who's screwing his wife, but vines and wine are a different thing. He's built up a good business over the years and he has a reputation as the best vintner in the district. Now he's faced with the prospect of all that going down the tube; worse, of Caeretan becoming the sort of junk you only find on the boards of Suburan slop-shops. For any self-respecting winemaker that'd be the equivalent of seeing your grandmother sell herself for a copper a throw under the Sublician Bridge. In fact—'

I stopped. Something was teasing at the back of my mind; something I'd missed. And nothing to do with Larth Papatius ...

'Marcus?'

'Hmmm?'

'Your eyes have glazed over.'

'Yeah?' I shook myself. 'Sorry, lady. Just wool-gathering. Where was I?'

'The Sublician Bridge.'

'Oh. Right.' I took another belt of wine. 'So. Papatius is still a prime contender. Points against.' I paused.

'Shit, there are no points against. We've got rid of these already. The guy had motive, means and opportunity, the whole ball game.'

'So he's guilty.'

'Yeah.' I was frowning; it didn't seem right somehow, but exactly why I couldn't put my finger on. Maybe it was something to do with his insistence against the teeth of the evidence that he'd gone into Caere. That just didn't fit, no way, nohow, never . . .

'Marcus, will you *please* stop doing that!' Perilla snapped. 'We're supposed to be having a discussion here!'

'Uh, yeah.' I blinked and refocused. 'I'm sorry, lady. Okay. Let's leave Papatius and look at some of the others. Larcius Arruns for a start. He's had his knife into the family for years over that stretch of vineyard.'

'Corvinus, is that a bad pun or was it an accident?'

I grinned. 'Accident. But it's true enough all the same. He's got a motive.'

'Has he? What exactly would he gain by killing Navius? It wouldn't get him the vineyard back.'

'It might open up a space for him. I've met Navius's mother, remember. She's got no other kids, she's not from around here originally, and she's a fancy fish in a muddy pool. Sure, she might decide to work the property herself through an agent, but it wouldn't surprise me if she didn't sell up and move somewhere the locals don't scratch their armpits and stink of garlic. In that case the fifty-year deadlock's broken. Arruns might be able to come to an arrangement with the new owner, especially if the guy's persistence is the constant embarrassment Sicinia says it is. And there's another thing. Navius's father didn't die from natural causes, or not in the narrow definition. The guy met with an accident out riding and bust his skull.'

Perilla stared at me. 'You think it could have been murder?'

'It's a possibility, lady. Both male relatives unnaturally dead inside a year is pushing coincidence. Arruns was getting nowhere fast through legal channels, and he's no spring chicken. Maybe he decided it was time to change his tactics.'

'Corvinus, you have an over-suspicious mind.'

'Yeah. Admitted. It would fit, though. And Arruns is definitely on the hook.' I topped up my wine cup. 'Next. Quintus Mamilius.'

'Mamilius is a nonagenarian!'

'He's a nonagenarian ex-First Spear, Perilla. That makes a difference. These guys are no shrinking violets, even at ninety, and Mamilius is as tough as old boots. Certainly he's got a hell of a motive: Attus Navius put his grand-daughter in the family way and she died of it.'

'You don't know that for certain.'

'Mamilius seems to. In any case he hated the boy's guts. And murdering the father would fit too. The bastard refused to marry his son to the girl because she didn't come up to social scratch.' I took a mouthful of wine. 'Added to which, Mamilius needn't've done either of the killings himself. I've seen the guy's son. He's built like a rhino and takes orders like a lamb.'

Perilla chewed thoughtfully on an olive. 'You're right,' she said. 'There are too many suspects.'

I reached for the wine jug. 'I haven't finished yet, lady. There're still Vipena and Clusinus.'

'Oh, for heaven's sake!'

I ignored her. 'Let's take Vipena. He's a vinegrower like Papatius, and Navius's scheme would hit him in the pocket as well. Also he quarrelled with the guy just before he died.'

'By his own admission.'

'Only because I caught him out through my extensive knowledge of Etruscan. That yarn about the dried-up well and trying to buy into the water rights may be straight enough, lady, but if it's the full story I'll eat my sandals. The bastard was covering. *What* he was covering I don't know yet, but I mean to find out. And I've got a gut feeling about our liver-reader. He knows more than he's telling, and he's crooked as a Suburan dice game.'

'Really?'

'Cut the sarcasm. You want to bet?'

Perilla sighed. 'No, Corvinus, I don't. You have the most annoying habit of being right about things like that, completely against the run of common sense.'

I grinned. 'Yeah. Okay. Last, Clusinus. In some ways he's the most obvious of all. Certainly he had opportunity. The murder happened on his own property, he'd arranged to meet Thupeltha at the same time but he didn't turn up. And finally he was the one who most opportunely caught Priscus with the corpse. As far as motive's concerned—'

'He'd been hunting. Priscus said he had the game with him.'

'He could've been out all day. A pair of bustards isn't much, not this time of year. And whatever applies to Papatius applies to him. He could've arrived when Thupeltha and Navius were having their argument, stayed hidden to listen, then instead of keeping the appointment followed the kid and murdered him. The knife would make sense, too. He'd've overheard Navius threatening suicide, so even if he'd used his own knife he could've replaced it with Navius's to bolster up the story. Then all he'd've had to do was go away for half an hour and come back when it was all over.'

'Why should he?'

I frowned. 'Why should he what?'

'Come back. If he really was the murderer. If he knew the corpse was lying there surely it would have been safer to keep well away. How could he be sure it had already been found?'

Yeah; the lady had a point. I'd been up that bit of the track, from the bottom, at least, and the place where Navius's body was was tucked away out of sight of the higher reaches. Shit. 'Maybe he saw Priscus coming and let him get there first.'

'Or maybe he didn't know the corpse was there at all.'

Right. Bugger. Failing Papatius, I liked Clusinus, I liked him a lot. But Perilla was spot on; that was a problem. I wished now that I'd walked that last bit of track, the stretch between Navius's place and the summit of the hill, to check the line of sight absolutely. Still, I could always do that tomorrow.

Perilla was looking thoughtful again. 'Marcus,' she said, 'one thing does puzzle me about this business.'

'Yeah? Just one?'

'What about alibis? Navius must have been killed within a very narrow space of time, an hour at most. Wouldn't it be sensible simply to ask everyone where they were and if anyone could confirm it?'

Fair question. 'Yeah, it would be,' I said. 'Very.'

'So why not do it?'

'Two reasons, lady. First, because officially this isn't my investigation and if I tried the buggers would quite rightly tell me to go and stick my nose somewhere else. End of interview. Aternius might've got away with it, sure, but Aternius has his man already. Second, because at this time of year any self-respecting farmer's out in his own fields and his own boss. There wouldn't be anyone to confirm. Sure, if Clusinus had been at home his wife and kids might've . . .' I stopped. 'Shit.'

Perilla looked at me. 'What is it?'

I waved her to silence. Oh, Jupiter! Jupiter, it was beautiful! I didn't know whether to laugh or cry, and it was my own fault.

I'd been making one glaringly stupid mistake all along: I'd equated sex with love. And because I'd done that I'd missed an explanation that was so head-bangingly simple that a six-year-old kid would've thought of it straight off.

Papatius couldn't have killed Navius. Papatius was the *only* guy who couldn't have killed him because Papatius was the only one of the bunch with a cast-iron alibi.

His problem was he couldn't use it.

15

Clusinus's place was pretty dilapidated: there were tiles missing from the roof, the shutters looked like they hadn't had a lick of paint since Augustus had swapped his sun hat for a halo, and the yard was littered with the sort of junk that people collect thinking they might get round to fixing it one day if they have the time. It also stank seriously of goat and chicken-shit.

I picked a careful path to the entrance, banged on the door and waited. Finally a kid of about six – female – opened up and peered round the jamb. There was another one behind her – male – a couple of years younger. They stood looking at me like I was a blue-rinsed Briton.

'Uh, your father in?' I said.

The six-year-old shook her head. Her brother shoved a finger up his nose.

Yeah, well, that figured, and I was grateful: if Clusinus had been at home things might've been a little tricky.

'How about your mother?'

Nod.

Not one of nature's great talkers, this little lady. 'What's your name, Gabby?' I said.

'Trebbia.'

The kid with the finger didn't introduce himself, he just stared and poked. I reached into my purse, took out a couple of coppers and held them out.

'Okay, Trebbia,' I said. 'You think you and Porsenna here can use these?'

'His name's Sextus,' she said; but she took the coins.

'Whatever. I'd like to talk to your mother. Any chance of arranging that for me?'

'Who is it, Trebbia?' The voice came from inside.

Trebbia stuck her chin over her shoulder. 'The Roman,' she said. 'The nosy one.'

I grinned. Well, there ain't nothing like a reputation.

There was the sound of light footsteps and the door was opened fully. Yeah, that was the girl I'd seen sure enough. And she looked even better without the cloak.

'My name's Corvinus,' I said. 'Marcus Valerius Corvinus.'

'Yes, I know.' Her voice suited her: barely a whisper. She didn't step aside, though. 'Titus isn't in at the moment. I don't know when he'll be back.'

'It was you I came to see.' That got me a quick, scared look. 'About Larth Papatius.'

I'd tried to make that last bit sound as unthreatening as possible, but she still went pale.

'Larth?'

'No hassle, lady.' I spoke quietly as if I were calming a frightened horse. 'None in the world. I swear it. But if you want to save the guy's neck we really do have to talk.'

She lifted the knuckle of her right forefinger to her mouth and nibbled on it. For an instant I thought she was going to slam the door in my face, but she didn't.

'Trebbia,' she said. 'Take Sextus and play with him in the yard for half an hour.'

The kids disappeared, with the smaller version being

trailed along by the wrist looking back at me with huge eyes. Vesia stepped back from the threshold.

'You'd better come in,' she said.

The inside of the farmhouse was laid out like Vipena's, with an inner courtyard and fermenting vats; but these looked filthy and unused, and there was more junk piled around the walls. She took me through another area with a press that looked like it had been used for squeezing olives once upon a time and still had the pulp to prove it and then down a short passage to the kitchen.

That at least was clean; it was better than clean. The stone-flagged floor and the big wooden table gleamed at me. She'd even polished the skillets. Meton would've approved, and where kitchens are concerned that bastard's as pernickety as they come. I'd guess that the farmyard area and the workrooms were Clusinus's province, but this was Vesia's.

'Sit down, please,' she said. Her voice had been low before, but now it could've done service for a ghost's. 'Have you eaten?'

'Yeah. Yeah, thanks.' I pulled up a chair. The wooden back felt slippy under my hand, and I could smell the beeswax.

'Some wine, then.'

'That'd be great.'

She poured. It was foul stuff – maybe these vats were used after all, but Clusinus just didn't bother mucking them out between seasons – but I drank it. The lady had enough problems without a picky guest adding to them.

'Now,' she said, sitting down facing me. I'd seen that look before on the faces of dentists' customers in Cattlemarket Square while they're waiting to have a tooth pulled.

It would be easier if I told her rather than asked, and like with the dentist it was best done quickly. I was pretty sure of my facts, anyway.

'Papatius was here the morning Navius was murdered,' I said.

She closed her eyes and nodded. 'Yes. Although not for the reason you think. We're not lovers, Valerius Corvinus.'

'No, I know that. But saying so wouldn't cut any ice in Vetuliscum, would it? Just the fact that the guy had visited – was in the habit of visiting – when your husband was out would be enough.'

'It was the first time. That he'd been here, anyway. We usually met in the vineyard at the edge of his property and ours. There's a corner hidden from the road and from our track where he likes to go to be by himself.' She was looking straight at me now. 'We don't do anything; he wouldn't, and I wouldn't, either. We just talk. That's where I was going later when you saw me, to talk things over, if he was there.'

'I believe you, lady.' I felt her relax; that had been important to her, and I was glad I could say it honestly. 'He came to tell you about Thupeltha and your husband.'

Another nod. 'She'd just told him. I didn't know.' A small smile, with no amusement in it. 'That's the difference between Thupeltha and Titus: she tells her husband about her affairs, I only find out about his by accident. If at all.'

'Normally Papatius couldn't care less who his wife was fooling around with.' I sipped the wine; it didn't get any better with further acquaintance. 'But with Clusinus it was different, right? It might hurt you.'

'Yes.' She swallowed. 'He'd seen her go out and he

knew where she was going. He gave her time to get
clear, then he followed her. He came straight here.'

'What about Navius?'

'Larth didn't know he was there. He was out of sight
by the time he left the wineshop.'

Uh-huh. That made sense: Papatius hadn't been 'following' either Thupeltha or Navius when the Gruesomes
saw him, not in the usual sense of the word. He'd simply
been heading in the same direction.

'Go on,' I said.

Vesia was twisting her fingers together; I noticed that
the nails were broken and bitten to the quick, like
a child's. 'Larth offered to stop it. Talk to his wife,
talk to Titus. I only had to say the word. He was ...
very upset.'

Yeah. I'd bet. Like he'd been 'very upset' with Thupeltha's
Caeretan butcher pal or the loudmouth in the wineshop.

'And did you? Say the word?'

She shook her head. 'It would've only caused trouble
for both of us. Certainly Titus wouldn't have paid any
attention, and in that case I don't know what Larth
would've done. It'll blow over eventually. She'll get
tired of him, or he'll get tired of her and that'll be
the end of it.'

'Until the next time.' Shit. I felt really sorry for the
kid – she wasn't much more – but there wasn't a lot I
could do.

'Yes.' Another smile which wasn't a smile. 'Until the
next time.'

'So when Papatius was caught out – by his wife and
by Gaius Aternius – he lied. He couldn't deny he'd been
following Navius because he'd been seen, but he couldn't
tell the truth either without putting your reputation on
the line. So he said he'd been going to Caere.'

'And stuck to his story. If it came to it, Valerius Corvinus, I would've told Aternius the truth. Believe that, please.'

I sighed. 'Yeah. Yeah, well.' I got up. 'Okay. I'll go and see Gaius Aternius myself, explain things.' If the bastard would listen. 'Don't worry too much, lady.'

She got up too and walked me to the door. 'Larth's a good man,' she said. 'Even if he hadn't been with me I would've known he didn't kill Navius.'

I didn't ask her about the Caere butcher; it didn't matter now, and she probably would've insisted it had been an accident whether she really thought so or not. Love's a funny thing, even the platonic variety.

Funny, and not necessarily very nice. The Alexandrian novelists would've had a field day with the poor saps. Me, I just felt sorry for them.

It'd been a long, hard day: time for a bath and a leisurely jug before Meton served up the beans and lentils. I went back home.

Perilla was waiting on the terrace with the Princess. They both looked upset, and the Princess was practically in tears.

'Oh, Marcus, thank heavens you're back!' Perilla ran over and hugged me. 'Marilla's found a body.'

16

The kid told me about it on the way.

She'd been up in the hills with Corydon and the mule had got thirsty. The Princess had seen an irrigation pond below, at what turned out to be the top end of Papatius's property: the sort of thing you get sometimes in the country, where the rainwater run-off or a small spring fills an artificial basin that feeds a system of sluiced irrigation channels for the fields below it. She was watering Corydon when she noticed further along the bank the ends of a hurdle sticking up from the surface; and stretching out from underneath it was a human arm . . .

So after she'd done a bit of screaming she'd got on Corydon and ridden home hell for leather. I'd been just round the corner at Vesia's, but of course she hadn't known that, with the result that Perilla had ended up fielding the whole crisis.

'It was horrible, Corvinus.' Marilla shuddered as she guided Corydon up the path through Papatius's vineyard. 'Like some huge bloated slug.'

I glanced down at her; I'd taken the horse, for speed, and in any case I'd done enough walking for one day.

I'd brought Alexis along, too, to help with the heavy stuff. He was riding along behind.

'Yeah?' I said, trying not to grin. The Princess was recovering fast. That shudder had been what's sometimes described as 'delicious', and she looked a lot more eager for the trip to be over than Alexis did. I'd bet she couldn't wait to tell Aunt Marcia the story when she got back up to the Alban Hills, too. An interesting girl, Marilla. Even although we weren't kin in the biological sense she'd a lot of me in her.

We got to the pond and dismounted. Everything was like the kid had described it. I looked around, but apart from the hurdle and what was underneath it there was nothing to see.

'Okay, Alexis,' I said. 'Let's do it. Princess, go and find Corydon a thistle or something, yeah?'

'Can't I watch?'

Hell. Kids today. Well, she'd see a lot worse at the Games in Rome, and who was I to stand in the way of her education? 'All right,' I said. 'At a distance. But don't come running to me if you have nightmares. I need my sleep.'

'I won't.' She took a hold of Corydon's bridle and stood wide-eyed as Alexis and me went over to the hurdle.

It was quite close in, easy to reach, and the pond being artificial the sides went straight down, so there were no shallows to be negotiated. Alexis took one exposed side, I took the other, and we heaved. The hurdle – it was the usual kind, no more than a screen of wickerwork – didn't move. Peering through the murky, red-clayed water I could see why. Piled on to its centre were five or six rocks, each the size of my head.

So. The guy had been thrown in, the hurdle put on top of him and then the stones added, pinning him to the floor of the pool; only he'd slipped partly clear in the process, enough for his arm to drift free.

Okay. So we could do this two ways. Either we waded into the pool and lifted the rocks off or went for the corpse itself. The second was easier, unfortunately. I gritted my teeth, took a firm grip of the wrist, slippery with fine red clay, and pulled ...

He came out from under like a dolphin breaking water. The rocks, dislodged, rolled across the width of the hurdle and it sank altogether.

'Hey, Alexis,' I said. 'You want to give me a hand here?'

He looked pretty green – Alexis is a sensitive soul – but he reached over and grabbed the scruff of the corpse's tunic. Together we heaved him ashore, face down, and let him drip. I noticed a nasty bruise – more of a cut – on the back of his head, between the crown and the neckline.

'Okay,' I said. 'Let's turn him over and see what we've got.'

I took the nearest arm and tugged. The dead man rolled on to his back and lay there staring up at us. He wasn't a pretty sight: the pool had been half mud, and the red clay coated him from head to foot as if he'd been dipped in blood.

He was fairly young – mid-thirties, a couple of years older than me – and he'd been well set up: tall, big-boned, plenty of flesh but most of it muscle. Good-looking, too, from what I could tell under the mud and all things considered. And I'd never seen him before in my life.

All of which put together could mean only one thing: Titus Clusinus's tomcatting days were over for good.

'Was he murdered, Corvinus?'

I looked back at Marilla standing behind my shoulder.

Her eyes were sparkling and she was staring down at what was left of Clusinus like he was the answer to a teenage girl's prayer. So; the kid took after Perilla as well as me. That lady never does what she's told either.

'Yeah, Princess,' I said. 'He was murdered.'

That made it three, in as many days. Someone was going for the record.

I sent Marilla straight back home, no arguments, then stayed with the body while Alexis went to round up a few guys with a stretcher. They'd take him back to his own place, of course, and I wished I'd had Alexis drop by there and break the news gently; not that I'd bet Vesia would be too upset. Still, Alexis was a smart cookie and he might think of it for himself.

I didn't have anything to carry water in, but I sloshed a few handfuls from the pool over Clusinus to wash off some of the clay. The face was puffy and waterlogged; I was no expert, but from his condition I'd say he'd been under for more than just a few hours. And that was strange, because I'd got the impression from Vesia that the guy was only out, not missing. That hurdle was odd, too: there weren't any others lying around in the immediate vicinity. On the other hand, I could see plenty in the field below, two hundred yards off. It must've been fetched from there special. And hurdles may not be all that heavy, but for one man they're a bugger to carry or drag.

So. What had we got? This wasn't Clusinus's property, although it was near the border, so he must've had a reason for being here; maybe he'd arranged to meet someone, or been suckered into thinking he would. Whatever the reason, having got him where they wanted him the killer had smacked him on the head with some sort of sharp, heavy instrument, a mattock maybe, and pitched him in the pool to drown. Unless the blow had killed him outright, of course. Then they'd gone down to the next field and brought up the hurdle, laid it on top of the body and weighted it down with stones. These, at least, weren't a problem: we were right at the edge of the farm here, outside the main cultivated area, and there were plenty lying around. Still, it would all have taken time and effort; and if Marilla could see the pool from above then so could any other passer-by, so it would've been risky, too.

Why not just leave the guy where he lay, like Hilarion? Why bother with all this hurdle crap?

To hide the body, obviously. It had been sheer luck that it had come to light so quickly at all. If the Princess hadn't happened along, if the hurdle had stayed submerged, if Papatius the owner of the property hadn't been under arrest in Caere and out of the picture, Clusinus could've lain there for days. Longer. Why should that be important? Important enough to take risks over?

That was another question I didn't have the answer to. They were piling up.

Alexis showed up finally. He'd found Mamilius sitting on the wineshop terrace. The old guy had rounded up his son and his two 'boys' – fifty, if they were a day – and come straight here. They hadn't bothered with a stretcher, but they unloaded the rocks and hauled the hurdle out of the pool.

While they were busy I took Alexis aside.

'Was, uh, Thupeltha around?' I asked quietly.

The slave grapevine is pretty efficient, and Alexis already knew the background. Also, like I say, he was no fool. He gave me a look and nodded.

'You tell her what'd happened?'

'Not directly, sir. But she heard me tell Mamilius.'

'Uh-huh. She make any comment? React in any particular way?'

'No, sir.'

'Which question's that an answer to?'

'Both.' Alexis's voice was neutral. 'She didn't seem particularly put out, sir. Or surprised.'

Well, that made sense. I couldn't imagine Thupeltha shedding tears for anyone. And certainly whatever she'd had going with Clusinus didn't involve much outside the basics.

'Decimus and the boys'll take him back the short way round.' Mamilius had come over. 'I'll go ahead myself to warn Vesia that he's coming.'

'It's Clusinus right enough?' I said.

'It's Clusinus.' Mamilius's voice was matter-of-fact, even cheerful, and it had me feeling almost sorry for the dead man. I wondered if I'd be the only one who did.

'You, uh, don't seem exactly broken up about it, friend,' I said.

Mamilius grinned and looked round at where the slaves were lifting the corpse on to the hurdle. 'Can't pretend I am,' he said. 'I always knew the bastard'd come to a bad end. And once Vesia's got over the shock she'll realise it's the best thing that could've happened.'

'Yeah.' I sighed; well, maybe the guy was right. I hadn't known Clusinus myself, but from what I'd heard he was no loss and the marriage was going nowhere. Still . . . I walked over to where I'd left my horse tethered to an oleander stump. 'Okay, we'll leave you to it. Come on, Alexis.'

I untied the lead rein and mounted. I was wheeling the horse to ride down the path to the main road when Decimus suddenly dropped his corner of the hurdle, spilling the corpse on to the ground. He ran towards me, waving his arms and gibbering. My blood went cold, and I pulled back on the rein. The horse shied . . .

'*Decimus!*' For a guy who'd been around when Actium was fought Mamilius could move pretty fast. He threw himself at his son and grabbed his arm.

I brought the horse under control finally – I'm no horseman, and I was pretty shaken myself – and patted her trembling flank.

'I'm sorry about that.' Mamilius was still holding on, although the big guy seemed quiet enough now. 'He didn't mean anything, he was just playing. Decimus, you'll apologise to Valerius Corvinus.'

The idiot gave me a hangdog look like a six-year-old kid caught with his spoon in the jam jar and muttered something. I shrugged and tried to stop my hands from shaking. Alexis was wide-eyed, but the two slaves were watching with incurious faces.

'That's okay,' I said. 'No harm done. I'll catch you around, Mamilius.'

Alexis mounted up on his mule and we rode back down through the vineyard towards the Caere road and home. All the way my brain was buzzing.

17

It was dinner-time when we got back. Jupiter, that'd
been some day! I was absolutely knackered, my belly
thought my throat was cut and I'd bet I smelled like
a barrel of stoats. I could murder a hot bath, a square
meal and an early night. Still, first things first. Bathyllus
was waiting with the wine jug and cup, and I downed a
straight half-pint.

'Perilla and the kid around, little guy?' I said.

'On the terrace, sir. I was just about to serve dinner.' He
refilled the wine cup. 'And Meton would like a personal
word with you when it's convenient.'

I groaned. Oh, shit, not Meton! Domestic problems
I could do without at this stage, and knowing that
single-minded bastard it could be anything from an
interrupted pickle supply to a complaint about the
quality of Flatworm's fish sauce. Certainly nothing more
earth-shaking; Meton's sense of priorities didn't exactly
mirror what you'd call normal.

'He deign to give any indication what it's about?' I
said.

Bathyllus sniffed. 'No, sir,' he said. 'And I didn't ask.'

Uh-oh. So there'd been ructions below stairs again and

the staff weren't on speaking terms. Bathyllus and Meton were like cat and dog: Meton was the original born-again anarchist, while the slightest change in household routine sent Bathyllus up the wall. Worse, the little guy didn't know a *boletaria* from a *sartago* and he couldn't care less. I was just waiting for the day when either we'd find our major-domo stiff and cold with a filleting knife between his ribs or our chef ditto with a feather duster shoved down his throat. 'Okay,' I said, 'tell the guy to make it after we've eaten. You manage that yourself or should I give you a flag of truce and a note?'

'No, sir.' Another sniff. 'That won't be necessary.'

'Fine. Fine.' I took the jug from him and carried it out on to the terrace.

Perilla and the Princess were already sitting at the table. I kissed Perilla and sat down on the other chair: that's the trouble with dining alfresco, no couches where you can sprawl, but we were in the country and the lady preferred the open air.

'So who was it?' Perilla asked.

'Clusinus.' I took a swallow of wine. 'Well, that's one suspect less, anyway. Maybe we'll be lucky and lose a few more.'

Perilla was quiet. 'He was married with a family, wasn't he?' she said at last. 'Do they know yet?'

'Quintus Mamilius said he'd break the news. But I doubt if his wife would be too upset.' I gave her an outline of my interview with Vesia.

'Perilla, isn't it exciting?' The Princess was still on a high. 'Three murders! Three! And I've never found a corpse before.'

Jupiter on wheels! Bathyllus and his minions were bringing out the starters, so I quickly shoved a plate of puréed squash and a hunk of bread in the Princess's direction. In Marilla's case I'd found the best method of sidetracking was to throw food at her.

'Here, Bright-Eyes,' I said. 'Get yourself round that and cut the crowing. It's not ladylike.'

Marilla tore off a piece of crust and scooped up some of the purée. 'He was under a hurdle,' she said through a mouthful of squash. 'Why would the murderer do that, Corvinus? Why drown him?'

Ah, hell; so much for parental authority. Still, it showed an enquiring mind, and it was a reasonable question. More than reasonable. 'He could've been drowned, sure,' I said, reaching for a plate of hard-boiled eggs in mustard sauce. 'But he was hit on the head first. And as for the hurdle, the intention would've been to keep the body out of sight.'

Perilla was frowning. I thought she was going to tick Marilla off for being too gruesome, or maybe just for speaking with her mouth full, but she said, 'You're sure about that, Marcus?'

I glanced at her. 'It seems a fair assumption. You have any other ideas?'

'No.' Perilla was thoughtfully spooning cucumber salad on to her plate. 'It's just that Marilla's right. It is a rather odd way of going about things.'

'Yeah. The same thought occurred to me.' I took a sip of wine. 'Especially since he'd have to bring the hurdle up from elsewhere.'

'When was Clusinus killed?'

'Jupiter knows. From the look of him he'd been in the pond for a while, maybe over a day . . .' I set down the cup. 'Shit!'

'*Marcus!*' Perilla snapped.

'Yeah, sorry, lady.' My brain was whirling. Oh, Jupiter!

Sweet holy Jupiter! 'Just a sudden thought. One I should've had before.'

'That's no excuse for bad language at the table.'

'I don't mind,' Marilla said.

'Then you should, dear. If—'

I waved her to silence. 'Hold on, Perilla. This is important. If the guy had been dead more than a day then we're back to square one.'

'Marcus, I hardly think—'

'Look. Larth Papatius was only arrested this morning, right? If Clusinus was killed before that then Papatius could still have done it.'

'Yes, but Papatius was with Vesia when Navius was murdered. Surely . . . ?' Perilla stopped. 'Oh. Oh, dear. Yes. I see what you mean.'

'Yeah. We only have Vesia's word that he was at her place, not even Papatius's. And with the third corpse being Clusinus's it opens up a whole new can of worms.'

'You think that Vesia and Papatius could have been in it together?' Perilla laid down her spoon. 'Marcus, that's horrible!'

'It's possible. Better than possible. Lots of people including Papatius may have had a motive for killing Navius, but Clusinus is a different matter. Sure, he wasn't popular, but so what? Papatius, on the other hand, has motive in spades: he was in love with the dead man's wife.'

'But he's already married!'

'There's such a thing as divorce. Maybe this new situation – with Thupeltha going for Clusinus – finally pushed him over the edge; or maybe he did it out of pure altruism. Papatius is a complicated cookie; personally I wouldn't like to predict which way he'd jump. And, like I say, he'd have reasons.'

'What about Vesia?'

'She needn't've been involved at all, not directly. Sure, she'd have to lie to me about Papatius having been with her when Navius was stabbed, and do it convincingly, but she's just as crazy about him as he is about her. I reckon under these circumstances she might manage it, especially since she's convinced he didn't do it anyway.'

'And her husband? You said yourself she'd simply told you he'd gone out. If he'd been missing for over a day she would have had to lie about that as well.'

'Not necessarily. Vesia's no Thupeltha. I'd imagine it wouldn't be the first time Clusinus had spent a night away from home, and Vesia's the type who'd cover up rather than blab, especially to a stranger. In fact, that's an argument for her not knowing anything about the death. She may be a good actress but I doubt she's that good. I'd bet the first she knew the guy was dead was when old Mamilius told her this afternoon.'

'You still haven't explained the hurdle. Why hide the body?'

'Yeah.' I frowned. 'That's still a bummer. Unless Papatius knew he was going to be arrested this morning and didn't want it found before then.' Shit, no. I discounted that angle as soon as I'd thought of it. It was stretching things too far; Papatius couldn't have known, and if he had the guy wasn't that subtle. 'Perilla, I just don't know about the hurdle, right? It's like Hilarion's death, it makes no sense.'

'Unless someone wanted to make sure Papatius was still a suspect.'

I'd been reaching for the wine jug. I paused.

'Run that one past me again, lady,' I said.

Perilla picked up her spoon and scooped up a slice

of cucumber. 'Let's say that Vesia is telling the truth. Clusinus was out all day, but not all night. If that's so, and you're not sure how long he'd been in the pond, then he could have been murdered this morning. If the body were left lying out in the open, as Hilarion's was, it would probably have been spotted quite quickly. However if the body were *not* obvious—'

'Then when it was finally found there'd be nothing to show one way or the other whether the guy had died after the arrest or before. And the longer it stayed hidden the better.' I nodded. 'Yeah, well, it's a tenable theory. The problem is, proving it either way depends on Vesia.'

'Surely she could simply be asked when she last saw her husband, this morning or yesterday?'

'Perilla, Vesia knows Papatius was arrested this morning and she doesn't want him nailed for killing Clusinus. The lady's not stupid. Truth or not, what answer do you think she'll give?'

'Then perhaps someone else saw him.'

'It's possible, sure. But it isn't likely.'

'Why not?'

'The pool's near the border of the two properties. He'd be on his own ground for most of the way, then on Papatius's. Besides, I don't think the guy wanted to be seen. I think he was meeting someone.'

'A woman? Thupeltha?'

'Not Thupeltha. They already had a place, in the oak grove on Clusinus's own land, and there was no reason to change the arrangement. On the other hand, Clusinus was off his own property and that argues a meeting of some kind.' I stirred the egg round on my plate, then put the spoon down in favour of my wine cup. 'The question is, why the hell there? If the killer came with murder and a hidden body in mind he could've chosen a dozen better places. The irrigation pond's got nothing going for it. There's no cover, it's exposed to view from above.'

'Perhaps that's the reason, Marcus. It wasn't the killer's choice of venue at all. It was Clusinus's.'

'And he thought he might be in danger if he chose somewhere more sheltered?' That opened up some interesting hypothetical lines I hadn't considered; it would imply that Clusinus knew a lot more about Navius's death and who had killed him than he'd said he did, for a start. 'Yeah, that might pass, but if so why not choose really safe ground, near the main road, for example? We're left with the same fundamental problem: why the pond at all?'

'So the killer could use the hurdle, of course.' That was the Princess. She'd been working her way through the starters and now she was coming up for air.

I didn't laugh. Crazy as it sounded, it was as good an explanation as any I could give, and it killed the two birds of the pool and the hurdle with one stone. The trouble was, assuming the murderer wasn't a total unmotivated head-banger it made no sense.

Bathyllus was oiling up with the main course, and my stomach rumbled in anticipation. Hell, shelve everything for the present, this looked good: a loin of pork stuffed with apricots and dotted with rosemary and garlic and a roast capon covered by a rich sauce. Plus the sundries. I topped up my wine cup and dug in.

By the time we'd all had enough and were ready to move on to the fruit and nuts the table was looking pretty empty. I pushed back my chair, set my feet against the terrace wall and called Bathyllus over. The beast had been fed. Now it was time for the master of the house to fulfil his duty to his staff. However unpleasant that might be.

'Hey, little guy,' I said. 'You want to tell Meton we're ready for him now?'

'What's this about, Marcus?' As Bathyllus left, Perilla laid down her napkin.

I shrugged. 'Jupiter knows, lady. Or possibly he doesn't, because not even Bathyllus has an inkling. Sit back with me and marvel.'

I'd been right about the ructions: Bathyllus brought the chef out like he was escorting a leper. Meton's a big guy, almost as broad as he's long, with hairy arms that wouldn't disgrace a gorilla, and he was looking straight ahead of him with the lowering intensity I'd come to know and love since I'd bought him at enormous expense from a Cappadocian gastronome twelve years back.

'The chef, sir,' Bathyllus said, as if I might not recognise him without expert help. No names, either: we were *definitely* not on speaking terms here.

'Right, right.' I filled up my wine cup. 'Fine. Buttle off and polish the spoons, Bathyllus, okay?'

Bathyllus sniffed and left.

Meton was grinning. 'You liked the dinner?' he said to me. No 'sir', you notice; I don't get a 'sir' from Meton all that often, and when I do I check for sarcasm.

'It wasn't bad.' That was an understatement: it'd been excellent as always, which was why we hadn't traded the culinarily fixated bastard in for a handful of beans years ago. Still, I wasn't going to tell Meton that. The guy had an ego the size of the Capitol. Bigger. 'New recipes?'

'Yeah. That's what I wanted to see you about, boss.' His eyes took on a manic gleam. 'I was especially pleased with the capon. In case you didn't notice, the sauce was made with walnuts, prunes, dried figs, green olives, cloves, sour cream and vinegar. You stuff—'

'Meton, please.' I held up a hand. 'Fascinating and informative as this is, pal, I hope it's not why you asked to see me. Because if it is then I'm afraid the next thing to be stuffed will be—'

'*Marcus!*' Perilla snapped. The Princess was watching with wide eyes.

'Yeah, well.'

Meton was looking hurt. 'You mean you're *really* not interested?' he said. From his tone it sounded like I'd just scored the double of committing mass murder and passing up a threesome with Helen of Troy and Cleopatra. Maybe by his way of thinking I had.

I sighed. 'Meton, listen. I've had a hard day, right? It may have slipped past you but we've had three murders around here recently and I'm trying to find out who's responsible before we have a fourth. Indeed at present a fourth is very much on the cards, although there won't be any connection between it and the other three. Do I make myself clear?'

'But that's what it's about!' The guy was flexing his huge fingers in agitation like they were two bunches of hairy bananas. 'I got the recipes from Tutia!'

'And who the hell's Tutia?'

'Gnaeus Vipena's cook.'

Hey! I sat back. 'Okay,' I said. 'You've got the floor.'

'Tutia has a lot of old Etruscan recipes, you see.' There went the eyes again. 'Boar marinated with juniper, oak and laurel, jugged hare and beechnut stuffing, that kind of thing. Did you know that the Etruscans used the gall bladder of the sturgeon to—'

Jupiter! Oh, hell! 'Meton, skip the inessentials, will you, please?' I said. 'That means' – I spelled it out, because

otherwise the guy wouldn't've got me in a million years
– 'anything whatsoever to do with food and cooking.
Right?'

He was staring at me in disbelief. 'You're sure?' he
said.

'As tomorrow's sunrise. Trust me. It's better that way.'

'All right. So long as you're absolutely certain.' He
paused. 'But this sturgeon's gall bladder, boss. They
used it to—'

'Meton!'

He fizzed a bit, then said, 'She overheard an argument.
Between her boss and Attus Navius.'

I sat up. 'When was this?'

'Five days ago.'

Shit; that would be two days before Navius was killed!
'You want to give me the details?' I said.

'She didn't hear much, just scraps. She was in the
kitchen and that's well away from the living-room. But
Attus Navius was shouting and some words came through.
There was something about wine – that came up a few
times. Navius called Vipena an old hypocrite. And she
heard a name, Tolumnius.'

'That's all?'

'All she told me, boss.'

Bugger! Ah, well. It was better than nothing, and all
the more so for being unexpected. 'Who's Tolumnius?
She know?'

'No. She's only been in the household a month. She
isn't a slave, she's a freedwoman from Fidenae.'

'Right. Thanks, Meton,' I said. 'You've been a great
help.' He turned to go. 'Uh, wait a moment, pal. Just
as a matter of interest, what's this Tutia like?'

He looked puzzled. 'I told you, boss. She knows a lot
of old Etruscan recipes.'

Jupiter! Did we talk the same language, or what? 'No, I mean physically. She young? Old? Have her own teeth and both legs?' I paused; I could see I wasn't getting through here. 'Married? Single?'

'Early middle age. And she's a widow.'

Oh, Priapus! 'Uh-huh. And how did you meet her?'

'She sent round a note saying that she had a lot of old—'

'Etruscan recipes. Yeah. And would you like to come round and see them some time. Right. Got you.' I didn't believe this; nobody could be that simple, *nobody*! 'Fine. Now bugger off, sunshine, okay?' Meton wandered back in the direction of his kitchen. Yeah, well. If this Tutia woman had any designs on the guy's chitterlings she'd have her work cut out, that was all I had to say.

Perilla had sat quiet through all this. Now she said; 'Vipena lied to you, didn't he?'

'Sure he did.' I drank what was in my wine cup and topped it up from the jug. 'At least the odds are on it. He told me he and Navius had quarrelled about letting Vipena buy into the water rights for the stream that goes through Navius's property. It didn't sound like that to me. And if Vipena had been the one wanting a favour he would've gone round to Navius's, not the other way round. Something smells, lady. I still don't know what it is, but it's there.'

Something else smelled: me. Whatever the ins and outs of it healthwise after a heavy meal, I needed a sweat in the bathhouse. I also needed to vegetate for an hour or so, switch off so I could sleep. Tomorrow was another day, and it was going to be busy.

It only occurred to me when I was lying on the bench in the hot room of Flatworm's bath suite that I'd forgotten to mention to Perilla the business of the horse.

18

The next morning after a fairly leisurely breakfast I went to pay another call on Navius's mother. I took the back way round, up Clusinus's track, just to check the bits and pieces of sightings I'd missed. The first was seeing whether the spot where Navius was murdered and the track up to it were visible from the higher ground, although that was pretty academic now, since it was only relevant to the theory that Clusinus had been the murderer. The answer was no and yes: because of the contours and the intervening trees and bushes I couldn't see the actual site of the murder from any point along the hill track, but most of Clusinus's road itself was overlooked.

The second sighting, the irrigation pond, was more important. I knew from what Marilla had said that you could actually see it from higher up, but not for how long. In fact, it wasn't so bad as I'd thought; Marilla must've been lucky and caught the window between the shoulders of the hills and the undergrowth screen. Even so, it was risky: the time taken for the meeting, the murder and – most of all – the business with the hurdle made it more than likely that there'd be somebody passing who would look down and see what was going on ...

Unless Clusinus had been killed before dawn, of course, when no one would be around, or late at night the previous day. The moon wasn't full, but it was past the three-quarters and we hadn't had any cloudy nights. In which case Papatius could've done it either way.

It probably was Papatius. The guy had both motive and opportunity for both murders, and if I couldn't account for Hilarion's then he was as good a suspect as any. Besides, every new twist to the case seemed to point in his direction. On the other hand there was that business with the horse, and Vipena. Which reminded me: I'd promised Vesia that I'd go into Caere and talk to Gaius Aternius. That I wasn't looking forward to, not with Clusinus dead and Papatius very firmly back on the suspect list. Nevertheless, it had to be done, and I could schedule it for the afternoon.

I was above Navius's place by now. I took the branch path off the track and headed down the slopes through the terraced vineyards. They were impressive. Arruns had been right: even I could see that the guy had put a lot of work in. The terracing was in first-class repair, a lot of the drainage and irrigation ditches I passed looked new, and the property looked tight, productive and well managed. Navius had certainly gone all out, and he'd known his business. For the first time I could really appreciate why the traditional vinegrowers like Papatius and Vipena were worried; if I'd been a vinegrower I'd be pissing myself.

Wine. Meton's culinary pal Tutia had said that it'd featured strongly in the argument she'd overheard, and that made a lot of sense. As far as Vipena was concerned, Navius's new farming methods were a real threat. But as a motive for murder? The more I saw of the guy's farm the more I was convinced it was possible; more than possible. We were talking financial survival here, and in the country that was everything. Vipena had a motive, sure he did; the evidence was all around me.

'Hypocrite', now, that was another matter: *hypocrite* I didn't understand at all. And why should Vipena want to kill Clusinus?

Yeah, well; we'd get there eventually, and when we did no doubt everything would make sense. At least I hoped it would. At the moment the case was a pig's breakfast.

Sicinia was having her hair done when I arrived, so I kicked my heels in the atrium until she came down. I thought about what I'd said to Perilla, about the lady being a big fish in a muddy pool. Yeah, that fitted: she wasn't quite in Mother's class, but she was definitely a looker, especially done up as she was this morning and wearing a mantle that must've come straight from the best couturier in Rome and cost her an arm and a leg. Not long after the funeral, either. I wondered how long it'd be before Sicinia Rufina decided she'd had enough of lonely childless widowhood out here in the sticks and branched out. With her money and looks she wouldn't be short of offers . . .

Something itched at the back of my skull, but when I reached for it it wasn't there any more.

'Valerius Corvinus!' She came over, and I caught the scent of her gold-piece-a-bottle perfume. 'What a pleasant surprise! Were you just passing or did you come specially?'

'Uh, the second.' That was some hairdo too, and I noticed the bits of grey I'd seen on my last visit weren't there any more. 'I've got a couple of extra questions to ask. If you don't mind.'

'Not at all.' She indicated a couch: I'd noticed the set as soon as I came in, top-quality antique with gold-leafed carving on the endboards and purple velvet upholstery. Pricey and tasteful both. 'Do make yourself comfortable. Have you had breakfast? It's a little early for wine.'

'Yeah, I'm fine, thanks.' Bugger; early, nothing. I could've managed another cup or two of that Falernian, especially after the walk. Still, I was on my best social behaviour. I lay down and she took the matching chair facing. 'I'll try not to take up too much of your time.'

'Oh, I'm quite free. This morning, at least.' She folded her hands in her lap. 'Now. What can I do for you?'

This was going to be tricky. 'I understand your son visited Gnaeus Vipena two days before he died.'

Was that a little hardening of the mouth? I couldn't be sure because of the make-up, and certainly the lady's voice was neutral. 'Yes, he did,' she said.

'You happen to know what they talked about?'

'I'm afraid I don't. Business, certainly. Vipena had been very concerned latterly about the failure of a well on his property. He wanted to rent a supply from the stream that flows through our own land near the property border. Perhaps the visit was connected with that.'

Hell. So that part of Vipena's story had been true, at least. Still, it would've been unrealistic to have thought otherwise: to be caught in a downright lie would've done Vipena no good at all.

'Your son was willing?' I said.

'No.' She hesitated. 'It's a perennial stream, but there isn't much water at this time of year. Attus needed all the water he could get for our own purposes. He had to refuse.'

'When was this exactly?'

'Some time last month, I believe. Or perhaps two

months ago now. Yes, it was July, just after the barley harvest.'

I sat back. Shit! Two months! And Vipena had given the impression, quite deliberately, that it had just happened. There was something out of kilter here after all.

'You think your son might've been reconsidering?'

Sicinia smoothed a fold in her mantle. 'That is very unlikely. He was quite firm about it. However, I can't really think of anything else that Attus would have wanted to discuss with Gnaeus Vipena, and a social visit, as I've indicated, is totally out of the question. He and his sisters really aren't our kind of people, and our connections with them are almost non-existent.'

'What sort of mood was he in when he left, can you remember?'

She frowned. 'It's strange you should ask that, Valerius Corvinus. Attus was . . . I can only describe his mood as very upset. Of course he always was a very emotional boy, quite unlike his father in that respect; he felt things too much, if you understand me.'

'And when he came back?'

'That was even more odd, and quite unlike his usual practice. On his return I happened to ask – which I don't always do – how the visit had gone and he categorically refused to discuss it. But whatever the object of the meeting was, it seemed to have been achieved satisfactorily.'

'Uh-huh. He seem happier, then?'

She hesitated. 'No, I wouldn't quite say that; but he gave the impression, as I said, of regarding the matter as closed.'

Hell's teeth; what was I to make of *that* little lot? It chimed with what Tutia had told Meton, sure: the guy had obviously been fit to be tied when he arrived, and whatever the argument had been with Vipena it'd been violent enough to provoke a shouting match. But why the secrecy where his mother was concerned?'

'Did, uh, Attus normally consult you on business matters?' I said.

'Not often, no.' She touched her impeccably arranged hair absently. 'As I told you on your previous visit I have no interest in or knowledge of the wine business per se. On major issues of policy such as his plans to increase production, yes, of course he consulted me. Personally, I wasn't in favour of that, but my cousin Publius – Publius Holconius the wine-shipper, I think I mentioned him to you – was, most definitely, and I bowed to his opinion. There's a growing niche in the market, you see, for cheaper wines, and being so close to Rome we would be at a definite advantage. It's so sad, though, don't you feel, when quality is sacrificed to quantity, whatever the arguments? The end of an era, almost.'

'One more question. Have you ever heard of a guy called Tolumnius?'

Her brow furrowed. 'I don't think so. Certainly he's no acquaintance of mine, or of Attus's either, as far as I'm aware. In what context?'

'That I'm not sure of. Maybe the wine trade, but it could be anything.'

'Then I'm afraid I can't help you.'

Ah, well: it'd been a shot in the dark, anyway. I got up.

'Thanks for your help,' I said. 'I won't take up any more of your time.'

'Not at all.' She rose and adjusted her mantle. 'It's a pleasure talking to someone from the outside world. Someone with a little' – she hesitated – '*culture.*' Jupiter! If Perilla could've heard that! 'And as I said I'm free until Gaius Aternius arrives later this afternoon.'

I paused. 'Aternius?'

'He's an old friend of the family, as I think I told you on your previous visit.' Was she blushing? Again with the make-up I couldn't say, but certainly her eyes lowered briefly. 'And he's been very kind over this business. Most assiduous.'

'Yeah.' I almost whistled. Given the lady's undoubted attractions, physical and financial, I'd bet the bugger had been just that, especially since his attentions seemed to be so welcome. Still, at least it stopped him from pestering Mother. 'Well, I'll be getting off. Thanks again.'

'Don't mention it.'

She saw me to the door. I was just leaving when a last thought struck me.

'Uh, Sicinia Rufina,' I said, 'forgive a personal question, but your late husband's accident. Where exactly did it happen?'

'He was found on the main road. By the bridge at the edge of Licinius Nepos's estate.'

Bull's-eye! 'Yeah. Yeah, right. Thanks.'

As the door closed behind me, my brain was buzzing like a hive of bees. Shit, now *that* had been interesting: the bridge spanned the boundary stream between the southern part of Nepos's land and Quintus Mamilius's property. Definitely food for thought, right?

The news about Aternius had been interesting, too.

19

I hadn't been into Caere before. As Etruscan towns go it's par for the course: think of a mountain with sides that go straight up far enough to give an eagle migraine, shove a wall round the top, fill the space with houses and the plain either side with fields and tombs and you've got it. Walking around the place, half the time you're going up, the other half you're going down, and there ain't no in-between. No wonder the Etruscans lost out to Rome; the poor buggers were probably too knackered to fight us off.

They must've been pretty good businessmen, mind. The wineshop looked like it went back to the Tarquins, and it was placed just where punters would see it the moment they came through the gate with their tongues trailing the dust from the climb. I crawled up to it, dropped my worn and shattered body into a chair and ordered up a jug of their best. It took me two full cups before I felt with it enough to forget about just breathing and take an interest in the local scenery. Part of which was an evil-looking guy with stubble you could use to grate cheese and a set of teeth like tent-pegs, sitting at the next table.

Sitting *grinning* at the next table.

'Better?' he said.

'Yeah.' I swallowed half my third cupful. It was good stuff, and it was a mark of how blown I was that I hadn't noticed. 'You got something against visitors in this town, friend?'

'Only when they're Roman. It's a local tradition.'

'Right.' I sank another mouthful and topped up the cup. 'The name's Corvinus. Marcus Corvinus.'

'Titus Perennius. You have business here, Corvinus, or are you in Caere for fun?'

I sat back. When she goes to a strange place Perilla likes to get the sights under her belt: temples, statues, libraries, you know the kind of thing. Me, what I like most is to find a good wineshop with good wine and spend the time shooting the breeze with a friendly local. It seemed I'd struck lucky straight off. This guy was obviously a kindred spirit.

'Business,' I said. 'You happen to know a man called Gaius Aternius?'

Perennius took a pull at his own cup before answering. 'Sure,' he said at last. 'The mayor's nephew.' He gave me a look that Perilla would've called 'circumspect', and most of the good humour had gone. 'He a friend of yours?'

'No. But I need to visit him.'

The guy grunted but didn't comment. 'He's got a house just off the Hinge.' That, I knew, was Caere's main street, running the length of the town. 'By the temple of Nortia. What kind of business are you in? Land? Grain? Wine, maybe?'

I pricked up my ears. 'Why these in particular, pal?'

'Just an assumption. They're Aternius's main ... call them interests.' His mouth twisted. 'Him and his uncle. Together they're the biggest landowners and property developers in the district.'

'Is that so, now?'

'That's so. That is indeed so. It's why the bastard's mayor.' Talk about flat; any flatter and you could've used the guy's voice to lay tiles on. 'A bit of advice, Corvinus, if you don't know Cominius or Aternius already: you've got any business with that pair of shysters, you be careful to count your fingers after you shake hands on the deal.'

'They're crooked?' Shit! This was an angle and a half, and one I hadn't been expecting!

'Let's just say they always come out ahead. It's a family feature. Old Cominius – Cominius's father – was the same, and Aternius is a shoot off the same stock. Slippery bastards, the lot of them. And I'm talking from personal experience.' He got to his feet, drained his cup and laid a handful of coppers on the table. 'Nice meeting you, friend. You be careful, right?'

'Right.' I watched him go, brain churning.

I found Aternius's house no bother: it was one of the snazziest in town, a two-storey job covering half a block with a garden at the side you could've run chariots in. I introduced myself to the door slave and got sniffed at despite my purple-striped tunic; the guy gave the distinct impression that he thought real Roman purple-stripers pulled up in litters with half a dozen attendants ready to pass bowls of cooling drinks through the curtains, and he wasn't going to be fobbed off with dusty pretenders reeking of wine and sweat. Nevertheless he let me in and left me to twiddle my thumbs in the hall while he fetched the master.

Aternius didn't seem too pleased to see me, either.

'Valerius Corvinus,' he said, shaking hands. 'This is a surprise. I can only give you fifteen minutes, I'm afraid. I'll be going out shortly.'

'Yeah, I know.' I followed him into the atrium. 'To

Sicinia Rufina's place.'

He stopped so abruptly we nearly collided. 'You're remarkably well informed,' he said. 'Curiously so.' Whatever residual friendliness there was in his tone had evaporated.

I shrugged. 'I was there earlier. The lady told me herself.'

'Indeed.' He lay down on a couch and waved me to another. 'So. What can I do for you?'

'I thought maybe you'd like an update on the Navius case. You know there was another murder yesterday?'

'Titus Clusinus. Yes. So I've been told.' The guy's voice was expressionless. 'It doesn't change anything, of course. I understand the body could've been submerged for a day, at least.'

Uh-huh. Who was the 'remarkably well-informed' one now? Still, I supposed he'd keep tabs on what was going on. 'Yeah. But there's one more thing. Papatius was with Clusinus's wife when Navius was murdered.'

His eyes came up. Good! I'd rocked the bastard after all! It was worth playing devil's advocate just to wipe the smugness off his face. 'Who said so?'

'The lady herself. Vesia.'

He seemed to relax. 'Corvinus, surely that's fresh proof of Papatius's guilt. If the two were lovers—'

'I said he was with her, pal. I didn't say they were lovers.'

'It's a logical assumption, although naturally it's not essential. And it explains why he refused to give an account of his movements.'

I was getting angry now. 'It explains nothing of the sort, friend. Just the opposite. If Papatius had killed Navius and Vesia was prepared to lie to back him up he'd fall over himself to tell you where he was.'

'Not if he and the woman were intending to murder her husband.'

That stopped me. Shit, I hated to admit it but the guy was right, in theory at least: if Papatius and Vesia planned to murder Clusinus they wouldn't put their scheme in jeopardy by tipping him and everyone else off in advance that they were an item, platonic or not. On the other hand . . .

'He wouldn't give Vesia on an alibi at all if he'd killed Clusinus,' I said. 'Before or after. It would point the finger straight at him.'

'But he didn't.' Aternius was smiling, the full teeth job. 'Vesia did. Perhaps it was her own idea; certainly I doubt if she thought the implications through, and meanwhile Papatius still isn't talking. And you're right about the finger of suspicion, Corvinus. That's just where it does point.'

Bugger. Yeah, well; there wasn't much more I could do or say, and I was hamstrung by the knowledge that, smug narrow-minded bastard or not, the guy was probably right. If you went by pure logic and common sense Papatius was guilty six ways from nothing. Maybe it was because Smooth-Chops was so sure he'd got the right man that I kept on going; that and a gut feeling that Vesia just couldn't be the scheming bitch she'd have to be for the theory to work. Also if Papatius had killed Clusinus during the hours of darkness surely Thupeltha would know he'd gone out. Unless they didn't actually sleep together in the literal sense, of course, and that was possible, too.

Aternius was saying something, and my attention snapped back to him.

'The praetor's representative from Rome should be in the area in ten days' time. The murders are capital crimes committed by a citizen, and so beyond my uncle's

jurisdiction, but we should be able to finalise things then.'
He smiled. 'I'm sure you'll be as glad to get this nonsense
off your hands as I will.'

Hell; I hadn't thought of that. We're a stratified society,
us Romans. Barring the off-chance of an execution if the
victim's family is important enough to have serious clout,
purple-stripers like Priscus accused of murder face exile
and a whacking fine, unless they do a runner voluntarily
first, which saves everyone's time and is a lot more
profitable to the accuser. No-account commoners out
in the sticks, on the other hand, get the praetor's rep and,
if they're found guilty, a fast appointment with a noose.
And Papatius would be found guilty, sure he would: this
bastard would make certain of it.

I'd got ten days to solve this thing, max; or at least
to be happy in my own mind that they'd nailed the
right man.

'Uh, you mind if I go round and see him?' I said.
'Papatius, I mean?'

Aternius frowned. 'Why on earth would you want to
do that?'

'He may want to change his testimony now I've talked
to Vesia. Besides, there're a few things I need to clear up.'
A few! Jupiter! 'He's at militia headquarters?'

The guy's frown hadn't lifted. 'Corvinus, this is neither
wise nor necessary. The case is solved. We have the
murderer in custody, largely thanks to you, and he'll
have every chance the law allows to defend himself.
Frankly, now your stepfather is no longer involved in
this affair it's none of your business. Why don't you leave
things alone and get on with your holiday?'

My fingers bunched, but I kept control of my temper.
'How I choose to spend my holiday's my concern, pal,' I
said equably. 'Besides, the guy'll need a lawyer.'

That got me a sharp look; very sharp. 'You're offering your own services?'

'If he isn't already represented – and from what you just said he isn't – then sure, why not?' That was one good thing about the legal system: I might not know the *lex Augusta de vi* from a kick in the pants, but I had the only formal qualification necessary for the job; I was willing to do it. And as Papatius's lawyer I'd have automatic right of access to him. 'Just write me the letter, sunshine, and I'll be on my way.'

He fizzed a bit, but I had him over a barrel and he knew it. He was writing out the note for the militia commander when I thought of something else.

'Incidentally,' I said, 'you happen to know a guy called Titus Perennius?'

The pen paused. 'I've met him, yes.'

'Business or social?'

'Business. I bought his farm from him several years ago.' Aternius rolled up the paper sheet and gave me it. 'There you are, Valerius Corvinus. Now if you'll excuse me I have other things to do.'

'Right.' I got up, tucked the letter into the belt of my tunic – no mantle, it was too hot for mantles and I've never liked these things anyway – and made for the door. 'I'll see you around, pal. Have a nice day.'

He didn't answer.

I'd passed the militia building on my way to Aternius's. It was on the main square, a grim-looking place built of the soft local stone and worn down so much it could've been there when Rome was just a gleam in Jupiter's eye. The militia commander wasn't exactly spruce and dapper, either. Or any less grim.

'You want to see Larth Papatius, you say?' He glared at

me like I'd just made an indecent proposal in the public latrine. 'Authorisation?'

I handed over Smooth-Chops's letter. He unrolled it, read it, grunted and handed it back. 'So what makes the bastard rate a fancy Roman lawyer?' he said.

'Maybe his charm and witty conversation. You should try it some time, sunshine.'

That got me no answer at all, not even a grunt. He heaved himself to his feet, picked up a huge key from a nail in the wall, and led the way along a passage that could've doubled for the one Pluto dragged Persephone down. I only hoped there wasn't a three-headed dog at the end of it.

We got to an oak slab that was just recognisably a door but looked like it hadn't been opened since Romulus got his first taste of wolf's milk. The guy put in the key, turned it and shoved.

'Bang on the door when you're done,' he said.

'Hey, it's a long way up, chum. You want to leave me the key instead and I'll find my own way back?'

He just looked at me. 'I've got good ears,' he said finally.

Yeah, well, that was a matter of opinion: I'd seen better soup-pot lids myself. But I wasn't going to say that, not with Charon here the only thing between me and the outside world.

There was a lamp on the floor. I lit it with the strike-light beside it and went in. The door shut behind me and the lock rattled. Footsteps retreated into the distance. *Easy is the descent to Avernus*: the real bugger is getting back.

Apart from the light from the lamp, the room was pitch-dark: no windows; we must've been twenty feet below street level, and it smelled of urine and worse. When my eyes got used to the dimness I saw Papatius sitting on a cot bed; just sitting, watching me. He had chains on his wrists and ankles.

'What the fuck are you doing here, Corvinus?' he said.

I could've asked myself the same question. There was no stool, so I leaned against the wall. The top of my head scraped the roof. It felt damp.

'Don't knock it, pal,' I said. 'I'm your new lawyer.'

He laughed; not that there was much humour in the sound he made. 'Cut the crap, Roman. You're the reason I'm down here.'

Well, I couldn't argue with that. 'I've been talking with Vesia,' I said.

He was off the bed in a second. If the guy hadn't been half-starved and leery with beatings he could've taken me easy. As it was, when he got to me I had to hold him up, and the lamp too. I took him back to the cot and sat him down.

'You bastard,' he said.

No argument there either: he had a right to his opinion, and from his angle he was justified. 'She says you were together when Navius was killed. That right?'

He was quiet a long time.

'If she says so.'

Jupiter! He wasn't giving much away, was he? 'Hey, look,' I said. 'I told you; I'm your lawyer. I'm supposed to be on your side and vice versa. So cut the crap yourself, right?'

He grinned, or tried to; he didn't have many teeth left. 'Okay, Roman. Yes, that's where I was. But we were just talking. Nothing else.'

'She told me that too. And what you talked about.'

Another silence. Finally, he broke it, softly. 'I'd've killed him for her, if she'd wanted me to. If she'd asked. You know that?'

He wasn't talking about Navius, or Thupeltha. 'Yeah,' I said. 'I know.'

'Only I didn't. Someone else did it for me. And if I could shake his hand I would. That clear?'

'Clear.' Jupiter! 'There anything you haven't told me?'

His lips twisted. 'That depends on what you know, doesn't it?'

It was my turn to grin. 'Okay,' I said. 'When Thupeltha left the wineshop that morning you gave her time to get clear. Then you went round to Vesia's. You told her about Clusinus and your wife and you offered to do something about it. Vesia said to leave things as they were. You talked for a while and then you left to work on your own property. You didn't see nothing nor no one for the rest of the day until you went back home and found out that Navius had been murdered. Finish, end of story. Is that right?'

'That's right. And, as you say, end of story. I didn't know anything about it then, and I don't now. Either about Navius or Clusinus. You can believe me or not, but it's the truth.'

Yeah. It probably was at that; at least my gut feeling told me it was. Maybe the guy deserved a lawyer after all, even if it was a legal lame-brain like me. Okay; so it cleared the ground. We could start on the other angles. 'You know anyone by the name of Tolumnius?'

He gave me a puzzled look. 'Sure. Two of them, Gaius and Titus. The first's a wine-shipper, the second makes wine jars. They're brothers, cousins of Gnaeus Vipena, and they're based in Pyrgi. So?'

I leaned back against the wall. Shit! Vipena's cousins! Maybe I was on to something here! 'Can you tell me anything about them?'

'Just the names and who they are. I've never met either.

Between them they handle Vipena's wine. He gets his jars from Titus and Gaius ships them to Ostia. It's a family business.' He shifted and his chains clanked. 'What's this about, Corvinus?'

'I don't know. Maybe nothing.' Nothing, hell! I had an itch at the back of my neck like a dozen fleas. In this place that's just what it might have been, but I doubted it. 'Pyrgi, you say?' Pyrgi was Caere's main port, eight miles to the north-west.

'Titus runs a potter's yard near the Caere Gate and Gaius has a place by the harbour.'

'Got you.' I turned and banged on the door. I just hoped Big Ears was listening. 'Okay, friend. Keep your pecker up. Your fate is in good hands.'

His ruined mouth split in another grin. 'Yeah. Right.' The grin faded. 'When you go back, Corvinus, say hello to Vesia for me, will you?'

'You've got it.' A thought struck me. 'By the way. You know why a winemaker would want a set of cisterns with a fire grid underneath?'

'Sure. That's standard equipment in some wineries. If a wine's not up to scratch you can mellow it by heating. I don't do it myself, mind: they say it puts ten years on in as many hours, but you'd have to be a pretty poor judge not to know the difference between jar- and flame-aged stuff.'

'Right,' I said, my brain buzzing. *Hypocrite!* 'Right. Thanks, pal.'

For a wonder, Big Ears showed up at last and let me out. After that dark, stinking hole even Caere looked good; but I didn't regret the visit.

I knew now what Attus Navius and Vipena had quarrelled about. Clusinus's death might be something else again, but the odds on our wine-making soothsayer having murdered Navius had just taken a hike.

20

I had a problem here. It may've still been early – the sun wasn't quite into its last quadrant yet – but Pyrgi was far too far to walk, and it would've taken time to have gone home and either picked up the horse or Lysias and the carriage. On the other hand, time was pressing. I mightn't have a hope of solving this thing in the ten days Smooth-Chops had unwittingly given me, but I reckoned I'd feel pretty sick when Papatius was strangled and I looked back on an afternoon and evening spent twiddling my thumbs and knocking back the booze. The answer, of course, was obvious: there're hack stables in every town where you can buy an animal or rent it, and I could get a horse there. Jupiter knew what kind of screw I'd end up with in Caere, but whatever it was so long as it had four legs and could go the distance it would have to do. I stopped the first guy I met outside the militia building and he gave me directions to the best glue factory in town; in fact, the *only* glue factory in town.

Before I left, though, I had one more thing to do. The records office was practically next door to Papatius's slammer, part of the temple of Jupiter Tinia. I went in and asked to look at a deed of sale.

'You know the buyer and the seller, sir?' The clerk behind the desk was human for a change. That doesn't often happen in these places, where they seem to have a policy of employing social misfits with a deep and abiding hatred of anything that isn't made up of glued-together sheets rolled round a roller.

'Sure,' I said. 'It's a stretch of vineyard. Sold by a guy called Arruns and bought by a Velthur Navius. We're talking fifty years back, mind.'

The kid – he couldn't't've been any more than nineteen – was frowning.

'Arruns, you say? And Navius?'

'Yeah. Yeah, that's right. Out at Vetuliscum.' I could've been imagining things – I probably was – but there was something in his tone that made the hairs stir at the nape of my neck. 'You got a problem with that, sunshine?'

'No. No, of course not.' He turned away. 'If you don't mind waiting I'll see if I can find the document for you.'

'Fine. Thanks.'

Whatever filing system they used it was pretty efficient. I'd hardly sat down and begun picking my teeth when he was back with the roll. I undid the leather tie-string and opened it up.

It was straightforward enough, and couched in the proper legal form that makes your head ache: the sale of X amount of land, boundaries specified, for Y amount of cash on date Z, the exchange being made between one Aulus Arruns and one Velthur Navius, signatures and seals appended; but the signature and seal I was looking for was under the heading 'Witnessed By'. There it was, large as life, and if I'd had any bets on what it'd be I'd've cleaned up.

I thanked the guy and left.

*   *   *

I hadn't overestimated what Caere had to offer in the way of horseflesh. The owner of the hack stable beside Hercules Gate led out something that was just arguably equine but which any place where any kinds of standards applied would've been recycled for cat meat ten years ago.

'You sure he'll last the trip there and back, pal?' I said. The horse's head drooped dispiritedly. He looked like he'd had the lot – glanders, mange, the strangles, you name it – and hadn't quite come out the other end of any of them.

'Fulgor's okay.' The man gave the animal a slap on the rump that nearly had him over. 'Just point him in the right direction and he'll take you there.'

Shit: *Fulgor?* 'Yeah, but I'd sort of envisaged sitting on his back while he did it,' I said. 'In his present state that'd seem to be pushing things.'

The guy sniffed. 'You don't want a horse then I can hire you a mule,' he said.

Uh-uh. 'No mules. I wouldn't trust these bastards as far as I could throw them. Or they could throw me.'

'Then Fulgor's the best I can do.'

I sighed. 'Fine, pal. How much?'

He named a price, I halved it, we dickered and I finally paid over as much as would've kept the brute in hay and barley mash for a month. They all see the Roman coming.

Gingerly, I lifted myself into the saddle. It was like balancing on a ruckle of bones. If I'd had a stick I could've played a tune on the bastard's ribs.

'Okay, Flash,' I said. 'Let's move.'

To be fair, when he got going he wasn't all that bad. With the run downhill from the town gate, once we hit the open plain we were moving at something between a trot and a canter, and there was still a chunk of the afternoon left when we reached Pyrgi.

The town wasn't much, even more run-down than Caere. Sure, it'd been a sizeable place in its day, but that had been three or four hundred years back when Etruria was still a viable proposition and the Confederacy's merchant fleet were having rings run round them by slick-as-virgin-oil market-conscious Cumaean Greeks. Now Pyrgi just sat there between the Caeretan plain and the sea like a faded old grandmother paddling her toes and sulked.

I found Titus Tolumnius's pottery business no bother, about fifty yards in from the gate between a wheelwright's and a line of butchers' shops. In contrast to them it looked prosperous: a yard stacked with every kind of pot from the big vats used to ferment wine to the sort of casserole that the local housewives cooked their beans and sage in. Just inside the entrance a couple of slaves were loading a cart with what looked like oil jars wrapped in straw. I dismounted and tethered Flash to a ring in the perimeter wall.

'The boss handy, lads?' I asked.

They nodded towards the back of the yard where a small, thin-faced guy in a sharp green tunic was supervising the unloading of a kiln. I gave them a wave and carried on over.

'Titus Tolumnius?' I said.

'Who wants him?'

'My name's Corvinus. Marcus Valerius Corvinus.'

He'd caught the purple stripe on my tunic now, and the frown changed to a smile: Roman purple-stripers aren't thick on the ground in places like Pyrgi, and seeing one tends to set the local businessmen's abacus fingers twitching.

'I'm Tolumnius,' he said. 'How can I help you, sir?'

Amazing the change the scent of money has on diction. No doubt one of Perilla's smartass Greeks has written a book about it. 'I'm interested in wine jars,' I said. 'The bulk carriage variety.'

'Amphorae?' The smile broadened. 'We can supply you with these, sir. How many would you be wanting?'

'Say seven or eight hundred. That's for starters, probably well over the thousand, but it depends on quality.'

His eyes bulged. 'Ah ... yes. A thousand amphorae. Well, now ...'

Shit; maybe I'd overdone it here. It was a bad sign that even the guys unloading the kiln had stopped to look at me with their jaws hanging. Still, I'd made an impression, and that was the main thing.

'You got a problem, friend?' I said, giving him my best patrician stare.

'No. No problem.' He was shaking his head so hard I was afraid it'd drop off. 'We can handle that for you. And the quality will be excellent, I can promise you.'

'Uh-huh. You won't mind if I check on that? Maybe have a look at a sample of what I'll be getting?'

'Not at all! Not at all!' He was practically rubbing his hands, and you could've used his tone of voice to deep-fry fish. 'If you'd like to come this way ...' He led me across the yard to where a dozen or so of the seven-gallon jars were stacked on their pointy ends against the wall. 'Here you are, sir. You won't find finer quality in Pyrgi. And if you happen to need a shipper I can recommend my brother. He has his own ship, very reliable. I'm sure we can work out a most attractive package.'

'Yeah.' I was examining the nearest jar. These things

are pretty standard, of course, except for the potter's mark. I'd seen this one before, although unlike the jars at Vipena's place it didn't have the disfiguring chisel scars. 'Nice stamp.'

He looked at me strangely. 'Sir?'

I pointed. 'TOL. That'd be short for Tolumnius, wouldn't it?'

I got the distinct impression that if financially induced politeness hadn't stopped him he'd be backing off a step or two. Coming from a bulk wine dealer like I was supposed to be the question was about as sensible as 'You pour the stuff in at the top and plug the hole afterwards, don't you?'

'Uh, yes, sir, that's absolutely correct,' he said.

'Fascinating. You use any other letters, ever?' I wasn't watching him, but I could feel him stiffen. 'Just for variety. Like HOLC maybe?' No answer. 'HOLC as in Holconius, for instance? Publius Holconius, the Pompeian wine-shipper?'

There was a long silence. I looked up. The guy had gone as green as his tunic. Bull's-eye!

'Who the hell are you?' he said.

'I told you, sunshine. My name's Marcus Corvinus.'

'Okay, Corvinus. Get the fuck off my property and don't come back.'

It was quite a change. Not only – understandably – was the guy a lot less friendly, but he sounded a lot tougher, too. I wondered if I'd underestimated Titus Tolumnius. However, it was too late to back down now.

'You've got a wine scam going with your brother and your cousin Gnaeus Vipena,' I said. 'Vipena's heat-treating his wine and passing it off as prime Falernian under Holconius's mark. He makes it, you jar it, your brother Gaius ships it to Ostia and sells it and you split the considerable profits three ways. Now's your chance to tell me I'm wrong. So go for it.'

I waited. Nothing. Finally Tolumnius turned away from me in the direction of the two slaves who'd been loading the cart.

'*Rufus! Grumio!*' he yelled.

They glanced up, straightened, and came over at a run. Uh-oh. Mistake. I stepped back; lugging seriously heavy industrial containers around for a living does wonders for your muscle development, and those guys looked like they wrestled gorillas in their free time.

'Throw this bastard out,' Tolumnius said quietly. 'He shows his face again, you flatten it for him. Clear?'

The two nodded and moved forward, grinning. I held up my hands, palm out, and they stopped. 'Okay, sunshine,' I said to Tolumnius. 'I'm going. And forget the amphorae order. I'll take my business elsewhere.'

'Now you listen to me, Corvinus' – Tolumnius was still speaking quietly – 'because I'll say it once and once only. Make trouble over this and you're dead, purple stripe or not. Remember that. Never ever forget it, or the gods help you. You understand?'

Now was not the time for heroics. 'Yeah, I understand,' I said. 'Have a nice day, pal.'

As I turned and walked back to Flash I could feel the three pairs of eyes burning into my back all the way.

Dead, Tolumnius had said. Like Navius. And he hadn't had a purple stripe to protect him. If I'd wanted another suspect I'd just got one in spades.

21

Even though I cut out the round trip and went straight home – I could take Flash into Caere the next day, or Lysias could – it was almost dark when I got back. I was starving. Perilla and the Princess had eaten hours ago, but I had Bathyllus scare up whatever they'd left and serve it up with a jug of wine on the terrace.

Perilla was there already, watching the sunset. 'You want to talk to me while I eat, lady?' I said to her, once I'd planted a smacker between her nose and her chin.

She sniffed. 'It seems the occasional hurried meal is the only time I *can* talk to you these days. I thought this was supposed to be a holiday.'

Uh-oh. She sounded seriously peeved, which was fair enough. Still, what could I do? I only had ten days, and if I hadn't nailed the killer by then I'd be standing up on my hind legs in court with nothing to offer but an ingratiating smile and a load of half-baked theories. Neither of which was going to do Papatius a lot of good. 'Yeah, well,' I said uncomfortably, pulling up a chair. 'We're getting there.'

She fixed me with a long hard stare. 'Corvinus, it's a mystery to me why you're going anywhere at all. And

181 •

I'd be grateful if you didn't use the plural. *You* may be getting somewhere but *I* am not, not to speak of. That is precisely the problem. Apart from one of your mother's dinners with the added fillip of a corpse cooling downstairs and an extremely boring visit to two gossipy old cats whom *you* wanted me to butter up for reasons of your own I haven't been out of the house. Oh, I beg your pardon, I was forgetting Hilarion's funeral. Compared to the other outings you arranged for us that was a positive pleasure jaunt.'

Ouch. Maybe I should go out and come in again, preferably as someone else. 'Uh, yeah.' I sank back into my chair. 'Yeah, right.'

Bathyllus oozed up with a loaded tray. 'Meton presents his compliments, sir,' he said. 'He asks me to remind you that he is a chef and that warming up leftovers is the province of a cookshop hash-slinger. Despite this he hopes you will enjoy your meal.'

I groaned. Shit. Of course I hadn't had a chance to let Meton know I wouldn't be back for dinner, and in that bastard's book missing one of his carefully orchestrated meals without letting him know beforehand is tantamount to treason. However, Perilla was one thing, Meton was another.

'Tell the pernickety bugger to go and fry himself!' I snarled.

'Certainly, sir.' Bathyllus poured the wine. Not an eyelid did the little bald-head bat.

A thought struck me. 'Hey, Bathyllus.'

'Sir?'

'You two talking again?'

'Yes, sir.'

'You mind telling me what the argument was about this time?'

He put down the jug and began setting out plates of lamb in a thick bean sauce, carrots in cumin and a meatball ragout. If they were reheats they looked okay to me, but then I only went by normal human standards of edibility. Besides, like I say I was so starved I'd've eaten boiled horsemeat.

'Sponges, sir,' he said.

Maybe hunger had affected my hearing, too. 'Uh ... sorry, little guy, but was that "sponges"? As in the things that grow on rocks and you use in lavatories to ... ?'

'Yes, sir.'

'Right. Right.' Jupiter! Don't ask, Corvinus, don't ask! 'Fine. So long as you're all pals again.'

'Indeed.' Bathyllus sniffed and left. I picked up my spoon and began to eat. Jupiter, that little bugger got weirder by the day.

'So, Marcus,' Perilla said. 'How is the case progressing, in actual fact?'

'You really want to know, lady?'

'Not particularly, but I suppose you'll tell me anyway.'

Snappy, but at least she'd expressed an interest. And I knew Perilla. Whatever front she put up, deep down she was just as keen to find out whodunnit as I was.

Probably.

'Forget Papatius,' I said. 'He didn't do it. Gnaeus Vipena, now, he's a real possibility. Him or one of his business associates. And I'll take side bets on Mamilius and Gaius Aternius.'

She stared at me. '*Aternius?* Marcus, you can't be serious! He was put in charge of investigating the murders!'

'Maybe so, but the guy's as bent as a wooden drachma. Him, his uncle and the rest of his family.'

'That's nonsense. You simply don't like the man because he's smooth, good-looking and sophisticated and he made a play for your mother.'

'Yeah, well, all that too.' I tried a meatball. Warmed over or not, the sauce – it had marjoram and lovage in it – was excellent. 'But I don't like his smell, Perilla. There's something rotten about that bastard. I don't know quite what it is yet, but if there isn't a connection between him and the case I'll eat my sandals.'

'But what makes you suspect Gaius Aternius, for goodness' sake? He isn't even local.'

I put down my spoon so I could count off on my fingers. 'One: he's in a hell of a hurry to put Larth Papatius in an urn. Two: in addition to trying to get Mother on a slow trip to Lake Sabatinus he's playing footsie with Sicinia Rufina who following the death of her son is now a wealthy childless widow with a gleam in her eye. Three: I have it on the authority of a certain Titus Perennius who fell foul of him that he and his uncle are two of the biggest sharks in Caere. Four: Cominius's father witnessed that document of sale that old Larcius Arruns has been causing trouble over for the past fifty years. That do you?'

Perilla sighed. 'No, it will not do me. In fact, I don't think I've ever heard such a farrago of nonsense in my entire life.'

'Nonsense it isn't, lady.' I picked up my spoon again. 'And what the hell's a farrago?'

'Marcus, even if all that is true it's neither relevant nor in any way evidence of guilt. You know yourself that there's a strong case against Papatius, Aternius has been a friend of the Navius family for years, he's a bachelor and by your own account Sicinia is still an attractive woman. As far as his business reputation is concerned, wineshop rumour ... I assume you met this Titus Perennius in a wineshop?' I winced. 'Exactly. Wineshop rumour is a long way from being hard fact. And as for your last offering the gods alone know what it has to do with anything whatsoever, on earth, above it or under it.'

Jupiter on a tightrope! Well, she had a valid point; several valid points. Maybe I was building sandcastles here. Still, I had that itch at the back of my skull that told me there was something screwy. And, like I said, I didn't like Aternius's smell. I scooped up the last meatball, ran a bit of bread round the dish to soak up the sauce, then started in on the lamb and carrots.

Perilla let me eat for a bit, then she said, 'What about Vipena?'

At least I was on better ground here. 'The guy's a crook,' I said. 'No theorising this time, solid proof.' I told her the story of the visit to Papatius and the trip to Pyrgi. Navius was right to call him a hypocrite. 'He was doing the same as Navius was planning to do and Vipena was slating him for monkeying around with wine, only where the kid was acting above board what Vipena was up to was actually criminal.'

'Selling heat-treated Caeretan as Falernian. Could he get away with that?'

'Sure.' I bit on a carrot and chewed. 'No problem. You get whacky Falernian in wineshops all over Rome; all over the empire, for that matter. Not just Falernian, any high-class wine; Faustinian, Caecuban, Setinian. Most ordinary punters've never tasted the real stuff, so they wouldn't know the difference anyway. All they're interested in is the chichi label on the flask their jug comes from that shows what big spenders they are. And the wineshop owners aren't complaining. They get their Falernian at a price that may be double what they pay for ordinary wines, but it's still a hell of a lot less than it should be, and it means they can put it up on their boards and raise the tone of the place with a clear conscience.'

'It sounds big business.'

'It is. Profitable, too, which means the wide boys who run it are no pushovers. On his own Vipena might be just a long drink of water but his cousin's another matter. Tolumnius is bad news. The scam could've been chugging along for years, and if Navius looked like causing trouble then I doubt if he'd've thought twice about shutting the guy's mouth permanently. And I'd guess his brother's the same.'

'What about Clusinus's murder? Not to mention Hilarion's?'

'Perilla, I just don't know, okay? Sure, on present showing they'd have no motive for killing anyone but Navius. On the other hand, with Papatius out of the picture the other deaths don't make sense anyway, and Vipena and his pals are as good a prospect as any.'

'So what happens now?'

'I have another talk with Vipena.' I drained my cup and refilled it. 'Maybe if he knows the game's up he'll cave.'

'Marcus, be careful.' She had on her serious look.

'No problem, lady. Vipena I can handle.'

'It wasn't Vipena I was thinking of.'

Yeah, well; she was probably right. Still, you didn't make an omelette without breaking eggs, and ten days was ten days.

'I'll be okay,' I said.

Which, as a prediction, was pretty much of a bummer. But then predictions never were my bag.

22

Early the next morning I sent Lysias back to Caere with
Flash and walked into Vetuliscum. I had a busy day ahead
of me: as well as bearding Gnaeus Vipena in his den if I
was going to find out anything about Titus Clusinus it
meant another talk with Vesia. Then there was Quintus
Mamilius and his blue-eyed boy Decimus. That I wasn't
looking forward to, but it was one interview I couldn't
put off.

Mamilius first, to get it over with. I called in at the
farmhouse but there was nobody around, not even a
housekeeper. I wondered what the old guy's domestic arrangements were, how he managed the ordinary
day-to-day things like eating and laundry. Pregnant granddaughter or not, I couldn't think of Mamilius as a murderer; which was strange because as far as Navius was
concerned anyway he had as good a motive as any and
better than some. The trouble was I could easily be
wrong. I had a soft spot for straightforward, no-nonsense
characters like Mamilius and a natural down on canting
frauds like Vipena and smoothies like Gaius Aternius,
and I knew it; given the choice, I'd rather have one of
the last two guilty. It might not be the way the world

worked, but it had what Perilla would call a dramatic rightness to it.

Well, we'd simply have to see. Certainly Mamilius had questions to answer, and neither of us could duck the fact.

He was harvesting apples in the orchard behind the farm: the two slaves beating the higher branches with poles and Mamilius and his son holding either end of an old blanket to catch the fruit. He looked up as I came over, and when our eyes met I saw his jaw tighten. He motioned the slaves to stop, then laid the blanket down and waited, his back straight like we were on a parade ground. Decimus was staring at me wide-eyed and slack-mouthed. He started to gibber something, but Mamilius reached over and put a hand on his arm. The slaves were watching too, and their faces wore the same expression as Mamilius's did. I felt like I'd just stepped on to a stage and the other performers were waiting for me to act my piece; that they knew the scene already, didn't like it but accepted that it had to be played out as written. It wasn't a comfortable feeling, either.

'You're up early, Corvinus,' Mamilius said.

'Yeah.' I picked up an apple from the blanket. It was as big as my fist, evenly shaped, and the peel was unmarked. I thought of the scraggy spotted abortions that I'd seen hanging on Clusinus's trees. 'Good quality.'

He nodded. There was a stiffness in the movement that had nothing to do with age. 'The best,' he said proudly. 'I may not be a winegrower but apples're another thing altogether. Go ahead, have a bite.' I bit; the apple was firm-fleshed and juicy. 'That's a Matian. I've Appians, too, grafted on quinces, but these're the real sellers. They store well, too.' He paused and looked away at Decimus. 'You've come about the business with the horse, right?'

'Yeah,' I said quietly. 'You're a smart man, Mamilius.'

He shrugged and turned. 'Fine. We'll talk inside.' Then, to the slaves: 'Carry on, lads. I'll be back later.'

We walked to the house in silence. He pushed open the back door and led the way in, down a short corridor and into a small kitchen. I'd expected the place to be untidy at the least, but everything gleamed like a new pin. No dust, no grime, not so much as a dirty plate in the sink. Vesia couldn't've done better.

Mamilius had seen me looking. 'I do the cleaning myself,' he said. 'Since my granddaughter died. There's a woman comes in to collect the washing once a week, but we manage well enough otherwise, Decimus and me.' He lifted the napkin from a jug on the table and poured wine into two cups. 'So. Sit down, make yourself comfortable. You want to start or will I?'

I sat on the bench that ran the length of the rough wooden table.

'Your son was responsible for the death of Navius's father, right?' I said.

Mamilius had sat down facing me. He nodded, slowly, his eyes on mine.

'Yes,' he said.

'Was it an accident?'

'Would you believe me if I said I didn't know?'

'I might.' I took a sip of the wine. 'You want to tell me the whole story?'

'There isn't much to tell.' He was turning his own cup round and round in his gnarled hands. 'Not as far as what happened goes, anyway.'

'Just start at the beginning, go through the middle and stop at the end. That'll do me fine.'

Mamilius's lips twisted, but he didn't smile. 'It was just over a year ago. Decimus, me and the lads, we were over in the corner field cutting wheat. Decimus was at the end of the line nearest the road. I saw Gaius Navius ride past. When he gets level with us I see Decimus suddenly drop his sickle and run at Navius waving his arms.'

'Like he did with me up at the irrigation pond?'

'Just like that. We don't have many horses round here. Maybe that's what put it into his mind.' His lips twisted again. 'Into whatever passes for his mind. In Vetuliscum most of us ride mules, or we just walk and use donkeys to carry stuff. Horses're for the nobs. No offence.'

'No offence. Gaius Navius considered himself a nob?'

'Gaius Navius,' Mamilius said carefully, 'would've ridden a fucking camel bareback if he thought it made him look good. He'd be about as competent on it, what's more.'

'Navius wasn't a rider?'

The old guy chuckled. 'He was what my cavalry mates used to call a tin-arse, Corvinus. That was what killed the bastard. The horse shied and threw him. Me and the lads ran over, but he was out cold so we carted him home on a hurdle.'

'And you didn't give his wife the full details, right?'

'Would you?' I said nothing. 'No. I just told her he'd had a fall and we'd found him lying on the road. We were lucky there were no other witnesses and he never woke up.' Mamilius was watching me levelly. 'That's all there is, the full story. If you want to call it murder instead of accident you can go ahead. Decimus wouldn't understand the difference anyway.'

'Uh-huh.' I took a swallow of wine. 'The obvious question is, why did he go for Navius in the first place?'

Mamilius was silent for a long time. Then he said, 'I told you he thought the world of his mother?'

'Yeah. You told me that.'

'He thought the world of Mamilia as well. The lad's always been good with young animals. He'll nurse a sick lamb or a kid you or me'd give up on, and nine times out of ten he'll pull them through. Trouble is, after that they're safe from the cookpot. To Decimus, Mamilia was just like one of his other foundlings. When she first came he was the one who looked after her, and he did it better than I could've done. He loved her, Corvinus. It nearly killed him when she died. And he knew why she died, too.'

'Because of Attus Navius?'

Mamilius nodded. 'After the . . . when she fell pregnant I went round to arrange the wedding with the boy's father. The bastard threw me out.'

'And Attus?'

'He wasn't there. His parents'd sent him down to their fancy relations in Pompeii.' Mamilius took a mouthful of wine and reached for the jug. 'Not that he kicked up much of a fuss about leaving. They were a pair, these two, father and son, both stuck-up bastards. Decimus knew what was going on. He may be slow, but he's no fool, not in that way. When Mamilia's time came and she died I had to keep him tied up for a month. And I warned Gaius Navius never to let his son come anywhere near our land when Decimus was around or—' He stopped.

'Or Decimus might kill him,' I said softly. 'Right. Did he?'

Mamilius didn't answer at once. He was staring into his wine cup. 'I don't know,' he said finally. 'I don't know, and that's the gods' truth. Usually Decimus is with me, or with the lads. They're family, they keep an eye on him as well.' He drank and refilled the cup; he still wasn't looking at me. I didn't say anything, just waited. 'The day Attus Navius died I was going round the farm checking on ditches. The lads were over in the far field burning the wheat stubble, but Decimus'd got a nail in his foot a few days before and he was resting it up, pottering round the house. I didn't see him until I got back.'

Shit. So that particular end was still flapping around loose. Navius, I knew from the talk with Thupeltha, had been working among the vines in the stretch near the road. If Decimus had come out the front door and caught sight of the guy, he could've followed him and committed the murder. That scenario left a few holes, sure – like why the Gruesomes hadn't seen him pass, and why he'd left it until Navius was up Clusinus's track – but it was still within the bounds of possibility.

Mamilius obviously thought so too. He sank the new cupful and reached for the jug again.

'You know the worst thing about all this?' he said softly.

'No.'

'It's that Decimus could've killed the bastard without knowing what he was doing.' He raised his eyes to mine. 'Me, I'd've enjoyed every moment of it, even if it meant I'd die myself. If Decimus is your murderer, Corvinus, then I envy him.'

He wasn't kidding, either. Maybe Decimus wasn't the only mad one in the family. The hairs rose on my scalp.

I stood up.

'Yeah, right,' I said. 'Thanks for the wine, pal. And the apple. I'll see you around.'

He didn't look up as I left.

23

I walked the short distance to Vipena's place. There was no sign of the Gruesomes, but the foreman Baro was hanging about the yard and I gave him a wave. I noticed that when he saw me he glanced round at a couple of slaves plaiting panniers, and he came over slow and careful, like he'd half a mind to throw me out and see how far I bounced. Which, when you thought about it, was interesting. We might be a fair way from Pyrgi, but I'd risk a pretty hefty bet that someone had made the trip already.

'Vipena at home this morning, pal?' I said.

'Maybe.' Baro was scowling.

'All of that, right? You think I could see him, perhaps?'

His scowl didn't lift. 'The boss is busy. We all are. We've a business to run.'

'Yeah. So I notice.' I wished I'd brought my knife. The guy probably wouldn't try anything but you never know with those obvious in-your-face types. If looks could kill then I'd've been rissole. 'I've been having words with one of the partners, as it happens. Your boss's cousin Titus Tolumnius.'

He grunted; no surprise, just pure dislike. That made
sense, too. 'Okay,' he said. 'Vipena's inside. Find your
own way.'

How to win friends and influence people. I went
across the yard to the farmhouse entrance. Out of the
corner of my eye I noticed Baro make a hand-sign to the
basket-plaiters before tagging along.

Vipena was in the wine-fermenting court where I'd last
seen him, counting jars. He looked up when I came in.
His face went grey, and he dropped the tablets.

'Valerius Corvinus.' He tried a smile that didn't work:
the guy was scared shitless, and it showed. 'I'm sorry, but
I've too much on today to socialise. Some other time,
perhaps.' He bent down and picked the notebook up.

I glanced over my shoulder. Baro was there, but he'd
stopped at the door. He was leaning against the jamb with
his arms folded, watching. I got the distinct impression
Vipena wasn't too happy about that, either. His eyes
flicked behind me, following mine, then away.

'That's okay,' I said. 'I'll keep it short.'

Vipena didn't answer, but I could almost feel him
shrivel. He tried another smile. 'Baro,' he said, 'Corvinus
and I have to talk. Go and make sure everything's in hand
for the picking this afternoon.'

The foreman didn't move. I turned to face him fully.
'You've got your orders, sunshine,' I said quietly. 'Why
don't you do as you're told like a good little slave?'

It was a close-run thing. Our eyes locked for a good
five seconds before the guy straightened, spat sideways
and ambled off the way we'd come. When he'd gone I
turned back to Vipena. His face was the colour of dirty
flour, and the muscle in his right cheek was twitching.

'I don't want to butt in on your staff relations, friend,'
I said, 'but where I come from that's called insolence.'

'Oh, Baro means no disrespect, either to you or to myself.' Vipena tried to tuck his pen behind his ear and missed. The pen fell and he ignored it. 'He simply takes his job very seriously.'

'His job? And what would that be exactly, now?'

Instead of answering Vipena turned away. 'So, Valerius Corvinus. What can I do for you?'

I walked over to the pile of wine jars. Vipena's eyes followed me like an anxious dog's.

'I've just been talking to a cousin of yours in Pyrgi.' I brushed the topmost jar with my finger. 'The guy who made these for you. We had a very interesting conversation. About potter's marks.'

'Indeed?' If Vipena's face had been grey before, now you could've used it for a dish-rag.

'Yeah.' I gave him my best smile. 'It turned out he'd made a mistake with the stamp he'd used, put HOLC on them instead of TOL. Strange, right? And I couldn't help noticing that you'd corrected it. As far as it could be corrected, naturally, once the jars were fired.' I waited. Silence. 'Two things puzzled me about that, pal. First, why the foul-up in the first place? And second, why take the trouble to fix things?'

'Corvinus . . .'

I ignored him. 'Of course, to a suspicious-minded bastard like me the explanation for the original mistake was simple enough. Publius Holconius is a big Falernian shipper. Fill jars labelled with his mark with heat-aged wine and you can sell them at twice the going rate for Caeretan easy, if the punters're either too stupid or too crooked to care what's inside. A winegrower who was less than scrupulous could make a packet on a scam like that, especially if he's got the distribution angle sewn up as well through a second partner in the shipping trade. Such as Titus's brother Gaius.' Silence. 'The snag is, Holconius turns out to be the uncle of a certain Attus Navius who's the winegrower's neighbour and who supplies the Navius family. So when Navius accidentally stumbles across a whacky version of his uncle's wine he's going to know it for what it is, and being family he'll take the trouble to find out where it came from. And when he gets his answer he isn't going to be too pleased.' I paused. 'How am I doing so far?'

Vipena's face was ashen. 'Corvinus, I swear to you by all the gods that I had nothing to do with—'

'No one's accusing you yet, friend. You'll get your say in a moment. Just let me finish.' I leaned against the pile of jars. 'So. Navius discovers that you and your two cousins are operating a wine scam. He could blow the whistle on you, but he doesn't because crook and hypocrite though you are you're also a neighbour of good standing locally and the kid's got scruples. Instead, he calls round to discuss the problem in private. The result is a deal: he'll keep his mouth shut but in exchange the scam stops there and then, and it stays stopped. As a pledge of good faith he insists you change the marks on the jars. Now. Do I win the nuts or not?'

'Changing the marks was my idea, Corvinus, not his.' Vipena's voice was so low I had difficulty hearing him. 'And if it's worth anything I was glad he'd found out.'

'Is that so, now? And would that go for your partners as well?'

There was a long silence. Finally Vipena said, 'I wasn't in touch with Gaius – he's away at the moment on business in Rome – but I discussed it with Titus. We . . . came to an agreement.'

'Which was?'

'I told him that I was no longer willing to continue with

the scheme. Just that. Gaius could dispose of the current stocks – he has a warehouse near the harbour – but I intended to sell the wine from this year's pressing and all future harvests legitimately, under a Caeretan label.'

'Uh-huh. And how did Cousin Titus take it?'

'He had no choice but to agree. As you say, Corvinus, if we'd carried on with the scheme Navius would have reported us to the authorities. It was profitable while it lasted, and it did no one any real harm.'

'Except for Holconius.'

'Not even him. The buyers weren't fooled. They knew that what they were getting wasn't real Falernian, not at the price we were selling. And if you think about it we were providing a service. The Falernian vineyards are far too small to supply the demands of the market as it is, and because we only sold to second-rate wineshops Holconius's trade wasn't really affected.'

Justifications, now: maybe confession was good for the soul after all, because the guy was easing off. He even looked more relaxed. It was time to go for the jugular.

'You're sure your cousin agreed?' I said quietly. 'About pulling the plug on the scam?'

'What else could he do?' Vipena gave a tight smile. 'Like I say, he had no choice.'

'Except with Navius out of the picture there wouldn't be a need any more. Would there?'

I was watching closely for the reaction, and I got it. Scratch relaxed: the guy gave me a look that was pure terror.

'I told you, I had nothing to do with . . .' he began.

'The grape-pickers've arrived, sir.' I turned round. Baro was back, slouched against the door post.

'What?' Vipena was gazing at him blankly like he was

a lifebelt that someone had thrown. Or maybe a cruising crocodile, I wasn't sure which.

'The squad from Caere. For the first picking.' The foreman's eyes were boring into me like bradawls. 'You wanted to talk to them.'

Vipena shook himself. 'Yes,' he said. 'You'll excuse me, Corvinus. We'll talk later.'

'Now just hang on, there, pal!' I stepped forwards. 'Your grape-pickers can—'

A hand gripped my shoulder. Jupiter, the guy was fast! I hadn't even seen him move!

'The master's got other business,' Baro said. 'He wants you to leave. Now.' The grip tightened and pulled me round slowly. I looked over his shoulder and saw the basket-plaiters waiting in the background like a heavy Greek chorus.

There wasn't much I could do. I shrugged and unprised the fingers one by one.

'Okay, sunshine,' I said. I glanced back at Vipena. His face was a white mask. 'But I'll be back. And the next time the conversation won't be so friendly. You understand me?'

'The choice is yours, Roman.' Baro stepped aside. 'Only if I was you I'd think very, very carefully before you make it.'

They were watching me when I left, all four of them. Only I had the impression that Vipena's eyes held a touch of desperation.

24

I shook the dust of Vipena's place off my sandals and
headed up the road towards the fork and Clusinus's farm.
What had been Clusinus's farm. That little interview had
been interesting, and not just because it confirmed a
theory. Now I reckoned we could take things further.

Okay. Scenario. Vipena, Titus Tolumnius and his brother
Gaius ditto are running a profitable wine scam, with
Vipena the weak link. Attus Navius rumbles them and
calls round at Vipena's threatening to blow the whistle
unless the partners mend their evil ways forthwith,
whereupon Vipena caves in and agrees. He goes to
Cousin Titus and tells him the whole sad story. Titus
lets the guy cry on his shoulder and then sends him
home with a promise to lead a reformed life from that
day forward.

So far so good, and if you believed Vipena that'd been
the end of it; only having met Titus Tolumnius I'd bet a
gold piece to a poke in the eye that it hadn't been. So.
Now comes the twist. Tolumnius has plans of his own.
Unlike Vipena the guy's no cream bun, and he decides to
solve the problem at source. Without consulting Vipena
he tells the foreman Baro who's his plant down on the

farm to zero Navius, which Baro does. As a result, Vipena
is in the shit up to his eyebrows with nowhere to go but
down. He's the one on the spot, his quarrel with the dead
man is on record and he's got a prime motive. Worse, his
cousin the tough cookie is putting on the screws through
Baro. If Vipena does feel the urge to blab then the odds
are that either he'll be for the noose himself or before
he has the chance to tell what he knows his minder will
send him the same way as Navius and whistle through his
teeth while he does it. Result: Vipena's caught between
the rock and the proverbial hard place without even
room to squeeze.

It fitted. Sure it did. And if the theory was right then
it was no wonder the bastard was scared.

On the other hand, if Vipena's a good boy and toes the
party line he's home and clear. With Papatius in jug and
waiting for his appointment with the praetor's strangler,
officially the case is closed. Once justice has been done
the scam can continue on its merry way and the silver
pieces will flow in uninterrupted. All he has to do for
that to happen is do nothing.

The perfect carrot-and-stick situation, in other words.

On the *other* other hand, I could be completely wrong
about Vipena being the cream bun of the partnership.
I already knew he was no blue-eyed innocent, and if I
didn't miss my guess by nature he was as slippery as
an eel in a grease bucket. I only had his word for the
fact that he'd blown the whistle on the scam himself.
And the marks on the jars could've been changed after
Navius's death just as easily as before to send me down
just this alleyway. He could still be both a crook *and* a
murderer . . .

Only of course in that case there were the other
murders to account for, and them the theory didn't

cover, nohow, no way. Navius, sure, no problem; but Clusinus? And *Hilarion*, for Jupiter's sake? I still hadn't a clue where Hilarion fitted in.

Ah, the hell. Leave it. One thing was sure: I'd better watch my back in future. Whoever Baro really worked for, he wasn't a card-carrying member of the Marcus Corvinus fan club. I'd been warned off in no uncertain terms, and warnings from big lugs like that you take seriously or live to regret it. If you're lucky.

I thought, when I knocked on Vesia's door, that I'd have to go through the kids thing again, but it was the lady herself who opened up. She looked a mess, as much as a stunner like Vesia could manage that: hair like a bird's nest and dark puffy bags under eyes with more red in them than white. Yeah, well; it couldn't't've been easy losing a husband and a lover both inside of two days, even if the husband was a bastard and the lover was only the platonic variety.

'What is it this time?' she said. There was a hardness to her voice that hadn't been there the last time I'd spoken to her, and the door didn't widen an inch.

'Nothing much, lady.' I kept my own voice mild. 'I've been to see Larth Papatius. I thought you might be interested.'

She hesitated, then stepped aside.

'You'd best come in, then.'

Grudging, but there again I couldn't exactly be her favourite person. And the day after a funeral is no time for a social visit.

'No Trebbia and Sextus?' I said as she shut the door behind us.

'They're with my mother. In Caere.' She hadn't moved.

'I'm sorry about your husband.' Trite, sure, and both

of us knew I didn't mean it, but I had the idea formal nothings like that might matter to Vesia.

'Thank you.' That was all. She hesitated again, and then seemed to reach a decision. 'You'd better come through.'

I smelled the perfume as soon as we hit the corridor: like I said, it was the kind of cheap, obvious stuff that smacks you between the eyes at the first sniff. Sure enough, Thupeltha was sitting at the kitchen table. She turned round as I came in, but she didn't speak. There were dirty plates on the table. Without a word, Vesia gathered them up, took them over to the sink and began scrubbing at them with a washcloth. She hadn't so much as looked at Thupeltha.

My brain was racing as I pulled out a stool and sat on it. Shit, what was going on here?

'Uh . . . you two know each other?' I said to Thupeltha. 'I mean . . .'

'You mean why should Clusinus's wife and mistress be sharing a meal only a day after the man's been burned?' Thupeltha shrugged. 'I invited myself, Corvinus. I've no quarrel with Vesia, I never have. I just wanted her to know that.'

I stared at her. Jupiter! Of all the brass-necked egotists I'd ever met this one took the cake!

'Besides, if what she's been telling me of her . . . relationship with Larth is true' – the pause before the word and the slant she put on it set my teeth on edge – 'then we're more or less even, aren't we?'

I glanced at Vesia. She still hadn't turned round.

'Not quite,' I said. 'I sort of think there's a difference somewhere along the line.'

Thupeltha laughed, and her big breasts shook. Her fingers were playing with a bracelet on her left wrist.

It was gold, with a design in fine granulation, and it looked old. I'd seen things like that in Phlebas's antique shop in the Saepta, with price labels that made my eyes bulge. 'What difference?' she said. 'You're a romantic, Corvinus. I told you, there was never anything between Titus and me but sex and we both knew that wouldn't last, so it didn't matter. If Larth had been screwing around without telling me I might be annoyed and I'd surely be surprised, but I wouldn't've been upset about a harmless friendship. Larth obviously thought otherwise, but that was his business. If he and Vesia got any satisfaction out of their arrangement then we've neither of us cause for complaint. Isn't that right, Vesia?'

The girl turned round. She had a plate in her hand, and for a moment I thought she'd throw it, but she carefully reached for a dishtowel, dried it and set it down to one side.

'If you say so,' she said. Quietly. Too quietly, and there was nothing mousey about the tone. I began to think that maybe I'd misjudged sweet little Vesia, and that more to the point maybe Thupeltha had, as well. 'How is Larth, Valerius Corvinus?'

'He's okay.' Well, one white lie wouldn't hurt. 'He sent his regards. And with' – I stopped and changed what I was going to say: tact may not be my strong point but I'm not that thick – 'with your husband dying when he did he may be off the hook.'

'I thought the body could've been in the pond for some time,' Thupeltha said.

Something cold touched my spine. I turned to face her. 'Is that right, now?' I said. 'And who told you that?'

'Mamilius.' Thupeltha's voice was bland. 'Stop it, Corvinus. If you want to find your murderer then don't look at me. Remember, I'm on your side.'

Yeah. That's what I'd thought. Still, I was beginning to wonder.

Vesia had finished with the plates. She came over, pulled up a stool and sat down. I noticed she'd avoided sitting next to Thupeltha, although there was plenty of room on the bench.

'You didn't come here just to pass on a message from Larth, did you?' she said.

'No.' Mild-mannered the lady might be, but she was no fool. And I was glad we'd moved on to less sensitive ground. Or at least I hoped it was less sensitive: you could still cut the atmosphere in the room with a knife. 'I'd, uh, hoped you might tell me a bit about your husband. Who his friends were.'

'What friends? No one liked Titus, Corvinus.' Well, that was candid enough, and she'd handed it to me deadpan. 'But no one hated him, either, as far as I know. Not enough to kill him, if that's what you mean.' Vesia's big brown eyes were on mine. It was unsettling.

'Why should no one like him?' I said.

'He wasn't a real farmer. And he'd poach on other people's land. Not just game: chickens, the odd lamb, even a sheep once in a while.' Vesia's voice was expressionless. 'We get wolves down from the mountains, sometimes, in the early months of the year, and he was careful not to be too greedy. Still, everyone knew. They just didn't make trouble.'

'Uh-huh.' I'd imagine one reason would be Vesia herself. Her and the kids. Country people are harder than townies as a rule, but they have their own weaknesses. If you like to call them that. 'And that's what you lived on? The farm and the . . . pickings?'

Vesia hesitated, then lowered her eyes. 'No,' she said finally. 'Not exactly.'

My stomach went cold. *Not exactly . . .*

'What, then?' I said. Silence. 'Come on, lady! I'm no praetor's rep, and I'm pretty broad-minded. If I'm to find out who killed your husband I need a lead. I can't work on air.'

'He had . . . I suppose you'd call it other business.'

'Like what, for example?' I was handling this all wrong, and I knew it: I never could get the measure of women except for dowagers and good-time girls. Perilla would've done better, but Perilla wasn't here. And Thupeltha was just looking on like it was a sideshow.

'I don't know! I swear I don't. He never told me.'

There was hysteria in there somewhere, I could tell, and not all that far away; the lady was wound up more than she seemed. Important or not, it was time to back off. 'Look, Vesia,' I said as calmly as I could manage, 'whoever killed your husband didn't do it because of a missing sheep. You must know something. A word, a hint, any fu . . . anything at all, right?'

She was trying, that was sure. Her eyes now were screwed shut and her hands clenched and unclenched on the table top.

Finally they stopped, and her eyes opened.

'Aulus,' she said.

'What?'

'About a month ago Titus mentioned a man called Aulus.'

'Aulus what?'

'I don't know. He just said Aulus.'

Hell! I tried to hide my disappointment. It might not be the most common first name going, but there had to be a couple of hundred Auluses within striking distance of Vetuliscum, starting with Priscus's pal Nepos. I needed more than that. Still, there was no point pressing her.

'Okay,' I said. 'So what business did they have together?'

'I don't know that either. Not exactly. Titus was selling him something, or hoping to. He seemed very pleased about it.'

'Selling him what?'

Vesia shook her head sharply. 'Titus wouldn't say. But it was something valuable. Very valuable. He was even talking about buying a little place in Rome when the deal went through.'

I sat back. Jupiter, now that was a facer. Valuable had to be right: for most hayseeds a move to Rome and on to the corn dole list is the impossible dream. In hayseed terms even the worst slum in Transtiber or the Subura costs an arm and a leg to rent, and as far as buying goes forget it unless you have serious cash under your mattress: landlords make more out of sitting tenants, and if the place collapses or burns down the ground's still there, there are plenty of cowboy builders around and you can always find punters who need a roof over their heads. Even if it does leak or brain you with a tile. So what did a no-hoper like Clusinus have to sell that was worth that amount of gravy?

'Did the deal go through?' I said.

'I don't know. Titus never mentioned it again.'

I almost howled. 'You mean that's all? All he ever said?'

She nodded. 'I'm sorry, Corvinus. I'd help you more if I could.'

Well, I'd got something, at least, although where it'd got me I hadn't the faintest idea. I turned to Thupeltha.

'How about you, sister?' I said. 'You have anything to throw into the pot?'

She laughed. 'Titus and I had better things to do with

our time together than talk about business, Corvinus. No, I can't help you at all.'

'Yeah, I just thought you might say that, lady.' I caught the barest flash of ... annoyance? amusement? assessment? I wasn't quite sure, but it was something. I stood up. 'Thanks, Vesia. I'll keep in touch.'

Aulus. Now who the hell was Aulus?

25

The sun was past its highest when I left Vesia's and my stomach was rumbling. Time for home and the feed bag.

That had been a real eye-opener, where Thupeltha was concerned especially. There was cold blood there, a calculating egotism with a touch of malice that was right at odds with her claims to directness. That first time I'd talked to her I'd believed she'd been telling the truth, as she saw it at least, but now I wouldn't lay any bets. The lady knew more than she was saying, that was obvious; but I had the distinct impression that she knew I knew she knew she was hiding something and it made her enjoy watching me flounder all the more. If you get what I mean. And I'd wager a dozen of Caecuban to a mouldy rissole that she got a charge out of watching people flounder, especially if she had the lifebelt. She mightn't be averse to kicking the feet out from under them in the first place, either.

Not a very nice person, Thupeltha.

Vesia was another problem. Call me jaundiced if you like, but I was beginning to feel that maybe she was just a little too squeaky-clean perfect to be true. Oh, she wasn't putting up as big a false front as Thupeltha, but there was a touch of steel there under all that powder-blue softness that I hadn't expected. Maybe I should've done: the woman couldn't've had it easy bringing up two kids and trying to stay respectable married to Titus Clusinus, and the quiet mousey types are often tougher than the brash in-your-face Amazons. Still, I had the impression that it was a side of her nature that Vesia didn't want to show. And that was interesting.

Bring the two together, and put both women in the same kitchen, and bad vibes or not you got something that was even more interesting still. I thought about that aspect, and the implications, all the way home.

Bathyllus was waiting with the wine jug, which was great because it had turned out to be a scorcher of a day and by the time I reached the villa my tongue was trailing the road. The first cup didn't even touch the sides; the second I took more slowly.

'Where's the mistress, little guy?' I said as I held the cup out for a refill.

'The bath suite, sir. She and Marilla went out riding this morning.'

'Is that so?' I felt a small stab of guilt. Perilla had been right: this was supposed to be a holiday, and I'd hardly seen anything of her. Let alone the Princess, and she'd be going back to Aunt Marcia's when we headed home to Athens. 'Look me out a fresh tunic, will you, Bathyllus?' I said. 'And ask Meton to hold the chickpea rissoles for an hour.'

That's one thing about lunch: it's usually cold leftovers anyway, and not even the world's most single-minded chef could object to a postponement. Also, I noticed Bathyllus's nostrils had twitched as he poured the wine, and although the little guy was far too polite to pass a

remark on the strength of the master's body odour a
bath before eating would be a kindness to the world in
general. After traipsing over half Vetuliscum on a roaster
of a morning I would've given a goat a headache.

I swallowed down the rest of the wine and made for
the bath.

One thing you could say for Flatworm: where life's little
luxuries were concerned he didn't stint himself. Out in
the sticks or not, the villa's baths were better than mine.
You could've put a couple of dozen people into the hot
room if they didn't mind squeezing up, and knowing
Flatworm his regular guests wouldn't. The mosaics and
wall paintings were something, too; in fact, the fresco by
the cold plunge was so much something that Perilla'd told
Bathyllus to cover it over with a sheet. Well, the artist
hadn't got the perspective right anyway. Either that or
his knowledge of anatomy was seriously flawed.

I stripped off in the changing cubicle, wound the towel
round my middle for modesty – Bathyllus hadn't said as
much, but I assumed the Princess would be bathing as
well – and headed for the hot room. Sure enough they
were both there, the colour of cooked Baian crayfish. I
gave Perilla the requisite nice-to-see-you-again smacker
and ruffled the Princess's hair: she doesn't like it done
up, and anyway no hairstyle ever invented can stand up
to an hour in a bathhouse.

'Well, Marcus, did you have a successful morning?'
Perilla said.

'Yeah.' I sat down beside her. 'How about you? Bathyllus
tells me you went out riding.'

'We saw a fox,' the Princess said. 'A vixen, really. She
had cubs.'

'Yeah?' The kid's mad on animals, as I think I said.
'Whereabouts?'

'Oh, just around. Up in the hills. I don't know the area well enough to be more precise.'

'I hope you didn't tell any of the locals, then, Bright-Eyes. Vixens and chickens don't mix except on the most basic level.'

'We're going into Pyrgi tomorrow. Bathyllus says he knows someone there with a tame bear. Are you coming?'

I hesitated. 'Maybe,' I said. 'We'll see. I'm kind of tied up at the moment.'

'Oh.' She looked down. 'Yes. Well.' There was a pause. Then she got up. 'I'll see you later, Corvinus. I have to go and brush Corydon. He walked through a thistle patch and he's still wearing half the result.'

When she'd gone Perilla and I sat for a while in awkward silence.

'I've got to solve this thing quickly, lady,' I said finally, not looking at her. 'The praetor's rep'll be here in nine days' time, and after that Papatius is crows'-meat.'

She sighed and put her head on my shoulder. 'Yes,' she said. 'I know. Don't let it worry you. Marilla understands.'

I kissed her. She tasted salty. 'The little guy's setting up his network already, then?' I said.

'It was Alexis, really. One of the farmers down the Caere road happened to mention the bear to him when he went to ask about Corydon.'

'Uh-huh.'

She was quiet for a long time. Then she said, 'Marcus, can't we move back to Rome? Sejanus is dead, you don't have to have anything to do with any senators if you don't want to, and you know you miss it. The Alban Hills aren't far away. Marilla could stay with Aunt Marcia and we'd still see her regularly. Much more regularly than we do now living in Athens.'

'Yeah. I'll think about it.'

But not now. I closed my eyes and leaned back, letting the heat leach away the tiredness. Jupiter, that was good! If we Romans'd given nothing else to the world that didn't have its downside at least we'd got bathing to a fine art.

'So.' Perilla had lifted her head, and the usual cool, businesslike tone was back. 'How are things going, in fact?'

I told her about the visits to Mamilius's and Vipena's. That last was the tricky one: Perilla's never liked the idea that one day I might stick my neck out a bit too far and be carted home on a board. Sure enough, I got the usual lecture about keeping out of trouble. This time I took it like a lamb, which was fair because I agreed with every word: the obvious guys, or the guys who bluster, you can take in your stride, but hard professionals like Tolumnius and Baro are another matter. These bastards don't threaten, they promise.

Then we got round to Vesia and Thupeltha. When I mentioned I'd found them together Perilla's eyebrows rose.

'Hardly orthodox behaviour, is it?' she said. 'On either side. If you'd just been murdered, Corvinus, I wouldn't expect your mistress to drop round for a meal and a chat the day after your funeral, however pushy she was. And I certainly wouldn't open the door for her if she did.'

That's what I like about Perilla: she's got a lovely way with words. 'Yeah, that's what I thought,' I said. 'Cut it how you like, lady, it smells. Sure, they didn't exactly give the impression they'd been swapping sisterly confidences before I arrived over the home-made must cake, but there was something screwy going on somewhere. And one thing I can't get out of my head.'

'What's that?'

'We're running round in circles trying to link Navius's murder with Clusinus's, right?' She nodded. 'Vipena's wine scam would give a motive for the first, but it doesn't explain the second. Or if it does the connection's not obvious. But put these two lovelies together and the problem disappears.'

Perilla frowned. 'In what way?'

'Thupeltha had a motive for killing Navius, okay? The guy was threatening to make trouble, split the marriage, and that broke all her rules. Clusinus was different: she'd no quarrel with him because the only thing the guy was interested in was a casual affair. So as far as Thupeltha's concerned motive-wise, then, tick Navius and scratch Clusinus. Vesia, on the other hand, has no beef with Navius. Her problem is she's stuck with a bastard of a husband who spends his time out tomcatting. Okay, so the consensus of opinion is that she's ready to make the best of a bad job and bring up her kids in honest poverty, at least honest on her side.' I shifted on the bench. 'But what if she's not the mousey little housewife people think she is? Clusinus owns the property. If there's a divorce she's out in the cold with two kids on her hands. Now with the guy dead she inherits. It may not be much, but if she sold up it'd give her enough for a fresh start someplace else. And on Thupeltha's side getting rid of a woman who's already planted a hook in her husband would be a definite plus.'

Perilla was staring at me in shock. 'Corvinus, let me get this straight,' she said. 'You're saying they might have planned the murders together?'

'Sure. Why not? They'd both benefit in different ways, and like I say, it fits the facts like nothing else does.'

'But that's horrible!'

'It's a tenable theory, lady. All there is against it is

Thupeltha's claim that she wasn't involved and the impression Vesia gives of being the goody-goody house-wife. Personally I wouldn't risk any bets now on either being true.'

'You're forgetting Papatius. If Vesia were as genuinely fond of him as she seems to be she wouldn't have put him in the position of prime suspect. Nor would Thupeltha, for that matter.'

I shook my head. 'No, I'm not,' I said. 'Papatius needn't've been a suspect at all, Perilla. Not if you go back to the beginning. He brought that on himself, partly at least. The day Navius was murdered Thupeltha left him pitching wine jars. If he'd stayed back home instead of following Thupeltha the Gruesomes wouldn't've seen him heading for Clusinus's track. And even as things turned out Vesia could supply his alibi herself. He's only in jug now because I fingered him and Gaius Aternius is the kind of pig-headed bastard who ignores facts because they don't fit his theories. Besides, if I'm right the case should've been open and shut from the beginning because the obvious killer was already to hand.'

'And who was that?'

'Titus Clusinus.'

'But—' Perilla stopped. Then she said, more slowly, 'Oh. Oh, yes. I see.'

'The killing was done on Clusinus's property. If Priscus hadn't happened along and screwed everything up the way Priscus does it would've been Clusinus who found the body, and six gets you ten Thupeltha would've been the first person the guy met. Put those facts together and once she'd told her story even if Clusinus had denied killing Navius until he was blue in the face the poor sucker'd've been in jug and legally strangled faster than you can spit. Two birds with one stone.'

'But what about motive? On Clusinus's part, I mean. And what possible reason could Thupeltha have given for being there in the first place?'

'There's always jealousy, one boyfriend killing the other, but that would've been a last resort. In the event I doubt if motive would've been an issue. Clusinus was Vetuliscum's bad boy. No one had a good word for the guy, there would've been enough circumstantial evidence stacked against him to convict him twice over with the locals, and the authorities wouldn't've cared a plugged copper coin so long as someone was chopped. As for Thupeltha, she could either say she was on her way to visit Vesia – which Vesia, being an accomplice, would've confirmed – or if the fact of the rendezvous with Navius did come out she could stick to the story she told that he'd run off and left her back at the grove. Whereas really they'd met further up the track and she'd knifed him herself.'

'But what about her claim that he'd threatened suicide?'

'That only came later, after Priscus had found the body and the whole plan was shot to hell. She had to say that. If Clusinus weren't to be the prime suspect after all then Thupeltha had to cover herself somehow. And it left her free to arrange another clandestine meeting with Clusinus and finish the job another way. Which she had to do to keep Vesia's mouth shut.'

Perilla stared at the opposite wall for a long time. Then she said softly, 'Corvinus, you have a really nasty mind. You know that?'

I grinned. 'It's only a theory. But it works. And it explains something else, too.'

'What might that be?'

'Vesia's attitude to Thupeltha. The way things've turned

out, the deal's gone sour. Instead of Clusinus being set up for Navius's murder, he's one of the victims and the guy the authorities have fingered is Larth Papatius. Thupeltha's a cold-minded bitch. If it's a question of her husband being nailed instead of her she's happy to go along with that. Vesia's different. Like you say, she's genuinely fond of the guy, only she's caught in a cleft stick: she can't save him without reopening the whole can of worms, and if she does that she risks everything. Sure, she's got what she wants – her husband's dead, she's home and dry – but in return she has to play along with her partner. And if Aternius won't accept Papatius's alibi for Navius's murder and insists that Papatius being in jug is no hindrance to his having killed Clusinus then she's got no way out. All she can do is send me off down another track and hope the mare's-nest at the end of it'll get him off somehow. But she's going to absolutely hate Thupeltha.'

'What about Hilarion? You still haven't explained his death.'

'Perilla, I don't *know* about Hilarion, okay? Obviously the guy saw something, or found something out, or otherwise stuck his nose in where he shouldn't have, but where he fits in is a complete mystery.' I closed my eyes. 'Shit. I'm tired and my brain hurts.'

'I'm not surprised.' She kissed me. 'Leave it for now. Let's go and eat.'

That was fine with me. Yeah, well. Maybe Thupeltha was our killer after all. But if so, how did I prove it?

26

Maybe the bath wasn't such a good idea after all: once we'd eaten I crashed out on the dining-room couch, and when I woke up it was too late to do anything else.

Not that I had anything else to do. We'd reached a dead end here. There were plenty of theories, sure, but they pointed in half a dozen different directions at once. What I needed were hard facts, and at that precise moment I had about as much idea how to go about getting them as a rhino has of crochet.

The hell with it; Papatius could take his chances, for another day, at least. I had family commitments, and anyway the case needed time to settle.

I broke the glad news to the Princess over breakfast next morning.

'You still want some company on your trip to Pyrgi, Bright-Eyes?' I said.

Her face lit up; at least, what I could see of it behind the half omelette she was stuffing it with. It was her third, and Meton doesn't skimp these things. I reckoned our step-daughter had put away most of the villa's egg production single-handed since we'd been here; certainly the chickens were looking seriously harassed. Eggs the girl can eat.

'You're coming?' she said.

'Sure. I've got nothing better to do.' I nibbled at a crust of bread soaked in olive oil: breakfasts have never been my thing, not the solid variety anyway, and Perilla had broken me of the other kind years ago. 'Besides, bears are my favourite animal. Especially the paws, fricasséed with juniper berries. Joke.'

'You're sure, Marcus?' Perilla said.

'Well, maybe not juniper berries. Plum sauce.'

'I'll go and saddle Corydon.' The Princess crammed in the other half of the omelette and raced off.

I watched her go. 'Jupiter! She's taking that brute? I'd kind of thought in terms of Lysias and the coach.'

'We can go with Lysias.' Perilla leaned over and kissed me. 'And Corydon's not a brute, Marcus. He's really quite sweet when you get to know him.'

Oh, Silenus! Maybe the lady was going soft on me. Still, if Marilla wanted to trust herself to that moth-eaten clothes rack that was her business. 'You, uh, have any other plans for things to do when we get there?' I said cautiously. 'Besides Alexis's bear, I mean?'

'There's a nice old temple of Velchans I'd like to see. The pediment and cult statue are supposed to be quite impressive.'

Yeah, I'd thought as much. There's always a temple. And whoever the hell Velchans was he could keep his bloody pediment as far as I was concerned. 'Is that right, now, lady?'

Perilla was grinning. 'Oh, I'm sure there'll be a wineshop somewhere nearby,' she said. 'We can drop you there and pick you up when we've finished.'

I brightened. A day out with the family's one thing, but sightseeing's another. And making the acquaintance of a new wineshop is always a pleasure.

'Fine,' I said.

'Then of course there's the shrine of Nortia, the sanctuary of Vertumnus, and if we have time . . .'

I stopped listening. Well, to each his bag. I just hoped the wine was good.

We saw the bear. I'd been afraid it might be one of those sad buggers with a chain through its nose that street musicians drag around and have a boy prod with a stick to make it dance – the Princess would've hated that – but it was a plump, cheerful little bastard the size of a big dog that was more of a family pet than anything else. The owner let Marilla feed it with lumps of bread soaked in honey, and the kid had the time of her life. Finally, about two hours later, we called it a day, washed them both down with a sponge and a couple of pails of water, and headed off to look for Perilla's temple.

It wasn't all that far from the harbour, which was all I noticed about the place. I waved Perilla and the Princess goodbye at the steps and left them to their pediments. The lady had been right, as usual: just up the road was a tight little wineshop with a plane tree outside and an interesting collection of wines on the slate. Top of the list was a cut-price Falernian, but remembering Vipena I gave it a miss and settled for a jug of Privernatian, a plate of the local goat's cheese and a bunch of fresh-picked dessert grapes. Good choice: Privernatian's not one of your absolute top wines, but for sitting outside under a plane tree on a hot day watching the world go by you could do a lot worse, especially if it's cellar-cooled and the alternative's a temple. The place's owner was quite an interesting guy, too; he had a cousin who ran a wineshop I'd been into once or twice near the Livian Portico on the slopes of the Esquiline, and we swapped memories of low life in the Subura until my bladder filled up enough to make the trip across the street to the local urinal something I couldn't put off any longer.

I suppose my brain registered the fact that someone had come in behind me, but I didn't pay him any attention: I had most of a jug of wine inside me and, besides, my nasty suspicious mind was out for the day gathering rosebuds. In the event I was happily adding my contribution to the Pyrgi Launderers' and Dyers' Guild's stocks of mantle-cleaning fluid when the latrine's roof collapsed, smacking me above the right ear, and everything went black.

I woke with a splitting headache and the knowledge that I had major problems. The biggest of these was leaning against the wall next to the only way out, watching me.

'That's him coming round now, boss,' he said over his shoulder without taking his eyes off me.

'Thank you, Baro.' Uh-oh. I knew that voice, sure I did. Well, at least they'd left my hands and feet free. Mind you, the way I felt at that moment I couldn't've fought past a five-year-old kid armed with a rag doll, let alone Big Bad Baro with the lump of seasoned oakwood he was hefting. If that was what he'd hit me with then I was lucky to wake up this side of the Winter Festival.

Baro moved aside and Titus Tolumnius came into the room. With three of us in it the place was looking pretty crowded. I'd guess, from the sacks I'd been propped against, we were in a small storeroom somewhere in the Tolumnius pottery. Which was more bad news, if I'd needed it.

Who the hell had suggested coming to Pyrgi anyway?

'How're you feeling, Corvinus?' Tolumnius asked.

Shit. As far as pointless, inane questions went that one took the nuts.

'You know what can happen to you for belting a five-star Roman purple-striper in a public lavatory, pal?' I said. Or that was what I thought I said; my tongue wasn't working too well either.

He grunted. 'You were warned. Still, if it's any consolation Baro was told to bring you in peaceable.'

'Is that so, now?' I reached up and touched the lump on my head. It was as big as a duck's egg, it hurt like hell, and it felt like a tacky sponge. 'Then we've got a problem here with basic semantics, friend. Or maybe your tame gorilla's a sadistic bastard with serious hearing difficulties. You like to choose, perhaps?'

'Shut it, Roman,' Baro growled.

'I'll handle this, Baro.' Tolumnius sat down on one of the sacks. He hadn't so much as given the other guy a glance. 'You've only yourself to blame, Corvinus. Like I say you were warned. And we had to talk.'

'About the murders of Attus Navius and Titus Clusinus?'

'Among other things.' Tolumnius leaned back against the wall. 'Baro, get Valerius Corvinus some water.'

Baro shifted. 'But, boss—'

'Do it.' His eyes hadn't left my face. He waited until the big guy had gone. 'Now. You think I was responsible, right?'

'You or your slippery cousin. Sure. Why Clusinus I don't know, but Navius—'

Tolumnius held up a hand. 'I'd nothing to do with Navius's death,' he said. 'Nor as far as I know had Gnaeus. Let's get that clear from the start.'

'Yeah?'

'Yeah.' He was looking at me straight, not smiling. 'Oh, I thought about it, and if the boy hadn't died we might've had to make certain arrangements, but in the event it wasn't necessary because someone else made them for us. Clusinus I'd never even heard of. That's part of what I brought you here to say.' The eyes bored into me. They were hard as chips of marble. 'The other part's to tell you one last time to get the hell off my back.'

'You chose a pretty drastic way of fixing up a meeting, friend. And why should I believe you all of a sudden?'

'Corvinus, listen. I'm a businessman, right? Hassle I can do without, and unlike Baro I'm no fool. If it's of any interest to you he wanted to put a knife between your ribs and get my brother to drop you over the side of his boat somewhere between here and Ostia. I could still let him have his way, but I wanted to try negotiation first. If that doesn't work, well, I'll have to think again.' His voice was calm, matter-of-fact. My stomach want cold and I said nothing. 'The four of us've been running this business for quite a few years. We're not greedy, and we don't harm anyone, but that doesn't mean I'm ready to sit back and let it go down the tubes just because some smartass Roman gets a fancy idea into his head and starts making waves. Clear?'

'What about Vipena? I sort of got the impression he was bowing out and taking the scam with him.'

'Gnaeus is a gutless wonder. I'll deal with him in my own way.' I must've looked as shocked as I felt because he chuckled. 'Oh, no; no killing. He's family, and I don't hurt family, not unless I have to. But the other three of us have too much invested to give up that easy. We'll make him see sense. Only it'd help if he didn't have you nosing around making him nervous. You get me?'

I swallowed. 'Yeah. I get you.'

'Good. I was hoping you would. I really was.' He looked up. 'Ah. Here's Baro with your water.'

The big guy came in holding a cup and a jug. He handed them over like he was the jailer passing Socrates the hemlock and stood back while I drank. Neat Setinian would've been better, and he must've taken the stuff from the bucket they used to wash down the pots, but I wasn't in any position to complain.

Tolumnius waited until I'd finished. 'Now,' he said, 'I told you I was a businessman. I don't expect to get something for nothing. Give me your word you'll leave us alone in future and we'll trade.'

I set the cup down slowly. 'Trade what?'

'Your word first.'

What did I have to lose? I was just surprised I was being given the choice. 'Sure,' I said. 'You've got it, pal, as far as the scam goes, at any rate. All I'm interested in's solving the murders; where whacky Falernian's concerned for all I care you can sell it by the bargeload and give the Wart a cash discount.'

Tolumnius glanced at Baro. The guy didn't look exactly cheerful, but he grunted and nodded. 'Fine,' he said. He stretched out his hand and we shook. 'We have a deal. Keep that well in mind, Corvinus, and you won't be troubled further.'

'What about this trade?'

'I said I'd never heard of Titus Clusinus. That was true.' Tolumnius stood up. 'But since the murder I've made it my business to find out.'

'Yeah?'

'I'll give you a name. Just a name: seeing where it leads is your affair, and there're no guarantees, but it may help. Agreed?'

'Agreed.'

He gave me another of his marble-chip stares. Then he looked away.

'A man called Aulus Herminius Bubo. He has a business in Caere, in Lampmakers' Street, off the market square.'

Hey! '*Aulus* Bubo, you say?'

Tolumnius's eyes came back to me, fast. I winced.

'You've heard of him already?'

'Only by his first name. At least, maybe I have.' I got up, too. The room spun a bit and I held on to the wall until it steadied. 'Thanks, pal, I'm much obliged. I assume I'm free to go now?'

Tolumnius shrugged. 'Free as air. Just don't forget we have an agreement; not now, not never. And leave Gnaeus alone.' He turned to Baro. 'See Valerius Corvinus gets back safely. He's still a bit delicate.'

Jupiter! Delicate was the word! Well, I supposed a clout on the head was a small price to pay for a fresh lead, but all the same I had the distinct impression the big guy enjoyed his work, and he was less than gruntled how things had panned out.

We didn't talk a lot on the way back to the wineshop.

27

I'd just settled in with another jug of Privernatian and was
taking things slow and easy when Perilla and the Princess
showed up from their marathon temple bash, full of the
joys of entablatures and acroteria. The lady took one look
at what Baro had left of me and blew her wig.

'And just what the *hell* happened to you?' she said.

I winced. 'Don't shout so loud or everyone'll want to
look like this. And don't swear, it isn't ladylike. Sit down
and have a fruit juice.'

'Corvinus, you do *not* get out of this by cracking
jokes!' She was prodding at the duck's egg lump all
the best purple-stripers were wearing that year. This
time I yelped in earnest: Perilla may be pretty hot-smart
in several departments, but a second Hippocrates she's
not. I've met less ham-fisted gladiator trainers. 'Merciful
Juno, you need a doctor! This is a cut! It's bleeding!'

'Yeah, they do that. Just leave it alone and don't encourage it. And no doctors.' I looked at Marilla, who was
staring at me with eyes like dinner plates. 'Hi, Princess.
You have a nice time?'

Perilla sat down. She'd gone very quiet suddenly, and
she looked pale. 'Marcus, please,' she said softly. 'No

jokes, no irrelevancies and no subterfuge. Just tell me what happened.'

So I did. Dwelling on the fact that it was a once-off, not to be repeated, and Tolumnius and I had done a deal. 'And I know now who the phantom Aulus is,' I said. 'He runs a business of some kind in Caere. If we start back now you can drop me off and—'

'We are *not* going to Caere,' Perilla said firmly. 'We are going to find you a doctor and then we are going straight back home. Is that absolutely clear, Marcus, or do I have to hit you again myself?'

Uh-oh. I knew that tone. When the lady was in this mood you might as well argue with a rock. Yeah, well, perhaps she was right: I did feel pretty woozy, and I was still having difficulty telling which of the two wine cups on the table in front of me was the real one.

'Okay,' I said. 'You've got it. Ask the guy inside. I think I'll just sit here and throb.'

We were lucky: doctors aren't too thick on the ground out in the sticks, but the wineshop owner pointed us towards an ex-army surgeon who'd settled in Pyrgi and had a freelance practice in the town square. While Perilla fussed over me the Princess ran to where they'd left Lysias with the carriage and had him pick us up. Then after a fairly unpleasant half-hour of medical treatment we went bowling up the road back towards Vetuliscum.

Despite the heat outside the temperature in the carriage was close to freezing: once she'd got me safely salved and bandaged, I'd drunk the disgusting concoction the surgeon had made out of his old legionary boots, and the Princess was carefully out of earshot on Corydon, Perilla finally let rip.

'Corvinus, I despair, I really do. I indulge you by leaving you for five minutes soaking yourself in a wineshop while the child and I improve our minds and you contrive to get your head beaten in by a gang of criminals. Why on *earth* can't you have a normal day out like a proper civilised person?'

Jupiter! Where do you start? 'First of all it wasn't five minutes, lady, it was more like three hours,' I said. 'Second, all I did was go across the street for a leak. Third, my head's still the shape it was, give or take the extra temporary bulge. And fourth, on the plus side, we're one more step along the road to finding who the killer is.' I paused; be fair, Corvinus. 'I'll give you the criminals, though.'

She sniffed; one thing about Perilla, once she's settled down, even when she's being unreasonable she's open to argument. 'You're sure? About the killer?'

'No. But at least it shows that Vesia wasn't spinning me a yarn. And it proves Titus Tolumnius's bona fides. Whoever this Aulus Bubo is, he's a guy I have to talk to.'

She settled back against the cushions; crisis over. I breathed again. 'Actually, Marcus,' she said, 'I've been thinking. Along quite different lines.'

'Yeah?'

'Your theory about Gaius Aternius being involved may not be so ludicrous after all.'

I blinked. In the stir of recent events I'd forgotten about Aternius. And for Perilla to backtrack or admit the barest possibility that she might be wrong or mistaken over something was as unusual as seeing the High Priest of Jupiter slide down the steps of the Capitol on a tin tray.

'Gee, thanks,' I said.

'Or at least not totally so.' Sarcasm just bounces off Perilla. 'You say he and his uncle have an interest in acquiring property, and that they're none too scrupulous.'

'Yeah. Yeah, that's right. At least that's what the guy in the wineshop told me.'

'Mmm. Then if you look at this business from the financial and sociological angles it might well make sense.'

'Yeah? From the financial and sociological angles, eh?' Jupiter! Those were a couple that had slipped past me somehow. 'You, uh, care to explain, lady?'

'Certainly.' She straightened a fold in her mantle. 'It's all about property. First, Clusinus's death frees his farm; at least there's a good chance Vesia will sell up, and with the condition the place is in the price won't be high. Second, if Papatius is executed for the murder then his land may be up for sale as well.'

'He's not the owner. Thupeltha is.'

'I know. But Papatius is the actual hands-on farmer of the partnership. Thupeltha would have to bring in a bailiff, and that would eat into her profits as well as being unsatisfactory in other ways. Also, life in Vetuliscum as the widow of a convicted murderer, especially when the victim was a local man, wouldn't be easy. If Papatius does die then personally I won't be surprised if Thupeltha decides to leave the district.'

'She could always stay put and marry again. Knowing that lady, finding another husband wouldn't be a problem.'

'A remarriage wouldn't wipe out the past, Corvinus. And however thick-skinned the woman is or pretends to be she's given rise to enough scandal to make her life here thoroughly unpleasant in future. Don't forget that it's only the threat of Papatius that's kept tongues from wagging publicly so far, and her affairs with both Navius and Clusinus must be common knowledge by now.'

'Yeah. Yeah, that's right.' I was getting seriously interested. 'Go on.'

'Third, there's the Navius property. Again with both the male members of the family dead continuity is far from assured. And you said yourself that Gaius Aternius is making eyes at Attus Navius's mother.'

I sat back. Shit! Long words or not, the lady might have something here. The three properties formed an unbroken line, and together they made up half of Vetuliscum. If Aternius could get the Navius place by marriage and tack the other two on at knockdown prices he'd be the biggest landowner in the area bar none; and with one property producing top-quality wines and a second ready to roll with mass production, this close to Rome he could clean up.

Was it worth murder, though? Not just once, but two times; three, counting Hilarion (why the *hell* had that guy died?). Maybe; I didn't know, although if you're going to kill someone you can do a lot worse than get yourself appointed as the officer investigating the case. It would explain why Aternius was so keen to see Larth Papatius chopped, too.

'Well, Marcus?' Perilla was looking at me. 'What do you think? Is it possible?'

I shrugged. 'Anything's possible, lady. Certainly it sounds good, and like you say it's another angle. I might do a little digging when I'm in Caere tomorrow seeing this Aulus Bubo. Go round and talk to Aternius himself, maybe, see if the bastard sweats.'

The chill was back. 'Corvinus, the doctor told you to rest for at least a day. Going to Caere is not resting.'

'These guys always overestimate recuperation time in case the patient dies and the family drop round with hatchets. I'm fine, Perilla. Or I will be after a decent dinner and a good night's sleep.'

'We'll see.'

'Yeah. We will.' I leaned over and kissed her. Actually, I wasn't spinning a line: whatever had been in that boiled boot stuff was working marvels, and my head didn't feel quite like a dozen sadistic-minded elephants were using it as a football any more. Half a dozen, sure, but at least that was an improvement.

Besides, I'd had experience of Perilla's brand of post-op care before. In essence it consisted of strained chicken broth and a total ban on wine, and it was as debilitating as hell. Me, I'd rather have the elephants.

28

I got my way. By breakfast time next morning the cut
wasn't looking nearly so angry and the swelling was
down. I could even manage without the bandage. Still,
Perilla insisted that I take Lysias and the carriage into
Caere, even if it was only a half-hour's walk.

Maybe the carriage was a good idea in any case. The
weather was changing, heading for the autumn break.
We'd had a scorching few days, but the morning was
close and muggy, with thunder rumbling in the hills.
It couldn't be long to the rains, and getting caught by
a cloudburst out in the open with nowhere to run to
would be no joke.

We were rounding the first bend when I caught sight
of Arruns. The old guy was on foot, and heading in the
same direction we were. I thumped on the carriage roof
for Lysias to pull up and leaned out of the window.

'Hey, Arruns,' I shouted. He turned. 'You going into
Caere?'

'I might be.'

'Want a lift?'

That got me a long slow stare.

'Maybe.'

I grinned. Jupiter! Talk about grudging! 'Fine.' I opened the door. 'Climb aboard.' He did, and Lysias whipped up the horses. 'You get the rest of your ditch cleared without my help?'

'Don't get cocky, Corvinus.' He was scowling. 'You did well enough, but ten days in the country don't make a farmer.'

'Make that nine, pal. And I've counted every joyous hour.'

'Is that so, now?' The scowl cleared. He chuckled and prodded the cushions before settling back against them. 'Nice carriage. First time I've been in one of these things. They're fine for long journeys, but I wouldn't like to use them that often.'

'Me neither.'

We trundled along for a bit in companionable silence. Then Arruns said, 'I hear that you were round at the Caere records office a day or so back.'

I glanced at him sharply. 'Yeah. Yeah, that's right. You've got big ears, pal.'

'Maybe, but this time I didn't need them. The boy who looks after it's my grandson Publius. His mother lives near the Fufluns Gate.'

'Uh-huh.' I tried not to let my surprise show; for some reason I'd thought Arruns was a bachelor, but then maybe his wife was dead, like Mamilius's. And if the clerk had been Arruns's grandson it explained why he'd done a double-take when I'd asked to see the bill of sale. 'He's a smart lad.'

'He is that. A credit to the family. Enjoys his work, too.' He was looking out of the window at the fields we were passing; I've noticed that about farmers, they pay more attention to what's growing on the ground either side of the road they're on than to the person they're talking to. 'So. You were checking up on that vineyard sale.'

There was no point in denying it. 'Sure.'

'And you found out that the man who witnessed it was Quintus Cominius's father. Aternius's grandfather.'

'Yeah.'

He turned back to me. 'I was wondering, after we talked, if you might've thought the vineyard was a reason for me to murder Attus Navius.'

Well, that was direct enough, anyway. 'Were you, now?' I said carefully. 'And why would I do that?'

'You'd have cause. And as far as the vineyard goes you're right, I want it back and always have done. Navius's death has improved my chances. His father's dead, and the family've got no real roots here; old Velthur was the first of them, he moved over from Veii seventy years back. With Attus gone too Sicinia Rufina'll be thinking of selling up and moving into town, maybe even to Rome. I've got a bit put by, and I'd be willing to offer any new owner a fair price for the land. More than a fair price.'

'Why pay good money for something you think is yours already?'

'Because that vineyard's important to me, Corvinus. It's family land, it's always been family land, and it belongs to us. I wouldn't pay a penny to these Navii crooks out of principle, but the money itself doesn't matter. A stranger would be different. Only there's one thing I want you to remember.'

'Yeah? And what's that?' I tried to keep my voice light.

His eyes held mine. 'I'm no killer. I wouldn't murder anyone just for a piece of land, however badly I wanted it. That stretch of vineyard's waited fifty years already, it

can wait a bit longer. We'll have it back eventually, if not
me then Publius or his sons or grandsons. The family's
got a long memory, and that's what's important. More
important than changing the name on a title deed. You
understand me?'

'Yeah.' I swallowed; the guy was serious, deadly serious.
But then I had the impression that Arruns was that sort of
person. 'I understand.'

'Good. That's all I wanted to say.' He opened the coach
door. Lysias pulled up. 'Thanks for the lift, but I think
I'll walk after all.' He paused. 'Oh. One more thing. You
might like to have a word with a man called Marcus
Veluscius. You'll find him in Three Heroes Street near
the Bronzeworkers' Guildhouse.'

'Yeah? And why would I want to do that?' I said; but
he was already out and striding up the road like a
thirty-year-old. He didn't look up as we passed, either.

I settled back to think.

So. It looked like turning out to be another busy morning.
I'd got Aulus Bubo to see, then Gaius Aternius. Now for
reasons of his own Arruns had added this guy Veluscius
to the list.

The agreement with Perilla had been that I'd take the
coach in, not ride around in it when I arrived or use it
for the return trip, so I got Lysias to drop me in the
main square and then sent him back to Vetuliscum.
Hair-splitting, yeah, and on the shady side of sneaky, but
I really hate using these things any more than I have to,
and the lady knew it. Besides, the threat of rain had gone
and it was too good a day not to walk.

With the help of a friendly local fruit-seller I found
Lampmakers' Street no bother: a long straight alley
running north-west from the centre towards the walls.

I'd gone about fifty yards down it when I met a funeral procession coming in the opposite direction. There ain't no way to beat one of these things. I squeezed as far as I could against the blank house-wall that edged the pavement and waited for it to pass.

Whoever was being burned may not've been from one of the top families – I couldn't see any magistrates' mantles among the fake ancestors escorting the stretcher – but they hadn't been short of a gold piece or two: there were a good half-dozen double-flutes wailing away and the same number of bugles, and the masked professional mourners playing the ancestors weren't the half-drunk specimens you sometimes get if you try to cheese-pare. The dead guy himself was wrapped in a good quality mantle, and although for some reason the face was covered I caught the glint of gold on his arms. The surprise was the strength of the burial party: I'd've expected a real crowd at a top-notch funeral like this, but besides the widow – at least I assumed it was the widow, a big woman in a pricey mantle with a hatchet of a nose I could see even through her veil – there were only a handful of tough-looking guys who looked as out of place as nightclub bouncers in a ballet class.

I stayed respectfully still until the tail-enders had passed me and then carried on down the street. Another fifty yards on, the houses gave way to shops, mostly belonging to the lampmakers who gave the street its name. One of these, next to a place with the shutters up and the padlock on, had a guy lounging outside it, obviously the owner touting for trade. I went up to him.

'Excuse me, pal,' I said. 'I'm looking for an Aulus Bubo.'

The guy gave me a strange look. 'Yeah?' he said.

Jupiter! All the tradesmen in Caere to choose from

and I had to strike lucky! 'I was told he had a shop around here.'

'You were told right.' The man nodded at the shuttered counter. 'That's Bubo's. But you've just missed him.'

'Is that so, now? You think he'll be back soon?'

'It isn't likely.'

I kept hold of my temper. 'Then you think you could possibly tell me where I can find him, friend?'

The man grinned. 'You could try the cemetery on the other side of town. After that it's anyone's guess.'

Oh, shit; the penny dropped. I turned round to look at the retreating funeral, then back to Smiler. 'You mean that was him? He's dead?'

'Well, if he isn't he's due for a hell of a shock in an hour or so.' The grin widened. 'It'd serve the bastard right, too. Give him a taste of what's to come.'

Jupiter on a tightrope! What had happened to *Of the dead, nothing but good*? I wasn't particularly superstitious, but I shivered and made the sign.

Smiler chuckled. 'Don't bother, Roman,' he said. 'Any god that's listening would agree. Bubo was a crook. He only got what he deserved.'

'Yeah?' I said. 'And what was that?'

'Some enterprising bugger dropped by a couple of nights back and flattened his head with a hammer.'

I stared at him, my jaw slack.

Oh, fuck.

29

'He was murdered?'

'Unless he managed to beat his own brains in and hide the weapon afterwards, sure.' Smiler was clearly enjoying himself. Either he was a complete bastard himself or Bubo had been a neighbour from hell. Probably both.

Jupiter! This I hadn't expected, and it was a real bummer. 'You care to tell me what happened exactly?' I said.

The man shrugged. 'I work normal hours, friend, and I wasn't here. All I know is that the shop was open when I turned up the next morning, which it shouldn't've been because Bubo didn't usually roll in until midday. Halfway through the afternoon he had a customer and the guy came straight out gagging.'

'You didn't think to check earlier?'

'Why should I?'

Yeah, that added up: conscientious fellow-tradesmen ever ready to keep a watchful eye on his neighbour's affairs this bugger wasn't. 'It might've saved you some embarrassing questions, pal. Like what was to stop you having slipped in sometimes over the previous few hours and croaked the guy yourself.'

Instead of answering, Smiler stuck his head round the doorway of his shop and shouted, 'Roach!'

A thin kid with acne and a wall eye came out.

'Yeah, boss?' he said.

'Where was I two days ago, the morning after Bubo was killed?'

'Here, boss.'

'All the time?'

'Sure. We was stocktaking. Then the priest from the Temple of Hercules came in with the bulk order, and that woman who runs the brothel on Turms Street—'

'Right. That's fine.' The kid disappeared back into whatever limbo he had his existence in and Smiler turned back to me. 'Even if I didn't have Roach to back me up there were plenty of other people around that time. The shop door wouldn't've been out of observation for two clear minutes after sunup. Besides, I'm secretary of the Guild and I've a reputation to lose. I wouldn't murder anyone if you paid me, not even Herminius Bubo.'

I sighed. 'Okay, pal. Forget the implied slur on your honesty. Now. What kind of business was Bubo in?' Some shops have signs above the door; Bubo's didn't. The dead man evidently believed in keeping a low profile.

'You name it, he did it.' Smiler grinned. 'I'm talking shady, you understand. But if you want to go by what he put on his citizen's papers you could call him a second-hand goods dealer.'

I nodded; yeah, that would cover a multitude of sins, all right. Like 'import-export agent' or 'entertainer'. A fence, in other words. 'And what particular brand of second-hand goods did he specialise in?'

Another shrug. 'Jewellery. Old statues. Silver tableware. That sort of thing.'

No surprises there, either. Anything that was worth

nicking and selling on, in other words. He must've been
doing well, though, to judge by his funeral. 'Was anything
missing from the shop?'

'Sure,' Smiler said smugly. 'According to the militia
the place was stripped. His wife had the shutters put up,
but that was only for form. There's nothing left in there
worth stealing.'

'His wife. That'd be the lady I saw in the procession
with the nose like the business end of a warship.'

'That's right.'

'And where would I find her, when all this is over?'

For the first time the guy began to look suspicious.
Me, I'd've smelled a rat long before this point, but he'd
been so busy crowing and generally playing the smartass
that he clearly hadn't wondered what the fancy Roman
bastard's business with the dead man was. Now you could
see the idea dawn.

'Here,' he said. 'What's this about?'

'I'm looking into a couple of murders as a favour to a
relative.' I thought about pulling out my purse and then
decided against it: the secretary of the Lampmakers'
Guild might get offended if I offered him a tip, and he
was talkative enough already. 'I think your neighbour
Bubo might've been involved.'

The smug expression came back. 'Murders, you say?
I never thought he was in that league, but I wouldn't
be surprised. This could be a revenge killing. Organised
crime, even. They say there's a lot of it about.'

Jupiter! In Caeretan terms 'organised crime' could
mean three men who shared the same crowbar. Still,
if I wanted his tongue to keep wagging I had to humour
the bugger. 'Yeah, I've heard that too,' I said. 'You happen
to know if a guy called Titus Clusinus was a frequent
visitor?'

'You think this Clusinus could've done it?' He was looking positively animated now.

'I doubt that, pal. But you don't recognise the name? Or maybe the description?' I gave him a thumbnail sketch of Clusinus, at least what I'd seen of him under his mud face-pack.

He shook his head, regretfully: I had the impression he'd've loved to have produced a diary with all Clusinus's visits noted down, the details of the heists the two had pulled together in red. 'I didn't know nothing about Bubo's business,' he said. 'But I can point you at someone who did. You go and talk to Pullia.'

'That's his wife?'

Smiler grinned. 'Nah. The wife's Arria Metella. She won't know nothing, he only married her for her connections. Pullia's the girlfriend. She's a—' He stopped. 'She works at the Cockerel in Half Moon Street near the baths.'

Uh-huh. 'I might just do that,' I said, turning to leave. 'Thanks for your help, friend.'

'Organised crime,' the guy called after me. 'Don't forget. This probably all hinges on organised crime.'

Well, even with Bubo murdered I couldn't complain about a lack of leads now, although how many of them would prove to be dead ends I didn't know. Also, there was the outside chance the guy's death had nothing to do with my business: a dealer in valuable goods working alone in his shop when all the other traders around him had packed in for the night is just asking for some local entrepreneur to drop in unexpectedly and close him down permanently. Still, it was strange that it should happen just when I'd got the guy's name and number ...

I stopped. Shit, that was right! Okay, so maybe Titus Tolumnius had been playing straight when he'd pointed me in Bubo's direction, but the fact remained that the guy was already dead when Tolumnius had fingered him. The obvious question was, had he known? Because if he had then the odds on his being the murderer were pretty short. So. I could be being played for a sucker here. With Aulus Bubo definitely an ex Tolumnius's trade was no trade at all; I might be chasing rainbows, and with only seven days before Papatius's appointment with the praetor's rep that was not a smart position to be in.

On the plus side, at least Smiler had given me a name. If I couldn't talk to Bubo then at least I might be able to work out Clusinus's connection with him – if it existed – some other way.

Pullia would have to stand in line, though. I'd decided to put off talking to Gaius Aternius – there wasn't much I could do there, really, even if the guy was guilty, except rattle his cage to see if he jumped – but Arrun's pal Marcus Veluscius, whoever the hell he was, was a definite next step. All I could do at the moment was keep all the balls in the air for as long as possible and hope that when the dud ones finally fell there'd still be one left.

Three Heroes Street turned out to be the other end of town, in one of these quiet respectable districts where the houses aren't particularly grand but you get the impression that the residents have their slaves up before dawn scouring the doorstep and deadheading the roses. I asked one of the scourers and deadheaders – he was scooping up a pile of donkey manure at the time – for directions to Marcus Veluscius's place. He pointed me to a neat little property with flowerpots along the wall and a knocker that positively gleamed.

The slave who answered the door gleamed too, like he'd just been laundered. I wondered if his drawers had creases in them.

'Yes, sir.' Smile.

'Someone called Marcus Veluscius live here, pal?' I said.

'Yes, sir. Indeed he does.' The smile widened, as if confirmation was a positive pleasure. He stepped back neatly, and his sandals squeaked on the fresh-scrubbed mosaic. Hercules cleaning the Augean stables, if you're interested. No joke; truth. 'Come in, please. Are you expected?'

'No. My name's Marcus Valerius Corvinus. Maybe you could tell your master that a man called Larcius Arruns sent me, and ask if I could take up a few minutes of his time.'

'Of course, sir. If you'd care to wait?' He hurried off at a pace that would've left Bathyllus nowhere. Impressive: slaves *never* run. Maybe I could take what he had, bottle it and feed it to the little guy. It'd certainly beat being sniffed at and sniped at all the time. But there again, maybe not; I had the idea that squeaky-clean bit of perfection would've had me climbing the walls inside a month.

I looked round the entrance lobby. It fitted with the neighbourhood: nothing flashy, nothing expensive, but nothing particularly interesting or unusual, either; everything just ... yeah, well, the word that sprang to mind was *nice*. It was a nice house, full stop.

The guy came back. 'The master's in the study, sir, if you'd like to follow me.'

I did. The slave showed me into a nice study with nice furniture and a nice, wrinkled old man sitting at a desk.

The bugger must've been pushing eighty. He was clean, though.

'Valerius Corvinus?' he quavered. 'I'm Marcus Veluscius. Pleased to meet you, sir. Have a seat.' I pulled up a chair. 'Candidus, bring us some wine, please.' Then, when Snow-White had vanished: 'You come from Larcius Arruns, I understand.'

'Yeah. He suggested I drop by and talk to you.' I had to lean forwards to hear him. 'Why I'm not quite sure, but I'm looking into three murders in Vetuliscum.'

'Murders?' The old guy's lips pursed; I got the impression that in this house murder was a four-letter word. 'Then I'm as puzzled as you are. I know nothing of any murders.'

'But you do know Arruns?'

'Of course. I knew him very well, in my working days. He comes from an old local family. A very old family. But *murders*?'

'Attus Navius.' I tried the names out on him, watching for a reaction. 'Titus Clusinus. And a Greek doctor by the name of Hilarion. The actual investigating officer's Gaius Aternius. He's the nephew of Mayor Cominius.'

'Ah.' Veluscius's lips pursed harder like he was sucking on a lemon. 'Aternius I also know. And Cominius, naturally. I knew Navius's father, but not the boy himself. Hilarion, no. But Clusinus, now. Clusinus rings a bell.'

'Yeah?' The hairs on my neck began to prickle. Maybe we were on to something after all: there was a brain there, under all the creases, and I could almost hear it ticking.

'Arruns didn't give any other indication of how he thought I could help you?' Veluscius asked. 'None at all?'

I shook my head. 'We were talking about an old vineyard sale, fifty years back. Arruns thinks Cominius's father and old Velthur Navius did *his* father out of the property.'

Veluscius's brow cleared, and he nodded. He was still doing his lemon-sucking act. 'Yes. Yes, that would be it.' He hesitated. 'Arruns, I take it, didn't tell you who I was? Before I retired, that is?'

'No.'

'I was the Cominius family's head clerk.'

I swallowed. Shit! Bull's-eye!

The door opened and Snow-White came back in with a tray. I noticed that there were two jugs.

'Ah, Candidus. Just pour and leave us to ourselves, will you?' Veluscius turned back to me. 'Mine will be mostly water, Valerius Corvinus. I don't imagine you'll care to follow my example.'

I took a sip of the wine Snow-White handed me. Nice.

'First of all, Arruns is quite right,' Veluscius said. 'Velthur Navius did forge his father's signature. And old Cominius did connive at the deception.'

Jupiter! 'Aren't you a bit late admitting that, friend?' I said. 'And why tell me?'

Veluscius shrugged. 'Fifty years ago telling the truth wouldn't have done any good. It was a matter of personalities. Cominius was mayor himself at the time, and the most powerful man in Caere. Velthur Navius was one of the biggest landowners in the district, a member of the Caeretan Town Council. And Aulus Arruns may have been one of Vetuliscum's oldest residents but like his son he was too cross-grained and standoffish for his family to win much support. Now, conditions haven't really changed, and the result of any modern court case would probably be the same, as Arruns well knows. The difference is in myself. I no longer have a position to lose and frankly, Valerius Corvinus, I'm too old now to care.'

'So the Cominii are crooks?'

'Most certainly, at least where property is concerned. It's a family tradition. And I'd include young Gaius Aternius with them. His mother, of course, is the mayor's sister.'

'You said the name Clusinus rang a bell.'

'Yes.' Veluscius took a sip of wine. 'That matter, naturally, is much more recent and quite above board. Or, I should say, within the limits of the law. Cominius and Aternius advance five-year loans to property owners on the security of the property itself. The terms are very favourable but there is no provision for renewal, and it is no coincidence that without exception the recipients are the sort of people who will default when repayment becomes due. At which time, of course, the property becomes forfeit. One agreement along those lines was entered into with Titus Clusinus.'

Hey! 'And when would the loan expire?'

'I left the Cominii almost exactly four years ago. If I remember rightly – and although I no longer have access to the company records there is nothing wrong with my memory – the contract had been signed in October the previous year, so repayment would be due quite shortly.'

I sat back. Jupiter! So Aternius had a definite link with Clusinus! I'd got the bugger! The only question was, why should Aternius kill him to get his farm when he'd default anyway? The guy had been broke, anyone could see that. All Aternius had to do was wait a couple of months and . . .

My spine went cold. No, cancel that: if what Vesia had told me was true then Clusinus may've been broke when he died, but he had prospects; big prospects that hinged on whatever deal he had cooking with Aulus Bubo. If that had gone through presumably he'd've had the money to pay off the loan and then, if he wanted to, sell the farm on the open market and recoup his outlay. Probably better than recoup, from what Veluscius had said, if he was willing to wait for even a half-decent offer. But whatever the deal was, it had died with him before it could happen. A month or so down the road, Aternius was going to show up at Vesia's place, wave the signed contract under her nose and tell her to get the hell off his land. And he wouldn't've been able to do that if Clusinus hadn't been dead.

It worked; sure it did.

'One more thing, pal,' I said. 'How exactly are the Cominii doing these days? Financially, I mean?'

Veluscius hesitated. 'Well enough,' he said. 'But my sources tell me they are overextending themselves. The cash flow, if you understand the term, is imbalanced.'

'In other words, the bastards've got plenty of irons in the fire but they're in danger of getting burned, right?'

'You put it very succinctly. That would certainly seem to be the case.'

'If Gaius Aternius made a good marriage would that help?'

'Considerably.' The old guy gave me a sharp look. 'Is he likely to?'

'If I don't miss my guess he's got his eye on Sicinia Rufina. And it might well be mutual.'

'Indeed? Then the lady had better consult a good lawyer concerning the future management of her financial affairs before she signs the marriage contract,' Veluscius said. 'Aternius has his own agenda.'

Yeah. I'd just bet he did. And I was beginning to think that part of it had been four murders.

30

Before I left, I asked Snow-White about the Cockerel.

'It's Caere's biggest cookshop, sir,' he said. 'With' – he coughed delicately – 'entertainment. Very popular with the younger set.'

Jupiter! Starched drawers was right: the guy must've been all of twenty-four and he came on like a dowager. No sniff, though. If it'd been Bathyllus I'd definitely have got a disapproving sniff; that bastard was so straight you could use him to draw lines.

'Sounds fun,' I said. I wasn't being sarcastic: I've always liked dens of iniquity, the more iniquitous the better. 'Near the baths, I was told?'

'That's correct, sir. In Half Moon Street, not far from the Veian Gate.'

All the way back to the centre of town, in other words. Hell. Walking I enjoyed, but these old Etruscan city planners had been real exercise nuts. Caere had stairs everywhere, and in some of the side alleys you practically needed climbing spikes. Well, it was good for the waistline. I waved Snow-White goodbye and headed for the Hinge.

So: Aternius was definitely a front-runner. I could

make him now for the murders of Navius and Clusinus, and more important the same motive would account for both. I might even stretch things to Bubo. If killing Clusinus safeguarded his investment that end then Bubo's death made doubly sure: beating the guy's head in with a hammer was a pretty effective way of making certain he didn't call round to Vesia's to find out why his business pal wasn't coming out to play any more. The only question was, in that case how had Aternius known about the deal in the first place? Sure, Clusinus might've told him in advance that he'd be coming into some money and intended to pay off the loan – in fact, he'd've had to've done to give Aternius reason for murdering him – but he wouldn't've let on where the cash was coming from, especially if there was some illegality involved. Above all, he wouldn't've mentioned Bubo. So how could Aternius have made the connection? It was a detail, sure, and there could be half a dozen plausible answers, but it niggled.

The way to the Veian Gate took me past the market square, and I called in at the clink to see Papatius. He was pretty low, which was understandable with the prospect of me for an advocate, but at least the militia heavies had stopped beating him up. Whether that was a bad or a good sign I wasn't sure; probably the former, since it implied they thought they'd got enough on the poor bastard to strangle him already. There wasn't much I could do about it either, least of all entertain him with a lively run-down of my current theories: I doubted if the news that the principal investigator and counsel for the prosecution might well have cogent personal reasons for putting him underground would have a very cheering effect, while any suggestion that his wife and girlfriend could be jointly responsible for the murders would've lost me a few teeth. So I confined myself to patting him manfully on the shoulder and telling him not to give up hope.

On my way out I pumped the guy on the desk – not my sharp-eared pal from last time but a younger, less jaundiced version – on the subject of Bubo's murder. Not surprisingly, the militia were treating it as straightforward burglary with related homicide. Smiler's run-through was accurate as far as it went, and I didn't get much more: at some time between sunset and dawn, Bubo had been beaten to death with a mason's hammer – it had been found in the gutter round the corner – which his wife Arria had identified as having been left behind by a workman carrying out alterations the previous month and not returned by him, the shop had been stripped of everything that wasn't nailed down, and no one in the surrounding houses and flats hadn't heard nothing, officer. I got the distinct impression that the militia guy, speaking for his colleagues, regarded the investigation as closed: like Smiler, they were fully aware of the nature of Bubo's activities and reckoned the bastard had only got what he was due. There was, of course, no suggestion that the murder was in any way connected to the ones in Vetuliscum, so Papatius continued to be banged up.

When I re-emerged into the sunlight it was past noon and my mouth felt dry as a shortass camel's scrotum. A perfect time for the Cockerel. I grabbed an itinerant pastry-seller and got directions to Half Moon Street.

Caere's biggest cookshop or not, I'd assumed that the Cockerel would be a pretty low dive, but the place had some pretensions. Meaning that there was graphic and pictorial decoration on the walls, some of it not just the product of freelancers expressing their political views or detailing the sexual proclivities of the local talent. Not that the management's contribution was artistically speaking much better, mind: the eponymous cockerel that faced you as you went in could've been anything from a constipated ostrich to a cabbage with legs and a beak, and I'd never seen so many cross-eyed ladies in my life. Early afternoon you'd think a place like that would be quiet – cookshops with 'entertainment' only get going after sunset – but it was comfortably full, and there was what I can only describe as an air of expectancy. I found a free table and ordered up a jug of Caeretan, some poached brains with fennel and a side plate of cheese and olives.

'Hey, pal,' I said to the waiter when he'd brought the stuff. 'Does a girl called Pullia work here?'

He grinned as he set the plates down. 'Sure.'

'You think I could see her?'

'No problem, boss.' He jerked his head towards a platform at one end of the room that I hadn't noticed. 'That's Pullia now. Look all you want.'

I looked, and my jaw hit the table. Jupiter! I looked harder, just for the fun of it. Yeah, well, that explained why there were so many punters this early. The girl who'd just come out of a side door and jumped up on to the stage was wearing enough make-up and flashy jewellery to fit out a whole cathouse, and not a great deal else. The noise level suddenly went up a couple of dozen notches.

I sat back with my wine and watched the show. Subtle it wasn't, but she was young enough to get away with it, and stacked into the bargain; that much was obvious after the first two minutes when she started peeling off in earnest. There were no gimmicks, no wrestling with amorous pythons or spinning judiciously attached tassels: this was a straight appeal to the audience's gut instincts, and they lapped it up and yelled for more.

Me – well, I've always preferred my poached brains with fennel cold, anyway.

The punters were still climbing over tables and yammering for seconds when she picked up the bits and pieces that she'd pulled off, slipped down, wriggled out of or otherwise removed in the course of her act and left the stage. I took a deep swallow of the wine – it wasn't bad stuff, which said a lot for the management's professional integrity – and waved the waiter back over.

'Now, friend,' I said. 'About that introduction. I'd sort of envisaged a more private chat, somewhere quiet. You think you could arrange that for me now the lady's done her bit out front for the boys?'

'Sure.' He looked down pointedly at the pouch on my belt and leered. 'No problem.'

I pulled out a silver piece. He waited. I made it two. He waited again and I added a third. Well, it'd been a cheap holiday so far.

The coins disappeared like rabbits down a hole. 'Follow me, boss,' he said.

I picked up the cup and jug – the brains I didn't mind, but there was no point in leaving good wine for some other bugger to filch – and tagged along behind him. He led me through the exit the girl had taken and up a flight of worm-eaten stairs, stopped outside a door at the top and knocked.

'Yeah?' A woman's voice, muffled.

'Visitor for you,' the guy said through the panelling.

'Damn! Wait a minute, Flavius.' There was a pause and the door opened.

She was older than I'd thought she'd be: at close quarters and with the make-up off I could see the beginnings of crow's-feet round the eyes. Also she was wearing a decent tunic, which tended to spoil things.

'Flavius, you little pervert, I told you never to—' she began. Then she took in my purple stripe and aristocratic nose and did a good imitation of a gannet swallowing. 'Oh. Ah. Right. Yeah.'

Well, at least we were starting on a plus here. 'The name's Marcus Valerius Corvinus,' I said. 'You think I could have a word with you, lady?'

'Sure.' She stepped aside quickly. 'Two. A dozen. As many as you like. I'll see you later, Flavius, okay?'

The waiter gave me another leer and went clattering off down the stairs.

'Come in.' Pullia closed the door behind me, walked over to the bed and lay down. 'Make yourself comfortable.'

I looked around. There was an open clothes chest, a couple of shelves with not much on them, an old bronze mirror thick with verdigris that could've come from the bargain heap of any third-rate junk shop, and nothing else. No chairs, no stools.

Uh-huh.

Well, it had to be done. I went over to the clothes chest, closed it and sat on the lid, setting the jug and wine cup beside me. Pullia watched expressionlessly.

'Words, lady,' I said. 'Just words.'

The tunic had slipped. She pulled it up a bit and sat higher on the bed, her back against the wall. Still she said nothing. I opened my pouch, slowly took out a half gold piece and laid it beside the wine jug. Her eyes went to it, then back to me. They looked puzzled.

'You're kidding,' she said.

'Uh-huh.' I shook my head. 'I enjoyed the show. Think of it as payment for that, if you like.'

She shrugged, shifted on the bed and swung her feet over so she was sitting on the edge. I had a tantalising glimpse of leg, but then the hem of the tunic was pulled down. I sighed; life is never easy.

'Okay,' she said. 'Then what do you want?'

'You're Aulus Bubo's girlfriend, right?'

That got me a considering look; the lady was no bubblehead.

'Was,' she said. 'The poor sap's dead.' Well, I'd heard gentler valedictories in my time. 'He was murdered two days ago.' She paused. 'That what this is about?'

'Yeah. I thought you might be able to tell me a bit about him.'

'Like what, for instance?'

'Jupiter knows, lady. Let's start with his business. He was a fence, right?' She hesitated. I glanced meaningfully at the half gold piece, and she nodded. 'Okay. So what sort of things did he handle, mostly?'

'Besides me?' Her lips twitched. 'The usual. Jewellery, plate.'

'Middle of the range? Top? Who did he deal with?'

'Top.' She was still looking at me like a cat at a mouse-hole. 'He specialised in antiques. And he had his contacts. Not many, but they were the best.'

'Uh-huh. And he sold the stuff on through his shop in Lampmakers' Street.'

'Sometimes. It depended. There's no real market for antiques in Caere. The best of it went to his brother in Rome.'

My scalp prickled. 'His brother?'

'Sure. His brother Publius. He has a business on the Sacred Way.' She leaned back. Maybe it was accidental, but her tunic was shifting again, and this time she didn't pull it down. 'You from Rome yourself, Corvinus?'

'Ultimately, yeah.'

'I've never been to Rome. It must be nice.'

'It's okay.' I glanced at the coin again, then back to her. 'Ever hear of someone called Clusinus?'

'Titus Clusinus?' She smiled. 'Sure. I've met him a couple of times.'

'At Bubo's?'

'There and elsewhere. He's a nice guy.'

'You know what his business with Bubo was?'

That got me another shrug. 'He was selling, Bubo was buying. That's all I know.'

'Something big?'

'Bubo always dealt big. I told you. But, like I say, that's all I know.' The tunic hem rode up another half-inch. 'You have a house in Rome?'

'No. Not any more.'

'I've never met a Roman purple-striper before. You don't see many of them in Caere, not at the Cockerel anyway. You really liked the show?'

'Sure. You've got real talent.'

'Bubo never complained. But now he's dead there's no one to appreciate it.' She wriggled. The tunic top slipped. 'Not properly.'

'I saw the funeral pass,' I said. 'You weren't there.'

She laughed. 'I'm a working girl, Corvinus. I've got commitments. Besides, I doubt if his wife would've been too happy about me turning up at the graveside.'

'No.' I kept my voice neutral. 'Maybe she wouldn't. Arria knew about you, then?'

'Sure she did. Arria may be a stuck-up cow but she's no fool. That marriage was a simple trade-off, connections for cash. She was happy enough so long as the money kept coming in.'

Smiler had mentioned connections, too. 'She come from a good family?'

'The best in Caere. Her brother married the mayor's daughter.'

Something cold touched my spine. *'Cominius's?'*

'Unless there's been an election I haven't heard about, sure.'

Jupiter! So Bubo's wife was a collateral relative of Aternius's! If I wanted an explanation of how the bastard had known about Clusinus's connection with Bubo I needn't look any further. It seemed like I'd have to talk to Arria Metella after all.

'Can you give me an address, sister?' I said.

'For Arria?' Absently, she reached up to the neck of her tunic and tugged at it, pulling it off the shoulder. 'I could. There's no hurry, though. The funeral'll be over by now, but she'll still be busy with the purification rites. Besides, I'm not on again until tonight.'

'Humour me.'

Our eyes locked. Then she sighed, twitched the tunic back and hugged her breasts. 'The big house at the top of Crows' Staircase,' she said. Her voice was dull. 'Near the Shrine of Atropos.'

I stood up. 'Thanks.'

'Don't mention it, Roman. Just fuck off and leave me alone, okay?'

I left the wine where it was and went back downstairs.

31

Crows' Staircase was well named: I was gasping for breath halfway up, and the back of my legs hurt like hell. The view from the top was something, though: I could see across the plains in every direction, down into the valleys either side of town where the tombs were and over to the north-west almost as far as Pyrgi. Bubo's place you couldn't miss. It was perched out on a spur like an eagle's nest, and just the thought of standing on the balcony gave me vertigo.

The front door was still hung with cypress branches. I knocked and a slave opened it. He had a chunk of hair missing in the front. Whoever had wielded the funeral scissors had taken his job seriously where the domestic servants were concerned.

'Yes?' he said.

This was the tricky part: the afternoon of a funeral is no time for a social call, especially if what you really want to discuss are the dead man's shady business affairs. However, I'd got my approach all worked out.

'Uh, I'm sorry, friend,' I said. 'This is Herminius Bubo's house, right?'

He gave me a look like he'd just caught me chalking a

nasty word on the door post. 'Yes, sir,' he said. 'But the master's dead. We've just burned him.'

'Yeah, I know.' I went into my routine. 'I was down at his shop earlier and I saw the funeral pass. Only I didn't know it was his at the time. I'm only in Caere for the day and I thought maybe I should come up and give my condolences to his widow.'

I'd let the guy have the full force of my patrician Roman's plummy vowels, and he blossomed like a rose, which was just what I'd been playing for: in my experience house slaves are the biggest snobs you could ever hope to meet, and he couldn't've had many purple-stripers standing on his doorstep.

'If you wait here, sir,' he said, 'I'll see if she's receiving. What name shall I say?'

I told him; all four bits, because I was out to impress. 'She won't know me,' I said. 'But we have an acquaintance in common. Gaius Aternius, the mayor's nephew.' Yeah, well, that was true enough. And good society runs on being able to name shared acquaintances. The fact that I thought the guy was a crook and multiple murderer and hoped to nail him as such had nothing to do with anything.

That put the icing on it: Baldy turned almost affable, and let me wait in the porch. Two minutes later I was being shown through into the atrium where Arria Metella was waiting to receive me.

Hatchet face was right: I could've used the lady's nose to split kindling. She was pleasant enough, though.

'Valerius Corvinus,' she said, stretching out a hand. 'It's good of you to come. I saw you when we passed Aulus's place of business, naturally, but I didn't know you were a friend of his or I would have spoken.'

'I wasn't.' No point in lying, especially when I didn't

have to. 'I was going to see him, sure, but I'd never met him. When the guy in the shop next door told me he was being buried I'd've come to the cemetery but I didn't like to impose. Still, I felt I should come and pay my respects in some way.'

'Most thoughtful.' She gave me a sad smile, then turned to Baldy who was hovering in the background. 'Sestus, a cup of honey wine for our guest. Do have a seat, please, Valerius Corvinus.'

Baldy bowed and left. I winced as I pulled up a chair and sat down. If I went before Perilla I'd leave instructions that for the duration of the mourning period unless it was actually asked for that muck should stay in the cellar where it belonged.

Arria turned back to me. 'What exactly was your business with Aulus, by the way? I doubt if I can help – I know very little of that side of things – but I'd hate to think your visit to Caere was entirely wasted.'

The question sounded completely natural. Either Bubo's widow had the art of dissimulation worked out to a T or she was genuinely ignorant of what the guy's business entailed. Probably the former: I'd met wives like Arria before, and they'd spent so long cultivating a blind spot to what their husbands got up to outside the family circle they'd come to believe the fiction themselves.

'Nothing in particular,' I said. 'I was told he dealt in high-class antiques. My stepfather's a bit of a collector. I thought I might drop in and look over his stock, maybe pick up something I could put by for a present.'

She preened; there couldn't've been many purple-stripers interested enough to paw through Bubo's merchandise. 'Aulus certainly did have some beautiful things,' she said. 'He had excellent taste.' Another sad smile. 'Taste, but no sense. I told him the shop was no place to keep them on a permanent basis, even with the iron shutters and that new strongroom of his, but he insisted. Of course, that was why the poor dear was killed. It was an open invitation for burglars.'

'New strongroom?'

'Yes. He had it built a month ago by one of the local masons.' Oh, yeah: the mason's hammer that he hadn't returned and the killer had used to bash the guy's skull in. Poetic justice. 'Not that he used it, to my knowledge. Silly man. Quite ridiculous.'

Baldy came in with the wine. I took a token sip and set the cup down. The hairs on my neck were prickling. 'Uh, he didn't?' I said.

'No. Not at all. And it must've cost thousands. Of course, there's no extra space in these Lampmakers' Street properties, and the foundations are solid rock. Aulus had to dig a small cellar and put in an iron trapdoor.'

The prickle became a full-blown itch. 'You're sure? That he never used it?'

Arria gave me a suspicious look. 'Certain,' she said. 'The thieves cleared the shop out, but the trapdoor was hidden by an empty storage chest and the padlock was intact. He'd left the key at home, and when I opened it the strongroom was empty. Valerius Corvinus, I'm afraid I fail to see what possible interest this can have for you.'

'Just curiosity,' I said. Was it hell! Jupiter on wheels! 'Uh, one more thing, Arria Metella. Did your husband ever mention a guy called Titus Clusinus?'

She stood up. 'Young man, I'm beginning to doubt your motives for coming here today after all. Perhaps you'd better leave.'

Well, maybe I had overreached myself. Pullia had said

the woman was no fool, and the turn the conversation had taken would make anyone smell a rat. Still, I had no regrets. That nugget about the strongroom and Arria's reaction to the name Clusinus were worth a little aggro. I stood up too.

'I'm sorry,' I said. 'My condolences again.'

She was giving me a look that would've put a coating of ice on a firebrick. 'Sestus!' she snapped. Baldy must've been hanging about outside to make sure the mistress's virtue wasn't threatened, because he was right there before she'd got the second syllable out. 'Valerius Corvinus is just leaving. Show him to the door, please.'

I went quietly.

So. I'd been right about Arria having passed on Clusinus's name to Aternius; or at least she'd realised what I was getting at or she wouldn't've jumped up like a startled pheasant and thrown me out. The question was, how did this strongroom business fit in? The lady had said it herself: to spend that amount of time and effort building a strongroom you didn't use made no sense at all. And Bubo hadn't used it: the fact that he'd left the keys at home instead of keeping them on him showed he'd no intention of using it. Not immediately, anyway. So what the hell was he playing at?

Not immediately, anyway . . .

I stopped. Shit! That was it, it had to be!

Bubo hadn't used the strongroom because he was keeping it for something special. And if he'd only had it built a month ago then whatever that was had only come on the horizon recently; about the time, say, that he'd begun to deal with Titus Clusinus. And the deal had never gone through . . .

So what was valuable enough to justify a guy like Bubo,

who was used to big deals, taking extra security precautions that involved him in a lot of unwonted personal expense? Whatever it was, it had to be big: physically big, because otherwise why a whole strongroom, why not a simple strongbox cemented to the floor like most people had to hold their ready cash and Great-Auntie's pearl and ruby necklace?

I started down the stairs. It wasn't much easier going down than it had been coming up; you only strained different leg muscles. No wonder the guy had spent so much time at his shop. There was a road, sure, but it zigzagged so much that it'd take three or four times as long to get down to the town centre. Also, there was the view. Downhill was even more impressive because you had it all the time. The sun glinted off the small stream far below, and the line of the road that wound its way through the old cemetery on its far side. I stopped to look and give my calf muscles a rest. Jupiter! There must be hundreds of tombs down there, plus hundreds more the other side. A real City of the Dead that made Caere itself seem like a village. A city with proper houses, too, that guys who'd died when Rome was a clutch of mud huts had built to spend eternity in and stocked with . . .

With . . .

And then it hit me. Oh, Jupiter! Jupiter best and greatest! Bubo handled antiques. And where did you find antiques by the barrow-load, just squirrelled away out of sight where no one would ever see them again or know if they'd gone missing?

Right.

That was what Clusinus had been up to, I'd bet my last copper coin on it.

The guy had been robbing tombs.

32

Which, believe me, sounds a lot simpler a proposition than it is.

Oh, sure, there're hundreds of the things in the cemeteries around Caere laid out and waiting, maybe even thousands, and the other Etruscan cities have just as many, even more. If we're talking just numbers, tomb-robbing should rank pretty high on the list of lucrative criminal activities. Only it doesn't, not at all, and there are good reasons why it shouldn't.

First of all, and most important, there's the religious angle. I'm no more superstitious than the next guy, but personally just the thought of breaking into a tomb gives me goosebumps, and the same would go for ninety-nine per cent of the population, even the bastards who'd slit their grandmother's throat for a jug of third-rate Surrentine. You don't mess with the dead, ever: that's a rule everyone knows. These buggers've got their own ways of getting even, and they don't play around.

Second's the law. Grave-robbing's a semi-religious offence, and there's only one penalty, crucifixion and half-burning. Sure, Perilla's philosopher pals could be right about the soul not surviving death, and if you're one of the free-thinkers who don't believe a proper funeral's important, then fine. Me, I'd hedge my bets, and so would most people, low-life included. The prospect of wandering around this side of the River for the next thousand years or so scares me silly.

Third's security. The tombs themselves are locked, or their doors are bricked up if the family isn't there to use them any more. Also, the cemeteries are patrolled at night. Get caught by the local militia hanging around a graveyard after midnight with a crowbar and a pickaxe and it ain't no use claiming you were digging truffles. And as far as your future prospects're concerned thereafter, see point two.

So. If Clusinus *had* been robbing tombs then it was no small deal. I'd never met the guy properly, so I couldn't make an assessment of his nerves, but he'd have to be some tough cookie, and I don't mean tough in the way that my pals Tolumnius and Baro were tough. Skulking around cemeteries alone after dark and breaking into tombs takes a special kind of courage. For a start he'd have to cope with the constant fear of the Watch butting in while his attention was on the business in hand. Because naturally he wouldn't know if or when the militia guys were going to come piling round the corner . . .

I stopped.

Jupiter, wait a minute. Wait just one minute.

Unless of course he did.

Let's go back a bit. The dead were one thing, the living were another. Sure, any tomb-robber would need iron nerves to do the job in the first place, but given these he was halfway there. If he knew he was in no danger of being disturbed then breaking into a tomb was easy-peasy. The cemeteries covered at least as much ground as the town itself, and there were three of them. So long as the guy was careful not to leave any traces and kept to the older, out-of-the-way piles which weren't even visited any more there was no reason why the thefts would ever be noticed. All he'd need was someone high up in local government who could make sure that, wherever he was that particular night, the militia wasn't.

Someone like the Caeretan mayor. The very *crooked* Caeretan mayor. Or, of course, one of his immediate family . . .

Okay; so how would it work? I'd already got a connection between Aternius and Bubo through Arria Metella to match the link between Bubo and Clusinus. The triangle was complete. So. A scenario. Let's say there was more than one scam involved here, the tomb-robbing and the property angle. Tomb-robbing first. Clusinus is the muscle, Bubo's the brains and Aternius and his uncle are the sleeping partners who make it all possible. Bubo goes to Clusinus – forget why he chooses him for the present – and sets up a deal: together they'll go into the tomb-looting business, with Clusinus doing the heavy work and Bubo selling on the result through his brother in Rome where the markets are. Bubo tells Clusinus their necks are safe, because part of the profits will go as kickbacks to the Cominii who'll see to it that the scam proceeds undisturbed. Everyone wins, nobody loses: Aternius and his uncle get to tap into a flow of hard cash which they badly need to pull their finances out of the hole, Bubo gains access to a major source of antiquities which is for all practical purposes inexhaustible, and Clusinus is making a hell of a lot more than he could pull in growing apples and breeding goats. As a scam, it's a literal gold mine, with maximum profit and minimum risk. Perfect, in fact.

Only something screws up before it properly takes off.

What that could've been was anybody's guess, but my bet reading backwards from what actually happened was that Clusinus, being Clusinus, had got greedy and had tried to pad out his share of the deal by soaking the Cominii. That would make sense, even if it was just a matter of threatening to spread ugly rumours: unlike simple fraud, tomb-raiding isn't a gentleman's crime, and Caere's an old-fashioned town. Come the election, even the barest hint that the Cominian ticket was being funded from the sale of black-market grave goods would have the guy's tail off the curule chair so fast his head would spin. So. The family decides to dissolve the partnership and plaster over the cracks. Being the clever bastards they are they don't just zero Clusinus and Bubo straight off; they work out a way to kill three birds with one stone. Hence the property scam. Old Navius is dead, his widow's loaded and looking round for a suitable replacement, and she's already got her eye on smoothie Aternius. The only fly in the financial ointment is young Navius, but if they can get rid of him with no risk to themselves then the Navius property is in the bag. So they set Clusinus up. Aternius kills Navius on Clusinus's land, making him the natural suspect; and with the Cominii running the local judicial system pinning the rap where it doesn't belong will pose no problems . . .

Except that Aternius couldn't know in advance that Navius would be around that morning to be murdered, or that Clusinus would conveniently happen along and find the body. Plus half a dozen other glitches that shoved their way in along the line.

I groaned. Shit. It didn't work.

There was something there, though, I'd swear that on my grandmother's grave. It only needed thinking through a bit more; preferably with the help of a jug or two.

I carried on down the staircase and headed for home.

Perilla, as usual, was reading; how that lady can waste so much valuable time on the sort of muck these soft-boiled egghead academics spew out beats me completely. I glanced at the title as I leaned over her shoulder and bit her neck: Alcidamas's *On Writers and Sophists*.

Enough said. She hadn't got that one from Flatworm's library, that was sure. It didn't have any pictures, for a start.

'Well, Marcus, did you have a nice day?' she said calmly. Her eyes hadn't lifted from the page she was reading.

Bathyllus oozed up and handed me my welcome-home belt of Setinian (yeah, Setinian: the little guy had found Flatworm's secret cache) together with the jug. I took a swallow, then another. Nectar.

'Not bad, lady.' I took the jug over to the chair next to the wall – we were on the terrace – and sat down. 'You, uh, fancy a trip to Rome?'

She set Alcidamas down on her lap and stared at me. Understandable: Caere might be practically within spitting distance of the Head of the World but after the Sejanus business I'd wiped my sandals of the place and sworn it was for keeps. Even the thought of breathing the same air as the smug broad-striper bastards who ran things there and had twelve-year-old virgins raped just so they could execute them legally for treason turned my stomach. Especially since it had been partly my fault.

'Why?' she said simply.

'There's a guy I have to talk to with an antique shop on the Sacred Way. A Publius Herminius Bubo.'

'I thought he lived in Caere. Didn't you go to see him this morning?'

'That was his brother. He's dead.'

'Dead?'

'He had his head smashed in with a mason's hammer two days ago.' I refilled the cup. 'And you haven't answered my question.'

'A mason's hammer?'

Jupiter, was she being dense, or what? I'd've thought she'd've jumped at the chance, and all I got was a set of responses that would've disgraced a parrot.

'Come on, Perilla,' I said. 'Cut it out. Forget murders for a minute. What about Rome?'

She hesitated, still looking at me. 'If you want to, yes. We could stay at your mother's house. And Marilla would love it.'

'Fine. We'll go tomorrow.' I took another swallow of wine. 'Where is the Princess?'

'Out with Corydon.' Another pause. 'Marcus, are you absolutely sure about this? I know how—'

'Sure I'm sure. But it's straight in and straight out, right? If that's okay with you. You and the Princess can do a bit of shopping while I'm seeing Bubo Part Two and I'll meet you back at Priscus's.'

She got up, laid Alcidamas on the table, walked over and kissed me. 'Whatever you like,' she said quietly. 'Only don't blame the city for the people who live in it, all right?'

'Yeah,' I said, sinking another quarter-pint of Setinian. The evening suddenly seemed a whole lot rosier. 'Thanks for the advice, lady. I'll bear it in mind.'

33

We set out at first light, in the carriage, Perilla, the Princess and me inside – Corydon was relegated to the stables for the duration, although getting Marilla to agree to leave him had involved a fight that made the Battle of Beneventum look like a honey-wine-and-sponge-cake klatsch – and Bathyllus and Meton perched on the roof behind Lysias's box. I'd wondered a bit about the wisdom of that, but Meton had brought along his recipe books to edit and he was happy as a lark agonising over whether his hare's-meat casserole tasted better with an acetabulum of Massic added to the gravy or a cyathus (don't ask; I don't know what they are, either). How the bugger could work at all stuck on top of a coach on the worst stretch of road this side of the Alps I didn't know, but so long as it kept him from practising his filleting skills on our major-domo it was okay with me. The gods know how Bathyllus amused himself. He probably brought a supply of spoons to polish.

The Princess was still half asleep and Perilla was busy watching the scenery. Me, I've never liked scenery: once you've seen one rustic hillside clad in shady arbutus and redolent with the heady scent of thyme you've seen them all. Besides, this was a business trip. I poured myself a cup of Setinian from the travelling flask and considered the Aternius-Bubo-Clusinus triangle.

It had to work, whatever the flaws, because it was far too good to drop. The only question was how. Okay. So let's see what we'd got. First of all, I was fairly sure about the tomb-robbing. Bubo's business was antiques, the empty strongroom argued storage in bulk, at least in the short term, and barring the proceeds of multiple burglaries which would've been noticed locally Clusinus wasn't in any position otherwise to guarantee that volume of fenceable merchandise. Given that, the involvement of the Cominii also made sense. If Bubo and Co. were robbing tombs on a large scale, which they'd have to be doing to make the business worth the candle, then they'd need the backing of patrons with clout, and there wasn't no one better: the Cominii were already bent as a Suburan dice match and I had old Veluscius's word for it that financially they were up against the wall with nowhere left to go. Also, Bubo's wife was a slip off the old olive tree. So far so good.

Second was the property scam. That I was sure of, too, at least in essence: marrying rich widows, especially when there're no kids to complicate matters, is a favourite way for good-looking entrepreneurs to pad out a shaky bank balance, and again thanks to Veluscius and my wineshop pal Perennius I knew Aternius and his uncle already had a land scheme up and running. And to provide factual back-up I had the business of Clusinus's loan to offer and – maybe – Aternius's interest in burying Papatius.

The problem was the murders. Clusinus's and Bubo's, no hassle: if I was right about the blackmail then Clusinus was two ways dead: once to shut his mouth, once to make sure his widow defaulted on the debt. And if Clusinus went, then Bubo would have to follow because the guy knew too much to live. Navius's murder was another matter. The Cominii had a motive in spades, sure, but no opportunity. And as for Hilarion the gods alone knew what foot that poor bastard had put out of line.

I took a brain-lubricating swallow of Setinian. Okay. So let's re-examine the Navius business, taking as our basic premise that the Cominii are guilty as hell.

The tomb-robbing scam's under negotiation, and Clusinus is pressing for the best deal he can get. He tries Bubo first, but Bubo sends him off with a flea in his ear: he's pulling his full weight already and he has his brother in Rome to square. So Clusinus goes to Aternius, or maybe to his uncle, it doesn't matter which because the two are an item. He doesn't use the word 'blackmail', because he's not that stupid; he just suggests that the Cominii might want to sub him out of their cut because after all he's the guy bringing home the actual bacon. Aternius, however, is no fool either. Maybe he and his uncle are having second thoughts about the whole business, and Clusinus trying to chisel them is the final straw; or maybe they've worked out the possibilities of a double-cross already, in which case he's playing right into their hands . . .

I paused.

Playing . . .

Oh, Jupiter!

I'd been lifting the cup for another mouthful; carefully, because although Lysias was a good driver and was missing as many potholes as he could we were still being bounced around like a pig in a blanket. Now I lowered it again, and my scalp began to tingle as the implications of that idea registered.

Shit! That was it!

I'd been wrong; or partly wrong, at least. The Cominii had never had any intention of getting mixed up with tomb-robbing: it was too tricky, it was too dangerous, and when you got down to it whatever the cash return it was just too low-class. All they were ever interested in was the property scam.

Hell! It was beautiful!

I sat back. Right. Let's get this straight. Forget the blackmail; Clusinus could never have made it work without fouling his own nest, and he'd know it. Concentrate on the scam itself.

So; the scenario. Bubo, knowing the Cominii are crooks, takes them the idea and offers to cut them in on the deal in return for their protection. They agree, but not because of the kickbacks: they know damn well that it's all academic, that the scam'll never get off the ground because by that time both Bubo and Clusinus will be dead. No; they agree because when he's making his pitch *Bubo tells them who his partner is.* That was the clincher. Bubo and Clusinus weren't murdered to cover up the Cominii's involvement in tomb-robbing; in the event, there was no tomb-robbing to cover up for, as witness the empty storeroom. They died because Clusinus was Navius's neighbour and already Vetuliscum's number one bad boy.

Forget whether the Cominii had already decided to target the Navii or if Bubo's proposition suggested it to them; either way worked, and it didn't really matter. The important thing was, they now had the perfect fall guy. Aternius – let's say it was Aternius, because the role fitted that smooth bastard to a T – invites Bubo and Clusinus round to discuss terms. Or maybe this was a private deal on the side with Clusinus alone. Whichever it was, he agrees to join in on one condition: that Clusinus act as his agent in putting Attus Navius underground and clearing the way for a profitable marriage with Sicinia Rufina. As a simple quid pro quo that would work: it put each party in the other's pocket and cemented the partnership. Clusinus is safe – he thinks – because with Aternius himself tagged to be the investigating officer any later investigation is rigged from the start, and the success of the tomb-robbing scam hinges on his staying alive and free. Also, no doubt, there's a considerable extra sweetener involved. What he doesn't know, crucially, is that once Navius is dead Aternius and his uncle mean to drop him and his partner like hot bricks. Worse, that they'll nail him for the murder after all; legitimately, because he'd actually have done it. And with his reputation he can make all the counter-claims he likes and still end up strangled by the public executioner nem. con., leaving Navius dead and the Cominii home and dry.

So when the opportunity arises Clusinus kills Navius as per contract, thinking that he's protected. Only then things start to go wrong for Aternius. Instead of an open-and-shut case with Clusinus as the only suspect the place is crawling with them. First and foremost there's bloody gormless Priscus, the Roman middle class's prize patsy. Then there's Papatius, who's followed Thupeltha who makes a possible third. Aternius is stymied; he can't go straight for Clusinus as planned because now there're too many variables involved and he'd have to justify his choice above the others. Also there's a smartass Roman purple-striper nosing around in the wings with ideas of his own.

So he changes his plans. Clusinus, remember, has no grounds for suspicion: he still believes he's safe and the deal is going through according to the agreement. Aternius invites him for a talk up by the irrigation pond, zeroes him himself and shoves him under the hurdle. That last is important, because the nosy Roman has dug up a fresh suspect and he can make a case, or enough of one to serve Aternius's purposes: all the guy's interested in is that *someone* should be nailed, and fast, so the whole thing gets buried and forgotten. Also, maybe, he smells a future chance of getting his hands on Thupeltha's land and consolidating his property into one big stretch that takes in half Vetuliscum. To make sure Papatius is in the running for Clusinus's murder as well – and so stitch the investigation up properly – the time of death has to be left uncertain, hence the hurdle. Then it's just a matter of pushing things on as quickly as possible by arresting Papatius and waiting for the guy with the noose. And if the nosy Roman doesn't like it then tough cheese.

I grinned into my wine. It all slotted together, sure it did. Bubo was no problem: robbery was enough of a motive to satisfy the militia, Aternius could've dealt with him any time, and because there was no link with the Vetuliscum murders the fact that Papatius was already out of the frame didn't matter. I might even manage a case for Hilarion. Sure, the timings were well out but Nepos could've been mistaken: the guy might've seen Aternius murdering Clusinus and been caught on his way back with the news.

Proving it all, though, was another matter. I didn't underestimate the opposition: the Cominii were tough nuts to crack, and purple-striper or not out in the sticks any clout I might have was limited. It was lucky we were on our way to Rome after all; sure, the original intention had been to interview Publius Bubo, and the tomb-robbing angle was a red herring now, but I still had friends there in high places. Maybe if I argued my case well enough at the praetor's office I could scare up some sort of official investigation from the city end.

Besides, I hadn't been back to Rome since Sejanus died. I hated to make the admission even to myself, but I was looking forward to it.

'You're looking pleased with yourself, Marcus.'

I let my eyes focus. Perilla was watching me, smiling. She looked relaxed and happy. Well, at least we could start having a proper holiday now. We might even go down to Baiae for the oysters, if I could swing the loan of a villa. I leaned over and kissed her.

'Yeah,' I said. 'The case is solved. Corvinus strikes again.'

'Really?' She sniffed. 'Now where have I heard that before?'

'Believe it.' We hit a pothole and the wine splashed over my wrist. 'Shit!'

'Hubris,' Perilla murmured. 'It serves you right.'

'Cut it out, lady.' I licked the skin clear and glanced out of the window. More scenery. Miles and miles of it. 'The gods don't speak through potholes.'

'Are we stopping somewhere for lunch?' The Princess had woken up. 'I'm starving.'

Yeah; come to think of it, I was hungry myself. Usually on these trips you bring your own food, but I'd had enough of coaches and being rattled around like a dry pea in a pod. We found a clean roadside cookshop and I watched the kid eat her way through a chicken while I explained to Perilla how everything fitted together.

34

We finally made Rome just before sunset. The Aurelian Road swings into the city from the west through a crease in the Janiculan, which is a chichi area of urban farmhouses that I don't know at all well, so the smell of ripe Tiber mud caught me almost unawares and brought tears to my eyes: Tiber mud, especially when there isn't an 'r' in the month, is about the most pungent substance known to man short of the Wart's boil ointment, and it doesn't take prisoners, either. The best smell in the world, bar none. I opened up my nostrils and drank it in.

Perilla was watching me while I did it. I couldn't quite place her expression: tolerant? amused? long-suffering? sad? It was all of these, and none of them.

'What's biting you, lady?' I said.

'Nothing.' She turned away. 'I'll be glad to get in. It's been a long day.'

The Princess, I noticed, was sitting quiet and eyes-front, which was unusual for her because breaks for sleep and omelette sandwiches excepted she'd spent the entire journey hanging out the window goat-spotting and chatting to Lysias. Then I remembered, and mentally kicked myself: she'd spent a large chunk of what should've been her childhood cooped up on the Janiculan before Perilla and I had sprung her, and the memories wouldn't be good. I was just glad she was sitting on the wrong side of the coach to catch a glimpse of the Tarpeian Rock once we were across the Tiber and in sight of the Capitol; but maybe that particular memory wouldn't register. She'd been up in the Alban Hills with Aunt Marcia when her father died, and she had no reason to remember that bastard with any fondness at all.

We crossed the Sublician Bridge that Horatius had defended against Lars Porsenna and the Tarquins – at least in its earlier version – and cut through Cattlemarket Square towards the Circus. It felt funny not to be making for the old Palatine house – that was sold, of course, long since – but Mother's house was straight on, on the Caelian, where the Staurian Incline met Head of Africa Road. We wouldn't be expected – I should've sent a slave ahead on horseback, but I hadn't bothered – but Mother for all her woolliness ruled the household with an iron rod, and we ought to be comfortable enough.

The streets were full: it was a beautiful evening and after their day's work people were out shopping, or maybe just strolling around taking the air. Ten hours in a coach, even with the extended lunch break, had left me fidgety. I shouted up to Lysias and got him to pull over.

'I'll walk the rest,' I said to Perilla. 'You mind, lady?'

'Not at all.' There was that expression again. 'Go ahead, Marcus. Enjoy yourself.'

I opened the door and jumped down, not bothering with the steps. I'd be just as quick walking anyway: the horses were tired, although Lysias hadn't been pushing them, and now we were inside Rome proper the going would be slow. In any case, now the sun was down the carts were out – wheeled traffic isn't allowed inside the city boundaries between dawn and dusk – and the Septimontium would be packed wheel-hub to wheel-hub.

It was good to feel stone under my sandals again. Sure, Athens has roads, of a kind, and they're far older than Rome's, but where they're paved the stone is smoother, less gritty. Slick, almost. The smells are different, too. You get roasted pumpkin-seed sellers in the Old Market by Twelve Gods and the Odeion, but somehow the scent that comes up off their braziers isn't quite the same. Maybe it's the overlay of Tiber mud. Foreigners say they can smell it as far east as Maecenas Gardens, and maybe that's true. For real Romans like me it's just the city's natural odour.

It must've been a race day. Oh, the Circus was closed by that time, sure, and the races would be long finished, but you can always tell when it's been a race day in the Circus district. People come in from all over and they don't go home when the gates shut; they hang around the local cookshops and wineshops eating and drinking and shooting the breeze until all hours, making a holiday of it. I saw one cheerful bastard – he looked like a Syrian – weaving his way past the Temple of Hercules clutching a wine jar like it was a baby and doling out cupfuls to everyone he met. The guy must've struck lucky on the cars – Syrians know their racing – and be blowing the proceeds; technically, organised gambling on the teams is illegal, but there're always touts, if you know where to get hold of them, and because they've got a reputation to keep up they usually pay out when they have to. Either that or sooner or later they're found stiff and cold up an alleyway or floating backside-up in the Tiber.

I saw another guy, too, mouth bloody, crawling along the pavement just short of Butchers' Market looking for his teeth while passers-by edged round him laughing. If he was another winner he'd obviously been mugged. Rome's no utopia, far from it. Sometimes it can hurt.

Still, it was good to be home.

I got to Mother's just behind Lysias. Mother's head slave, plus of course her mad chef Phormio the Dinner-Guest Poisoner, were with her and Priscus back at Vetuliscum, so there was only a scratch staff. Bathyllus, as was the little guy's wont, went through the buggers like a dose of salts and the result was that by the time I'd wrapped myself round a pre-dinner cup of Priscus's Falernian the baths were hot, the domestic arrangements were somewhere on the excellent side of average and Mother's slaves were wondering what the hell had hit them and which way was up. Credit where credit's due. I know I knock Bathyllus from time to time, sure, but that's not to say the little bald-headed hernia-sufferer isn't an organisational genius. If Bathyllus had been put in charge of the Second Punic War he'd've had that bastard Hannibal washing down the front steps of the Senate House and polishing Jupiter's thunderbolt before you could say 'elephants'. There wouldn't've been any backchat, either.

So by dinner-time I was nicely steamed and sweet-smelling. According to Perilla, as soon as he'd arrived Meton had gone off in the direction of the local market with the fixed expression of a sleepwalker, and despite the late hour the result was pheasant in a saffron nut sauce, truffles with spiced celery and half a dozen sweet cinnamon tartlets to follow. Plus the wine. Priscus may be no drinker, but for a fluffbrained academic he's no bad judge of quality, either; which means that his cellar's stacked with top-notch stuff that's sat there untouched for maybe ten or fifteen years and was drinkable when he bought it. I checked the label on the jar myself before Bathyllus dug the clay stopper out and took the stuff away for mixing: consuls Augustus Caesar for the twelfth time and Lucius Cornelius Sulla, which meant it was almost forty years old. And it wasn't from the reserve bin, what's more.

Beautiful!

'So.' I moved the dessert plate away and took an appreciative sip from my fifth cup. 'What're your plans for tomorrow, lady?'

Perilla glanced at the Princess who was tucking in to half a vineful of grapes. That on top of more than her fair share of the pheasant and three tartlets. Jupiter! You'd think she hadn't eaten for a month! 'I thought we'd have a look at the mantle shops in Augustus Market,' she said. 'Then perhaps up to the Saepta.'

'Unless you want to take me with you, Corvinus,' Marilla said. 'I've got all the mantles I need, and I've nothing else to get except a present for Aunt Marcia. Sleuthing would be a lot more fun than shopping.'

Yeah, well, I'd go along with that. Shopping I hate. If the concept had been around when Prometheus was nailed for fire-smuggling, instead of being chained to a cliff while a vulture ate his liver the gods could've had him tag along while his wife chose a new pair of earrings. 'Sorry, Bright-Eyes,' I said. 'I'll have a lot of ground to cover.'

'You're seeing Lippillus?' Perilla said. Lippillus was a guy I'd known off and on for years, currently the head of the Public Pond district Watch. What he didn't know about what went on in Rome – or anything else you could think of, for that matter – wasn't worth quoting.

'I thought I might.' I took a pull at the Falernian. 'Then up to the praetor's office on the Capitol. Plus the Sacred Way, of course, for Publius Bubo.'

'Take your time, then. Don't hurry back.'

I grinned. 'You got two or three ex-lovers you want to visit while we're here, lady?'

'No. I just thought you'd like some time to yourself.'

Jupiter! Sometimes I couldn't make Perilla out. Back in Vetuliscum she'd been complaining that I was spending all the hours the gods sent out and about talking to potential candidates for a murder rap; now we were in Rome she couldn't get rid of me fast enough. If it had been anyone else but Perilla my last question might not've been a joke.

'Yeah. Right,' I said. 'You can keep Lysias and the carriage, incidentally. I'll walk. And I'll see you back here for dinner.'

She yawned suddenly. 'Juno, I'm tired,' she said. 'I think I'll go to bed.'

I glanced at her over my wine cup. Well, I know when I'm being propositioned. 'Fine,' I said, downing the last of the Falernian. 'Good idea. You want to pack in too, Princess?'

Marilla's eyes were already closing. She nodded.

'Okay. Let's call it a day.'

We made love in the main guest bedroom to the sound of carts rumbling back and forth beneath the window. Afterwards, I thought the noise would keep me awake – you don't get much passing traffic in Diomeia and of course at Vetuliscum one guy on a mule is news – but it didn't, any more than it ever had in the house on the Palatine. I went out like a light and stayed out until I was woken up just after dawn by our door slave arguing with the neighbour's over whose turn it was for the dung shovel.

35

I left Perilla sleeping, ate a quick breakfast and set out
for Public Pond.

The Pond is Rome's Twelfth District, lying south-west
of the Caelian and taking in half of the Aventine and the
Remuria: everything, in fact, between Ostia Road to the
west and the Capenan Gate to the east. As one of the
seven Regional Watch Commanders, Lippillus was in
charge of both it and the Circus district that stretched
up towards the Sublician. No sinecure, in other words.
I had a lot of time for Flavonius Lippillus. When I'd
first met him about ten years before he'd looked like
a fresh-faced kid just into his first adult mantle, and he
had the sharpest brain I'd ever come across. Since then
he'd come a long way. He'd lost the fresh-faced look and
matured into something between a dwarf and a pixie,
but the brain was still there. It was a mark of how good
the guy was at his job that he'd made commander status
fifteen years early and kept it, even in a business where
names are everything: you can search the old consular
and tribunician rolls until you're blue, but you won't find
no Flavonii Lippilli.

Maybe that was another reason why I liked him.

I called in at Watch headquarters and got one of the squaddies. I'd missed Lippillus by about ten minutes: there'd been a late-night break-in at a house near the Temple of the Good Goddess, and the owner had got fatally in the way. The squaddie gave me more precise directions and I went round to see if I could catch him up.

The house was easy to spot, largely because of the dozen or so ghouls hanging about round the doorway waiting for the corpse to be lugged out. It was an upmarket property by Aventine standards, which meant it wasn't a tenement, and whoever had built it had cleverly sited the little garden so it got watered for free by the drips coming from the Appian Aqueduct overhead. There was a squaddie on the steps keeping the ghouls at bay, but I gave him my name and Lippillus's and he let me through.

When I went into the tiny atrium Lippillus was kneeling by the dead man examining the wound on the side of his head.

'Festus, get—' he began, and then did a double-take when he looked round and saw me. 'Corvinus? What the hell are you doing in Rome?'

I grinned. 'Breaking promises.'

He set the man's head down gently on the tiled floor, stood up and wiped his hands on his tunic. I noticed they left red smears.

'You made them, friend,' he said. 'You can break them.'

'Yeah.' I nodded at the corpse. While it was still erect and breathing it'd been a wizened-looking man in his sixties with warts and a penchant for brightly coloured bathrobes. Now it was just sad. 'Anything interesting?'

'No. Just the usual. The bastards got in through the garden door. They probably thought the house was empty, because the neighbour says the rest of the family were at the races. Unfortunately for this old guy he had a bout of rheumatics at the last minute and stayed in bed.' He frowned. 'We'll get them. Maybe. If we're lucky.'

'How's Marcina Paullina?' Marcina was Lippillus's 'stepmother': definitely in inverted commas, because the lady was long widowed, only a couple of years older than he was and built like an African Praxiteles Venus. Also, I'd seen their sleeping arrangements.

'She's okay. Eating too many honeyed dates, though.' He grinned suddenly, and his ugly face lit up. 'You here for long?'

'Only a couple of days. We've borrowed a place near Caere.'

'Perilla's with you?'

'Sure. And the Princess.'

'Business or pleasure?'

'Business.' I hesitated. 'You know of a guy named Publius Herminius Bubo? Has an antiques store on the Sacred Way?'

'The Owl?' He hadn't even paused for thought, but that didn't surprise me: what Lippillus didn't know about Rome and Romans you could write on a bust sandal strap and forget. 'Sure. Just round the corner from Venus's Temple. What sort of business?'

'Maybe nothing.' I gave him a quick run-down of the Vetuliscum situation. 'I just need to talk with him. Tie up the loose end.'

'Uh-huh.' He was rubbing his jaw. Obviously he hadn't had time to get shaved that morning because I could hear the rasp. 'Loose ends I don't know about, but you're right about him being a crook. And about the high-class fencing angle. We've had our eye on the bastard for years.'

So. The brothers had been two of a kind. That added up nicely.

'Only an eye?' I said.

'More than that sometimes, but nothing serious so far. Or nothing we can prove. The Owl's sharp but he'll step out of line some day.'

Yeah; that made sense, too. Aulus Bubo had been so sharp that he'd cut himself. Still, that was the risk guys like that took. The grey area between legal and illegal was lucrative, but put a foot wrong and you could find yourself in an urn. 'You have time for a cup of wine, pal?' I said.

Lippillus glanced back at the corpse. 'Sorry, Corvinus. Not now, I've got people to talk to. Later, sure, if you want.'

Yeah, well; I supposed the guy did have his living to earn, and though he hadn't said as much he'd have other things on his mind than entertaining layabout aristocrats. 'No problem,' I said. 'Perilla's given me the whole day off. Just tell me a time and place.'

'Hold on. We can do better than that.' His brow creased. 'You in a hurry to see the Owl?'

'No.' I wasn't; I'd been meaning to call in at the Foreign Praetor's office on the Capitol first to see what I could arrange in the way of an investigation of the Cominii, and like most officials these guys tended to get grouchy if you infringed on their afternoon siesta. 'I'd planned that for after lunch.'

'Fine. There's a cookshop halfway along Tuscan. They do good tripe with fennel. Meet me there an hour after noon and have a jug waiting and we'll go together once we've finished it. I wouldn't mind the chance to sweat the Owl myself.'

'Great.' I paused. 'Uh . . . you're sure you're not tramping on anyone's corns here, pal?' I wasn't just being polite: the question needed asking. Whether Lippillus chose to put it that way or not he was doing me a big favour here because having a Watch Commander at my shoulder when I talked to the Owl would give me clout in spades; but at the same time he was putting himself out on a professional limb, and he knew it. Lippillus's patch was the Eleventh and Twelfth Districts, full stop. The Venus's Temple stretch of the Sacred Way is Fourth District, and one thing you learn early in any business is not to poach.

'Screw that, Corvinus.' Lippillus laughed. 'The Three and Four commander's Ummidius Quadratus. He's a nice guy, and he doesn't like crooks. Especially crooks he can't get to. If we can nail the Owl he'll pick up our cookshop tab and whistle while he does it. He might even throw in a couple of jars of Caecuban to make up the difference.'

'That desperate, eh? Fair enough.' I turned to go. 'Thanks, Lippillus. I'll see you at the cookshop.'

'Right, pal.' He was already bending to re-examine the corpse. 'Order Setinian. Their Falernian stinks.'

I crossed the Septimontium and cut across the Palatine for old times' sake, even if it did mean climbing unnecessary stairs. Mind you, I hardly noticed the extra effort involved: one thing about a holiday in Caere, your calf muscles end up like knotted cord. I had meant to make a detour to take in our old place but I changed my mind: that was finished with, and I've never been one to cling to the past. Still, it would've been nice. In front of the House of Augustus and the slightly grander Palace of Tiberius, where the Wart, of course, wasn't, and hadn't been for some time, was the usual crowd of gawping tourists, and

I had to push my way through; these bloody Egyptians get everywhere, and they don't move for you, either.

Nice curses, though.

Finally I cut my losses, went down Cacus Staircase into the Velabrum and turned right along Tuscan Street. I spotted Lippillus's cookshop straight off; sure enough, it had tripe with fennel on the board, and I'd bet it would be as good as the guy had said. I'd timed it perfectly: the sun was just past its full quarter and I wasn't all that far now from the Market Place and the Capitol.

This could be tricky. Having been away from the political scene for so long – and I'd never been part of it in any case – I wasn't sure how things were going to go. If I was lucky, I'd find that the relevant praetorian official was one of my old cronies. That, at least, was a distinct possibility: most of them would be in pretty senior positions by now, and they were the guys I needed, especially if they had a pedigree you could measure by the yard. Prominent Italian provincial families like the Cominii might still not have the clout of the Junii Silani or the Aemilii Lepidi, but things in the social world were changing fast and you couldn't be sure any more who was related to who. And unless your bastard was a bigger bastard with better connections than the bastard you were trying to nail you might as well go home and grow radishes.

That's how the world works. You can knock it, sure, but you can't change it. Not even Augustus could do that.

I found the praetor's office and waited for the guy on the desk to finish picking his nose and ask what I wanted.

'Caere?' he said. 'That's part of the Latium district. The rep's office is third corridor, second on your left.'

'Who is the rep, pal?' I said. 'You know?'

He shrugged. 'Search me. I only know the offices. These buggers come and go like punters in a cathouse.' And he went back to bursting his boils.

I made my way down the corridor, found the door and knocked.

'Come in.'

My heart sank. Shit. I knew that voice. Forget lucky; forget persuading the guy to mount an investigation, too. I might as well try whistling Pindar's Second Pythian through my left ear.

I pushed the door open.

'Hi, Crispus,' I said.

36

If anyone is ever nicked for pissing on my grave after I've gone it'll be Caelius Crispus. Not that it's my fault, I've got no particular down on the guy; it's just that whatever evil-minded god or goddess arranges these things has managed to bring me into contact with the oily little bastard more than either of us have liked, and it's invariably led to tears. His, mostly, but like I say that isn't my fault. Call it fate.

The clang of his jaw hitting the desk when he saw me had been almost audible. Now he was looking at me like I'd just taken my head off and waved it at him.

'Oh, gods,' he said. 'Marcus bloody Corvinus.'

'Right.' I closed the door behind me, pulled up a chair, sat down, and grinned at him across the desk. 'How are you, Crispus?'

No answer; he was still in shock.

I tried another angle. 'This is a surprise. I thought you worked in the Treasury, pal.'

A muscle beside his right eye twitched. He was still staring like if he did it long enough I'd fade into philosophical atoms.

'I moved,' he said.

'Yeah. Yeah, so I see.' I looked round. 'Nice office. I like your taste in dados.'

'You still married to that Perilla female?'

'Last time I looked.' I don't know what Crispus has against Perilla. Sure, she was largely responsible for getting him chucked out of the Happy Bachelors' Club when we gatecrashed their tutu evening on the Pincian, but you can only hold a grudge for so long. And she didn't mean it.

Well, not really.

Well . . .

'What the hell are you doing back in Rome?' The guy was slowly getting some of his bottle back. He looked a better colour, too. 'I thought you'd settled permanently in Athens.'

Good; we'd got past the social niceties stage and down to business. I gave him my best smile.

'Actually,' I said, 'that's why I'm here. We're holidaying with my mother and stepfather at a place called Vetuliscum. Near Caere.'

Crispus frowned. 'Vetuliscum? That rings a bell.'

'It should. We had a couple of murders there and you'll be trying the case in five days' time.' That was another total bummer; with Crispus on the bench and me defending Papatius had about as much chance of staying alive as a fly in a meat-grinder. Still, the effort had to be made. 'I thought you might be interested to know that the guy they nailed didn't do it.'

'Is that so?' He puffed up like a Calabrian doughnut. 'Don't you think that as the judge I'm the best person to decide that?'

Uh-huh. Same old Crispus, right in with both feet. Yeah, well, some openings are too tempting to ignore, however polite you're trying to be.

'You want a straight answer to that, pal?' I said. 'And with or without the colourful language?'

'I'm the praetor's representative, dammit!' he snapped.

'Only because you've got something on him he wouldn't want made public when he runs for consul.'

It was a shot in the dark, sure, but I was fairly certain it would hit the target. Crispus and I went back a long way. He might be well on the sunny side of respectable these days, but I'd bet his modus operandi hadn't changed since I'd saved his balls for him – literally – fifteen years before. Crispus lived and thrived by knowing things about important people, things that in most cases if they came out would get the buggers the Rock, or at least make animal lovers everywhere seriously displeased. From Treasury clerk – disgraced Treasury clerk, thanks to me – to praetor's rep for a whole district was quite a hike, but a praetor makes his own appointments. Whatever seedy hold the guy had over his boss it must've been a beaut.

Hit the target it did. Crispus went white, and then puce. He opened his mouth to say something but no sound came out. I smiled at him and waited.

'All right, Corvinus,' he said. 'Who do you think did it?'

'A guy called Aternius.'

'That name's familiar as well.'

'He's the investigating officer.'

There was a long silence.

'He is *what*?' Crispus's eyes were bulging. If he'd been an older man I'd've thought he was having an apoplectic seizure.

'The investigating officer. The bastard in charge of the case. His uncle's the Caeretan mayor. One gets you ten he's mixed up in it too.'

There was another long silence. Only this one was longer than the first, and you could've used it for pickling walnuts. When it had finished, Crispus said quietly; 'Get the fuck out of my office. And don't come back until hell freezes over, if then. You understand?'

I sighed. Ah, well. It had been a thought. But I'd known as soon as I walked in the door I was on to a loser. I stood up.

'Right,' I said. 'Thanks, pal. I'll see you around.'

'Not if I see you first.'

I was on my way out when he said, 'Corvinus! Wait a minute!'

I turned. 'Yeah?'

'What makes you think this Aternius is responsible?'

'He and his uncle are involved in a property scam. Then there's the possibility that—' I stopped. Maybe it was the gleam in his eye that warned me, but I suddenly decided baring my soul to the praetor's rep wasn't such a hot idea after all. Not if the rep was Caelius Crispus. 'Never mind. Thanks for your time.'

'Don't mention it. Just go away and don't come back.' He was already shuffling memo tablets like a good administrator should. 'And tell that bitch of a wife of yours to keep her distance.'

I left him to his dados.

It wasn't quite noon when I came down the Capitol steps and pushed my way through the Market Place crowds. An hour before I was due to meet Lippillus. Hardly worth going anywhere: I'd've liked a stroll through the Subura, but I'd no sooner have got there than I'd've had to come back. Also my stomach was rumbling. I took a right down Tuscan and headed for the cookshop.

It was busy already, and most of the tables were full:

a good sign, because cookshops where you're liable to
end up with gutrot half an hour after you've eaten tend
to be pretty empty, even if they are in the city centre.
That's if they manage to hang on to their licences at all: a
couple of stonemasons or a pig-herder knocked off their
perches by a stew that glows in the dark might slip by
unremarked in the wilds of the Thirteenth District, but
when you've got punters from the Public Health and
Sanitation Department up the hill among your customers
that kind of thing gets noticed. I parked myself at a table
by the door and followed Lippillus's advice by ordering
up a jug of Setinian, plus a plate of cheese and olives to
keep me going until it was time for the tripe.

That had been a narrow squeak; in fact, I might've
already scuppered myself as far as the trial went. Now
Crispus knew there was something whacky about Aternius
I wouldn't put it past the bugger to indulge in a little
pre-trial blackmail. If – when – the case came to court
he might well have come to an arrangement with the
Cominii whereby in return for a backhander the accused
was found guilty whatever evidence there was to the
contrary, because the alternative would be to reopen the
whole can of worms; and that, if he was guilty himself,
Aternius couldn't risk.

Which meant that Papatius was more cooked than
ever. After that little interview I couldn't even hope for
an unbiased judge. Nice one, Corvinus. I'd've done better
to have stayed at home.

So where the hell did I go from here? Aternius was
the murderer, sure he was: of Navius by proxy, Clusinus,
maybe Bubo, actually, and Hilarion probably. The theory
fitted the facts like a glove. My only problem was proof,
and that I didn't look like getting. Nohow, no way,
never.

I hadn't got any further thinking about it when Lippillus showed up. I'd been hoping that he'd solve the problem once I'd explained it with a brilliant flash of insight, but he didn't. Ah, well. That was fair enough. The one drawback to Lippillus is he's a Roman first and last, in the city sense. If the murders had happened in the Subura, or even up on the Janiculan, he'd've been full of ideas because Rome's his patch, it's relevant. Anything beyond the city boundaries, forget it. It's not that he's not interested or willing to help, it's just as if his brain refuses to work outside the fourth milestone, over little things like murders, anyway. So in the end we ate our tripe, drank the wine, ordered another jug and talked about how life had treated us since we'd seen each other last. Then I fought him for the bill and we set off to talk to Publius the Owl.

37

The Sacred Way's one of the oldest streets in Rome, a blend of magnificence and squalor. The squalid element's made up of buildings that look like they've been around since Brutus threw out the Tarquins. Their walls are timber and mud-brick, with more patching and holes than a street-sweeper's tunic, and every so often in among the graffiti and scrawled adverts for personal services a black streak from pavement to roof that could've been made by one of Brennus's cookfires. Most of them are used for storage or as squats by the city's drifting population, but some are mansions belonging to hard-line Republican families that've been living in them since Cincinnatus ploughed his first furrow and ain't never going to move nohow for no one.

The newer properties are a lot more upmarket. They only date back fifty or so years to the time when Augustus was on his marble-for-brick jag, and they stand out like ivory false teeth in an old woman's grin. The Owl's shop was one of these, on a prime corner site with a nice view of the Palatine to the south. Even from the outside, it smelled of money. Crooked or not, the guy must've been pulling it in hand over fist. There was a slave on the door, which again made sense: upmarket traders don't encourage riff-raff on the lookout for somewhere to shelter from the rain or a quick see-and-grab, and a bouncer's standard equipment. He wasn't the usual gorilla squeezed into a sharp tunic to make him blend with the decor, either; we got a bow that wouldn't've disgraced a high-class major-domo.

Impressive.

The inside was impressive, too, more like a private house than a shop, even down to the pool in the middle and the hole in the roof above to let in light and catch the rainwater. No counter, and although there were more statues and bits of furniture around than you'd ever get in an ordinary property they weren't obtrusive. Money again: the trick, when you're dealing with the market the Owl was obviously targeting, is not to show everything you've got at once. Bulk's vulgar; space makes room for a bigger price tag.

The guy himself fitted the part. Forget the greasy shopkeeper in a tunic with bits of last night's dinner sticking to it: the Owl was sitting in a chair like a consul's and his mantle was better than mine and three shades cleaner. He rose and came over smiling.

'Good afternoon, gentlemen,' he said; shit, we had a real smoothie here. 'And how may I help you?'

'The name's Valerius Corvinus, pal,' I said. 'This is Watch Commander Flavonius Lippillus.'

'Yes?' The Owl's eyes flicked to Lippillus and a lot of the smoothness disappeared. 'Correct me if I'm wrong, but I thought the commander of the local Watch was Ummidius Quadratus. With whom, may I say, I'm on excellent terms.'

'Come off it, Owl.' Lippillus was grinning. 'Save that for the customers. Quadratus wouldn't touch you with gloves and a ten-foot pole.'

The guy stiffened and blinked slowly. 'Owl' was right: his eyes were grey and round, with the biggest, blackest pupils I'd ever seen. There was a drowsiness about him, too, that didn't quite square up; maybe he was on something, like that whacky *qef* stuff I'd come across in Athens. He stared at Lippillus for a long time then turned back to me.

'What exactly is it you want?' he said.

That was better; me, I've always preferred short sentences and simple grammar. 'You're Aulus Bubo's brother, right?'

Another long pause. The eyelids went down and up. 'Aulus is dead. I had the news from his wife three days ago. Unfortunately I wasn't free to attend the funeral.'

'You were pretty close, I understand. Partners, even.'

'We're in the same business, yes.'

'He supply you with stuff to sell to the rich punters here?'

'Sometimes. Naturally enough. The Roman market is more buoyant, and as you say the customers have more to spend.'

'You know where the goods came from?'

Pause. 'Where do antiques usually come from? Aulus had his sources of supply, as do I: private individuals, auctioneering firms, even collectors who for reasons of their own decide to part with a particular piece.'

'Crooks?'

He blinked again. This time I was the one to get the death-stare. 'Corvinus, or whatever your name is,' he said softly, 'that is defamation. No doubt your friend here will confirm the fact if you know no law yourself. Also that it's actionable. Now if you're not bona fide customers I'd be grateful if you would leave my premises, please, before I call my slave and have you removed forcibly.'

So we were back to the long sentences. Lippillus grunted and muttered something profane under his breath, but we'd agreed in the cookshop that this was my show. I didn't move. 'You ever hear of a guy called Clusinus?' I said. 'Titus Clusinus?'

'No.'

He was lying; sure he was.

'How about Gaius Aternius?'

His eyes shifted. 'I've warned you once,' he said. 'I won't do so again. You're clearly not here for legitimate commercial purposes and I would like you to leave.'

I moved up close, and he flinched. 'What's the penalty for robbing tombs, pal? Maybe you can tell me that. Also, why your law-abiding brother should have his head stove in with a hammer.'

For the first time the Owl's bland face showed a spark of expression and his tongue licked out over his lower lip. 'Aulus always did think too little of security,' he said. 'He was killed by a casual robber.'

Yeah, I might believe that at a pinch, but the Owl clearly didn't; the guy was shit scared, and it showed. I had my lever and I knew it.

'He thought enough of security to build a new strong-room under his shop,' I said. 'One he never got round to using. What was he planning to put in there that he didn't already have? Tomb goods that his crony Clusinus stole for him and he was going to ferry down to you when he'd collected enough?'

The Owl glanced at Lippillus and his mouth opened but no sound came out.

'Your brother's dead, pal.' I lowered my voice. 'So's Clusinus. That's two out of three. Now if I were feeling particularly bloody-minded I'd walk out of here right now and forget the whole thing. Sure, the murders happened in Caere but I have the feeling that whoever was responsible wants the partnership completely dissolved with no loose ends. You a betting man, Owl? You want to bet he doesn't know about you or where to find you, or that he hasn't got the fare to Rome? Because that's just what you're doing here.' Silence. I turned away. 'Ah, the hell, Lippillus, let's—'

'I wasn't involved. At no point was I involved. I wish to make that perfectly clear.'

I turned back. Got the bugger!

Big grey eyes blinked at me. 'It was Aulus's scheme. Aulus and Clusinus. I asked no more than my usual commission.'

Yeah, sure; and my name was Tiberius Caesar. 'Go on,' I said.

There was a single bead of sweat on the Owl's forehead. 'Clusinus came to Aulus. He said he'd found a way into a tomb. He couldn't get there very often but if Aulus would handle what he brought out he was willing to make a deal for a cash advance and a half share of the proceeds. That's all I know.'

I frowned; there was something wrong here ...

'Where was this tomb?' That was Lippillus. He'd obviously decided that he'd played the stooge for long enough.

'Somewhere in the Caere cemeteries. Clusinus wouldn't tell him the exact location.'

'He mention any more partners?' I said. 'Your brother, I mean?'

'No. Not to me. Only him and Clusinus.'

'Not a smoothie lawyer called Gaius Aternius?'

'You asked me that before. I've never heard of the man.'

'You said that about Titus Clusinus too, pal.'

305 •

'It's the truth, nevertheless.'

Uh-huh. Well, there was no reason for Bubo to tell his brother about any arrangement with Gaius Aternius. Not that that would save the Owl once the bastard got around to . . .

I stopped and backtracked as the implications of what we were being told caught up with me.

Shit.

We weren't talking tombs at all. The Owl had said one tomb; *one* tomb, precise location unspecified, with a secret way in . . .

Hell. If the guy was telling the truth then we were screwed. I'd been basing my theory on tombs, plural, looted over a period of months or years; also on the assumption that both the other partners would know which tombs Clusinus would be robbing at any particular time. Or at least the area involved. They'd have to, because the Cominii would need that information to work their trick with the militia.

One tomb 'somewhere in the Caere cemeteries' that only Clusinus knew about and was robbing in his free time made the whole thing a nonsense. There was no point to an arrangement with the Cominii at all. And if that went then everything went.

Jupiter's balls on a string! I felt like weeping!

'Corvinus? You all right?' Lippillus was staring at me.

'Sure,' I said. 'Just a touch of wind.'

That got me another strange look, but Lippillus was no fool and he didn't chase the subject. Oh, well, it wasn't the end of the world. We weren't beat yet. Maybe Clusinus had had his own deal going with the Cominii and Aternius had just hired him to kill Navius. When you got down to it the tomb scam didn't actually need to have anything directly to do with the murders at all,

I'd already worked that out. Not Clusinus's or Navius's, anyway. And Bubo's death could still be coincidence. It was just a case of letting the pattern rearrange itself.

I turned back to the Owl. 'How far gone was this scam, pal?' I said. According to the original theory it'd never got further than a gleam in Bubo's wicked little eye. Now everything was back up for grabs I just didn't know what to assume any more.

'Clusinus was still . . . negotiating with my brother, as I understand.'

'Yeah? Using what as bait?' The eyes blinked, but that was all I got. Something cold touched my spine. Why I'd asked the question I didn't quite know, but it'd gone home. I felt Lippillus tense up, too. 'Come on, Owl! Your brother was a smart businessman. A small-time crook from out in the sticks tells him he's got a private tunnel into a big Caere tomb but wants some money up front before he starts stripping it, Bubo's going to send him away with a flea in his ear. If he can still talk for laughing. Unless the guy happens to have a couple of samples to get him hooked, prove the whole thing's on the level. And in that case Bubo would want to test the market, see how much the deal was likely to be worth. That means you. So give!'

Silence. Lippillus cleared his throat.

'Or of course if you prefer instead,' he said conversationally, 'while Corvinus here carries on his chat with you I could go round to the local Watch headquarters and bring back Quadratus and a few of the lads to turn over your shop. In which case the provenance of everything we find – and I mean everything – will be investigated very carefully indeed, and should the requisite purchase receipts not be immediately forthcoming we will then pin your crooked hide to your fancy front door with the rustiest set of nails we can lay our hands on. How does that sound?'

The Owl blinked at him. Then without a word he went over to the strongbox that stood against one of the walls, took a key from his mantle fold, opened it and brought something out. He handed it to Lippillus.

I looked. The thing was a gold bracelet with a raised granular decoration. It was old, very old, and one of the most beautiful bits of jewellery I'd ever seen. Jupiter alone knew what it'd sell for, but I'd've hated to be picking up the tab.

'Thank you,' Lippillus said formally. 'I'll give you a receipt, naturally.'

'Don't bother,' the Owl said. 'Just take it and get the hell out of my shop.'

'As you like. That's all?'

'All I got. All my brother ever got. I swear it.'

Lippillus weighed the thing in his hand and looked at me. I nodded.

'Well, I hope you're right, Owl,' he said. 'I really do. Because if we find you're lying you'll be lucky to end up peddling good-luck charms from a tray in Cattlemarket Square with both your hands attached.'

The Owl swallowed and said nothing.

As we left, my brain was buzzing. I'd seen a piece like that before; another bracelet, not nearly so fine, sure, or so big, but the style was the same. Thupeltha had been wearing it when I'd last seen her in Vesia's kitchen.

38

There wasn't much else I could do in Rome, not as far
as the case was concerned. In a way it'd been a wasted
journey: finding out that Crispus was the praetor's rep
for Caere had been a real bummer, and all my talk with
the Owl had done was pull the plug on my pet theory.
Or part of it, anyway. On the other hand, at least I knew
now that the rep *would* be Crispus and that particular
avenue was a dead end, and on the personal level I was
quite looking forward to the trial. Maybe Aternius hadn't
passed on my name to the Roman authorities or more
likely Crispus hadn't bothered to read the preliminary
info sheet properly; but whatever the reason was he
obviously didn't know who Papatius's lawyer would be,
and I'd been very careful not to tell him. I could just see
the look on the bastard's face when he came into court
and saw me on the defending counsel's bench.

Another plus was that I'd got the bracelet. I'd thought
Lippillus might've hung on to it as evidence against the
Owl, but he'd shrugged as he'd handed it over.

'Evidence for what, Corvinus?' he'd said. 'Sure, we've
got his witnessed admission that it came from a tomb,
and maybe we could nail him for fencing stolen goods.

But the admission is all we've got. His partners're dead, the scam's buried and we don't know which tomb it came from. The Owl's slid out from under too many raps already, and this time I want him stitched. If you can use it to find the information from the other end go ahead with my blessing.' He grinned. 'And if the bastard does happen to get his head bashed in like his brother in the next few days Quadratus won't be shedding any tears.'

I winced. A nice guy, Lippillus, but all Watch commanders have that hard streak to them; it goes with the job. And he didn't like crooks.

I'd planned to go straight back to Vetuliscum the next morning, but I decided that wouldn't be fair to Perilla and the Princess: two ten-hour coach journeys inside three days doesn't constitute much of a holiday, and the lady still had the other half of the Saepta to buy up. So we spent the day bumming around. I took my walk through the Subura – it hadn't changed much, except some bits of it had fallen down and been replaced with other bits that looked the same, only in worse condition – and called in at Scylax's Gym to check that the financial whizz-kid Daphnis wasn't screwing me over the accounts. The place was doing pretty well. The ex-centurion I'd got in when Scylax had died to handle the practical side of the business had gone on the wagon – when he'd started to see little green and pink Illyrian tribesmen crawling up the walls his long-suffering daughter had finally blown the whistle and pocketed the wine cellar key – and the punters were getting real value for money. He was no masseur, though, and Daphnis had hired a big guy from Patavium with muscles like rocks and hands like grappling hooks. I risked one session and decided to let my flab stay where it was. In the evening we had

Lippillus and Marcina round to dinner, and I sent one
of Mother's slaves to Agron's place in Ostia to ask him
and his wife as well. Meton went overboard and cooked
us an ostrich. Jupiter knew where he'd got it from –
high-class poultry you need to order days in advance,
unless it's featured on the programme at the Games
in which case there's a temporary glut – but it made
his holiday, too, and a happy chef is a thing of pure
delight.

We made the return trip next day.

That bracelet of Thupeltha's was preying on my mind
the whole journey. Yeah, the natural assumption was
that she'd got it from Clusinus as a love-gift, but I had
reservations about that explanation: the lady had said
herself that there'd been nothing between the two but
sex, and if both parties had been happy with that arrangement, which they seemed to have been, then love-gifts
just didn't figure. Also, like I'd noticed at the time, the
thing was worth serious money. I hadn't known Clusinus
when the guy was a viable proposition, but from what I'd
heard about him he didn't seem the kind to throw pricey
presents around. Added to which with Larth Papatius
growling away in the background it was in his interests
to keep his affair with Thupeltha low-key.

So if not from Clusinus then where had she got it?
Not from Bubo; as far as I knew there was no connection there, and in any case I couldn't see that sharp
entrepreneurial bastard dishing out gold bracelets either,
especially when he already had a girlfriend who'd no
doubt show herself more than usually grateful for a
snazzy piece of jewellery like that. And why should Bubo
give Thupeltha a present of any kind?

The only other candidate was Gaius Aternius.

Sure, the Owl had said he wasn't involved in the tomb-robbing scam, and if Clusinus hadn't needed anyone to watch his back as far as the militia were concerned then he didn't have a role to play there anyway. Still, like I'd said, that was no reason for scrubbing him out of the picture altogether. If he wanted Navius dead, which he did, and a suitable fall-guy to frame for the killing, which he also did, then Clusinus was as good as any and far better than most, and the connection between them still held. At the same time, Clusinus had his own scam cooking with the tomb-robbing angle, and in his free moments he was screwing Thupeltha. So. Let's put Aternius, Thupeltha, Clusinus, the tomb and the murders together and see what came up.

The first point was the lady's credibility, or rather lack of it. I'd rate Thupeltha's honesty and frankness quotient pretty low now, if not at absolute zero. She knew about the tomb, sure she did: the fact that she had the bracelet alone proved that, because you don't find these things at your friendly local jeweller's. Which meant either that Clusinus had told her or she'd found out about it some other way. And if Thupeltha knew about the tomb then we were looking at a whole new ball game.

Second there was her susceptibility where men were concerned. I didn't like Aternius myself, but the guy obviously had an attraction for women: he'd hooked Sicinia Rufina, I'd seen the effect he'd had on Mother and even Perilla had started out on his side. If for reasons of his own Aternius had made a play for Thupeltha then I wouldn't've laid any bets against her having taken him on: Clusinus may've been up to par as a local stud, but the mayor of Caere's nephew would be a real catch.

Okay; so let's work on the assumption that Aternius and Thupeltha are an item, and that they're in this together for their own separate reasons. Or maybe that Aternius is using Thupeltha to further his own schemes. How would it work?

Scenario. Aternius has fixed it with Clusinus to get rid of Navius as per the theory. Now what he has to do is to set up the actual murder so that Clusinus is sure to take the rap. The problem is that both the prospective victim and the prospective killer are free agents. He has to bring them together at a place and time of his own choosing without either of them knowing they've been manoeuvred, whereupon things will take their natural course; and that's tricky.

The answer's Thupeltha. With her on the team the problem disappears because Thupeltha's got an in with both Navius and Clusinus and she can swing the deal without arousing either guy's suspicions. On the chosen day she arranges a meeting with each of them separately, but for the same place and the same time; not in the holm-oak grove, like she said, but further up the track. She goes as far as the grove and hides in the bushes while Navius goes past. Then she waits for long enough to fit in with the story she'll tell later about talking to Navius and sets off home. Meanwhile Navius has met with Clusinus, who chops him according to contract and leaves the scene of the crime. At which point Priscus strolls up unexpectedly, does his bit with the knife and junks Aternius's whole plan for him.

So far so good, and it fitted the facts as well as anything else did. Now for the cover-up.

Thupeltha's running scared. Clusinus doesn't know about her connection with Aternius, but he knows damn well that she's lied and is lying about the grove being the meeting point, and soon he's going to start wondering why, which neither she nor Aternius want. According to the original plan it wouldn't've mattered because he'd already be behind bars and to have raised the point would've put the noose round his neck faster than he could spit, but now he isn't even on the list. Nevertheless, both he and she know he did the killing. So she talks it over with Aternius. They decide that to give them breathing space she'll offer, out of the goodness of her heart, to do Clusinus a favour: she'll tell the world that Navius left her vowing suicide.

For Aternius it's only a stopgap, sure: Clusinus knows too much to live. The problem is, he's already been tagged as the honest citizen who reports a murder, and first impressions are hard to shift. So instead of being zeroed by judicial process he has to be killed personally, and that's a bummer because as soon as it happens people will start thinking again in terms of foul play. Luckily this smartass Roman comes up with the perfect theory which lets him pin both killings on Thupeltha's husband Larth Papatius . . .

That was the stumbling block. Sure, the marriage was no marriage at all in the real sense, and Thupeltha was a cold bitch, but was she cold enough to stand by and see her husband set up for a murder he hadn't committed? Because this, if anywhere, was where the bracelet had come in. I remembered her telling me categorically the morning Papatius had been arrested that the guy hadn't done it; telling *me*, not Aternius, and that was the point. Him she hadn't spoken to at all. She hadn't said a word, in fact, from the moment we came in to the time they'd left taking her husband with them, and maybe that had been significant. Jupiter knew how Aternius had found out about Clusinus's tomb – maybe he'd known all along, or maybe he'd forced the information out of the guy before he'd killed him – but if the theory was right Thupeltha had traded her husband's life for a cut of the deal, and that I just didn't like to think about.

Yeah. It was all possible, sure. Whether it was true was another matter. What was certainly true was that I'd have to have another talk with Thupeltha.

39

The day after we got back was another one of these close,
thundery ones with lightning flickering in the hills to the
east. The rains couldn't be far off now. I had an early
breakfast and set off into Vetuliscum. I'd got the Owl's
bracelet in my pouch to show Priscus in the hopes that
he might be able to tell me about it, maybe even suggest
a tomb it might've come from.

I called in at Thupeltha's first. She was in the yard
round the side of the wineshop, collecting eggs. Pleased
to see me was something the lady wasn't.

'Corvinus.' She straightened. She was still wearing the
bracelet. It winked at me in the sunlight. 'I thought you
were in Rome.'

'I was. I found this.' I pulled out the Owl's bracelet.
'Snap.'

She looked at it, then slowly set the bowl down and
wiped her hands on her tunic. 'So?' she said.

If I'd thought she'd show some signs of guilt I was
disappointed. Cold was right. I pushed a bit harder. 'Who
did you get yours from, Thupeltha? Gaius Aternius? And
why did he give you it?'

I wasn't expecting what happened next. She took two

steps towards me, brought back her fist sideways and slammed me hard across the face. It was like being slugged with a marble column.

'Now you get out of here,' she said quietly.

At least I'd managed to stay on my feet. I felt my jaw. It moved, but it hurt like hell, one of my teeth felt loose and I could taste blood. Jupiter, the lady packed a punch! I'd been socked before, but not often as professionally as that.

'Clusinus was robbing tombs,' I said. 'Or rather a tomb. That's where the bracelets came from. I had this one from a guy called Herminius, Bubo's brother in Rome. So how did you get yours?'

'Titus gave me it.' She picked up the eggs. 'I wouldn't touch that slimy bastard Aternius with a barge-pole. Now get off my land, Roman, and don't come back.'

Maybe she was lying, but it sounded true. And that clout had carried conviction. Well, maybe I had overtheorised a little here. Still, it was too late to back out now.

'Uh-uh.' I shook my head. 'Not this time, lady. That's stolen property you've got there. You can tell me about it, or you can tell the authorities, but you'll have to tell one of us. The difference is the second way you'll be facing a receiving rap, maybe worse.'

She stood glaring at me, her heavy breasts rising and falling above the bowl she was clutching to her stomach. Finally, she nodded.

'All right,' she said. 'So Titus robbed a tomb. He was a crook, but then I knew that. It had nothing to do with anything.'

'Which tomb? Where?'

'How would I know? The bracelet was a gift, Corvinus. You never met Titus. He could be generous when he could afford it. And he obviously thought he could afford it.'

'He never told you?'

'No.'

She was lying, or at least hiding something: there was hesitation there.

'Look, Thupeltha,' I said, 'this is important, right? I couldn't care less about the bracelet itself, but I have to know where it came from. Clusinus is dead, but I've a fair idea now who killed him and why. And the why has something to do with the tomb; maybe not directly but it's a factor. Anything you can tell me might just pin the guy responsible.'

'Aternius?'

She was sharp, but then I'd always known that. And the way she said the name suggested she didn't like the bastard at all and never had. So much for the conspiracy theory.

'Yeah,' I said. 'Yeah, I think so.'

That got me a long level stare. Then she said, 'Come into the house.'

I followed her inside. She set the bowl of eggs on the kitchen table and disappeared through the door at the back. She was away so long I thought she might have done a runner, but ten minutes later she came back holding something wrapped in a cloth. She handed it to me without a word. I unwrapped it.

It was a drinking cup chased with a hunting scene: that guy whatever-his-name-is being torn apart by his own hounds while Artemis-Minerva watches. The goddess had those lozenge-shaped eyes and that smile you see on really old carvings. And it was gold; solid gold, from the weight. I whistled silently and turned the thing over. There was an inscription on the base, but it was in Etruscan and I couldn't read it. Another job for Priscus.

'Clusinus give you this?' I said.

'He left it with me for safe-keeping.' She wasn't looking at me. 'If it'll help you can take it. I don't know anything else.'

'You sure this time?'

'I'm sure. And Corvinus?'

'Yeah?'

'What you said. That hurt. I'm no whore. I told you once that I only took one lover at a time, and I meant it. And none of them's been Gaius Aternius. So watch your mouth in future, understand?'

'Yeah. Right. Thanks, lady.'

I went.

Mother and Priscus were still at breakfast when I got to Nepos's villa, although Nepos himself was out supervising the first stages of the grape harvest.

'Marcus, dear.' Mother put up her cheek to be kissed. She was wearing a light-green mantle and a perfume that would've corrupted an octogenarian Chief Priest. 'What on *earth* are you doing here? I thought you'd all gone to Rome.'

'We did.' I lay down on the third couch and cut myself a piece of cheese. 'We got back last night.'

She stared at me as if I'd grown an extra head. 'But that's silly,' she said. '*No one* can spend less than ten days in Rome when they've been away as long as you have, even at this time of year. I mean, really!' She turned to Priscus. 'I'm right, aren't I, Titus?'

'Mmmaaa.' Priscus was sogging his way through a crust: the guy had perfect teeth, but from the way he ate you wouldn't know it. 'Good morning, my boy. What's that, dear? Marcus going to Rome?'

Mother closed her eyes for a moment, then opened

them and reached for an olive. 'And I suppose you've dragged poor Perilla and the child back too?' she said to me. 'You have *no* thought for other people, Marcus, none at all. Sometimes I look back on your upbringing and wonder where I failed.'

Jupiter! 'Mother,' I said, 'I only have four days before I'm due in court to defend Larth Papatius on a murder rap. I haven't got the fu— I haven't got the time to mess around in Rome.'

'Oh.' She carefully cut the olive stone out with the point of her knife. 'So that's it, is it? Forgive me, dear. I thought perhaps it had something to do with that silly decision of yours not to go back after Sejanus's family were executed.' I said nothing. 'And it was silly, Marcus, that's the only suitable word. There's no earthly reason for you not to live there. Quite the reverse, in fact, because now the pushy little so-and-so has got his just desserts you're in no danger at all. As for the Senate, I can appreciate your feelings, but they can't help it if they're a pack of vacillating, self-serving, vicious-minded idiots. Your father was just the same, if we except the vicious-minded, which for all his faults the poor dear wasn't, and stress the other three qualities.' Ouch. 'And although I do have my reservations about young Gaius Caesar he is almost certain to be our next emperor and you seem to have made quite a hit with him.'

Oh, hell. Jupiter, there had to be a conspiracy here; everybody I talked to seemed desperate to get me back to Rome. 'Yeah, yeah, right,' I said. 'Look, Mother, do you think we might just bypass the ticking off and get round to why I'm here?'

'If it pleases you, dear.' She sniffed. 'I suppose you must have some reason beyond simple filial courtesy.'

'Fine.' I'd brought out the bracelet and the cup. I

handed the bracelet over first. 'Priscus, you want to cast your eye over this for me?'

It was like a rose unbudding. The gods knew what particular plane of reality the guy had been on up until now, but he snapped back as soon as the thing cleared my pouch. He reached across and took it like it was made of gossamer.

'Oh, now,' he said. 'Mmmaaa! This is really rather . . .' He turned it in his hand. 'It's not from Caere, or not originally. I would guess it was made in Clusium, the work of one of the court goldsmiths, perhaps Velthar Fufluna. Not an apprentice, either; the master himself. Porsennine, of course, in any event. The treatment is quite distinctive. A beautiful piece of work.'

'Uh, Porsennine?' I said. 'You mean Porsennine as in Lars Porsenna?' Jupiter in spangles! The thing was five hundred years old!

'Certainly. The uniformity of the granulation, in conjunction with the—'

'Could it have come from one of the Caere tombs?'

He blinked. 'Yes, I suppose so. But no ordinary tomb, Marcus. This is a very fine piece, very fine indeed. Uniquely so, in my opinion. Where did you find it?'

Instead of answering I handed over the cup. 'There's an inscription on the bottom,' I said.

'Marcus, dear, *what* . . . ?' Mother began. Then she stopped.

We were both looking at Priscus. The guy had set the bracelet down, taken the cup and turned it. His mouth opened in an O that should've been comical but wasn't. It closed, then opened again.

'Titus?' Mother said. No response. '*Titus!*'

'Mmmaaa!'

Jupiter! Whatever the whacky writing was it'd produced

one hell of an effect. The guy's mouth was waggling like a manic sturgeon's and he was the colour of plaster. I hadn't seen him look like this since he'd drunk a quarter-pint of fish sauce thinking it was tamarind juice.

Mother was looking as seriously worried as I felt. 'Marcus, do something!' she snapped. 'He's having a seizure! *Titus!*'

'Mmmaaa!'

I got off the couch, picked up a couple of fingerbowls and threw the contents into Priscus's face. He stopped bleating and blinked at me like a constipated owl.

'Marcus, if you've . . . !' Mother began.

Priscus waved her down. The water was running off his face on to his mantle, but he ignored it.

'Marcus, my boy, where did you get this?' he said. His voice was quiet and level, not like Priscus's at all.

'Uh, it came out of a tomb,' I said.

'And where is this tomb exactly?'

Jupiter! For the first time since I'd known him the guy sounded almost rational. It was as if someone had clouted him from behind and he hadn't actually realised it yet. 'I don't know. Somewhere in the Caere cemeteries.'

'I doubt that,' he said. 'I doubt it very much, unless the records have been lost, and that is most unlikely. The bracelet, yes, but not this.'

I felt the first prickle of excitement. 'Yeah? So what does the writing say?'

'It says "I was made for Lars Tarquinius, king of the Romans".'

I didn't take it in at first, in spite of Mother's gasp. Then I did.

No wonder Bubo had built himself a special cellar.

Clusinus had found the tomb of Rome's last king.

40

I left Nepos's with my head swimming. So; Tarquin the
Proud's tomb. I didn't know where it was supposed
to be, and nor for a wonder did Priscus, but it sure
as hell wasn't Caere, Priscus had been adamant over
that. Still, there wasn't any doubt that that was what
Clusinus had found, and if the grave goods had hit the
black market then illegal operation or not he and Bubo
could've written their own ticket: it ain't every day you
auction off a king of Rome's dinner service. Sure, I
could see Clusinus's reasons for claiming that it was
somewhere in the Caere cemetery complex, because
anyone trying to pull a fast one on him would have
their work cut out finding it before they started; but
if it wasn't there after all then where the hell was it?
Tombs tend to stick together, and an isolated one was
queer as a three-legged cat. Also queer was the fact
that no one seemed to have noticed it. Even in death
– especially in death – there's such a thing as cutting a
social figure. When you go you like to leave something
behind somewhere prominent, to remind the passing
punters what a rich, powerful, well-respected guy you'd
been, and if you're a king that applies in spades. Only

this time, obviously, it didn't. Why not? That didn't add up, either.

Another thing was, it had to be close: close enough for Clusinus to get to it in his free time. That was queer too, in a different way; the guy was no farmer, he had free time by the barrow-load. If for some inexplicable reason the tomb was out on its own in the hills somewhere pretending to be a lump of earth then why couldn't he just have foregone the pleasure of hunting hares for a month or so and cleaned it out?

It didn't make sense; none of it.

I was passing the Navius property, where a gang of grape-pickers were at work among the trellised vines by the road. Over to my left, the thunder rumbled in the hills: east, the favourable direction, Vipena would've said. Maybe it was a good omen. I looked up towards the higher ground, behind Vetuliscum. The sky was broken with clouds. Certainly the rain couldn't be long in coming now, and when it did the ditches would have their work cut out. If the pickers on the terraces didn't . . .

I stopped as if one of the lightning bolts had strayed a couple of miles out of line and fried my brains.

Shit. Oh, Jupiter! Jupiter best and greatest . . .

I knew where the tomb was. Where it had to be. And knowing that, why Navius, Clusinus and Bubo had died. Or at least I knew part of the why.

And of course I knew who had killed them. That bit was simple.

But why Hilarion? And why should the guy bother? It wasn't as though he had a vested interest. Still, he had practically told me; told me himself . . .

Something was coming towards me. I looked: a mule without a rider, running like the clappers with its tether trailing. My spine went cold.

Jupiter, no! Not the Princess!

As it came closer I stepped into the middle of the road, yelling and waving. Corydon slowed, bared his teeth, then stopped and backed. I jumped forward, grabbed the bastard's nose-rope and pulled. I'd got him reduced to some semblance of docility, which meant that instead of biting me he was trying to turn round and kick my teeth through the back of my skull, when Marilla came charging up behind, red-faced and out of breath.

'Oh, you've caught him!' she gasped.

I was still shaking. 'You okay, Princess?'

She took the nose-rope from me and made gentle cooing noises. The change was amazing: Corydon stopped throwing himself around and stood stock still, grinning. That kid really has a way with animals.

'Of course I am,' she said, looking up. 'Why shouldn't I be?'

'Uh, I just thought maybe you might be lying somewhere with your neck broken, that's all.' I tried to keep my voice light. Jupiter! That had been a bad one! 'Nothing important. What happened? He throw you?'

'Corydon wouldn't do that. Would you, dear?' She kissed the bastard's nose and he snickered. 'He just ran away. He does that sometimes.'

'Ran away?'

'I'd stopped for a . . .' She hesitated. 'I'd tied him to a branch and gone into the bushes for a minute. While I was busy he undid his tether.'

I stared at her. 'He what?'

'Undid his tether. Oh, he's very clever. Aren't you, darling?' She kissed the brute again. Sickening. 'He can unpick knots with his teeth. And of course when I came back he'd gone.'

'Hey, that's . . .' I stopped. Suddenly everything went

very still and clear as the last piece of the puzzle slipped into place.

'That's what?' the Princess said.

'That's quite smart. Very smart indeed.'

'Corvinus, are you all right?'

'Sure.' I fondled Corydon's ears; the bugger looked surprised but he didn't object. Lovely animals, mules. 'Sure. Never better.'

'Only your eyes have gone funny.'

'Yeah, well.' So. That explained why he'd never been claimed or recognised. And because Alexis had touted the brute round all the neighbourhood farms, including Nepos's, it explained why Hilarion had been killed, too.

'Are you on your way home?' She was still looking at me like I'd dropped a few marbles on the road. 'I really think you should be. You don't look well. If you want I can—'

I shook my head. 'No, Princess, I'm fine. You can head on there yourself now, though, and tell Perilla I've gone on into Caere on business. I shouldn't be long.'

'Well, if you're sure.' She swung herself up on to Corydon's back and gave me a doubtful look. 'I'll see you later.'

I watched the two of them trot back down the road ahead of me. Then I followed them, past the track up to Flatworm's towards Caere.

There was just one last thing I had to check before I confronted the murderer.

The guy at the stables where I'd hired Flash for the trip to Pyrgi was mucking out. He put down the fork, wiped his hands on his tunic and came over grinning.

'Good morning to you, sir,' he said. 'You want to hire a horse? Fulgor's out at the moment, but—'

'Not today, friend.' No way. I took out my purse. 'You sell mules?'

'Sure. Mules and donkeys.' The grin widened. 'If you'd like to look over the stock I've got one or two that might suit you very well.'

'I'm not buying.' I pulled out a silver piece. 'I just want some information.'

'No problem.' His eyes went to the coin. 'Ask away.'

'You sell a mule ten days back? Idiosyncratic bugger with a white flash on the left fore?'

The grin slipped. 'I might have done,' he said. 'It depends. Some trouble? We're always willing to take an animal back, with a small reduction for wear and tear, naturally, but you have to take into account that—'

'No trouble, pal. None at all. You happen to remember the customer's name?'

'Not the name. The customer, sure. Old man from Vetuliscum. He came in early. His mule'd just died and he wanted a replacement.'

'Uh-huh.' Bull's-eye! 'Could you describe him, maybe?'

He could. Five minutes later I was out and heading for home, a silver piece down and up one murderer. I didn't like it, but there you were; you can't pick and choose.

The guy I wanted, of course, was Larcius Arruns.

41

The only question left was why?

Oh, sure, part of it was okay: the tomb was on what had been Arruns's land before Navius's grandfather had diddled the family out of it. And Arruns himself had told me, the day I'd given him a lift part-way into Caere, that he wouldn't kill just for a patch of vineyard. That much, at least, had been true; it'd been, in a way, a kind of confession, or a justification, rather, because – again, like he'd said – Arruns was no killer, not by nature. I'd stake my sandals on the truth of that. The land itself didn't matter. What mattered was that Navius – and later Clusinus – had found the tomb; and that Arruns couldn't ignore.

Still, the fact remained that he'd killed four people. Not being a natural killer made that even stranger: tomb-robbing's a crime, and a word to the authorities would've had the same effect and caused a lot less grief. So why had he done it? Not because he wanted to loot the tomb himself; if he'd known it was there – and he must've done, for all this to make sense – he could've done that any time this past fifty years. And a five-hundred-year-old tomb don't carry no loyalties.

I spent the walk back thinking about how to play this. Arruns had to be nailed, sure, if only for Papatius's sake, but I'd liked the thrawn old bugger and I wasn't looking forward to pointing the finger. When I turned up Flatworm's drive I still hadn't decided. And I felt sick as a dog.

Perilla was on the terrace with (surprise!) a book open on her lap. She kissed me.

'I didn't expect you for hours, Marcus,' she said. 'Marilla said you'd gone into Caere.'

'Yeah.' I slumped down into my usual chair.

Perilla paused. 'She also said that you were acting rather strangely. Or at least more strangely than you usually do. The case isn't going well, is it?'

'The case is solved, lady.' She shot me a startled look but I ignored it. 'Finished, over and done with. All I've got to do now is shop the murderer. What's the book?'

'Another copy of Aulus Caecina's *Etruscan History*. I bought it in Rome to replace the one Corydon ate. Marcus, are you sure you aren't ill? If the case is solved – really solved – then who—'

I put a finger to her lips. 'Don't ask me, Perilla. Please. Not just yet, okay? I'll tell you later.'

Bathyllus soft-shoed over with the tray. I let the little guy pour me a belt of Caeretan – we'd finished the Setinian – downed it in one and held the cup out for more.

'I did come across a very interesting passage,' Perilla said brightly; gods, I hate it when the lady tries to cheer me up. 'I thought perhaps it might be relevant.'

'Yeah?'

'It's about hurdles.'

I was just about to ask what the fuck hurdles had to do with anything when I remembered Clusinus's death.

We still had the problem of the hurdle. If Aternius had been the killer then sure, it made sense because of the time element. With Arruns firmly in the title role that explanation didn't fit any more.

'Go on,' I said.

'It seems that when Tarquin the Proud called his Latin allies to a conference at the Grove of Ferentina—' Perilla stopped. 'Marcus, are you *positive* you're all right?'

I'd sat up. 'Yeah,' I said. 'Yeah, I'm fine. The Grove of Ferentina, you say.'

'Seemingly there was a bit of trouble. A man called Turnus Herdonius tried to stir up a revolt. The king viewed it as treason and had him executed using a method invented by himself.'

'The guy was drowned beneath a weighted hurdle, right?' I said.

'Oh. You've read it already.'

'No, just an educated guess.' I took a swallow of wine. So. That was that one explained, along with a lot of other things. 'Tarquin invented the hurdle business himself, yeah? A sort of private family punishment for treason.'

'Caecina doesn't exactly say so, but yes, I suppose it might be seen that way.'

That put the seal on the business. Well, it had to be done eventually, and the longer I put it off the worse it would be. Bathyllus was still hanging around on the fringes. I beckoned him over.

'Go and find Alexis, little guy,' I said. 'I want a message taking over to Larcius Arruns.' Perilla looked at me wide-eyed, but she didn't speak. 'Tell Alexis to ask him to meet me in the vineyard at the top end of his property in an hour's time. He'll know the one I mean.' Bathyllus turned to go. I caught his arm. 'No. Wait a minute. Scratch that. Ask him to meet me beside his family tomb.'

I knew the whole of the why now. Maybe I should've written the request out formally. After all, how often do you send messages to a king in exile?

The sky above the hills to the east was looking black as a Nubian's armpit when I climbed the last stretch of path between the terraces. Arruns was already there, standing next to the wide catchment trench that led to the vertical shaft of Attus Navius's half-completed storm drain. I'd tucked my knife into its wrist sheath, but I didn't think I'd need it: the time for killing was past, on either side.

'So, Corvinus,' he said when we were close enough to talk. 'You know.'

'Would you rather I didn't?'

It should've been a stupid question, but even as I asked it I knew it wasn't. He shook his head.

'No. I wouldn't have let Papatius die in any case. And it doesn't matter now anyway. The tomb's safe. There's no one left alive outside the family who knows it's here.' His eyes flickered. 'Except you.'

Uh-oh. Maybe I'd been wrong about the killing being over. Slowly, so he didn't think I was reaching for a weapon, I undid the fastenings of the small bag I'd brought with me and took out the contents.

'I won't tell, friend,' I said. 'You have my word. And I think these belong to you.'

He looked down at the things, then back to me: a long, slow, appraising stare. Then he grunted and held out his hands. I put the cup and the Owl's bracelet into them. The atmosphere suddenly felt a lot lighter.

'All right,' he said. 'I might just believe you. You want to see it before we go and finish this?'

I didn't have to ask what he meant by 'it'. The hairs lifted on my neck.

'Maybe,' I said. 'In a minute. Let me just check the facts first. For my own satisfaction.'

'If you like.'

'Navius found the tomb when he was digging his new storm drain shafts to carry water from the mountain under the terracing.'

'No. He never knew it was there.' Arruns nodded towards the shaft. 'That stops three feet short of the roof. I was lucky; he had an accident and broke his arm. Trouble was, it was only a matter of time before he started digging again, and I'd no way of stopping him.' His lips twisted. 'Bar the one, of course. There I only had to wait for an opportunity.' Yeah; I remembered now: Sicinia had said that her son had broken his arm in a fall from a ladder and been laid up for a month. Well, it'd given him that much longer, I supposed. 'I was sorry about Navius, even if I didn't like his family. He'd the makings of a good farmer. The real bastard was Titus Clusinus.'

'Okay. Let's leave Clusinus for a moment,' I said. 'Next bit. The morning Navius died you'd been in Caere buying a mule. On your way back just shy of Vetuliscum you saw him turning up Clusinus's track after Thupeltha.'

'I didn't see the woman, Corvinus. Not at first, anyway. I thought Navius was alone. An opportunity, like I said.'

'Yeah.' Jupiter, the guy was calm enough! It was like we were discussing the price of pigs. 'So. You left the mule tied up in the bushes out of sight of the road and followed him from above along the high ground. You waited until he'd left Thupeltha, then went after him and killed him. After that you went back to where you'd left the mule and saw it was gone.'

The old guy grinned. 'Bastard must've slipped his tether,' he said. 'I couldn't understand that. I still can't because I put a knot in the nose-rope. I assumed some bugger'd stolen him until your slave came round the next day asking questions about a stray.'

'Yeah. So you carried on into Vetuliscum on foot. You weren't too worried about the missing mule giving you away because even if he did turn up no one locally'd know he was yours.' I paused. 'Only someone did: a guy called Hilarion who was staying with Licinius Nepos and who'd seen you that morning in Caere. Right?'

'Right. I was lucky. Your lad came to me before he went to Nepos's place. Hilarion mightn't've made the connection but he was a friend of your family's and I couldn't take the risk. He had to die. I'm sorry about him as well.'

'Uh-huh.' His matter-of-fact tone was chilling. I kept my voice level. 'Okay. Now we come to Clusinus. He was the one actually found the tomb. Was that an accident too?'

He shrugged. 'That I don't know. I have my theories. Clusinus spent a lot of time hunting on the high ground. The day after Navius broke his arm I was up here checking the shaft. If Clusinus had seen me from above I wouldn't put it past him to put two and two together because the bastard had a nose for things like that. Certainly the next time I checked, about ten days later, the hole'd been deepened and the tomb breached.'

'So you watched.'

'I watched, but I never saw anything. It wasn't until I'd killed Navius that I found it was Clusinus. Then I followed him to Bubo.' Yeah; that made sense. Clusinus would already've taken the bracelet he needed to set up the deal, plus Thupeltha's bracelet and the cup; there was no point in pulling any more stuff out before he had things off and running. And by that time he was dead. 'I've no regrets about killing these two. They deserved everything they got.'

'The hurdle? That was in memory of Turnus Herdonius, right?'

'It was.' Another mirthless grin. 'I'm impressed, Corvinus. You've done your homework. Bubo I meant to knife, but then I saw the hammer leaning against the wall and used that instead.'

'Yeah? And why would you do that now, pal?'

'It was for Charun, the underworld demon who protects the tomb. Charun kills with a hammer. I wanted both of the bastards to go below knowing Tarquin had sent them there himself. By proxy, if you like.'

Jupiter! Talk about warped! Even Perilla hadn't spotted that one! Still, there was a sort of crazy logic to it.

He was looking at me with a half-smile on his lips. 'So? No more questions?'

'No. I think that about covers it.'

He paused. 'I have one. What do you intend to do now?'

The hard ones first. 'That depends. Clusinus and Bubo, I'd have no quarrel with you there, pal. Like you say, they're no loss and they brought it on themselves. Navius and Hilarion are a different matter. Sure, I take your arguments, but they weren't executions, they were murders. And there's still Larth Papatius.'

He nodded. 'Yes. And like I said it doesn't matter. The tomb's safe, and Publius – you remember Publius? My nephew in the records office? – Publius knows it's here. He's a good boy, a credit to the family, and he'll have my land after I'm gone. He'll look after it.' Another shrug. 'Don't worry, Corvinus. I'll give you no trouble. There're no hard feelings, either.'

I swallowed. 'Fine. You want to go, then?'

'Of course. Once I've said goodbye to the king.'

42

He'd brought a rope and a couple of lamps with him.
While I watched he climbed down the shaft of the storm
drain – these things have steps built into the sides – then
paused and looked up.

'You coming?' he said.

I felt the cold sweat break out all over. I wasn't scared of
Arruns; murderer he may've been, but the guy was honest
by his own lights. What frightened me was staring down
that black hole and knowing (or rather not knowing)
what was waiting at the bottom. Like I say, you don't
mess with the dead. Still, if I funked out now I knew
I'd regret it all my life. After all, how many people get
to see the inside of a tomb belonging to a legend?

Curiosity won. I offered up a quick prayer to whatever
god or goddess looked after brain-dead smartasses who
didn't have the sense they were born with and set off
down the shaft.

There was just room enough at the foot for both of us
to stand with what proved to be the capstone of the tomb
between us. Somebody – Clusinus, probably – had ham-
mered an iron staple into a crevice in the shaft wall, and
Arruns tied the rope to it. Then he lifted up the capstone.

Blank darkness yawned at me, and a chill breath touched my legs. I shivered, the hairs crawling on my scalp.

Arruns threw one end of the rope down. I heard it hit the floor somewhere below. He took a firm grip and eased himself over the edge. The top of his head disappeared into the blackness under my feet.

I waited. There was the sound of a strike-light and then the glow of a lamp. I could see the floor now, or part of it: stone slabs, about ten feet down.

'Come on, Corvinus. It's safe enough.'

Jupiter, the guy wasn't even whispering! A drop of sweat ran down past my ear. I wiped it away with the back of my hand.

Okay. So here goes . . .

My legs wouldn't move. I didn't blame them. Me, given the preference, I'd rather jump into a tiger pit.

'Corvinus!'

I swallowed, took a hold of the rope and went down it. My sandals hit stone and I let go.

Arruns was lighting the other lamp. I looked round . . .

We weren't alone. The third man was lying on a couch as if he were at a dinner party, watching me closely. He had a neat pointed beard, almond eyes and a faint smile to his mouth. I almost screamed before I realised he was a life-sized clay figure and the couch was the top of a clay coffin.

So that was what Rome's last king had looked like. I glanced at Arruns. Yeah. Same cheekbones, same bone structure. Family tomb, right enough.

The back of my neck felt cold.

Then I noticed what else was in the room. The place wasn't big, sure, no more than ten feet by ten, but apart from the bit of floor we were standing on it was packed:

chests, jars, a jumble of vases, weapons. Even a big old
shield you could've used to fricassée a sheep in. Most of
the chests were open, and from some of them came the
glint of gold and silver.

Then there were the walls . . .

Paintings have never turned me on, but these were
something else. We were in the middle of some sort
of huge eternal party, with flute-players and acrobats
and gladiators. And the figures were alive. They moved
and flickered in the lamplight, spinning and turning like
they were dancing to music I couldn't hear. I let my eyes
wander round the room, taking it all in, pushing down
the thought that maybe it wasn't my imagination, maybe
the bastards *were* alive. Or something. Finally I looked
back at the man on the couch. The fingers of his right
hand had been contoured to hold a cup – the cup I'd
returned to Arruns with the bracelet: that was on the
statue's wrist, just as the cup was back in his hand – and
he was raising it to me, like you would in a toast. Only
this toast had lasted five hundred years.

That felt eerie. Eerie as hell.

'Shit,' I whispered. Finally I remembered to close my
mouth.

Arruns was standing beside the couch, perfectly at
ease like he belonged there. He laid his hand on the
man's head.

'Meet Lars Tarquin,' he said.

I swallowed, and the spittle tasted harsh. I could've
murdered a cup of neat Setinian. There was probably
wine in one of those jars, but even if it'd been drinkable
I wouldn't've touched it for a Parthian satrapy.

'Family secret, right?' I said.

'From the beginning. He died at Cumae, a guest of the
Greek Aristodemus. That was after that bastard Porsenna

captured Rome and broke his promise to bring him back.'

Despite my other preoccupations I frowned. 'Hang on, pal. Porsenna never captured Rome. His army withdrew.'

'History's written by the winners, Corvinus. Forget Horatius and the bridge, that was a lie, it never happened. Lars Porsenna took Rome and set up a puppet government. It was only after the Latins and Cumaean Greeks joined together and killed his son Arruns at Aricia that your ancestor Publicola and his shower got to keep what they'd stolen. Forget the story of the rape, too. Lucretia never existed, or if she did Sextus Tarquin never touched her.'

Uh-oh. Did I detect a smidgin of fanaticism here? Sure, the guy might be right – I've always distrusted these stories of stiff-lipped squeaky-clean heroes and heroines renouncing evil and winning out against incredible odds – but what did it matter after five hundred years? Besides, I've made it a rule never to mix with religion or politics. Sex, sure, no problem, but not these two.

I backpedalled.

'So if he died in Cumae why's he buried here?'

'The family owned all the land round Vetuliscum. My property's all that's left, the bit we hung on to. He didn't want to be buried an exile, among Greeks, and Rome was obviously impossible. At the same time, Caere'd rejected him. Clusium and the other cities of the League, too.' Arruns's hand still lay on the statue's head; it was almost a caress. 'So he chose to come home without anyone knowing, after he was dead. No big tomb, no ceremonies, no records. Only the family. He's been here ever since.'

'In that case how—' I began; which was as far as I got before the world erupted.

The bang came from directly overhead, and it nearly lifted me out of my skin. Both of us looked up towards the opening in the ceiling. A moment later water began pouring through it like someone had sawn through an aqueduct. My sandals were covered before I could even yell.

Shit. The rains. The storm had broken directly overhead. And of course with the capstone removed the tomb was acting like the outlet to Navius's drain. The difference being that there was no outlet hole . . .

I went for the rope and started to climb. The water slammed down in a solid mass, filling my eyes and ears and nostrils so that I couldn't see or hear, or even breathe. It was like trying to scale a waterfall. I felt my hands slipping. I opened my mouth to shout, only to have that filled too. I choked and let go of the rope altogether . . .

And there were shoulders under my feet, and someone gripped my ankles and pushed up. I reached through the water and grabbed blindly for anything I could get. My outstretched fingers met stone, scrabbled across it and hooked themselves over an edge.

I gripped it, pulled myself up and through the gap. I was still under water but the shaft was much wider than the hole, and the current was less. I stood. The shaft was full to waist depth and water was pouring in from above as fast as it flowed out, but at least there was air. I took in several long, shuddering breaths . . .

Arruns.

Sweet Jupiter; he was trapped! The rate water was flowing down into the tomb the place would be flooded to the ceiling in minutes. Sure, I could put the capstone on and it might block the base of the shaft, but the shaft itself would still fill up: Navius had done a good job, and most of the rain that fell on the hill slope above us was being channelled into it. The ground wouldn't absorb much either: after the baking it'd had over the summer months it was bone dry, and water ran off it like oil dropped on a hot skillet.

I took another deep breath and went under again with my eyes open. This time it was easier, because the current was with me. I found the hole and shoved my head and shoulders through, leaning sideways to where the jet thinned out and there was air.

I strained back against the pressure from above and shook the blindness out of my eyes. The place was a quarter full already. It looked like the blunt end of a shipwreck.

Arruns was standing next to the king's coffin, holding both the lamps, looking up at me.

'Grab the rope!' I yelled. 'I'll pull you out!'

He shook his head. 'No.'

Jupiter! 'You stupid bugger! If you stay down here any longer you'll drown! Now *grab the fucking rope!*'

Another shake of the head. 'I'm staying here, Corvinus. Put on the capstone. At least that way we might save the tomb.'

'You can put the bloody capstone on yourself from up here! Arruns, for Jupiter's sake . . . !'

He smiled. 'That's why I'm doing this. The god sent the rain. He's punished me himself. It's a fair solution. I'd have to die anyway and I may as well do it here. Now put on the capstone and leave me in peace.'

Shit; that was all I needed: the bastard had gone religious on me. I gripped the rope and turned so my legs could clear the edge of the hole . . .

'No! Wait!'

I stopped and turned back. Arruns had put the lamps down beside the king's left elbow.

'That's more like it,' I said. 'Now come and get the fucking rope while I still have the strength to pull.'

'In a moment. I've something to do first.'

I should've realised there was something wrong with his voice, but I didn't. Not that it would've mattered because I couldn't've done anything anyway. He reached into his tunic, brought out a knife, put the point against his throat and shoved.

Blood spurted. He was dead before he hit the water.

I looked down, numbed. The king was still smiling. The party still went on for ever in the lamplight. There was nothing I could do; not now. Nothing.

I hauled myself up out of the hole and put back the capstone, like he'd told me to.

43

It took me what felt like an age to climb back into the
real world. The worst of the storm was over and the black
clouds were moving away westwards, but water was still
pouring like a river from the higher ground. With its
outlet blocked the shaft was almost half full already, and
there was more to come. Not that it mattered now, of
course. I walked down through the terraces to the road
and set off in the direction of home, dripping all the way,
feeling shattered.

So that was that.

Yeah, well, maybe it was for the best. Arruns had been
right; he'd had to die in any case, and at least he'd got
to choose his own time and place. A propos which, I
wondered about the knife. He'd been carrying it inside
his tunic, not stuck through his belt, so he'd wanted to
keep it hidden. The obvious explanation was that the
plan – the original plan, anyway – had been to kill
me before or after he'd got me down the tomb, but I
had my doubts about that. My gut feeling was that the
poor bastard had had enough of killing already and was
glad himself that it was over; he'd come close enough
to confessing unprompted that day I'd picked him up

on the Caere road. Also, if he'd wanted to add me to his tally he could've done it easy when I first hit the flagstones because at that point I was in no condition to worry about a simple, human thing like a knife in the ribs.

Last and not least, of course, far from trying to make a hole in me when I wasn't expecting it the guy had actually saved my life. That was the real bummer. Arruns might be a murderer four times over but I *owed* him, and one thing the old aristocratic code drums into you like it or not is that you pay your debts. The moral ones, anyway.

He'd got me over a barrel, and I knew it.

No; the knife wasn't for me. Arruns had meant to stay down there in the tomb all along, even before the flooding. That thought made me feel a bit happier, but not all that much. Mostly I just felt empty.

The sun had almost set by the time I got to Flatworm's track, and Jupiter was growling away in the hills again, working himself up for another spat. A stiff breeze had picked up, too, and what with my still-sodden tunic I wasn't all that warm; in fact, my head felt muzzy and I was beginning to shiver. Hell, that was all I needed: the case was over, I was free to do what I liked, and all the signs were I was coming down with a bad cold or worse. Some holiday. Perilla would be thrilled to bits.

Ah, well; at least we were into wrapping-up time, with a whole three days before Rome's answer to Solon came oiling up from the big city. I'd go and talk to Gaius Aternius tomorrow and see what I could swing . . .

I sneezed. Bugger. Call it a day: hot bath, dry tunic, a pint or two of wine, a square meal and an early night. I was sorry that smoothie bastard hadn't turned out to be the murderer after all, but then that's how things go, you can't have everything.

Arruns was dead; fine, that part of the business was settled and the account was closed, as far as it ever could be. There was only the private side of things left. So. How did I go about paying the guy back for the fact that I was still breathing?

That I'd have to think about.

Maybe the hot bath did the trick because I felt a lot better the next day, although my arm muscles were stiff as hell. The weather had improved too: we'd had another blaster of a storm in the night but the god had obviously blown himself out for the time being and when I set out for Caere and Aternius's place there wasn't a cloud in the sky.

The reception I got wasn't any more cordial than it'd been the first time. Aternius's door slave checked with the master, then led me through the atrium and into the study like he'd have been happier pushing me at the end of a pole. Aternius was on one of the two reading couches, in conversation with another man with silver-grey hair and the sort of stern, noble features you associate with portrait busts by sculptors angling for a follow-up commission. He looked up and frowned.

'Corvinus. This is a surprise. I thought you were—'

'In Rome. Yeah, everyone does.' I grinned at the guy on the other couch. 'Quintus Cominius, I presume?'

'Indeed.' The mayor's voice didn't fit his face; it was thin and high-pitched. I'd just bet that under that snazzy mantle he'd have spindly legs and knock knees.

'Nice to meet you at last. I've heard a lot about you.'

'Indeed?' Shit, maybe I was wrong and he was some weird variety of giant parrot done up to look human.

'As you can see, we are rather busy.' Aternius indicated the pile of wax tablets on the table between them.

'Yeah, I can see that. I really can.' There was a chair near the table. I pulled it up and sat on it, then gave him my best smile and waited.

A pause. Aternius's frown deepened.

'I assume it's in connection with the Vetuliscum murders,' he said, 'although this close to the trial I'm surprised as the defendant's counsel you should be visiting the prosecutor.'

'There won't be any need for a trial, pal. I came to tell you you can let Larth Papatius go. The real murderer's dead.'

Both men were staring at me. 'What?' Aternius said.

'Larcius Arruns. He confessed to me before he killed himself.'

Cominius pursed his lips. 'Most irregular,' he said. '*Most* irregular.'

'Why should Arruns kill Attus Navius and Titus Clusinus?' Aternius was looking blank. 'Not to mention your mother's friend Salvius Hilarion.'

I'd got this bit ready. 'He wanted his family vineyard back. With her husband and son both dead he thought Sicinia Rufina would sell up to an outsider and he could buy the terraces from the new owner.' I caught a quick glance between Aternius and his uncle. Uh-huh. 'Clusinus witnessed the murder and tried to blackmail him. Hilarion's more complicated, but basically the guy saw Arruns here in Caere with a mule he shouldn't've had.'

There it was: thin, sure, although I'd kept to the truth as far as possible, but what I couldn't mention – and this was part of the payment of my debt to Arruns – was the existence of the tomb. Physically, it had gone: Lysias and Alexis had sloped up there before dawn with a couple of shovels and filled in the shaft level with the ground.

With any luck Navius's drain would be forgotten like it had never existed.

As far as Bubo was concerned, I'd no need to account for him: Aternius had never linked his death with the others in any case.

'It's a bit thin,' Cominius said.

So. There was a brain there, after all. I shrugged. 'Maybe. But it's the truth. Arruns is already dead, like I say, but I'm willing to take any oath you like on that.'

'Where is Larcius Arruns?' Cominius again. Bugger; the guy was a *lot* smarter than he sounded. That was the question I'd been dreading, because I couldn't answer it. Sure, I could've gone back to the tomb before the lads had reburied it, pulled Arruns out and carted him somewhere innocent but I didn't want to do that. Not just for the obvious reasons: he had a right to stay where he'd chosen to be, and I'd fight to the last inch to keep him there.

I put on my best straight face. 'I don't know,' I said.

Cominius clicked his tongue. 'Then how the hell d'you know he's dead?' he said.

Reasonable question. And again not one I could answer. 'I'm willing to swear that too,' I said. 'Also that he killed himself.'

Aternius shifted irritably on his couch. 'Corvinus, we can't go to the praetor's representative with this. Even if it is the truth, you're expecting him to take your pure unvarnished word for the fact. Where's your evidence, for heaven's sake?'

I was on firmer ground here. 'I've already met the rep,' I said. 'He's an old friend of mine.' Jupiter! I could just see Crispus's face! Still, this was the way things worked, and a pair of grafters like Aternius and Cominius would appreciate that. 'He'll take my word. Just tell him that if he's at all unsure my wife and I will be very happy to come specially to Rome and explain things to him in full at his new club.'

Cominius looked doubtful. 'And you believe that will be sufficient?'

I tried not to grin at the thought of how Caelius Crispus would react to *that* little guarantee. 'Yeah,' I said. 'Yeah, I think that would about do it.'

Aternius sighed. 'Well, we can certainly try. As far as Papatius is concerned, though, I'm afraid we'll have to keep him in custody until the representative arrives and authorises his release.'

Well, you win some, you lose some, and you've got to compromise. It was only three days, and the guy was safe enough: to avoid another embarrassing meeting with Perilla Crispus would've accepted my oath that the Wart had come up from Capri and done the murders himself.

'Yeah, okay,' I said. 'There's one more thing.'

'Yes?'

'That scrap of vineyard. I understand you might come into ownership of it yourself quite soon. By marriage.'

The guy coloured and glanced briefly at his uncle. 'I don't know where you got your information from,' he said, 'but yes, that is possible. Very possible, in fact.'

'Fine. There's a young guy called Publius, last name I don't know. Works in the records office in the main square. He'll be inheriting Larcius Arruns's property and he may be making a bid for it. You think you might be interested?'

Aternius stared at me coldly. 'Corvinus, first of all I don't answer hypothetical questions of that nature; second any interest I might or might not show would be none of your business. And third as a convicted murderer Larcius Arruns's property is forfeit to the state and subject to public auction. Now I'm sorry, but we really have a lot to do this morning and—'

'I suggest you allow Publius to inherit in any case. After all, Arruns took his own life, and surely that must weigh in his favour. When the lad makes his offer let me know you've accepted it and I'll send you a banker's draft for the same amount, cash, payable on transfer of the deed.'

'Good gods!' Cominius murmured.

Aternius's eyes had widened. 'You will *what*? Why on earth should you do that?'

'Call it payment of a debt,' I said. 'You can collect the draft from a man called Marcus Veluscius in Three Heroes Street. Interesting guy, I don't know if you know him. We had quite a conversation a few days back about forgery and property scams.' Cominius squeaked quietly but I ignored him. 'In fact, I was thinking of inviting Veluscius and yourselves, plus your new fiancée, of course, Aternius – or is she your fiancée yet? – round to dinner when the praetor's representative arrives. She'd be fascinated, I'm sure. Oh, and the rep as well, naturally. I imagine he'd be quite interested too in his professional capacity.'

'Ah . . .' Aternius's jaw had gone slack. The other guy looked like he'd swallowed a poker butt-end first.

'Yeah. Well. Think about it.' I gave them another grin. 'Oh, and before I forget. I understand Gnaeus Vipena over at Vetuliscum has some cash for you that Titus Clusinus left with him before he died. A loan settlement. It may've slipped his mind, but when you ask him about it mention my name and remind him he put it for safe keeping inside a wine jar. The one with the faulty potter's mark.'

'Ah . . .'

That should just about do it. I stood up. 'Okay,' I said. 'I'll leave you to your business. A pleasure to talk to you, gentlemen.'

The snooty door slave watched me leave like he was thinking about frisking me for illicitly acquired spoons, but I didn't care. Jupiter, I'd enjoyed that! It's not often I got to indulge in a gentle bit of aristocratic in-fighting. And I reckoned Arruns would sleep a little more peacefully now.

The holiday started here. And Rome . . .

Well, maybe I'd think again about Rome.

AUTHOR'S NOTE

Most people will have some recollection of Horatius's defence of the Sublician Bridge and the subsequent withdrawal from Rome of Lars Porsenna, king of Clusium. In fact, Arruns's claim that Porsenna actually captured the city is probably historically correct, and indeed the Romans themselves, although understandably reluctant to admit to an Etruscan occupation, were aware of the alternative tradition. This is not to say that my siting of Tarquin's tomb near Caere – the modern Cerveteri, approximately 30km north-west of Rome – has any factual justification; it does not. According to tradition, the king ended his days as a guest of the Greek Aristodemus of Cumae, some 20km from Naples, and was buried at that place.

On the other hand, apart from that bald statement there is no other record in ancient literature of the tomb itself, and its site (unlike, say, that of the king's son Arruns on the edge of the Valle Ariccia some 25km from Rome) remained and remains unascribed. More useful still, for my purposes as devil's advocate working within the laissez-faire sphere of fiction, is a further tradition that following the expulsion certain members of the Tarquin family moved to Caere, where they had property; an interesting confirmation of this being the discovery in 1875 of a tomb containing the inscription AVLE TARCHNAS LARTHAL CLAN (Aulus Tarquinius, son of Larth). Perhaps, then, my suggestion of a secret interment in less alien ground for the exiled king himself is not totally unreasonable.

One last word about Vipena's wine scam. The Romans did indeed heat-treat their wines occasionally as I have described – the process is closely akin to the modern one of Madeirisation – to age them artificially, although I doubt if any serious wine-lover such as Corvinus would have approved. However, the ancient world was no different from our own in producing smart entrepreneurs eager to make a fast if questionable buck; and this fact, combined with the snob value of an upmarket label, the low production of the quality vineyards, the rapid expansion of the wine market and the rudimentary state of quality control safeguards, puts the scam, on a commercial scale, well within the bounds of possibility.

Finally, a little puzzle for Latinist readers. I've included among the characters – unremarked – two names with historical Tarquin connections. If you spot them, award yourself a celebration glass of wine with my good wishes.

My thanks, yet again, to my wife Rona and the staff of Carnoustie library for finding me books; to Professor Christopher Smith of the University of St Andrews for supplying me with information and guidance on Roman wine production; and most especially to Roy Pinkerton and David W. R. Ridgway, both of the Department of Classics, University of Edinburgh, for their limitless patience in fielding and answering questions on the historical background to the story. Any factual errors which may have crept in, despite their generous help, remain my own.